New York

Also by Eric Brown in Gollancz

New York Nights: Book One in the Virex Trilogy
New York Blues: Book Two in the Virex Trilogy
Penumbra
The Fall of Tartarus
The Web: Untouchable
The Web: Walkabout

http://ericbrownsf.port5.com/

New York Dreams

Book Three in the Virex Trilogy

Eric Brown

The right of Eric Brown to be identified as the author
of this work has been asserted by him in accordance
with the Copyright, Designs and Patents Act 1988.

First published in Great Britain in 2004 by

Gollancz
An imprint of the Orion Publishing Group
Orion House, 5 Upper St Martin's Lane,
London WC2H 9EA

A CIP catalogue record for this book
is available from the British Library

ISBN 0 575 07494 9

Typeset by Deltatype Ltd, Birkenhead, Merseyside

Printed in Great Britain by Clays Ltd, St Ives plc

This book is dedicated to
the memory of Chris Burgess,
fellow writer, my very first editor,
but, most of all, a great friend.

One

Halliday climbed the path to the highest point of the headland and stopped. A huge boulder was embedded in the sandy soil beside the path, and as usual he leaned against it and took in the view.

The sky had the silver-blue sheen of burnished aluminium, merging at the horizon with the deeper blue of the ocean. The coastline was an intricate series of islands and inlets, and directly below was the bay beside which Halliday had his camp. The circular surface of the bay fitted perfectly between the twin headlands like the lug of a jigsaw puzzle piece, no movement discernible at this elevation but for the occasional ripple as the warm wind raked across the shallows.

Perfection, Halliday thought. There was a time when all North America looked like this, unspoilt in its natural beauty.

He came to this stretch of Virginia coastline on average three times a week, leaving behind New York and his life there. His only regret was that he could not leave his memories of the city, too. They were a constant nagging presence, preventing his total appreciation of the scenery.

He closed his eyes, felt the warm wind against his skin. The scent of the pines, the juniper bushes that flanked the path, hit him like a drug rush. He heard the ripsaw cawing of a bird, and when he opened his eyes he made out, high above the shelving foreshore, the majestic sight of an eagle soaring stiff-winged on a thermal.

Perfection.

He heard the sound of voices behind him and turned. A family of four was making its way along the path towards him, junior and sis leading the way, thwacking at the high grass with custom-made sticks. They looked African. At least, they dressed that way; the mother and father wore psychedelically patterned jellabas. But they might have been from anywhere. They might even, for that matter, have been any nationality: whites trying on Senegalese personas for the hell of it.

They smiled and said hi as they passed him in single file. Halliday turned away, ignoring them. He watched as they disappeared down the precipitous path, stung by a ridiculous feeling that they had trespassed on his territory. Even here he could not leave the world behind without being followed.

He gave the family ten minutes to lose themselves in the vastness of the coastline, then stood and made his way slowly down the track.

He stopped from time to time and left the path to examine the occasional tree that caught his attention. He gave every specimen its common name, and rummaged in his memory for their Latin titles. He still had the Natural History DVD his father had bought him for his tenth birthday, one of the few possessions he had kept from his childhood. He'd been obsessed with trees as a kid. They had filled him then, as they still did now, with a sense that he could never be alone when in their presence. There was something mighty and powerful, and at the same time mysterious, about the giant lifeforms: they existed in a kind of self-sufficient disdain of the materialistic doings of humankind.

The path dropped towards the bay and deposited Halliday on the pebbled foreshore. He picked up a small, flat stone and skimmed it across the water. It hopped once, twice, a third time, and then sank.

He continued around the curve of the bay. His tent was a

hemispherical crimson blister pitched in the shade of a fir tree, and beside it Casey was crouching over a heater, frying bacon.

Halliday felt a sudden, surging regret that his allotted immersion time was almost finished.

She looked up as he approached and gave him a dazzling smile. 'There you are, Hal. Breakfast's up!'

She stood and hurried over to him, and the feel of the seventeen-year-old in his arms was the physical equivalent of the smell of the cooking breakfast, the beauty of the surrounding scenery.

Casey pulled away. 'You hungry, Hal? I'm starving!'

They sat beside the tent and tucked into plates of bacon and eggs.

Casey wore denim shorts and a red-checked lumberjack's shirt. She was blonde and pretty in a thin-faced, waif-like kind of way that Halliday found enchanting.

'Hey, guess what!' she managed past a mouthful. 'We got neighbours.' She jerked her thumb inland, towards an emerald family tent erected beyond a stand of spruce.

'The Africans? I saw them earlier.'

She shrugged with off-hand teenage unconcern. 'Guess the place is big enough for all of us.'

Halliday wanted to argue with her, but knew better.

He'd booked this stretch of Virginia coastline for exclusive use, and had expected just that. He'd demand a partial refund when he got back, but he knew what the operators would say. Sometimes, exclusivity could not be guaranteed. The system became so overloaded that visitors had to be shunted into already occupied sites. He knew he was being small-minded, but he had paid well over the odds to be alone.

Alone with Casey, that was.

After breakfast, she sat on his lap and laid her head on his shoulder, and Halliday held the girl in his arms, marvelling at her reality.

3

He'd programmed a platonic relationship with Casey. The parameters of her persona stipulated a full and trusting friendship, and no more. He could have programmed a sexual relationship with her, of course, and had sometimes wondered what had prevented him from doing so.

He told himself that it was because to have initiated a physical liaison with Casey in virtual reality, without the knowledge of her real-world self, would have been betraying her trust . . . But he knew he was kidding himself. He knew himself well enough to understand the truth. The only reason he wasn't making love to the ersatz Casey right at this moment was because to do so would remind him that she was unavailable in the real world.

As ever, virtual reality only served to point up the inadequacy of the real world – in this case, though, the inadequacy was wholly his own.

Not long ago, after a well-paid job had given him the cash to spend on the luxury of VR, Halliday had surfed the various cyberverse realities on offer. He'd used the sex-zones to excess, until the pleasures palled and reminded him of his isolation in reality. He'd travelled in space and time, experiencing wonders he had never thought possible. But again and again he'd returned to VR's more prosaic delights: nature sites and historical zones which showed the world as it had been in a more pristine, earlier era. He'd often come to be alone, to walk in the natural splendour of oak forests and jungles.

Then it came to him that he was missing something. Casey had stopped visiting him months ago – too busy enjoying life with her new boyfriend – and he admitted to himself that she was the only person he really missed from his former life.

So he'd invested in an expensive program and synthesised Casey's persona from the computer data he had of her on file, visual and aural. He'd come up with a pretty faithful likeness, even down to the content of her conversation, her irreverent teenage sarcasm.

'Hey, sleepy!' she called out now. 'Let's walk, okay? Show me the trees. Tell me all their funny foreign names!'

She pulled him to his feet with both hands, straining comically as if taking on a tug-o'-war team.

They strolled towards the pines, away from the bay, and up a winding, shadowed track.

Over the past year, the legally allowed immersion time in VR had risen from four hours to twenty-four. One day was as long as a citizen could spend in a jellytank, though there were measures under way to increase the upper limit. Halliday had heard that volunteers had spent weeks fully immersed. It was only a matter of time, according to those in the know, before people would be able to live indefinitely in virtual reality.

Halliday spent perhaps every other day in his own tank, which he'd bought with the proceeds of the Artois case. After twenty-four hours sunk in the jelly, he felt wrung-out and wasted. In the early days he'd maintained a regime of physical fitness to combat the effects of so many inactive hours; he'd eaten well and worked-out down the gym . . . But laziness had got the better of him. He'd stopped putting in the hours on the running machine, and he'd gone back to snacking at the local Chinese and Thai stalls.

He'd even wondered about getting a pirate tech in to tamper with his jellytank, fix it so that he could spend longer than the stipulated twenty-four hours away from the horrors of the real world – but the thought of the heavy fines, and the physical dangers involved, had stayed his hand.

In the meantime he wondered when he'd become tired of the nature sites, and his paternal relationship with Casey, and want something just a little bit more exciting.

She danced ahead of him. 'What's that, Hal?' she asked, pointing to a stately spruce.

He stared at her small, denim-clad bottom and thought: Oh, Christ, give me strength . . .

They climbed through the forest, up the steeply inclined hillside to the ridge path, Halliday making Casey laugh with his knowledge of Latin arboreal nomenclature.

When they reached the path, they paused and gazed out to sea. Casey slipped an arm around his waist, and Halliday found himself caressing the nape of her neck.

She made a small, kittenish sound.

'This is my favouritest view in all Virginia,' she said.

This simulacrum of the real-life Casey looked like the real thing, and sounded like the kid, but its verisimilitude was limited by the degree of information Halliday had been able to supply to the identity program. The VR Casey had none of the real girl's memories, though the program running her was stocked with banks of popular current knowledge the programmers assumed would be within the ken of an average seventeen-year-old New Yorker. Halliday had had to supply Casey's intelligence quotient, and he thought he'd erred on the low side. It had been difficult: she was uneducated, almost illiterate, and knew next to nothing about the arts and sciences – but to counter that she was a sharp, wise-cracking street kid who'd lived by her wits for years before Halliday had befriended her.

They walked along the ridge path, Halliday pointing out things he thought might interest her. She responded with genuine-sounding enthusiasm, and then, like the kid she was, began prattling about the last time they had been here. 'Remember the grizzly we saw by the fallen pine, Hal? You think he'll be there today?'

He laughed and told her that he was sure it would have moved on by now.

He smiled as he listened to her chatter. He wondered what he'd do if the speculation was right and the VR companies did come up with the technology capable of sustaining citizens in virtual reality for extended periods.

6

Would he turn his back on the real world, sign up and live out a life of dreams in some fabulous ersatz reality?

The trouble was, of course, that no matter how realistic the physical reality of a VR site, no matter how convincing the world appeared to the senses of the participant, you always knew where you were. You knew that you were living an incredibly realistic cyber-dream ... Your memories of who you were would not be banished.

That would change, of course, if the VR companies succeeded in producing memory-suppressant drugs. Then, in the not too distant future, a citizen would be able to enter VR and live a life in blithe ignorance of who and what they had once been. VR would effectively become the real world.

Halliday considered losing himself in such a reality, being able to forget his worries, assume a new, carefree identity in a perfect world. Perhaps after a while he'd become tired of who he was and desire a change, become yet another person ... Wasn't it a dream that everyone had considered, at some point?

He wondered if his real life had become so destitute that he was serious about signing on the dotted line, come the day.

They followed the path as it dipped towards the small, sheltered cove where Halliday often bathed when he came here by himself. The blue sea shrugged itself ashore with a rhythmic, lulling susurration.

'Hey!' Casey cried, skipping across the sand towards the waves. 'This is great!'

Halliday was aware that his mouth was suddenly dry. 'Why don't we go for a swim, Casey?'

She twisted a frown. 'Haven't brought my costume, Hal.'

His heartbeat thudded in his ears. 'Neither have I. So what? Come here ... '

She came, innocently. He reached out and began unbuttoning her shirt. She bent – at first he thought she was

7

attempting to avoid his hands: then he saw that she was enthusiastically unfastening her shorts.

She unbuttoned the rest of her shirt and shrugged it off, and Halliday saw that she was wearing no bra. She lowered her shorts and panties together, kicked off her sneakers and, naked, skipped into the shallows.

Halliday stared at her skinny nakedness, her small breasts and tuft of pubic hair, as she danced laughing in the waves.

He wondered how the program that was Casey might react when he undressed and joined her in the sea, pulled her to him and kissed her.

He was aware that what he was about to do was somehow wrong, but for the life of him he could not stop now.

He was unbuttoning his own shirt when he was alerted by the tingling of his right hand. He stared at the metacarpal quit decal: it was flashing on and off with the upper time-limit warning. He had been in the Virginia site for twenty-four hours, and in seconds he would be automatically ejected.

He smiled to himself as he stared at the naked girl frolicking in the sea, and a surge of regret was replaced by relief that he had been saved from what could only have been a harmful and demeaning intimacy.

Seconds later he made the transition.

Two

Halliday stood up, forcing his way through the cloying medium of the amber suspension gel. He pulled off the face-mask and the electrodes that adhered to his limbs. He felt weak, and as he stepped from the tank he was forced to reach out and make a grab for the wall as his legs buckled beneath his weight. He pushed himself across the sticky carpet, trailing goo, and made it to the shower-stall.

He stood beneath the spray with his arms braced against the tiled wall, head hanging. He took a series of deep breaths, fighting the urge to vomit.

Ten minutes later, revived by the steaming jet of water, he turned under the blow-drier. As the condensation evaporated from the glass of the stall, he caught a quick, unexpected glimpse of his face. He looked as bad as he felt: a two-day growth of beard lent a desperate quality to the dark, sunken eyes that stared back at him.

He looked down the length of his body, his flesh sallow, his arms and legs wasted. He was developing a pot-belly from all the junk food and beer he was putting away. He was thirty-six and he looked, if he were honest with himself, about fifty.

He thought of the naked simulacrum of Casey in the Virginia site, and experienced only a bitter feeling of self-loathing at the thought of what he had been about to do.

He would scrub her program from his files, he told himself, spend time alone in the site, next time. Yet, even as he thought this, he knew that he would be too weak to do anything of the kind.

He quit the stall, dressed in an old pair of beige chinos and a frayed white shirt, and stepped from his bedroom into the office.

Dust coated every surface. The fan on the ceiling turned languidly, doing nothing at all to cool the room's stifling humidity.

He walked around the desk and opened the window. A panting wind, freighted with a chemical cocktail of varied airborne pollutants, added to the office's intolerable heat.

He brewed himself a strong coffee, then sat on the swivel chair and lodged his feet on the desk.

He recalled some good times here in the office with his ex-partner. He'd worked with Barney for eight years, Barney doing days, Halliday taking the graveyard shift through the night. He'd preferred it that way, had liked the anonymity of darkness, when the buildings of Manhattan wore gaudy holo-façades like Cinderella's magical fineries. Days in New York were depressing; even in summer the sunlight rarely made it through the smog, and in daylight the holo-façades were wan ghosts, doing nothing to conceal the architectural decay and dereliction beneath.

Now, night or day, Halliday never ventured further than Olga's bar on the corner, or the closest fast-food stall. He couldn't remember the last time he'd left El Barrio for a trip into Manhattan.

He realised that he had no idea whether it was morning or night. He switched on his desk-com. The screen read: 11:59. Midday, then. A full day in the Virginia site . . . No wonder he felt like he'd died and been brought back to life against his will.

He took another swallow of coffee. The caffeine began to kick.

Yeah, there'd been good times. He pulled the bonsai tree across the desk and sat with it in his lap. A miniature English oak, its infinitesimal leaves coated with dust. Despite the heat, the pollution, it seemed to be thriving.

He recalled the day the VR-star Vanessa Artois walked into the room, a year ago now. Walked in like a predatory animal and demanded that he find her sister, and left the oak as a gift. It had been his last big case. Kim had been six months gone from his life at the time, Barney likewise – riddled with bullets in a darkened back-alley.

His thoughts were interrupted by the chime of the desk-com. Halliday accepted the call.

A familiar lean, swarthy face stared out, seemingly looking *through* him.

He leaned forward. 'Wellman?' he said, surprised.

'Halliday,' the executive said, 'I hope you can hear me?'

'Why shouldn't I?' he asked.

Wellman went on, 'This is a one-way communiqué, by necessity, as I'll explain later. Please listen.'

Halliday sipped his coffee, wondering what the hell the Cyber-Tech exec might want.

'Okay,' Wellman said, 'this is what's happening. Any minute now two of my men will come around to your office. They'll supervise your tanking and you'll meet me in VR, and I'll tell you more then.' He smiled. 'Apologies for the amateur theatricals, but you're a very difficult man to track down. You seem to spend most of your time in VR, though I'm gratified to see that you patronise Cyber-Tech.'

'This is a recording, right?' Halliday shook his head. 'I don't understand, Wellman. Why—?'

But the executive was saying, '. . . done some detective work of my own. I'm concerned that you haven't taken a case in six months. And you're spending too much time tanked.' He paused. 'I have a job I think you might be interested in. This might just kick-start your career, my friend. And before you tell me where to stick my job, let me tell you that it involves someone who was once close to you. And that's quite enough for now. I'll fill you in later.'

The image on the screen vanished, and Halliday was left shaking his head in confusion. Who could he be referring

11

to – someone who was once close to him? Kim? Vanessa Artois?

Why hadn't Wellman been able to communicate with him in real time? Why the pre-recorded message?

And why the hell hadn't the bastard the decency to leave him alone?

He looked across the room. The door was locked, the shutter down. The green paint that Kim had so meticulously applied, after insisting that the office needed a make-over to boost its flagging chi, was beginning to peel. The stand of flowers she'd installed in the south-west corner to bring good luck had died months ago. The wind chimes worked still, though, tinkling sporadic melancholy notes in the hot breeze.

He was surprised by the sudden rattle of the door handle as someone tried to enter the office. Then impatient knuckles rapped on the pebbled glass.

He stood and walked around the desk. A sharp pain shot up his left leg, as if he'd strained a muscle while standing. By the time he reached the door he was limping and out of breath.

Two heavies in silver-grey suits stood in the gloom of the landing. They had the build of thugs but the faces of executives, bodies inflated through steroid abuse and skin the unnatural bronze that comes from too much artificial sunlight.

'Halliday?'

He left the door open and limped back to the desk. He picked up his coffee and watched them as they entered.

They looked around the room, taking in the squalor without comment. When their eyes came to rest on Halliday, he could sense their contempt.

'Wellman contact you?' the first guy asked.

Halliday sat back in his chair. 'What does he want?'

'That's between you and him, buddy,' the heavy said.

The second guy moved to the bedroom. Through the

12

door, Halliday could see him checking the monitor at the head of the jellytank.

What had Wellman said? That his men would supervise his tanking? He smiled to himself: he wouldn't be doing any more tanking in this unit for another twenty-four hours, sadly.

The heavy stepped from the bedroom, shaking his head. He conferred in a lowered voice with his sidekick, who turned to Halliday.

'Wellman needs to see you in VR,' he said. 'We can't use your tank, so we'll have to take you downtown, okay?'

'And if I don't want to go?'

The heavies exchanged glances.

'Look,' Halliday said. 'I no longer work in the business. I've retired, okay? Tell Wellman to find someone else to do his running around.'

'Wellman said you'd want this case.'

'Would I? And why's that?'

The first guy shook his head. 'Like I said, that's between Wellman and you.'

The second guy spoke. 'Listen, Halliday. Wellman's ill. He's dying. Word is he has a matter of weeks. He wants you on the case before he goes.'

Halliday stared at the heavies. 'What's wrong with him?'

'We're not his doctors, pal.'

He hesitated, considering. Wellman was dying ... He owed the executive a visit, at the very least.

He stood and moved to the bedroom. He shrugged on his body-holster, then picked up his jacket from the back of the chair beside the bed.

He followed the heavies from the office and locked the door behind him. They'd left their silver Mustang parked in the street. He climbed into the back and sank into the genuine leather seat. The interior was air-conditioned, and the sudden chill after the midday heat sent a shiver across his exposed flesh.

The car started almost without a sound and eased its way through the crowds.

He stared out at the food stalls that lined the street. He saw faces he recognised, stall-holders and street kids and refugees. So many people, he thought. The sight of the packed crowds, so soon after the vastness of the Virginia site, filled him with despair.

The driver craned his neck to look at him in the rear-view mirror. 'What line of work you in, pal?'

'Like I said, I've retired.'

'So, what *did* you do?' the passenger asked.

Halliday ignored the question. He saw the heavies exchange a glance, but his silence had the desired effect. They got the message and quit the interrogation.

It was a while since he'd last ventured further south than 96th Street. As the Mustang wafted down Park Avenue, one of the few private vehicles on the road, he stared out at the families encamped on the sidewalks, homeless refugees who'd fled to the city after the Raleigh and Atlanta meltdowns. There seemed to be as many refugees living rough these days as there had been years ago, despite the government's routine promise to allocate funds for accommodation.

They turned left, and left again, and headed up Madison Avenue.

He leaned forward. 'Where's Wellman?'

In reply, the passenger pointed ahead, indicating a mirror-fronted skyscraper that gave Halliday vertigo merely looking *up* the length of its towering façade.

'Hospital?'

'Private apartments. Wellman has the penthouse.'

Great view, Halliday thought as the Mustang eased into the kerb.

The hot air hit him like the backblast from a jet engine as he climbed from the car and crossed the sidewalk. He was sweating, more from the unaccustomed exertion than the

14

heat, by the time he limped up the steps to the sliding glass doors.

In the arctic chill of the air-conditioned elevator, he rested against the panelling and watched the numbered display as they rose through a hundred floors.

The doors opened onto a carpeted corridor. They stepped from the lift and turned right. The first heavy produced a key-card and swiped open a pair of genuine timber double doors.

They entered a lounge with the floorspace of a basketball court. He was right about the view. Floor-to-ceiling windows on two sides gave a panoramic vista of Manhattan's crammed, man-made canyons.

'Take a seat. Drink?'

Halliday selected a minimalist rocking-chair positioned before a south-west view of Staten Island. 'Orange juice.'

A minute later the heavy passed him a tall glass of freshly pressed juice. He heard a door open and close. He looked around and saw that he was alone in the room.

He sipped the juice and stared out at the view. He wondered what state Wellman might be in. Pretty bad, if the medics had given him only weeks to live. How old was the Cyber-Tech exec, anyway? Halliday guessed around fifty. Too young to be given a sentence of death.

He tried to analyse his feelings. He'd hardly known Wellman, worked with him for a week eighteen months ago. He was more surprised than shocked that a rich exec was dying of some incurable disease. Death comes to us all, he thought, even the filthy rich.

A door opened. 'If you care to step this way, Halliday.'

The heavy was standing in the entrance of another room almost as vast as the lounge. Halliday drained his juice and stepped through. The second heavy was kneeling beside a jellytank positioned like a catafalque in the centre of the room.

15

Halliday looked from the tank to the guy beside him. 'Where's Wellman?'

'Just strip and enter the tank,' the heavy said. 'It's pre-programmed. All you have to do is go through the usual procedure.' His gaze scanned the length of Halliday's body. 'I can see that you're familiar with VR protocol.'

The heavy at the tank stood and nodded to the first guy. They left the room. Halliday heard the clunk of the lock as a key-card was used on the other side.

So if he was to meet Wellman somewhere in VR, why hadn't the exec simply communicated with him in real-time?

He undressed and piled his clothes on a nearby chair. Naked and suddenly self-conscious – he imagined the heavies watching him via a hidden camera – he applied the electrodes, pulled on the face-mask and stepped into the jelly. It gave, almost reluctantly, beneath his foot like soft rubber. He sat down and sank slowly into the goo. Fully submerged, he spread his arms and legs and floated free.

His vision blacked out. He soon lost all bodily sensation. He felt a quick heat pass through his head as he made the transition.

He opened his eyes. He was standing in a room identical to the first lounge. He was wearing a default suit, a smart black side-fastening affair, with a crisp white shirt and black laceless shoes. He raised a hand before his face. As far as he could tell, he was here as himself.

And, most amazing of all, he was free of aches and pains. He felt as though he had been lifted from his old body and dropped into a younger, fitter version. Only then did he notice the view through the wraparound window. He no longer looked out over the grey sprawl of twenty-first-century lower Manhattan. The scene showed a rocky terrain of snow and ice, and canted at a rakish angle just above the near horizon was the planet Saturn.

The door through which he'd entered the lounge in the

16

real world opened suddenly, and the man he recognised as Wellman, unchanged in eighteen months, stepped through.

He wore a dark suit, almost funereal in its sombreness, with a blood-red carnation in the button-hole; Halliday wondered if the suit was a macabre comment on the man's impending demise.

Wellman advanced across the room, hand outstretched. 'Halliday, it's good to see you again.'

They shook hands. Wellman had chosen a persona that betrayed no sign of his having aged in the intervening eighteen months, nor of having suffered the ravages of disease.

He gestured to the armchair, and as Halliday sat down Wellman seated himself on a settee opposite. 'You're spending a lot of time in VR, Halliday.'

He sensed a note of censure in the executive's comment. 'Isn't that what it's there for?'

'Of course, but there are . . . shall we say *drawbacks*, to spending so long tanked.'

'That's quite something, coming from the head of one of the world's biggest VR companies. Can I quote you on that?'

Wellman smiled. 'Only if you quote my full comment,' he said. 'I was going to say that there are drawbacks to spending twenty-four hours out of every forty-eight, as you do, in VR without taking the necessary care of yourself when you detank.'

'Is that why you got me here, to lecture me on my health?'

'I understand why you took to VR,' Wellman said. 'You haven't had an easy time of it, what with Barney, and then Kim . . .'

'The past's the past,' Halliday said, aware of the cliché as soon as he'd said it. 'There's nothing we can do to change it.'

'But you lose yourself in VR in the hope of forgetting the past, no?'

'That doesn't work, Wellman. The past is still up here.' He tapped his head. 'I use VR because it's easier than the real world. And I can afford it now.'

Wellman stared at him. 'Perhaps the question I should be asking you isn't why you use VR, but why you can't use the real world.'

Halliday lifted his right hand, looking for an exit decal. He tried his left . . .

Wellman was shaking his head. 'You're not getting away that easily.'

'What do you want with me, Wellman? Why the hell couldn't you tell me what you wanted back at the office?'

'That was impossible.'

'Why the elaborate charade? The recorded summons, the heavies, all this . . . ?' He waved at the surrounding spacescape.

'What do you think of this site? This is Tethys, a moon of Saturn. I always wanted to travel the solar system.'

'Wellman . . .'

The executive stared across at Halliday. 'Okay, no more games. Did Roberts tell you I was ill?'

'The heavy?' Halliday nodded. 'He said you had a few weeks.'

'If I'm lucky I'll see out three weeks, perhaps. Leukaemia. The medics have done all they can.'

'I thought nowadays . . .' Halliday began.

Wellman smiled. 'Not the form of the disease I've contracted. They can cure some patients, but not me.' He stared across at Wellman without the slightest trace of self-pity. 'That's why I couldn't talk to you directly at your office,' he said.

Halliday frowned. 'Because you're ill?'

'No, because I'm here, in this site. It's somewhat special.'

Halliday shook his head. 'You've lost me.'

18

'Did you notice what time it was when you tanked?'

Halliday shrugged. 'Not especially. Around twelve thirty?'

'Actually it was twelve twenty-seven precisely.'

'I don't see—'

'And when you quit the tank, only a few minutes will have elapsed. Two, three minutes at the most.'

Halliday stared at the executive. He knew what Wellman wanted him to say, so he said it, 'But I've already been in here what, five minutes?'

'If you remain in this site for one hour, subjective, only fifteen minutes will have elapsed in the real world. That's why I couldn't make the link, because of the time difference.'

'Christ . . .' Halliday combed his hand through his hair. 'That's why you're here, right? You said you had a few weeks out there, but in here you'll be able to live for . . .' He shook his head, the arithmetic beyond him.

Wellman smiled. 'Maybe two, three subjective months. I'll live without pain while my body is tanked, pumped full of analgesics and whatever else the medics recommend to keep the meat alive a while longer. Every day in the real world is approximately four in here – or in the other sites I've had customised for my use.'

'I didn't know this was possible.'

'We've kept it under wraps, Halliday. We know that other companies are working on it, but we're ahead of the field.'

Halliday pressed his thumb and forefinger into his eyes, massaging. He looked up and gave a laugh. 'This'll revolutionise VR, the way people use it.'

'The ramifications are manifold,' Wellman agreed. 'Business will benefit, of course. Think of all the man hours of work done in the real world, which could be accomplished here in minutes. The field of theoretical science will never be the same again. We're expecting some exponential leaps in research and development when we get the requisite sites up and running.'

19

'What about the general user? I mean, I could spend twenty-four hours in a site and be gone from the real world just six hours. I wouldn't feel so wrecked when I came out.'

Wellman laughed. 'Think about it, Halliday. What would happen? Users like you would spend twenty-four real-time hours in the tank, and live in a site, or various sites, for four days.'

'But it'll cost, right? I mean, you won't be charging the usual rates for this service?'

Wellman cocked a finger at him. 'You got it in one, my friend. Cyber-Tech isn't a charitable institution, after all.'

'So when will it come on-line?'

'For businesses, we're thinking about a year or there-abouts. It'll be maybe eighteen months before the first time-extended site is open to the public. If, that is, some other VR company doesn't beat us to the draw.'

The way Wellman was looking at him suggested to Halliday that this was where he came in.

'And you think that might happen, right?'

'We're increasingly worried, after recent developments.'

'Go on.'

'I've had a team of programmers working on time-extension for the past year. We've always been on the verge of a breakthrough, without actually getting there. Then about six months ago I transferred a kid from the matrix division, on the recommendation of the matrix director. She was one hell of a brain; my assessment team bombarded her with problems, and this kid just came up with the right answers time after time. A child prodigy.'

'How old.'

'You won't believe this, but she's thirteen.'

'Whatever next? Cyber-Tech exploiting child labour.'

'She was doing a PhD at MIT when we discovered her last year. She worked part-time at Cyber-Tech, three days a week.'

'Worked?' Halliday said. 'Past tense?'

'Right. She vanished last week.'

'I can smell the distinctive scent of *déjà vu*, Wellman.'

'But I hope this isn't going to end like the Sissi Nigeria case. No messy deaths and assassinations with this one.'

'So what happened?'

Wellman shrugged. 'One day she was at work, the next she wasn't. She was due to come into the labs last Friday, and she didn't show. She left the house where she lives with her mother in White Plains and caught the train south. Eyewitnesses saw her alight at Grand Central, but after that, nothing. She vanished.'

'You've had people looking for her?'

'We called the police in, naturally. They didn't get very far. I've also put a company detective on the case.'

'What's the worst-case scenario?'

'You mean, looking at this from Cyber-Tech's perspective?' Wellman sighed. 'Well, of course we fear that she's fallen into the hands of one of our competitors, either defected, or been forced against her will . . . Then again, speaking as a concerned citizen, I simply fear that some schizo out there might have—'

'But at least that'd leave you high and dry with the time-extension golden egg.'

Wellman stared at him. 'I'll pretend I didn't hear that, Halliday.'

He reached out and took a manila envelope from a small occasional table. He drew a photograph from the envelope and passed it across to Halliday.

'Susanna Charlesworth. She prefers Suzie. Thirteen last May.'

Halliday stared at the image of the teenager: she looked young for her age, but otherwise pretty typical of your average white American rich kid: blonde hair in bangs, braces strapped across smiling teeth. Halliday would never have guessed that she was a computer genius.

21

Wellman said, 'You can't tell from the photograph, but she's autistic.'

'She is?'

'She has severe socialisation problems. She doesn't mix, hardly communicates, other than with the other techs, and then only about work. She finds it hard to function on an interactive personal level, but give her a complex program to write . . .'

Halliday considered what the exec had told him. 'If she's autistic . . . I don't know, would she be able to travel alone on a train?'

Wellman nodded. 'She had a fascination about trains,' he explained. 'Timetables, specifications, the engineering . . . You could say she was obsessed. She used them all the time.'

Halliday regarded the pix of Suzie Charlesworth. He looked up. 'You said she disappeared three days ago, so why the delay in getting in touch?'

'We called the cops in a few hours after she didn't show up. Next day I thought of you. But you weren't taking calls. It took my techs the better part of another day to trace you to the Virginia site.'

Halliday nodded. 'You didn't know I'd retired?'

'That's news to me.'

He recalled what the recorded image of Wellman had told him. 'You said that someone I was close to is involved in the case, right?'

'That's right.'

'You going to tell me, or you want me to guess?'

'I'll tell you, and I think you'll be interested enough to come out of retirement.'

'Try me.'

'The night before Charlesworth disappeared, she was seen in Carlo's, a restaurant in White Plains. She was with a silver-haired guy in his sixties—'

'That doesn't sound like anyone I know.'

22

'Let me finish. With the guy was a woman, a young woman, about twenty-five. Eyewitnesses report she was Asian. The cops did some digging, learned she was known at the restaurant. She owns a string of her own restaurants in the city.'

Halliday felt his pulse surge. 'Kim?'

'The cops questioned her a few hours after the kid vanished. She said she didn't know the kid, but she was friendly with the old guy. She said the guy was a writer, a scientific journalist, doing a story on child prodigies. When the cops tried to find this guy, they drew a blank. They went back to Kim and she played dumb, said she'd known the guy a week, and that the name she'd given the police was the name the guy had given her. She knew no more, or so she claimed.'

'You think otherwise, right?'

Wellman spread his hands. 'Come on, Halliday. Kim's seen dining with Mr X and the kid, and the following day the kid vanishes, and Mr X can't be found. What do you think?'

Halliday nodded. 'You're right – about the retirement. Premature. I'll see what I can do, okay?'

'You don't know how pleased I am to hear that.'

'And since last time, my rates have gone up. I've got a VR addiction to pay for, after all.'

'Name your price.'

'How about five grand per hour and two hundred thousand when I find the kid?'

Wellman nodded. 'Very well. I think we can see our way to footing the bill.'

Halliday tried not to let his surprise show. 'How do I contact you?' he asked.

'Roberts will give you my private code when you detank. He'll also have photographs of the kid.'

'You were pretty confident I'd accept the case.'

The executive smiled. 'And another thing, Roberts will

equip you with a few state-of-the-art devices you might find useful. You wouldn't believe some of the technology developed over the past year.'

'Can't wait.'

He meant it sarcastically, but Wellman just smiled, stood up and held out a hand. 'It's good to have you back on the team.'

Halliday took the executive's hand in a firm shake, and a second later the plush lounge, and the panoramic view of Tethys, dissolved like a dream.

Three

Kat was haranguing customers entering the VR Bar on Fulton Street, TriBeCa. The nightly monsoon downpour had just quit, and the tarmac was slick with rain reflecting smears of neon light.

'Excuse me,' she said. 'Do you know that by patronising this bar you're directly contributing to the social decay of America?'

The couple hurried past her towards the brightly lit portal of the Bar. She ran over to a group of young girls. 'Hiya, there! Look, don't go in there, okay? You might think it's a great laugh – but psychologists' reports confirm that even as little as six hours' immersion every other day can be enough to undermine your social skills.'

The girls looked at each other and giggled, pushing on past her.

She tried a single white male. 'You ever thought about what VR's doing to you in here, pal?' she jabbered, matching his stride as he approached the Bar. She tapped her head. 'Think about it. You get everything you want in there, it's all so easy. There's no hardship. Then you emerge into the real world, and you know what, pal? You can't function. You've lost all your social skills—'

The guy turned on her, grabbed a bunch of her black T-shirt and said, 'Fuck you, bitch!'

He pushed her away. She lost her footing and fell on her butt in a puddle. Scrambling to her feet, she yelled, 'Bet you overdose on the sex-sites 'cos you can't get any in the real world, motherfucker!'

There were no other customers in sight. She paced up and down the sidewalk, her stride manic and fidgety. A thin, white-faced woman dressed in black leggings and a matching T-shirt, talking to herself. She might have been pretty once, but she was haggard now through stress and spin addiction.

A police drone turned the corner and approached her at head height, beacon flashing blue.

It paused before her, bobbing. 'Hiya, pepperpot,' she said. 'How's things?'

Its single lens regarded her, matching her retinal prints with those on file. 'Katherine Kosinski,' it purred. 'You are in breach of public order statute 27, sub-section 5a. If you do not move on, I will issue a warrant for your arrest.'

'No kidding?'

'This is your first warning, Katherine Kosinski.'

Another warning, and the drone would summon a flesh cop, and she'd be lucky to get away with a beating, as well as a fine.

'Hey, pepperpot,' Kat said, pushing her nose up against the drone's staring lens. 'See me? I'm outta here! See this Bar, it stinks. They can all go fuck 'emselves. All the fucking morons who use the . . .'

She turned on her heel and strode away furiously, her words turning to tears.

She walked north-east towards Chinatown through the cloying heat, her wet leggings uncomfortable. She often spent the nights on the move, restless, unable to sleep. She left her apartment at midnight and walked the streets of lower Manhattan, every damned street there was. She knew them all, every sidestreet and back alley, every passageway and short-cut. She was out so much she had a map of the area imprinted on her neo-cortex.

Everyone knew her, the woman in black, high on spin, fast and furious, ripping into the sheep queuing outside the VR Bars . . . Except they didn't queue any more. Came in ones and twos. Trade was bad for the Bars. Most people had their own tanks now. Could you credit that? Just eighteen months ago the first VR Bar opened for business and now most people had their own jellytanks.

She hit Canal Street and strode into the Jade Garden. She banged the counter with a flattened palm. 'Hey, chicken rolls and French fries. Service here!'

Mr Xing peered at her. 'Spinning, Kat? Calm down, okay? You make yourself ill.'

'Just give me some damned food, huh, Mr Xing?'

She had an arrangement with a few take-out places in the area. She fixed their com-systems and they supplied her with all the food she could eat. It was an okay deal, kept her from starving.

A tray bearing three chicken rolls in a Sargasso of congealed vegetable oil appeared on the counter. She stood and ate, stuffing food into her mouth with quick fingers.

She found herself running an entertaining fantasy number almost every hour or so. Her mind just slipped into it. She imagined the best way to end it all. A gun in the mouth in a crowded subway train, blasting the top off her head and covering all the moronic commuters with her brains. Or slitting her wrists in a busy street and spinning, spinning until the shoppers were drenched in the spray of her blood. Or better still, but impossible, she'd erect a jellytank in Times Square and die a tank death, and then the tank and her body and all would be freeze-dried and become a public monument to the folly of the technological age.

She often considered these fantasies in her more lucid moments. She might have been mad, but she wasn't stupid. All her dreams consisted of killing herself in public, not 'cos she wanted to die that much, but because she wanted to make a statement, shake all the brain-dead fuckers out of their tunnel-blind complacency.

She was reduced to fantasising about making the ultimate

statement because that seemed increasingly like the only way to make any impression at all.

She gagged down the last of the chicken roll, pushed the tray away, and quit the Jade Garden. She walked, no destination in mind, just walked to work off a lot of surplus nervous energy. She found it impossible to sit at home, the four walls closing in on her, suffocating her with claustrophobia. Her thoughts would become maudlin, and she feared that one night, when her head was really bad, she might do something stupid like kill herself, all alone. So she hit the streets and walked. In the streets there were distractions, taking her mind off things, most of the time.

Eighteen months, and she'd lost three men. Her brother went first. Joe, a cyber-fucking-scientist for one of the big three. He was fried good in some kind of freak jellytank accident. They'd been close, despite their opposed views of the VR industry. He'd worked for it and she worked against it. How opposite could you get? But, fact was, despite that, she loved him. Simple as that. He was . . . had been . . . her kid brother, and she'd always looked out for him, always protected him from the bullies at school, and she hadn't been there when he needed her most. She should have leaned on him more, tried to convince him of the inherent evil of the industry he worked for.

And then there was Sanchez. She'd only know him a couple of months. They'd been cell-partners for Virex. He was a weak kid, a loser, a cyber-nerd who'd turned against the company he'd worked for, and against VR in general. They'd been just about to get close, mean something to each other, when a fucking hired assassin working for Mantoni took him out with a laser . . .

Kat walked. She saw the Mantoni VR Bar across the way on Bowery. She thought about crossing the street and telling the fuck-wits entering the place to wake up . . . But what was the point? They wouldn't listen to her.

Sometimes it seemed like she was a lone voice, crying into the wind.

She walked on, shoulders hunched, staring down at the sidewalk and seeing only the face of her third guy, Colby, staring back at her.

Colby ... He'd been another weak, weasel-thin, hairy little geek assigned to her by the Virex controllers. They'd worked well together, vracking into some important sites, burning some big names. They'd made a great team. As was the way of things, seeing as how they agreed on most everything – and shared a passionate hatred of modern life and VR – it wasn't long before they hit it off in the sack, too. She was head over heels, like a schoolgirl again. What did it matter that he was an ugly, gap-toothed little runt? What mattered was what was in *here*, in the heart.

What was that nasty, invidious advertisement some VR Bar had used a month back? *'Image is all!'*

Well, fuck 'em! Image meant *nothing*.

She'd loved Colby.

Every so often, every six months or sometimes every year, Virex did a shuffle for security reasons. They didn't want their cells getting too cosy, too settled. They liked to shift their members around the city, so in theory the assassins gunning for 'em would have a harder time.

So, as she knew would happen, she and Colby were assigned new cell-mates. The protocol was that they couldn't make contact again, for security reasons. Kat was so stuck on Colby that she wanted to flout the unwritten rule. Colby, for whatever reasons – maybe it was true what he said, that he believed in Virex, and wanted it to work – took himself off somewhere uptown, and she'd never seen anything of him again. And that had hurt like hell.

And Kat was assigned a stuck-up bitch of a cell-mate, some Harvard-educated know-all, except she knew fuck all, and around that time the bombing campaign, the last resort to shake the complacency of the masses and the VR

29

companies, had been put on indefinite hold. Just when Kat had been cat-on-a-hot-tin-roof-eager to get out and start bombing.

She'd had a God Almighty bust-up with her cell-mate about that, and they'd ended up fighting, and when they next met their controller they were parted.

Kat had never had a partner since.

She'd seen little active service for Virex for the past few weeks. They seemed to have given up trying to burn the big three VR companies with viruses. In frustration, Kat had taken to the streets, arguing with whoever she could, harassing total strangers outside VR Bars.

Desperation calls for desperate measures.

Everything she had fought for, everything she had *thought* for, for the past eighteen months, was falling to pieces.

She was slowly going mad and there seemed to be nothing she could do to help herself.

Her com chimed.

She pulled it from the back pocket of her leggings and kept on walking. 'Yeah?'

A small face looked out at her. Temple, her controller.

'Kat, we need to meet.'

'Where and when?' She felt a stab of apprehension. She knew what this was about. Someone had seen her losing it outside some VR Bar, and it had got back to her controller.

'Thirty minutes. Do you now Connelly's on 42nd Street?'

'Sure I know it. I'll be there.' She cut the connection.

42nd Street? She could make it in thirty minutes if she upped her pace. She turned and headed uptown.

Of all the controllers she'd had, Temple was the only one she didn't get on with. The others had been good guys, who seemed to understand her. Temple was a slick, supercilious prick in his thirties who dressed like a prosecuting attorney and gave Kat orders as if he were talking to his rebellious teenage daughter.

What if word had got back to him about her behaviour? What if Temple said that Virex had decided to drop her? They'd take all her stuff, all her com-systems and monitors, and Kat'd be like a snail without a shell.

She got in thirty-five minutes later. The bastard was waiting for her, sharp in his immaculate navy blue suit. He was dark, Italian-looking. Gold watch and cuff-links, an emerald tie-clip, for Chrissake. It unsettled her that Virex was using suits like Temple.

His look, as she entered the bar and ordered a pint of Guinness, suggested that he resented having been kept waiting.

She took a thirsty gulp of the bitter liquid and wiped her mouth with the back of her hand as she slipped into the booth. Her knickers squelched with rapidly warming rain-water.

'Temple, what gives?'

He slipped a small manila envelope across the tabletop. She pocketed it, feeling a needle through the paper. Her heart pounded. Work, at last.

'A burn, right? The techs have cooked up a virus that'll fucking work this time?'

He had a unique way of expressing his distaste for her. He would simply stare at her, stare her down, until she looked away.

She took refuge in her beer.

'You know how unsuccessful the attempted viral attacks have been, Katherine.'

That was another thing she hated about him. She'd told him early on that she disliked her full name, and he'd used it ever since.

She slapped the tabletop, causing him to wince. 'Fuck this!' she snapped. 'First the bombing goes down the john, then the viruses! Jesus Christ, we'll be buying shares in VR next!'

He stared at her. 'Surveillance,' he said. 'Those in control,

31

in their wisdom, want you to check the sites catalogued on the pin. Record the programs that run the Cyber-Tech core site, in particular. They're progressing with their time-extension research.'

Kat nodded, overcome with the heavy, suffocating sensation of defeat. She sometimes wondered what was going on. For months, before her lay-off, she had been doing nothing but record what the big three were doing, and relaying the information to an unknown source.

The lack of perceived progress was sickening.

'I'll be in touch, Katherine,' Temple said, holding the flaps of his suit jacket together as he rose.

'Yeah,' Kat said. 'See you around.'

She watched him step from the bar and hail a taxi. She slipped further down into her seat and rested her feet on the opposite cushion.

At least, she thought, she would have something to occupy her mind for the next couple of days.

Her com chimed, and she wondered who the hell else might be calling her. 'Yeah, who is it?'

The tiny screen flickered. A face looked out at her.

She stared. 'Jesus Christ,' she whispered, her heart jumping.

'Hi, Kat.'

She found her voice. 'Colby? It's really you, Colby?'

He grinned at her, all snaggle-toothed and hairy. 'Course it's me.'

She shook her head, amazed. 'What's happening?' She ran a little fantasy number: Colby had quit Virex, was coming back for her.

'Things've happened, Kat. Big things. We need to talk.'

She nodded. 'Sure. Great. You in town?'

'I'm in Canada, checking something out. I'll be in New York by the weekend. I need to see you.'

She laughed. 'Sure. Can't wait, Colby.'

'See you then.'

32

Kat leaned forward. 'Hold it! What do you mean, big things?'

But he'd cut the connection. She tried to return the call, without luck.

She sat and stared at his stilled image on the tiny screen, grinning to herself.

And just when everything had seemed to be going from bad to worse . . .

Four

Once, around the turn of the century, White Plains had been an affluent satellite city of New York. Over the years the economic recession that had swept across North America had taken its toll. Businesses had closed, and sites marked for development had been left undeveloped or abandoned. Select outlying suburbs still maintained an air of defiant affluence; Maple Avenue, where Suzie Charlesworth lived, was one of these last bastions of wealth and privilege, and it showed.

Driving up on the Interstate, Halliday had passed vast tracts of diseased and stunted trees, elm and elder mostly, with the occasional plantation of genetically enhanced pine, developed in the vain hope that it might withstand the blight that had ravaged the country just as remorselessly as the economic recession.

Turning onto Maple Avenue, he was greeted by a startling sight. He wondered what would have been more surprising, evidence of real live maple trees in every front garden, or this: a display of holographic maples that stretched the length of the avenue in a blaze of bronze glory – a gesture at once visually arresting and intellectually futile.

He brought his old Ford to rest outside a tall, three-storey weatherboard house, luminously white amid a lawn so green that it was either a holographic projection too, or genetically modified.

After his VR meeting with Wellman, Halliday had tried to contact Kim. He'd called one of the restaurants she ran, but the manageress told him that she wasn't there and that she had no idea where she might be. He'd tried her old com number, which he'd last used well over a year ago, but as he expected it was no longer connected.

So he'd put off questioning his ex-girlfriend, relieved that the inevitable encounter had been delayed, and yet puzzled by her involvement with Suzie Charlesworth.

He left the Ford in the street and walked up the sloping driveway. He climbed a flight of steps to a long verandah and paused before the screen-door. He was out of breath from the short walk. He stanchioned an arm against the woodwork and wiped his forehead on his shirt-sleeve. He would have to start back at the gym again, begin eating properly.

He pressed the door-bell and awaited a reply. Was he as out of condition mentally as he was physically? He hadn't worked for six months, hadn't had to think through a case in that long, and he wondered if he'd be up to the task.

A child's voice issued from a speaker beside the door. 'What do you want?' According to the dossier Wellman had prepared, Suzie was an only child. So who was the kid with the brusque tone?

'I need to talk with Ms Charlesworth. Ms Anita Charlesworth?'

He heard the lock open automatically. He hesitated, waiting for a summons, and when none came pushed inside.

He was in a cool, shaded hallway at once strangely familiar and yet unusual. It was a museum piece, something from fifty years ago with its flower-patterned wallpaper, parquet flooring and framed oil prints. The hall had the evocative aroma of beeswax polish and freshly brewed coffee.

It was familiar because it reminded Halliday of his father's old house.

'Hello?'

'In here. You want coffee?'

The voice sounded from behind a door to his right. The kid's voice, again.

He pushed open the door and stood on the threshold.

It was a facsimile reproduction of his father's front room in the house he'd owned before his death last year: a similar three-piece suite, dark wood cabinets and, in the corner, something he recognised from his childhood: an old Sony television set.

He was wondering if it was still working when he saw the girl.

She was sitting on an upright chair by the window, her bare feet inches shy of the carpet. She was wearing a pair of cut-down denim shorts and a white T-shirt. She was blonde, perhaps thirteen years old, and her teeth were in braces.

'I said, do you want coffee, Mr Halliday?'

Like an actor fed the wrong lines, Halliday did his best to extemporise. He lowered himself onto an ancient sofa and sat back. 'Don't mind if I do . . . Suzie, isn't it?'

She pointed to a tiny hexagonal table beautifully fashioned from what looked like mahogany. 'Help yourself.'

He nodded, but made no move to comply. He was dealing with a deceptively bright kid here, despite appearances. If she wanted to play games, he was equal to the contest.

'Where's your mom, Suzie?'

'She's upstairs, resting.'

He nodded. There were any number of ways she might have learned his name. The house, despite its *fin de siècle* aspect, was possibly rigged with the latest surveillance devices, linked to some powerful mainframe directory.

'I can't disturb her,' Suzie went on.

'That's okay.' He took a bone-china cup from a tray and poured himself a black coffee, no sugar.

He sat back, the delicate cup poised before his lips. He felt

36

as though he were playing tea parties with someone who should have known better.

'Actually, it's not your mom I want to talk to. I came looking for you.'

'Well, in that case, Mr Halliday, you've found me.'

It was going to be, he thought, the easiest two hundred grand he'd ever worked for.

But, even as this occurred to him, he realised that there was something about the situation that was not quite right. As he sipped the lukewarm coffee, buying time, he understood what it was. Wellman had said the kid was autistic.

He could think of several words that might have described the precocious kid before him, but autistic was not one of them.

He returned the cup to the tray and leaned forward. 'Listen, Suzie, I'm a private detective and I've been hired by your employers to find you. According to Wellman, you didn't show at work on Friday. You've been missing for three days, you didn't ring in, and your employers were naturally concerned. If you can tell me what happened, and reassure me that everything's okay and you'll turn up at work next time, I can tell Wellman and things'll be fine.'

She was swinging her legs, staring down at her feet with a deep frown on her pretty face. She looked up at him, her eyes startlingly azure.

He'd expected a hurried, maybe embarrassed explanation, even an apology. What she said left him openmouthed.

'But I don't work, Mr Halliday.'

He massaged his tired eyes. 'You are Suzie Charlesworth, right? According to Wellman, who hired me to find you, you work for Cyber-Tech, in the time-extension division or whatever—'

'I'm Suzie, but I don't work. I very rarely leave the house. You see, I'm ill.'

Halliday nodded. Was this a part of her illness, then? Did

37

her autism have other psychological effects? He didn't know enough about the subject to hazard a guess.

'But last Thursday night you did go for a meal at Carlo's, with a silver-haired man and a woman called Kim Long, right?'

She was frowning at him, shaking her head. 'I haven't been out of the house for weeks.'

He decided to call it quits. He'd talk to her mother, get Suzie to call Wellman and explain the situation, and then pick up his cheque from Cyber-Tech for services rendered.

'I don't think this is funny. You're old enough to know that lying isn't . . .' He stopped himself; he was beginning to sound like his late father. 'I'd like to talk to your mother. Could you go and wake her?'

She shook her head, defiant. 'That's impossible.'

He sighed. More games? 'And why's that, Suzie?'

'Mother is tanked.'

He nodded. 'Okay, fine. When is she due out?'

'I don't know.'

'Well, could you go upstairs and check the monitor?'

She hesitated for a second, then jumped off the chair without a sound and hurried past him. He watched as she left the room, dancing around the partly opened door as if wary of coming into contact with the polished wood.

Come to that, he hadn't seen her touch anything else in the room, either. She hadn't opened the front door for him, or passed him a cup, or even opened the front-room door further to allow herself an easier exit.

She either had a contact phobia, or . . .

She returned a minute later, again moving around the door with the quick twist of a slalom skier.

As she resumed her place on the chair, Halliday watched the crimson brocade cushion.

'She'll be in there another twelve hours, Mr Halliday. She left instructions not to be disturbed.'

He nodded and moved from his chair. He knelt before the girl, staring into her bright blue eyes.

He had to admit, it had had him fooled.

She was almost perfect.

She smiled at him, shy. 'What?' she said.

He reached out, as if to cup her cheek, and his fingers passed through her flesh. His hand appeared to be buried, surreally, up to the wrist in the girl's head. His fingertips touched something, and he made a grab, his fist closing around a small, cold metallic object.

Instantly, Suzie Charlesworth disappeared.

He returned to his seat, hand grasped before him triumphantly as if he'd managed to snatch a fly in mid-air.

He held the device between his thumb and forefinger. The projection, released, relayed a partial image of the girl. Halliday's hand was still planted in her skull; her torso was complete. But her legs were cut off where they came into contact with his lap. The visual effect of the holographic projection was as if their two forms were melded, some face-to-face bi-sexual Siamese twin.

His hand vibrated as the device relayed her words. 'Pretty clever, Mr Halliday. You really are some super detective.' And she smiled, sweetly.

He released the device. For a second, the image of Suzie remained standing with her legs buried in his lap. Then she retreated and sat on the high-backed chair.

'Why the lies?' he asked.

'I didn't lie, Mr Halliday. I told you I didn't work for Cyber-Tech, I told you I hadn't left the house for absolutely ages.'

'And you also told me you were Suzie Charlesworth.'

'I never! You said you were looking for her, and I said you'd found me.'

'Who programmed you, Suzie?'

The projection hesitated. Checking the parameters of what she was allowed to divulge?

39

'Suzie did.'

'Can you tell me why?'

Another hesitation. 'Mother had me installed, as a kind of rehabilitation program for Suzie. It's called mirror-behaviourism. Suzie was supposed to see what I was doing and saying and want to compete.'

'Did it work?'

Suzie gave a sly smile. 'Suzie is okay as she is. She reprogrammed me, made me into what *she* wanted me to be.'

'Which is?'

The hologram girl swung her legs. 'Someone who can communicate with her.'

'A friend, right?'

She sneered. 'Suzie doesn't need friends. She programmed me as a mental co-processor, if you like. A tool.'

'To help her with her work at Cyber-Tech?'

The projection nodded.

Halliday poured himself another coffee. Far from feeling disappointed that he hadn't after all located Suzie Charlesworth, he was intrigued.

'What was she working on? Can you tell me that?'

That sly smile again. 'I don't think you'd understand a word, Mr H.'

'Try me.'

'Okay, Suzie was the star researcher on the time-extension team—'

'I'm with you so far.'

A flash of azure eyes. 'I haven't even begun yet, Mr H.' She hesitated. 'She was mapping neural interfaces in subject volunteers and correlating reaction times in and out of VR, trying to come to some definitive paradigm concerning cognitive dysfunction in temporal paradox sets—'

'Okay,' Halliday said. 'How about rephrasing that in simple language?'

Her gaze held his. 'That *was* simple language,' she said.

'Fine. Well, perhaps we'd better skip what she was working on.' Halliday smiled to himself as he realised that he was feeling inadequate in the presence of what was after all nothing more than an advanced computer system.

'Was she happy with her work at Cyber-Tech?' he asked.

She shrugged. 'We never discussed things like happiness.'

'What about sadness? Or what she was feeling?'

'We never discussed feelings. They don't matter.'

'You mean, they don't matter to you.'

'I mean, they don't matter to Suzie. They're unimportant. They're what other people have, which makes them what they are like.'

Halliday hesitated, phrasing his question. 'And what are other people like?'

'Other people are irrational,' she said. 'They say one thing and mean another, they act one way today, and another way tomorrow, with no apparent reason or methodology.'

Halliday sipped his coffee. 'And Suzie didn't like that?'

She gave him a look which he interpreted as contemptuous. 'It isn't a question of liking anything!' she said. 'It means that other people cannot think like Suzie. Even the people she works with are constrained by their feelings.'

'But with you, it's different, yes? She could talk with you, and you'd understand each other, with no interference from things like feelings and emotions?'

She nodded. 'We could talk for hours, overcome problems, work out avenues of investigation.'

'So would you say that you understood Suzie?' he asked.

She regarded him, obviously working out her reply. 'I know what she knows,' she said, 'and I understand what she wants.'

'So . . . what does she want?'

Suzie closed her eyes. Halliday wondered what exactly a thirteen-year-old autistic cyber-genius might possibly want from life. It certainly wasn't going to be a pony for Christmas and a party at the local KFC-McDonald's.

41

She opened her eyes and looked at him. 'Suzie,' she said, 'is trying to determine whether or not there is materialistic evidence for the existence of the human soul.'

Halliday opened his mouth, but a wisecrack was not forthcoming. He simply nodded. 'The human soul,' he murmured. 'Is that a fact?'

'It's what she's striving towards in her investigations.'

'Tell me, how far along the road is she towards discovering the truth about the soul?'

'Science isn't an exponential curve,' she said. 'It's more like a series of immeasurable leaps. Suzie will know when she gets there.'

Halliday nodded, at a temporary loss for words. So the missing autistic savant was on a quest to discover the human soul, was she? He wondered what Wellman might have to say when he reported that little gem.

'Do you have any idea why she didn't report in to work on Friday?'

Suzie shook her head. 'I don't know.'

'Do you know where she might be now?'

'I don't know that, either.'

'She never talked to you about people at work, people she knew outside work?'

'Suzie didn't know anyone outside work.'

'She was seen in a restaurant last Thursday evening with two people, an old guy and a young woman. Do you know if she'd ever met them before?'

'I don't know.'

'She didn't mention these people to you?'

'No, she didn't.'

'Did she program you to give these answers to anyone who asked, private investigators, the police?'

'If she did, then she kept the knowledge that she was doing so from me.'

'So in other words, what you've told me so far is the truth as you understand it?'

'The truth,' she smiled at him, 'and nothing but.'

Halliday stood up. 'I want to look around the house, if that's okay with you?'

She jumped to her feet. 'I'll give you a guided tour.'

Halliday moved to the door. 'Where's her bedroom?'

Suzie jabbed a forefinger at the ceiling. 'Third floor, attic.'

'Let's take a look.'

He climbed the stairs, Suzie following. The second floor was decorated in the same dark, old-fashioned style. He'd never seen so much wooden furniture in years. He smiled to himself. Lumber, his father had called it.

Suzie indicated a door giving onto a narrow, curving flight of steps. Halliday made his way carefully up the staircase. At the top he found a light switch and turned it on.

He supposed that if the rest of the house could be described as retro-twentieth-century, then this ivory tower of ultra-modernism might be termed cyber-minimalist.

A narrow bed occupied one corner, next to a bank of impressive-looking monitors and terminals. A state-of-the-art touchpad lay on the duvet. Not a doll, teddy bear, or holo-poster of a VR star in sight.

In fact, there was nothing at all in the way of possessions to indicate that this was the bedroom of a thirteen-year-old girl.

The hologram Suzie stood at the top of the steps, watching him.

Beside a computer monitor was a stack of perhaps fifty needles. Halliday sorted through them, squinted at the titles printed in tiny lettering along their shafts. He read them one by one, taking his time. They were all technical programs or com-texts.

He looked for blank needles, but found none.

'Suzie didn't keep a diary?'

'She didn't need to. Suzie never forgot a thing.'

Halliday nodded. 'Some girl, our Suzie,' he said to himself.

Two needles had titles containing the word eschatology.

He held up the needle. 'What does eschatology mean, Suzie?'

She corrected his pronunciation. 'Eschatology. With a hard *ch*, like *k*. It pertains to the study of death.'

'She certainly knows how to enjoy herself.'

'She is interested in the theory of existence beyond this life,' Suzie said.

'She's frightened of death, in other words?'

She looked at him. 'Not frightened. She sees death as illogical, a waste of valuable resources. She told me that it's a redundancy, a failure in an otherwise efficient system.'

Well, he supposed, you could put it like that.

'What does she believe in? Life after death? Some kind of reincarnation?'

'Suzie doesn't hold doctrinaire beliefs, as such. She understands that beliefs are the refuge of people who have failed to continue the process of learning.' If it were possible for a computer program to emanate intellectual superiority, then the Suzie hologram was emanating it in gigabytes.

'But she believes ... I mean, she *thinks* that humans possess souls, right?'

Suzie sighed. 'She is intrigued by the possibility that such a phenomenon as souls might have a materialistic basis.'

Halliday nodded and stared around the room. 'I stand corrected yet again.'

He'd seen enough. He moved towards the stairs and paused beside the hologram girl. 'You said Suzie's mother is tanked?'

'She has another twelve hours in VR.'

Halliday considered. 'How often does she use the jelly-tank?'

The projected girl looked at him. 'Every other day.'

44

'For the maximum twenty-four hours every time?'

'Sometimes, yes.'

He made his way down the stairs. 'And how long's she been using VR like this?'

Suzie paused on the step above him. 'I couldn't possibly say. Suzie's had me for only the past three months.'

'Where's the jellytank?' he asked, looking across the landing towards three closed doors.

She indicated the middle door and Halliday turned the handle and stepped inside, aware as he did so that he was violating established VR protocol. But what the hell: he was trying to locate the woman's missing daughter, and every bit of information he could gather along the way would be of value.

The jellytank stood in the centre of the room, one of the new art deco models that looked like nothing so much as a big aquarium. It was, not surprisingly, a Cyber-Tech tank.

Anita Charlesworth hung naked in the solid block of gel like some mummified specimen of womanhood preserved in amber. Halliday moved towards the tank, aware that Suzie had entered the room behind him.

He stared down at the woman. She was emaciated, yellow flesh shrink-wrapped around prominent pelvic flanges and bowed rib-cage. Fortunately, her face was concealed by the visor. From time to time her wasted limbs twitched in the gel as she lived out her fantasy existence in the cyberverse.

Anita Charlesworth, according to the information Wellman had supplied him, was thirty-eight years old – just two years older than Halliday. But the woman in the jellytank looked not a day younger than seventy.

He moved around the tank to the monitor. He tapped the touchpad, bringing up the history file. She had used the tank every other day for the past eleven months – the absolute maximum allowable by law.

He thought that Anita Charlesworth's physical state was a great advertisement for total abstinence.

He should really cut down, he told himself, or get to the gym.

Most of the sites she'd visited were hosted by Cyber-Tech. He read the list of zone codes: some he recognised as sex-zones, others game- and adventure-zones. He wondered what her daughter might have thought of her choice of virtual venues, if she had considered her mother's existence at all.

Could Anita Charlesworth's addiction to VR, he thought, be a consequence of having a severely autistic daughter?

From the door. Suzie said, 'If you've seen enough, Mr H . . . ?'

He followed her from the room and down the stairs into the shadowed hallway. He paused by the door, watching the hologram girl.

The content of the airborne projector, the program it contained, would be of interest to Wellman and his techs.

'Can you tell me if Suzie ever goes out, other than to work? Does she ever go into the city?'

Suzie pursed her lips. 'She does go into Manhattan from time to time.'

'Do you know where to, exactly?'

She shook her head. 'She's never told me.'

Halliday nodded. 'Okay. Well, I guess that's it. I'd better be going.'

He made to turn to the door, then reached out, quickly, before she had time to react.

His hand sank into the side of her head, and his fingers closed around the projector. He felt it surge as it attempted to free itself. He held on tight.

He hurried out, closing the door behind him, and jumped into the Ford. In the driver's seat, he slipped the projector into his pocket.

He should have known that Suzie would not be silenced so easily.

Her face appeared, bizarrely, at his crotch, staring up at

him. 'Once you get out of the car, Mr H, I'll scream and screa—!'

He clapped a hand over his pocket and her protests became muffled. 'Then I'll have to use force to ensure that you're a good little girl, won't I?'

He locked the device in the glove compartment, wadded into an old rag to disable the projection.

All the way from White Plains to Manhattan, he could hear Suzie's muffled contralto as she demanded to be let out.

Five

He left the holographic projection device with Roberts at the penthouse suite on Madison, then made his way back to the office. The sun was going down as he parked the Ford outside the Chinese laundry, but the temperature was still in the nineties and the humidity was choking. Soon the rains would begin, bringing temporary respite to the sultry, tropical atmosphere.

The street was packed with traders and customers; entire families sat out on the steps, calling back and forth like spectators at a sporting venue.

He bought take-out from a Thai stall, then returned to the car for the case that Roberts had given him. He made his way to his office, hit the fan and sat behind his desk. He blew the dust from the leaves of the bonsai oak, gave it a little water, then brewed himself a coffee.

He placed the case on the desk and thumbed open the catch.

The first surprise was the fact that the case was a small, self-contained computer, with a screen set into the lid and a touchpad that folded out.

He started it running, and seconds later a face smiled out at him.

'Halliday,' Wellman said. 'Hope you find some of the items in the case of use. They're the latest gadgets on the market. Good luck.' The executive disappeared, to be replaced by a menu listing the contents of the case and their use.

Halliday went through the devices. The first was a

capillary holo unit, or chu. He pulled it from its wrapper and held the mask before him, activating the slide control and watching as a hundred different faces emanated one by one from the fine mesh webbing.

Next out of the case was a neural incapacitator, a simple hand-held device no bigger than a pack of cards. One jolt from the incapacitator could scramble an assailant's neural network, leaving him or her temporarily paralysed.

There were a couple of surveillance devices, a vision aid a little thicker than a contact lens, and a series of disposable bugs tuned to an ear-piece.

Halliday had seen, and sometimes worked with, examples of all these devices, though he had to admit that these were the best that money could buy.

Then he came across something that he'd never seen before. They seemed to be a series of disposable surgeon's gloves, each one packed flat in a thin, transparent envelope.

He scrolled down the menu until he came to: *Cellular tracer [gloves]*. The fingertips of each glove, he learned, were coated with nano-monitors used frequently these days in surgery; the monitors invaded the target's bloodstream and relayed to the computer the state of the subject's health, everything from blood pressure to brain patterns. The monitors also reported the subject's precise whereabouts directly to an on-screen map.

He calculated that the contents of the case were easily worth the two hundred grand he'd requested for locating the Charlesworth kid. Wellman was clearly serious about finding her.

Outside, the rain began. It drummed on the fire escape beyond the window, lashing against the glass and filling him with an odd sense of reassurance. One thing you could always be certain of in this uncertain world was the arrival of the evening rain.

His spiced beef take-out, overlooked in his absorption with the devices, had grown cold and congealed in the silver trays. He hurriedly ate the meal and poured himself another black coffee. He was stuffing the empty trays into the trash can when his desk-com chimed and the dollar sign in the top left corner – which Barney had installed years ago – flashed on and off, signalling the arrival of a potential client.

He closed the case and slipped it into a drawer, then pulled himself closer to the desk in the swivel chair and tried to recall how to assume a professional attitude before a customer.

Not, he told himself, that he intended to take on another case while working for Wellman.

Someone knocked on the door, then entered without waiting for a reply.

The woman was slim, attractive, her short blonde hair spangled with rain. She was maybe in her mid-twenties and well-dressed. She paused by the door, one hand still on the handle, and smiled at him. 'Hiya, Hal.'

Halliday stared. 'Christ . . .'

The woman grinned. 'How's things?'

'Casey? I mean, Jesus Christ, what's happened?'

Where was the scrawny street kid he'd taken in a year ago, the barefoot refugee from the Atlanta meltdown?

He stood up and indicated the chesterfield beside his swivel chair, and as he watched her walk around the desk – watching how the dress hugged the curves of her hip and breast – he felt a sudden pang of guilt.

He considered the Casey persona he'd created in VR, and how lifeless it was beside the real, live human being.

She sat down on the chesterfield, kicked off her shoes and drew her legs up beneath her.

How many times had he seen her curled up like this, but dressed back then in soiled shorts and a ripped T-shirt, her feet bare and her hair a tousled mess?

He sat back in his swivel and laughed. 'Well, I don't know what to say . . .'

She blushed. 'Hey, Hal. It's still me. All this,' she indicated the sleek dress and fashionably styled hair, 'it doesn't matter, y'know.'

'It's just a surprise, that's all. You look about ten years older.' He leaned forward, staring at her. 'And you're wearing make-up.'

She shrugged. 'Just a little blusher and lipstick, is all. Aren't you going to offer me a coffee?'

He indicated the percolator. 'Help yourself.'

He watched her as she poured a mug of coffee and sat with it in both hands, held up before her rouged mouth. How many nights had they sat like this a year ago, just chatting as he waited for work?

She was no longer the thin-faced urchin he remembered: her face had filled out, become quite striking, with high cheekbones and full lips. He found it hard to believe that she was still only seventeen.

'Well, it's good to see you. How long's it been? Six months?' He was aware of a note of censure that he had not consciously intended.

She looked at him, eyes narrowed. She had always given as good as she got. 'Six months? Listen, pal, I was here last month. Dropped by to see how my old buddy was getting along.'

He frowned, shook his head. 'A month ago?'

'Can't remember, can you? Well, Hal, you were out of it. Blitzed on VR. You'd just quit the tank. I found you collapsed in the shower. You were not a pretty sight.'

'You did? I mean . . .'

'I got you out and dressed, bought you a take-out. You could hardly eat. I wanted to call Doc Symes, but you said you were okay. I tried to contact you a few days later, but you weren't taking calls. No doubt tanked again . . .'

Walking through the Virginia site with you in my arms, he thought. *Or, rather, some pale imitation of you.*

He shrugged. 'I'm working on a case,' he said feebly.

'Look, I'm eating again, see?' He pointed to the scrunched silver foil tray in the trash can.

Casey wrinkled her nose. 'When you going to get some real food down you, Hal? I mean, if you use VR so much, you need to really look after yourself.'

'Yeah, okay . . .' He busied himself, embarrassed, by pouring another coffee.

'I'm concerned for you, Hal. You never call round these days. I miss you.'

He shrugged again. About six months ago, feeling pretty low, drunk and maudlin for the good times when Barney was alive, he'd driven around the block to where Casey lived with her Chinese boyfriend. He'd hoped to catch her alone, see how she was keeping. He'd pulled up outside the tenement building and seen them walking along the street towards him, Casey and her man, hand in hand, and he'd been rendered breathless by a sudden stab of some strange and powerful emotion, part jealousy, part despair. He'd started the engine and roared off, gone back to Olga's bar and consoled himself with a few more Ukrainian wheat beers . . .

Not long after that he'd had the idea of creating Casey's persona in VR.

He took a mouthful of coffee. 'So . . . how's things with you, anyway? Still seeing Ben?'

She twisted her lips into a half-humorous, half-wistful pout. 'Ben's history, Hal. It was good while it lasted, but . . .'

'Too bad.' He was about to ask if she was seeing anyone else, but stopped himself in time. 'Still working for Kim?'

The last he'd heard, Kim had owned half a dozen restaurants around the area. She'd sold her street-stalls one by one and invested in real, sit-down, cutlery and chop-stick eating houses. Casey had worked for Kim on a stall, and when Kim moved upmarket she'd taken Casey on as a trainee manageress.

Halliday had seen one of her places reviewed on the

leisure channel, but the thought of dining there, and maybe happening across Kim and whoever she was screwing at the moment, did not appeal.

Casey replaced her empty mug on the desk. 'That's what I came to see you about.'

Something in her manner alerted him. 'What is it?'

'See, Kim sold all her restaurants a few weeks ago. Every one of them. She didn't even tell anyone, not even me. Yesterday the new manager came in and said he was laying a few of us off.'

'Hey, I'm sorry.'

'It's not the job I'm worried about, Hal.'

'So what is it?'

She hesitated. 'Last night I went around to Kim's apartment. I just wanted to know why she hadn't told me what was going down. You see, I thought we were friends, you know? I didn't want to make a scene.'

He was aware of his heart, thumping. Kim had sold her restaurants, was seen in the company of an old guy and a girl who a day later mysteriously vanished . . .

'And? What did Kim say?'

'Kim didn't say anything. She wasn't there. I talked to the neighbours, but they hadn't seen her for more than a week. I went round all her old restaurants today, but no one there had seen her, either.'

'What about the guy she was seeing? The Chinese guy who owned a restaurant?'

'He's long gone, Hal. Kim blew him out weeks ago. She was with a new guy, last I heard. A Vietnamese kick-boxing star.'

The thought of Kim with someone, even after a year, twisted something deep within him. 'So maybe she's shacked up somewhere with this guy?'

Casey shrugged, staring down at her fingernails. Halliday recalled them as being constantly bitten-back, the varnish

53

chipped and grown out. Now her nails were long and oval, with a chic mother-of-pearl lustre. Real sophisticated.

She said at last, 'So why hasn't she been around? Why hasn't she dropped by to tell her staff she was selling up? It just isn't like her, Hal.'

They were connected, of course. Kim's disappearance, and the Charlesworth kid. Halliday experienced a once familiar feeling: the visceral kick of initiating an investigation that would end in either success or failure. He wished, though, that he could be more objective about this one. The thought of Kim's involvement in the affair, in whatever capacity that might be, filled him with apprehension.

'You know where this kick-boxing champ lives?'

Casey shook her head. 'I tried to find out from his agent, but he wouldn't say. But I do know he's fighting tonight. Madison Square Gardens. His bout's scheduled for ten. Some title fight.'

'That'd be the place to start. I'll go along, see what the champ knows. What's his name?'

Even as he asked it, he realised that he'd never before wanted to know the name of the guy Kim had been seeing. Without a name, these people were less real, Kim's infidelity abstracted.

'He fights under the name of Jimmy King. I don't know his real name.' She hesitated, not looking at him, then asked, 'Hey, how about I come with you? I've nothing to do tonight.'

Halliday thought about it. Why not? It certainly beat the hell out of pretending with some lifeless VR ghost.

'Okay, sure.'

Casey grinned. 'Great. Thanks, Hal.'

He made to leave the office, then remembered the case Wellman had given him. He'd take it with him, stow it in the car.

They left the office and emerged into the night. The rain had ceased, freshening the air. The lights of a hundred fast-food kiosks dazzled across the wet tarmac. Halliday gunned the Ford and headed downtown on Park Avenue. Buildings clad in holo-façades flickered by like so many colossal Halloween lanterns.

Casey pulled the case from the passenger footwell where Halliday had placed it. 'Can I look?'

'Go ahead.'

He smiled across at her. For all her assumed sophistication, she was still a kid at heart: this time, a kid on Christmas morning.

'Hey,' Casey said, pulling a package from the case. 'Looka this.'

Halliday smiled. 'Not bad, eh? The latest in capillary holographic hardware.'

'Remember when I wanted one of these?'

A year ago, Casey had gone though a phase of thinking she looked ugly. She got it into her head that she needed a chu to hide behind. Halliday had talked her out of it, telling her that she was good-looking enough not to need one.

'Yeah,' Halliday said, 'and now look at you. Cinderella, right?'

He recalled the cheque Vanessa Artois had presented him with on the completion of the case a year ago. A cool half million dollars. He had dreamed of how he might go about spending the money. He had promised himself that he'd set Casey up in business, or pay for her education.

In the end he'd done none of these things. Casey had moved out and shacked up with her boyfriend, and perhaps understandably he'd seen less of her, and his resolution to make her a gift had foundered on apathy and his own very real need to fund his increasing VR addiction.

Now he felt a stab of guilt: he hadn't even mentioned a word of his windfall to her.

She was rummaging through the case. 'You bought all these, Hal?'

'A client. Like I said, I'm working on a case.'

'The first in how long?' she asked, slanting a glance at him.

'Oh . . . I don't know.' He opened his palms on the apex of the wheel in a dismissive gesture. 'Thing is, I'm working again.'

'And you gonna cut down on VR, right?'

The image of Anita Charlesworth's emaciated body flashed in his mind's eye.

How could he tell Casey that he had no intention of reducing the hours he spent in his jellytank? He'd simply make sure that he looked after himself when he quit VR.

'Yeah, sure.' He glanced across at her, saw a look of dubiety in her eyes. 'I mean it. See, I saw something today that gave me the creeps.'

'Yeah? Tell me about it.' She closed the case and replaced it in the footwell.

He hunched his shoulders in a *where-to-begin* shrug. 'Working on this case, upstate. The mother of someone I was questioning. Well, she was using VR to the limit, twenty-four hours in every forty-eight.'

Casey pulled a *yucky* face. 'You saw her, Hal?'

He nodded. 'Looked like something from the Egyptian Room of the National History Museum. Yellow and wasted, all skin and bone.'

Casey was quiet. He glanced at her. 'What?' he asked.

She said, 'Listen to the kettle . . .'

He didn't get the reference. 'What you mean?'

'You've got some room to talk. Looked in the mirror lately?'

'Come on, Casey . . . Okay, I've been overdoing it. But I'm not that bad.'

'No? Listen, I walked in the office and I said to myself, who's the moving skeleton in the swivel chair? That's how bad you look.'

He looked at her. 'And I suppose you don't use at all, Casey?'

'Matter of fact, I don't. Used it a few times, then decided it wasn't for me.'

'Listen to miss-holier-than-thou. You must be the only citizen in America not tanking.'

She stared straight ahead, stung. 'That suits me fine.'

He let the seconds pass, then said gently, placating, 'So, why don't you like it, Casey?'

She let out a long sigh and turned in her seat. 'You want to know what I think, Hal? I think it's a bad influence. I don't like what it's doing to people.'

'What is it doing to people?'

'I read something the other day, some professor writing on the Net. He said something about VR changing how people related to each other. He said the VR experience was too easy. I mean, you get everything you want in VR. You only have to think of yourself, not other people. So when you get back into the real world, you find it harder to relate . . . Except he used all these big words to back up his argument.'

'So you read one article and you're immediately down on VR?'

'No! The professor just wrote what I was thinking, or perhaps not even thinking, but *feeling*. I don't know . . . I look at people around me, see, and they don't seem to be relating to other people, they don't seem to be thinking about anyone else but themselves.'

She fell silent and looked away, embarrassed.

Halliday grunted. 'So when's it been any different, Casey?'

She turned and stared at him. 'What I'm trying to say is, look after yourself, Hal. Don't tank so much, okay?' She reached out and squeezed his thigh, and something in her expression, as her hand closed on the slack, atrophied muscle, turned his stomach.

'Hey,' he said. 'Here we are.'

The exterior of the arena was fitted with a gargantuan

and tasteless holo-façade depicting two Thai boxers head to head. The promoters had obviously lavished thousands on the display: from time to time a fist or leg lashed out with sickening authenticity. Halliday left the Ford in a sidestreet and made for the entrance between the boxers' dancing legs.

They bought tickets for ringside seats and made their way towards the focus of what seemed like a million dazzling spotlights. A bout was already under way, the last round of the fight before Jimmy King was due to defend his world middleweight title.

They took their seats to a chorus of grunts from the fighters in the ring. They were close enough to see the ejecta of sweat and blood that exploded, scintillating in the lights, whenever a fighter landed a blow.

Halliday looked around the banked arena. Despite the cacophony of noise, the partisan cries of supporters, he guessed that the venue was only half full. Since the advent of VR, attendances at sporting events all across the United States had gradually dropped. Why attend a live event when you could actually participate in a sporting fixture yourself, irrespective of your ability to play the game, and with no risk of pain or injury?

Casey held onto his arm and squeezed. 'What do people see in this?' she said above the noise.

He watched the antics of the marionettes in the ring, their expressions horribly contorted with every blow delivered and received. He bent his head to her ear. 'I can think of better ways to spend my evenings.'

The fight came to an end, and one participant was adjudged to have outfought the other. The verdict produced euphoria in one section of the crowd, matched by boos and cat-calls from another. The winner was carried precariously from the ring on the shoulders of supporters, holding a belt the size of a car fender high above his head.

'Can I get you a drink, Casey?' The heat of the night,

combined with the humidity in the arena, had given him a thirst.

'Love a beer,' she said. She looked at her programme. 'Jimmy King's on next. He's fighting someone called Han Ki Sin, from Taiwan.'

'Can't wait,' Halliday muttered as he left his seat and hurried down the aisle. In fact, if he was honest with himself, he was intrigued to see just what kind of guy Kim was currently dating.

He carried two ice-cold bottles of German lager back to his seat and watched as the promoter announced the night's main attraction. The beer cut a cryogenic swathe down his gullet, and he realised that it was the first alcohol he'd tasted since quitting the tank at midday. Some record, he thought to himself. Usually, his first stop after the tank was Olga's bar, to ease his way back into the real world.

A combination of work and Casey's company was having a beneficial effect on him already.

The fighters leapt into the ring. Jimmy King was short and squat. His body appeared to be constructed from variously sized blocks of solid muscle, each one highlighted in oil and shining in the spotlights. He sported a pair of scarlet shorts, a good size too big for him, and a white headband like a latter-day kamikaze pilot.

The Taiwanese boxer was his mirror image, physically; only his blue shorts and absence of headband distinguished him from Jimmy King.

Halliday sank into his seat, tipped his beer and looked forward to watching the Vietnamese fighter get beaten to a bloody pulp.

The bout began, and it soon became obvious that he was going to be disappointed. King had the advantage from the outset, kicking and punching with swift and brutal economy. Casey winced behind raised hands at every blow.

'Where the hell did Kim meet this monster?' Halliday asked.

'He came into one of her restaurants after a fight,' Casey said.

'Wonder what the hell she sees in him . . .'

Casey smiled to herself and squeezed his arm.

King disposed of his opponent a minute into the fourth round, laying the guy out with a lightning combination of punches to the head and a telling kick to the midriff.

Cue the clichéd victory celebrations, the hoisting of the champion from the ring. It struck Halliday, as did every sporting event he'd had the misfortune to find himself watching, as a microcosmic example of the overwhelming futility of human endeavour. But then what had Kim called him, more than once: something along the lines of a heartless cynic?

Halliday gave it five minutes, then turned to Casey. 'Wait here, I'm going to talk to the champ.'

'Can I come with you?'

He hesitated. 'You met this guy before?'

'A couple of times, with Kim.'

He nodded. There was a chance that Casey's presence might have the effect of loosening his tongue. 'Okay, follow me.'

They moved around the ring, towards a corridor thronged with jostling pressmen. Halliday fought his way through, pulling Casey after him. A big cop stood before the door to the dressing rooms.

Halliday flashed his old NYPD ID card and the cop stood aside. He passed down a half-lit corridor high with the odour of sweat and oil. Stewards in blue overalls moved back and forth. A bodyguard stood outside the door of a dressing room, legs spread, arms behind his back.

'Jimmy King in there?' Halliday asked.

'Who wants to know?'

Halliday hung his ID.

'A cop? What you want?'

'Well, I'm not an autograph hound, buddy. Tell the

champ I'm investigating the disappearance of Kim Long, okay?'

The bodyguard hesitated, then turned and ducked into the dressing room, pulling the door shut behind him.

'What if he won't let you in?' Casey asked.

Halliday drew the neural incapacitator from his jacket pocket and held it up for Casey's inspection. Before she could reply, the door opened and the guard appeared, bulking from the small opening like a genie from a lamp.

'Jimmy says he'll see you when he's dressed.'

Halliday nodded. 'That sounds reasonable.'

They waited in the corridor. Halliday said, 'Some fight?'

The guy grunted. 'Every bout fixed weeks back, so what the fuck?'

'And I thought the great tradition of American sports was unsullied by such things.'

The guy just looked at him, expressionless.

Someone rapped on the other side of the door, and the bodyguard stood aside and pulled it open. Halliday stepped into the dressing room, followed by Casey.

Jimmy King was dressed in a black tracksuit, and he still wore his trademark headband. Out of the ring he looked reduced, much smaller than Halliday had imagined.

He had the sudden, involuntary vision of Kim and the champ in bed.

Someone, his coach or whoever, was jabbering to King in Vietnamese. Halliday displayed his ID to the coach and gestured to the door. 'Get out.'

The coach glanced at Jimmy, who nodded. The guy quit the room.

Jimmy King shifted a quick glance from Halliday to the girl, who was standing by the door. 'Hey, Casey, how's things?'

She smiled shyly. 'Fine, Jimmy.'

Halliday indicated a bench. 'Sit down. Make yourself

61

comfortable. You must be tired after all that running around?'

Watching Halliday with suspicion, Jimmy King sat down.

Halliday sat on a bench across from the boxer, rested his elbows on his knees and looked across at King. Casey remained by the door.

'When was the last time you met Kim Long, Jimmy?'

King shrugged. 'I don't know. A month ago, maybe more.' He looked from Halliday to Casey. 'Why, what's happened? You said Kim was missing.' He picked up a towel and mopped the sweat from his face.

'She's been gone around a week.' Halliday stared at the boxer. 'What do you know about it?'

'Me?' King gave a fine imitation of pained incredulity. 'Listen, friend, I haven't seen Kim for weeks. We split up. She found someone else—'

Halliday digested this. 'She did?' He realised he was sweating. His fist clenched around the incapacitator in his pocket. 'You didn't like being dumped, so what did you do to Kim, champ?'

'Me? I did nothing. Last time I saw her, we talked.'

'Who's she seeing?'

King shrugged. 'I don't know.'

'You'd better tell me, champ.' Halliday pulled the incapacitator from his pocket. The boxer watched him, his eyes wide. 'Was it a silver-haired guy, old, in his sixties?'

'I told you, I don't—'

He surprised even himself, then. He leapt up and rammed the incapacitator into the guy's midriff, squeezing out a small charge – just enough to have the champ squirming on the floor as the voltage scrambled his neural network.

Casey gave a small shriek and covered her mouth with her hand.

Halliday had heard that the pain inflicted by an NI was exquisite. He stood over the boxer, staring down at the tortured expression on his face.

He reached down, took hold of a handful of tracksuit, and pulled King to his feet. He dropped him onto the bench, grabbed him by the neck and lowered his mouth to the boxer's mashed ear.

'If you don't tell me who the fuck she's seeing, champ, and anything else you might know about what's happened to her, I'll make damned sure you never fight again. Got that?'

'I . . .' The guy worked his mouth, trying to speak. 'I don't know who's she's seeing. But—!' he screamed, hands raised, as Halliday moved to make good his promise. 'Kim . . . she's been strange. Acting strange. Secretive. She was involved in something. I don't know what. I heard her talking on her com. Mentioned something about some Methuselah Project.'

Halliday raised the incapacitator. 'What else you heard, champ?'

The boxer's eyes widened in fright. 'I . . . she's been seeing someone. A friend. They're both involved.'

'The friend's name?'

The boxer was obviously struggling to recall the name. 'She . . . she's called Anastasia.'

'Surname?'

'Dah. Anastasia Dah. She has an apartment in the Kennedy building, off Broadway.'

Halliday knelt and patted King's sweat-soaked cheek. The champ flinched. 'Anything else you think I might need to know?'

King shook his head. 'That's everything . . . everything I know. Wish – wish I'd never met the bitch!'

Halliday smiled. 'That makes two of us, champ.'

He dragged King from the bench and dumped him behind a row of lockers, so that he'd be hidden from view when the door opened.

He looked up and saw Casey, staring at him. 'What? You

wanted to come along, Casey. How do you think I conducted interrogations?'

She just looked away.

'Come on, let's see what this Anastasia has to say for herself.'

He took her hand and they hurried from the dressing room. Another bout was in progress in the diamond-bright glare of the ring. They left the roar of the crowd in their wake and emerged into the hot night.

As they walked to the car, Casey said, 'I'm bushed, Hal. Is it okay if you drive me home?'

'Sure. No worries.'

She was silent in the passenger seat as Halliday drove uptown towards El Barrio. He looked across at her. 'Casey . . .'

She said in a small voice, 'You didn't need to have done that to him.'

'Hey, Casey, he got off lightly—'

'He would've talked without you using that thing on him.'

'Like hell he would. He wouldn't have said a damned thing. I had to find out what he knew, and I found out. And now I have a lead or two. You want me to find Kim, yes?'

She avoided his glance, muttered, 'What do you think?'

He fell silent. He wondered if Casey was right, if perhaps there might have been a more humane way of going about extracting the information he desired from King. How much had his actions been provoked by simple jealousy?

They turned onto East 106th Street and headed west. They passed Thai Joe's VR Bar where, before he'd bought his own jellytank, Halliday had spent a lot of tank time. Fat Joe was waddling up and down the sidewalk, resplendent in a multicoloured Hawaiian shirt. Halliday wondered how trade was, now that citizens could afford their own jellytanks.

'You're not going to use that thing on the woman, are you? On Anastasia?'

Halliday looked at her. 'I'd never—'

'What?' she said, meeting his gaze. 'You'd never use it on a woman? Not even if you needed to know something real bad?'

He didn't reply. He knew the answer to that one. He remembered one time back when he worked for the police . . .

'I'm just going to talk to her. I won't even mention I'm a detective. I'll tell her I'm a friend of Kim's, okay?'

She gave a small nod.

'Casey, all I want is to make sure Kim's safe. And I'm gonna do whatever I need to do to find out.'

She nodded again, not looking at him.

He drew up outside her apartment block.

'Hey, if you want to go out sometime, Casey . . . Just give me a call, okay?'

She smiled and touched his hand. 'Yeah, okay. I'll do that, Hal.'

She slipped from the car and hurried across the sidewalk.

He watched her go, then pulled out into the street.

The Methuselah Project, he thought, as he turned onto Fifth Avenue and headed downtown towards Broadway.

What the hell was the Methuselah Project?

Six

The Kennedy building was a four-storey apartment block on East Houston Street. Built during the boom period twenty years ago, it was the residence of fifty or so seriously rich citizens. Halliday found all this out from the Net as he sat in the Ford across the street from the building. He also learned that Anastasia Dah was the director of a casting agency in the VR entertainment industry. Kim was certainly moving in elevated circles, these days.

He considered whether he should use his police identification and go in there in a supposedly official capacity, or play on Dah's sympathies – if she were the type of woman who had such things. He could say he was a friend of Kim's, concerned for her whereabouts.

He tapped her code into his com and waited.

The small screen flashed, and the head of a striking black woman stared out at him. 'Anastasia Dah. Who is this?'

'Halliday. You don't know me. I'm a friend of Kim Long.'

He watched the woman, looking for the slightest reaction.

She merely nodded, non-committal. 'I think Kim mentioned you, once. What do you want?'

'I want to talk to you about Kim,' he said.

'Is she in trouble—?'

'I'll discuss that with you in person, Ms Dah. Now, if you don't mind. I'm right outside. If you could spare a few minutes . . .'

'I'm afraid that's impossible. I'm extremely busy.'

He hung his police ID card before the screen. 'We can do

this one of two ways. Either you can give me a few minutes of your precious time, or I can take you down to the station. That might take a little longer.'

Anastasia Dah glanced off screen. 'I can give you fifteen minutes, Mr Halliday. I'm on the fourth floor, apartment two.'

He cut the connection, pulled the case onto his lap and lifted the lid. If Dah was still in contact with Kim, then he'd be wise to plant a transceiver in her apartment. He slipped a cache of bugs into his jacket pocket, then considered the surgical gloves.

He slipped a hand into the transparent envelope and pulled on a glove. The membranous polymer material shrank around his right hand, visually indistinguishable from his flesh. He tried to detect any sign of the nano-devices that apparently coated the palm of the glove. All he saw were the lines that criss-crossed his skin – the life-line that Kim had once happily announced indicated a long and prosperous existence.

He locked the Ford and crossed to the building. A liveried concierge allowed him into the air-conditioned chill of a lobby full of artificial palms. He rode the elevator to the fourth floor, avoiding his reflection in the mirrored interior, and emerged into a sumptuous corridor of polished timber and thick carpeting.

He found Dah's apartment and knocked. The door opened almost instantly, swinging back to reveal a vision of sybaritic excess. The carpet resembled thick white fur, and the furnishings, two huge sofas and three armchairs, were upholstered in similar fashion. The effect was as if a family of polar bears had been sacrificed at the whim of some crazed interior designer.

Halliday stepped into the room, his feet snagging on the thick pile. The door swung shut automatically behind him.

Anastasia Dah wore a scarlet wrap that contrasted strik-ingly with the ebony perfection of her skin. The electronic

67

image of her as relayed by his com-screen had failed to do her beauty full justice: she was perhaps the most glamorous woman Halliday had ever met. He guessed that she was in her mid-twenties, with high cheekbones and lips that appeared constantly amused.

'I appreciate you taking the time to talk to me, Ms Dah,' Halliday said, holding out his hand.

Dah took it, and Halliday squeezed. 'As long as we can conclude the interview within fifteen minutes, Mr Halliday.'

'I don't see why it should take any longer.' He looked around the room. 'Quite a place . . .' He noticed, through a door that stood ajar to the right of the entrance, the sleek shape of a Tidemann's jellytank. The console at the head of the tank sequenced through a series of menus.

She was barefoot, and the wrap was drawn tight around her voluptuous form without a hint of any clothes beneath.

Halliday indicated the tank. 'I'm sorry if I've delayed your immersion,' he said.

'Likewise,' she said, her gaze taking him in from head to foot. 'I'm sorry if I've dragged you away from your own.'

He shrugged, damned if he was going to let her see that her barb had found the target. 'I use VR a lot in the line of duty, Ms Dah.'

'Then that's something we have in common.' She smiled, gesturing to one of the furred sofas. As Halliday sank into the cushions, she went on, 'I tank for an hour every day, Mr Halliday. It's one of the perks of the job.' She sat on the opposite sofa and crossed her long legs.

He noticed, with satisfaction, that she was absently scratching the palm of her right hand.

'You're the director of a VR casting agency?' He looked around the walls of the apartment. Perhaps a dozen large pix showed Anastasia Dah in the company of holo-actors and VR stars. 'I understand that the stars are computer-generated these days. So why the need for casting agencies?'

'I cast the actors and models who provide the original templates for the computer-generations,' she explained. 'We're always looking for new faces, as well as creating new personas from scratch, of course.'

'Pity the poor actors who find themselves out of work,' Halliday commented. 'I know Vanessa Artois. She quit the business when all they wanted from her was her identity. She wanted to act.'

'I hear she's doing well in Hollywood,' Dah said. 'Isn't she working in live theatre these days?' There was something insufferably smug in the way Dah phrased the question.

'So I believe,' he said, 'but I didn't come here to drop names.' He set his com to record and placed it on the glass-topped coffee-table between them.

'How long have you known Kim Long?' he asked.

'We met at a party perhaps six months ago,' she said. 'Can you tell me why you're interested?'

He watched her. 'Kim went missing some time last week,' he said. 'I'm questioning her friends and acquaintances. If you've any idea at all where she might be . . . When did you last have contact with her?'

Dah frowned, twisting scarlet lips in a moue that managed to be both sensuous and almost ugly. 'Perhaps last week some time,' she said. 'We spoke by com.'

'And Kim didn't mention that she was planning a trip, going away anywhere?'

Dah shook her head, a tumble of midnight ringlets falling prettily over one eye. She brushed back the offending curls with a lazy hand. 'She said nothing about any trip, Mr Halliday. In fact she said that she'd be in the city for the next few weeks – she suggested we meet for dinner. I said I'd get back to her.' She leaned forward. 'It isn't like Kim to do something like taking a vacation, even a short break, without telling friends. Do you have any idea what might have happened to her, Mr Halliday?'

'We're following various leads, but at the moment we have nothing definite. How well do you know Kim?'

'We're good friends, Mr Halliday. We have a lot in common.'

Halliday took in Dah's painted toenails, the gold rings sparkling on her long fingers. He found it hard to see what the practical, down-to-earth girl he'd known and loved would have in common with the affluent director of a VR casting agency.

'Do you know any of the men in Kim Long's life?' he asked.

'I've met her boxer friend once or twice.'

'What about an older man? He'd be in his sixties, silver-haired?'

She shook her head. 'Kim didn't go for the older type,' she said.

'Might she have had an acquaintance who would fit that description?'

She held his gaze. 'She might.'

'Do you know if she knew a young girl by the name of Susanna Charlesworth, a computer technician?'

'If she did, she never mentioned her to me.'

He picked up his com and switched it off. 'I might need to talk to you again, Ms Dah. I'll be in touch.'

'I am planning to go away for a while next week.'

'In that case I'll call you before you go.'

He replaced the com in his pocket and stood up.

Dah glanced down at the palm of her right hand, frowning as she scratched the skin with long, crimson-lacquered nails. She looked up as Halliday hesitated on the way to the door.

'One thing I thought I'd mention,' he said. 'Could you tell me what the Methuselah Project is, Ms Dah?'

She made a convincing performance of repeating the name and frowning. He had hoped to catch her by surprise, but Anastasia Dah would not be fooled so easily.

'I don't believe I've ever heard of it,' she said.

He smiled. 'I'll leave you to tank in peace, Ms Dah. Thanks for your time.'

He moved to the door, and turned before stepping from the room. She was watching him, drawing the gown tight across her chest and scowling with what appeared to be displeasure.

He quit the air-conditioned sanctuary of the Kennedy building and crossed the street to his Ford. He sat in the driver's seat and stared up at the strip of lighted windows on the fourth floor. Over the years he had developed the ability to intuit when someone was not telling the entire truth. Anastasia Dah had appeared superficially convincing, replying to his questions with just the right answers, but something in her performance convinced him that it had been just that.

As he stared up at the windows, the lighting dimmed. A darkened window to the left – presumably that of the VR room – flared with illumination. Halliday imagined Anastasia Dah slipping the wrap from her body and stepping into the jellytank.

He pulled the case onto his lap and lifted the lid. He activated the computer and accessed the nano-med file.

A fluctuating graph filled the screen. It took him several minutes to work out exactly what was represented, and then he had it: the horizontal slide-bars calibrated Anastasia Dah's physiological state: heartbeat, blood pressure, alpha- and beta-wave emissions . . .

As he watched, the slide-bars retracted. Her pulse dropped along with her blood pressure; her alpha-wave emissions slowed, indicating a sudden soporific state deeper even than that of sleep.

Dah had tanked and entered VR.

Halliday climbed from the Ford and crossed the street. He shook his head as the concierge swung open the glass door. 'Left my com in Ms Dah's apartment . . .'

The concierge waved him through.

In the elevator he took half a dozen key-cards from the breast pocket of his jacket. He always carried enough to get him past most of the modern electronic security systems. He recalled one occasion when he was confronted with a lock that consisted of an ancient tumbler mechanism, opened by the simple expedient of an old-fashioned key. He'd admitted defeat, and considered obtaining something called a skeleton key, without ever getting round to doing so.

At the door of Dah's apartment he swiped the first card through the lock mechanism. Nothing happened. He tried the second with the same lack of effect. The third, to his relief, sprang the lock. He pushed open the door and slipped inside.

He upped the lighting and moved to the door of the VR room. The dark shape of Anastasia Dah floated in the suspension gel. He looked around the lounge, wondering where to start. Dah had told him that she spent an hour in VR every day, which meant that he had about fifty-five minutes before she quit the tank.

He checked the other rooms, a large bedroom, kitchen, bathroom, and a study. There was no sign of a computer system. He guessed that Dah worked from an office elsewhere. Next, he looked for her personal communicator. It was likely to be in the lounge, or in the VR room if she carried it on her person. He searched the lounge without finding the com, then moved to the VR room.

On a chair beside the jellytank was a pile of clothing, with her scarlet wrap draped over the back of the chair. On top of the clothes was her com.

Halliday accessed the memory and found Kim Long's code. He tried getting through to her, but as he'd expected there was no reply. Then he went through the com's history and found that Dah had been telling the truth: the last time she had spoken to Kim had indeed been last week – on the Wednesday, the day before Kim had been seen at the restaurant with the silver-haired guy and Suzie Charlesworth.

He replaced the com and moved to the head of the jellytank. Anastasia Dah hung suspended in the gel, floating in a state of total relaxation. Halliday found something eerie in the sight of a human form in so unfamiliar a position, as if floating in the air without support or volition.

He accessed the tank's history and scanned the list of sites she had visited over the past few months. As she had told him, she spent an hour every day in VR, very rarely any longer. Most of the sites she frequented were the entertainment zones of the various big virtual reality companies: Mantoni, Tidemann's and Cyber-Tech. Occasionally she indulged herself and visited a sex-site; he read half a dozen listings for Aphrodesia and a couple for Eros Island.

Then, he saw a code that he could not immediately identify, and yet which seemed maddeningly familiar. He read the address out loud, wondering where he'd come across it before. Dah had accessed the site four times over the past couple of months: vrus~mp/ss/797.

He entered the code into his com, and then stared at the screen: mp . . . Was he being over-optimistic in hoping that 'mp' might stand for the Methuselah Project?

He looked around the VR room. It was empty apart from the jellytank. He returned to the lounge. He went though the drawers of a bureau, various shelves bearing nothing more than ornaments, pix and holo-cubes, not sure what he was looking for but aware from experience that he would know when he found it.

He froze, heart hammering, when the chime of the doorbell sounded through the lounge. He willed whoever it was to go away. The chime sounded again. He calmed himself. He had nothing to worry about. Whoever was out there would soon get tired of waiting when their summons was ignored.

Then he heard the sound of a key-card in the lock.

He was a metre from an interior door. He moved towards it, pushed through and found himself in the bathroom. He cursed. He should have made for the kitchen. It was more likely that a casual visitor would use the bathroom than the kitchen. He heard the pounding of his pulse in his ears and realised that he was sweating. He felt sick and faint, and wondered how much that was because of the situation, or the fact that he was so out of condition.

He shut the door, allowing a gap of a centimetre for him to observe whoever it was who had a key-card for Dah's apartment.

'Hello . . . Ana? Charles here.'

A man's voice, a low, rich tone. Halliday immediately supplied a face to the voice: over-fed, cultivated, grey-haired.

He peered through the gap.

A man appeared from the short hallway, and Halliday saw that his visualisation was not that far from the mark. Charles was tall, perhaps in his sixties or seventies. He wore a fashionably cut grey suit and sported a full head of long, silver hair.

Halliday told himself that it was a coincidence, of course. How many old, silver-haired men were there in Manhattan?

'Ana, you home?'

Charles moved to the door of the VR room. He stepped inside and approached the tank. Halliday knew he should have taken his chance, while the man's back was turned, to get out. Instead, he watched the guy as he stared down at Anastasia Dah's naked body.

Charles left the room. He moved across the lounge to the

bar in the corner and made himself at home. He poured a glass of beer and carried it to an armchair facing the door behind which Halliday was concealed. He wondered how long it might be before the guy's bladder decided that it had had enough beer and needed a leak.

Halliday could easily overpower him, but he would have to do so before Dah quit the tank, and without the guy catching a glimpse of him.

He would make his move when Charles finished his beer and was fixing himself another, while his attention was on the drink. He looked around the bathroom. On a peg by the shower was a pink robe. He'd pull the robe over Charles' head and be out of the apartment in three seconds.

It was a measure of his lack of confidence that he considered how he might react if his plan went wrong. What if the guy was fitter than he appeared, and decided to make a fight of it? Christ, Halliday hadn't worked out in months. He'd find it hard to go three rounds with a ten-year-old schoolkid, these days.

Charles looked big, solid around the shoulders, as if at some time in the past he'd known how to handle himself in an emergency.

Halliday tried to convince himself that he had nothing to fear. If only Barney could have seen how chicken-shit scared he was acting . . .

The guy drained his beer. He held up the glass, admiring the pattern of froth on the side, as if considering whether to help himself to another. He stood.

Halliday tensed himself to move. He reached out and lifted down the pink gown, holding it in both hands like a thuggee assassin.

Charles was moving towards the bar. Halliday was about to step from the bathroom when he saw movement in the VR room.

Charles half-turned and smiled as he watched Anastasia Dah emerge, naked and statuesque, from the tank.

She saw the guy and waved. 'Charles, I'll be with you in a minute. Help yourself to a drink while I shower.'

Halliday cursed himself. Great . . . Now he'd have to use the robe on Dah when she came into the bathroom, and attempt to get out before the guy reacted. He'd pull his automatic and threaten him if he looked like trying anything.

But it was unprofessional, a damned mess. He wanted to get out without being seen, without leaving a trace that he'd been snooping around.

Perhaps he should have refused Wellman's commission and stayed retired.

The seconds became a minute, and then two, and Anastasia Dah failed to appear from the VR room. Halliday let out a pent breath. He was damned lucky . . .

The VR room evidently had its own shower unit. He might yet get out without making a fool of himself.

Charles had poured himself another beer. He was sitting in the armchair when Dah emerged five minutes later, dressed in a full-length black evening dress that clung to her curves like a second skin. They kissed cheeks.

'A cop was round earlier,' Halliday heard her say.

'What did he want?'

'He was asking about Kim and Suzie.'

Charles stared at her. 'What did you say?'

Dah smiled, her eyes alight with mischief. 'What do you think I said, Charles? I said I didn't know a thing.'

The guy nodded. 'Good.'

'But . . . Charles, he asked me if I'd ever heard of the Methuselah Project.'

The man's back was turned to Halliday, his expression concealed. 'Damn it, Ana. How much do you think he knows?'

She twisted her lips into a familiar moue. 'He sounded as if he were casting about in the dark. I don't think he knows much at all.'

'I hope not. This is all we need . . . Okay, you ready?'

It would be just like her, Halliday thought, if she decided that she needed to use the bathroom.

Anastasia Dah looked around the room. She found a handbag the size of a cigarette case and said, 'All set.'

'You sure you don't need anything else?'

She laughed. 'How much do you think I need, where I'm going?'

Charles smiled. 'True enough. Let's go, then.'

Halliday watched as they left the apartment and closed the door behind them. He waited perhaps three minutes, his forehead resting against the cool paintwork of the door. Then he sank to the floor, his back against the wall, and considered everything he'd heard.

So they did have something to do with the disappearances of Kim and Suzie Charlesworth, and they were involved in the Methuselah Project, whatever the hell that was.

He'd contact Wellman, make his report. As things turned out, he'd struck lucky. Barney would have just shaken his head and called him the most fortunate son of a bitch in New York State.

He quit the apartment, took the elevator and hurried past the concierge. He stepped out into the sauna-like humidity of the midnight street and slipped into the Ford.

He opened the case in his lap and activated the screen. He accessed the nano-med file and initiated the surveillance program. A street map of Manhattan Island filled the screen, in the centre of which was a flashing red star indicating the location of Anastasia Dah.

She was moving west on Houston Street, towards Broadway. Halliday started the Ford and headed in the same direction. The red star turned left at Broadway, heading downtown, and seconds later Halliday caught up with a taxi whose position corresponded with the star.

He kept his distance, wondering how far they might be

77

travelling. The taxi turned onto Canal Street, moving into the bright glare of neons and holo-façades that was Chinatown.

Seconds later the taxi drew up at the kerb. Halliday braked a hundred metres behind, and watched as Anastasia Dah and Charles climbed out and entered the Happy Valley Chinese restaurant.

He considered waiting until they'd finished their meal, and then continuing the chase. They might be an hour or two, and anyway he would be able to trace Dah wherever she went from now on. He decided to return to the office, contact Wellman with what he'd come up with so far, and maybe access the site he'd noted in the apartment.

As he drove north through the bright streets empty of traffic, he felt a quick and involuntary pang of sadness that Barney wasn't around to work on the case.

Seven

He woke suddenly, swung his legs from under the thin cotton sheet and sat on the edge of the bed. Clean, pure sunlight, the like of which he hadn't seen for twenty years, filled the room with the radiance of a gold ingot.

He gazed down at his hands, then the rest of his body. They were young, strong hands, and the body was younger too, leaner, packed with slabs of hard muscle that were a distant memory of his youth. He looked up, through the window of the villa, and gazed across the foreshore to the crashing sea.

He turned. Estelle was sleeping soundly beside him. She was around forty here, at the height of her beauty, her short hair flecked with grey and her sun-browned face bearing the lineaments of maturity that served only to emphasise her natural good looks.

He dressed quickly and made his way downstairs.

He dispensed with breakfast; he never seemed to have an appetite here anyway, and whatever he ate seemed insubstantial and dissatisfying.

He was about to leave the villa for one of his regular long walks when he heard a sound behind him.

Estelle was hurrying down the stairs, hastily cording the peach wrap around her slim body.

'Barney, what's the rush? You're always up so early and shooting off!'

She hurried over to him and took him in her arms, kissed his cheek and smiled. 'Let's have breakfast on the verandah and plan the rest of the day, okay?'

He consented, as ever. He could not bring himself to disappoint her with a refusal, as ludicrous as he knew his reluctance to be.

He stepped out onto the verandah and sat down at the table. The natural power and beauty of this stretch of Californian coastline never ceased to amaze him. He had walked for miles, north and south, marvelling at the fidelity of the rocks and plants, the giant redwoods that made him puny by comparison. Hal, he thought, would love it here, obsessed as he was with trees. He wished Hal was with him now, to provide some variation in the conversation, some excitement. Life with Estelle, his wife of thirty-five years, was becoming unbearable.

He knew why that was, of course. Estelle was merely a construct – a brilliantly realised and faithful construct, but artificial all the same. Her programmed parameters were limited; she had memories, a stock of conversation, but after a time she became predictable: she did not have the near infinite resource of a real human for sustained and varied discourse.

Barney had assumed that this would be no disadvantage; she was lifelike enough to satisfy the yawning loneliness that had filled his life since her death six years ago. For the first hour or so of their initial meeting here, that had been so. He had marvelled at the touch of her flesh, the sight of her familiar beauty, the sound of her voice; they had talked of old times, and then made love ... But the hour had stretched, become days, and her limitations had soon become apparent, her conversation limited. Even the sex had palled.

For some reason ... He wondered if that reason was purely the intellectual knowledge that none of this was real, that it was all a dream lived out in some cybernetic nirvana. Or was it some failing in himself that did not allow him to appreciate that which, a week ago, out there in the real world, he could only fantasise about?

He wondered why he could no longer *feel*.

Estelle stepped through the sliding French window carrying a tray. She set it down on the table before him and smiled, oblivious of his introspection.

That was another thing which dissatisfied him: the real Estelle would have picked up on his mood instantly, would have questioned him, concerned.

This Estelle was like a programmed doll, ever ready to please, but with little or no insight or understanding. Her physical likeness to the real Estelle only pointed up and made painful the psychological differences.

'We're running low on provisions again, Barney. Let's drive into town and do a little shopping, shall we? I might even buy myself a new dress.'

He said nothing, poured himself another coffee.

'And we could stop off at that great seafood restaurant for lunch. You know, that place at the end of the jetty.'

'The Oyster Cabin,' he supplied.

'That's the place. They do heavenly lobster.'

She poured coffee and fixed herself a bowl of muesli. Barney sipped his black coffee.

He wondered if he could come to terms with existence here if there was more variation. It seemed that their life was locked into a perpetual round of shopping and eating, inane conversation and perfunctory love-making. Once or twice, unable to take it any longer, he had snapped at Estelle, asked her if she could think of nothing else but shopping and eating – but she had continued as if nothing had happened, smiled at him and said that she would go down to the store alone, then. And, dammit, he'd felt guilty at his outburst, and then had cursed himself for falling prey to such a conditioned response: the fact was that Estelle was a very clever computer-generated construct, with no feelings to hurt, no emotions to betray.

Barney looked up from his coffee. 'I want to go for a walk

81

this morning, okay? But lunch sounds great. We could go to the store this afternoon.'

She smiled. 'Fine. Can I come with you this morning? We could explore the cove you found the other day . . .'

'I'd rather be alone.'

That complacent smile again. 'Okay. I'll fix something for dinner tonight.'

At first, he had found sanctuary in going into town with Estelle, luxuriating in the illusion that he was out there in the inhabited real world again. The town was small, but there were always dozens, hundreds, of people about – only they were not people, he reminded himself. They were, like Estelle, computer constructs, though not as individually defined. Holding a conversation with one of the townsfolk was like trying to talk to a parrot. In the early days, he could make believe that he was in a real town, the bustle of people, the noise of the simulated conversation, satisfying some craving in him.

Recently, though, having seen through the sham of artifice that was this site, he had taken to retreating along the coast by himself, coming across no one for miles and miles and relishing the solitude and the opportunity it afforded him to consider his thoughts.

'Remember the lobsters we had in Virginia in . . . was it '21, Barney? You know, the holiday in Norfolk where we hired the boat and explored the coast . . . ?'

He nodded. 'The lobsters were great, Estelle.'

She went on, 'And remember that little island we found? We were all alone, no one for miles. Wasn't it wonderful?'

He forced a smile. The tragedy was that this Estelle had only so many programmed memories – recollections of shared events which, ironically enough, he had supplied to the Mantoni VR technicians. Over the past few days she had gone though her repertoire of memories, stories, repeating each one *ad nauseam* to the point where he thought that if he heard another of her reminiscences he would go mad.

All the more painful was the fact that these often regurgitated memories provoked in Barney his own recollections of events and incidents, of which this artificial Estelle had no memory.

Once he had recalled a holiday on Coney Island, a simple Italian meal they had shared on the sea front, and a leisurely stroll home through the warm summer evening.

He had said to her, 'Remember the pasta on Coney Island, Estelle?'

He had often reminded the real Estelle of that day, with these simple words, and the shared memory had suffused them, then, with a glow of mutual pleasure. They had gone home, after the meal, and made love as they had never made love before.

But when Barney mentioned the day for the first time in VR, Estelle only frowned. 'It's slipped my memory, dear. But do you recall . . .'

He finished his coffee and stood. He almost leaned over to kiss her cheek, but stopped himself. He was a puppet to conditioned responses that had no real meaning, now.

The fact was that he had no feelings for this Estelle; she provoked only bitterness that he had lost the original, a painful reminder of her death. This Estelle was merely an impostor, an interloper mocking him and the charade of this existence.

'I'll see you around one,' he said, turned and stepped from the patio, heading towards the dunes that backed onto the beach.

He heard her blithe farewell and hurried on without acknowledgement.

He climbed the dune and paused at the top, gazing out at the vast expanse of the ocean and the long curve of the beach. He set off down the seaward side of the dune, half-walking, half-sliding through a demerara avalanche of golden sand.

He walked towards the sea and stopped at the edge of the solid, wet sand that marked the extent of the high tide. It was the sight of the sea that caused him the most wonder in this virtual world; it bore not only a remarkable visual fidelity to the real thing, and sounded like the Pacific in full throat, but also recreated the original's effect of boundless power and might. He had marvelled at the technicians' ability to reproduce reconstructions of human beings in VR, but something about the energy of the ersatz ocean before him seemed an even more remarkable achievement.

He removed his shoes and socks and left them on the beach, out of reach of the greedy incoming lick of the waves.

He walked north, the sun hot on his skin. He considered his life in the real world, his existence in the hell-hole that was modern New York; his old self would never have thought it possible that he might become bored by this virtual paradise.

But something had gone very wrong since his immersion in the jellytank at the headquarters of Mantoni Entertainments, and Barney was at a loss to explain why.

He had agreed to Lew Kramer's offer a few months ago: it had seemed like too good an opportunity to turn down. Kramer and his techs in the Research and Development division were working on the reconstruction of famous people in virtual reality, with the aim of bringing back to life, for the education and entertainment of modern VR users, the legendary figures of yesteryear.

To begin with, the R&D team had experimented with the construction of non-famous people in VR. Lew had contacted Barney and offered to produce a simulation of his dead wife, Estelle, in a VR site of his choice. The simulation would be based on old pix, video footage, recordings of her voice, even the scent of her favourite perfume. Barney had supplied shared memories – not nearly enough, as it turned out – and over the months Lew and his team had worked to bring Estelle to virtual life.

Then Barney had immersed himself in the tank and met his wife for the first time since her death six years before.

It had been an incredible moment, freighted with a gamut of emotions from love and wonder to a strange but undeniable sense of guilt that he was in some way being unfaithful to the memory of the real Estelle. But he had been so lonely, had missed her so much, that for the first hour in her company it was as if he had died and been resurrected in heaven . . .

They had talked, and then moved upstairs to the bedroom, and he had made love to her with a body twenty years younger than his overweight, out of condition, real-world body.

He had been due to quit the virtual villa, take his leave of his resurrected wife, at the end of the hour. As he held her in his arms, conscious of the fleeting minutes that remained, he had wished that the moment could have gone on for ever.

Minutes later he had been overcome with a strange and terrifying sensation that he had never before experienced when quitting VR.

Instead of the bedroom scene vanishing and his finding himself in the warm grip of the suspension gel, he lived through what seemed like an eternity in which he teetered on the edge of a vast blackness, and then he fell, was diving through a kind of interstellar void in which he could make out sharp points of light like distant galaxies. The immensity of the scale, and his apparent insignificance beside it, was at once vertiginous and existentially appalling. It was as if he were plummeting into the immensity of existence but was himself too infinitesimal ever to land on anything solid. As if he might go falling through the universe for ever . . .

And then he had heard the voices.

'Reconfiguring the basal matrix . . .'

'. . . Check. Reconfigured. Establishing . . .'

The voices were tinny and distant and made no sense at all.

What seemed like a second later – but, paradoxically, as if he had been falling through the dark interstices of nothingness for ever – he was back in the sunlit bedroom of the coastal villa.

He marked the beginning of the terrible change from that very moment.

He had opened his eyes and found himself lying in bed with the sleeping Estelle in his arms, but he was unable to bring himself to register the slightest emotional response. He distantly recalled what it was like to feel emotion, the combination of affection and the need to protect that was known as love – but it was as if he had an intellectual understanding of these emotions, and nothing else.

He had his memories of their time together, a recollection of the love he had felt towards her, and the grief he had experienced at her death, along with his anticipation of this long-cherished moment. But it was as if these feelings belonged to another person entirely, as if a stranger had reported these emotions to Barney and expected him to be able to simulate their effect.

It was impossible. He felt nothing. He had left the bedroom and walked from the villa, wondering what had happened in that strange moment of timeless eternity when he had slipped though the interstices of the universe. He should have been returned then to the real world, but here he was, still in the dream world of the Mantoni VR site.

And here he had remained for days – even though, according to the experts, the safe upper-limit of immersion time was just four hours.

So he had gone through the charade of living with Estelle

in what before he might have considered an idyllic paradise, but his inability to generate any emotion, his knowledge that all this was nothing more than a cybernetic sham, had worried at him like a constant, nagging migraine.

As the hours had turned to days, he had rationalised his inability to feel emotion. He told himself that it was the insufficiency of Estelle's programming that deterred him from being able to empathise fully with the construct. But something within him feared that he was deluding himself. For the first hour in her company he had been so full of emotion and feeling that it had been painful. Then suddenly he had been robbed of the capacity to feel, and no amount of rationalisation could blind him to the fact that it had been at the very end of the first hour, after his bizarre cosmic experience, that this inability had begun.

Something terrible had happened, then – and not merely the beginning of his imprisonment in VR.

Eight

Halliday bought three spring rolls at the food stall outside the Chinese laundry and began eating as he climbed the stairs to the office. He brewed himself a coffee; he'd prefer an ice-cold beer to wash down the take-out, but he had none in. He briefly thought about having an hour in Olga's on the corner, but conscience got the better of him. He was working, after all, and he needed to be sober when he tanked.

He finished the spring rolls and carried his coffee into the bedroom. His jellytank was set against the far wall, an old model he'd bought cheap from Thai Joe almost a year ago. He'd told himself at the time that it would be necessary for his investigations, but he'd known full well that he was only using it to escape.

The tank was battered, and scaled on the outside with some repellent fungal growth, and the gel could have used a good cleaning. The effect of immersion, though, was the same whatever the state of the tank.

He activated the computer set into the head of the tank and tapped in the code he'd copied from Anastasia Dah's history file. The screen would come up with some information about the site, give him some idea what it might contain.

Instead, the screen came up with nothing – or rather a terse message that flashed on and off: *vrus~mp/ss/797: site unavailable. Restricted access.*

He decided to tank and attempt to access the site from one of the clearing zones. He tapped the zone code into the touchpad then stripped, peripherally aware of his naked form reflected in the wall mirror. He turned away, not wanting to be reminded of his physical state.

He attached the faceplate and electrodes and stepped into the warm, cloying goo. He lay back, sank and floated, waiting for the bliss of total immersion to take away the aches and pains in his body.

The transition hit him in a physical rush, a burst of sensory information that left him temporarily reeling. The first sensation was the absence of his old body, as if an unpleasant weight had been lifted from him: he no longer felt the aches in his muscles, the nausea that was for ever with him in the real world. He felt light-headed with relief, in possession of a new-born body as pristine and perfect as that of a child.

He was standing in the silver concourse of a vast city, a sprawling metropolis that seemed conjured magically from some far-flung and idyllic future Earth. The sun shone with a brilliance that, after the smog-muffled New York, seemed artificial.

A hundred citizens appeared in the plaza every second, establishing solidity in a quick fizz of pixels. They hurried over to tall, silver columns set in the tesserae of the concourse, consulted codes and pix of destinations, and tapped their choices into touchpads. Instantly they vanished, fizzing into non-existence in an eye-blink.

A fanfare of synthesised musical notes sounded, followed by a pleasant female voice: 'Welcome to the Cyber-Tech clearing zone. Please select your destination from the columns. A thousand worlds at your fingertips. Welcome to the Cyber-Tech clearing zone.'

Whenever he used a clearing zone, or experienced a site for the first time, he was always amazed at not only the fidelity of the ersatz world of which he was a part, but at the sheer physical difference of the site. The new reality seemed cleaner, brighter, somehow even more optimistic than the world he had just left.

Also, the choices were endless, here. You could spend a lifetime experiencing the multitude of worlds offered by the many virtual reality companies. A year ago, new to the idea of the gaming and adventure sites, he had spent hours exploring a variety of strange alien worlds, revelling in the roles of a starship officer, the survivor of a crash-landing, a scientist charting a new world for colonisation. Each site had convinced him utterly, and the only hindrance to his complete acceptance of the site and his role within it was the memories he carried from the real world.

He considered Wellman's time-expansion innovation, and the reported development of memory-suppressant drugs. He imagined a time when citizens could make a new life for themselves in VR, create a new identity and live a full and productive existence in some clean, Utopian world without the constant, nagging reminder of self.

He knew it was a futile dream, an escapist fantasy born of a society that had managed to destroy one world and was searching for impossible alternatives.

He moved to the nearest silver column. A woman flashed out of existence before him, and he was momentarily startled by the physical impossibility of what had happened.

He tapped the code into the touchpad on the silver column. Instantly the rectangular screen displayed: *Requested site inaccessible from major VR conveyors. Code suggests private access/limited user availability.*

After an initial stab of disappointment, he felt the quiet satisfaction of knowing that, with the discovery of the restricted code, the chances were that he was onto something important.

He cleared the screen and typed in the code of Wellman's time-extended site.

He blinked, and he was no longer in the futuristic Cyber-Tech plaza.

He found himself sitting in a high-backed leather arm-chair before a roaring log fire. He was in a small room lined with leather-bound books. A mahogany writing desk stood in one corner, a big globe of the world in another. It was as if he had stepped back in time a hundred and fifty years . . .

The view through the mullioned window to his right still showed the spectacular panorama of Tethys, a landscape of ice and rock stretching to the near horizon of the small moon. Ahead, Saturn was rising visibly, vast and majestic with its encircling system of rings aslant.

A door to his left opened quickly and Wellman stepped through, dressed in keeping with the room. He wore a frock coat, a waistcoat with a fob-watch, and carried a cane.

Halliday stared.

Wellman drew up a chair before the fire and sat down. 'Halliday, it's been four days since we last spoke.'

'Just over a day, my time,' Halliday said.

'Roberts told me about the Suzie hologram.'

'Have the techs come up with anything?'

Wellman shook his head. 'Nothing, to be honest. Suzie was careful when she reprogrammed the hologram. She gave nothing away. The hologram contains not much more than what we knew about Suzie already, other than her obsession with death and the soul.'

'She didn't tell the hologram where she was going?' Halliday asked. 'I thought she might have mentioned her meeting with Kim and the silver-haired guy.'

'She might have, but the memory of the hologram device could be edited. We think Suzie wiped anything she didn't want anyone to know about.'

Halliday nodded. 'So . . . it looks as though when Suzie disappeared, she went voluntarily?'

'So it would seem.' He looked across at Halliday. 'What about you? Have you come up with anything?'

'You heard about something called the Methuselah Project?'

Wellman shook his head. 'Nothing at all. What is it?'

He told Wellman about his meeting with Jimmy King and Anastasia Dah. 'The guy Suzie and Kim dined with on Thursday night is called Charles – that's all I know about him. They're both involved in something called the Methuselah Project. I have a few leads I'm working on. I'll keep you posted.'

Wellman was nodding slowly, seemingly impressed. 'In one day you've done very well. I've had a company detective on the case since the day Suzie vanished, for all the good it did.'

'I've been lucky. Been in the right place at the right time.'

'As long as you get results, Halliday, that's all that concerns me.'

'I also came across a code. I don't know, it might be nothing. I found it in the history of Anastasia Dah's jellytank. It contains the initials MP – I thought maybe it had something to do with the Methuselah Project.'

'Did you access the site?'

'Tried to. I came up with access-restricted errors, things like that. Maybe your techs will have more luck.'

'I'll get them onto it.' Wellman reached out and took a pen and a writing pad from the desk and passed them to Halliday.

He clutched the pen awkwardly, wondering when he'd last used one. He printed the code on the pad and handed it back to Wellman.

Halliday gestured at the room. 'Some place, Wellman.'

'Do you like it? Victorian, circa 1900. A hundred and forty years ago. I like the juxtaposition with the stellar scenery. Striking, don't you think?'

Halliday smiled. 'You spend all your time here?'

'By no means. I still have company business to conduct.'

'What about pleasure? Leisure time?'

'I have unlimited access to all the sites, Halliday. When I want to go somewhere, I just import the site into the time-extended matrix, or rather my techs do all that for me. When I use the leisure sites, I have various constructed personas to keep me company, so I'm never alone. From time to time my wife visits.'

Wellman consulted his fob-watch. 'It's time I wasn't here, Halliday. I have meetings to attend. Keep up the good work.'

He stood and hurried from the room.

Halliday remained seated, considering. It was almost midnight in the real world, time he caught up with some sleep. Or he could spend a further hour or two in VR . . .

On the back of his left hand was the decal to return him to the clearing zone. He hit it and found himself standing in the plaza, bathed in brilliant sunlight. He approached a silver column and entered the code of the required site.

Instantly he was phased from the Cyber-Tech plaza to the reassuring vistas of the Virginia site.

He stood on the ridge path overlooking the burnished blue water of the ocean. To his right, the coastline stretched away to the hazy horizon, an immense panorama of forested hills extending for as far as the eye could see. The sight never failed to fill him with a sense of wonder, and at the same time a throat-tightening sensation of regret.

He made his way down the path, through the pines, to the pebble beach that fringed the bay. His tent was a familiar red blister a hundred metres away in the shade of a fir tree.

Casey, the simulated version, sat on a deck chair. She waved as he approached. 'Hi, Hal. See anything interesting? I'm just taking a little sun.'

He smiled and shook his head.

He sat on the pebbles beside the tent and she came to him, as he knew she would. She sat beside him and leaned her head on his shoulder. He recalled the last time he had been with the Casey-construct in VR, how he had watched her splashing naked in the shallows . . .

Absently, tears misting his vision, he laid a hand on her head and felt her warmth.

'Hey!' she said, looking up. 'Why don't we go for a walk? Know what I saw earlier, Hal? A whale, a real blue whale out there in the ocean!'

He smiled. 'Maybe later, okay?'

She returned her head to his shoulder, and he resumed stroking her hair.

He had never really spoken to this Casey, never told her what he was thinking or feeling. He had always assumed that her mere presence would be enough to give him what he had wanted . . . which was, what? Companionship? Friendship? The reassurance in VR that he was not alone?

And the hopeless fact was that until the other day he had been perfectly satisfied with whatever Casey's simulation had given him, or so at least he'd tried to convince himself.

But this version of the real girl was no more than a shallow puppet, a fantasy figure dancing attendance on his warped and inadequate desires. His relationship with her was easy because she was not a real person, did not have thoughts and hopes and desires of her own.

Last night, with the real Casey, he had found how difficult it was to maintain a genuine relationship. The fact was that he'd had to consider her, acknowledge that she had thoughts and feelings that could be affected by his words and deeds. And he had made a mess of it, had driven her away with his gratuitous show of violence towards Jimmy King.

Casey looked up now and smiled at him. 'Hey, why so quiet, Hal?'

He stood quickly, spilling her. He walked away, stumbling.

'Hey, Hal!' her childish cry sounded behind him. 'What's wrong, Hal?'

Choking, he hit the exit decal on the back of his hand and quit the site.

He struggled from the embrace of the gel, his stomach heaving. He hung over the side of the tank and vomited. His head pounded and his body was racked with shooting pains.

Nine

Barney walked along the margin of sand made solid by the touch of the sea. When he came to the northernmost extent of the beach, where the sand curved to the point of a short headland, he turned right and walked through stands of shock-haired marram grass towards a plantation of pine trees fifty metres inland.

He had experienced the cosmic void, as he called it, on two occasions after the first. Each occasion caught him unawares, and was all the more terrifying for that. Once he was walking by himself along the foreshore when he was plunged into a blackness at once familiar and strange. He had experienced again the sensation of plummeting through light-years, of being a tiny part of a much larger fabrication. As before, the sensation seemed to last an eternity – and yet, when he emerged from the abyssal fall, he found himself completing the stride he had begun a fraction of a second earlier.

On the second occasion he had been in town with Estelle, strolling along the sidewalk. The darkness had overtaken him, enveloped him and challenged his sanity, and yet when he returned to his senses it was as if no time at all had elapsed.

But what was even more disconcerting was the feeling experienced after these cosmic falls that weeks, maybe entire months, had been removed from his life, great missing chunks of time that registered somewhere deep in his mind despite the evidence of his senses that only a fraction of a second had gone by.

He came to the pine forest and slowed, looking around for the anomaly he had discovered just yesterday.

He had come upon the first of the anomalies, as he called them, three days ago. Since then he had happened upon half a dozen more. The first time, he had been driving the car along the coast road ten kilometres to the south. From the corner of his eye he'd seen a sudden and startling shimmer of blackness, an obsidian lozenge laid out at the side of the road. He braked and quickly reversed, sure that his senses had been playing tricks.

But there it was, lying in the shadow of a pine tree like a puddle of oil. He climbed from the car and approached with a caution born of experience. Even when he was still within metres of the jet-black pool, he was aware of its irresistible attraction. He slowed his pace, but found himself walking on. He stopped two metres away, leaned forward and peered into the slick like someone on the edge of a mineshaft.

His vision had swirled. He was looking down into a miniature version of the blackness he had experienced after his first hour in VR, and on two occasions since.

There had been something subtly different about this blackness, however. It did not posses the all-encompassing and overwhelming quality of the others. He felt he could control it, keep his distance. He was attracted to it, undeniably, but it did not have the power to draw him in and engulf him entirely.

He had remained by the side of the road, staring for what seemed like hours into the mysterious pit that seemed at once to possess a slick jet surface and yet infinite depth.

He had come across other anomalies over the course of the next few days. Yesterday he had found the largest yet, spread like a perfectly level slick of crude across the surface of scrubby ground all around a pine tree, like a shadow too geometrical and intense to be believable. Again it had exerted its mystifying allure. He had stared into its depths, from a safe distance, for hours.

Now he saw the patch of blackness through the trees. He approached slowly, step by slow step, and then lowered himself onto his hands and knees and moved forward on all fours.

He came to the margin of the obsidian pool and stared over the side, like an enchanted child peering into fairyland.

He made out, scintillating in the depths of the jet pool, a million points of firefly light. They were like stars in space, or more accurately like galaxies in the vastness of the universe, for each light was not a point but a swirl made up of any number of infinitesimal individual lights. He felt himself being drawn into the blackness, lured head-first to fall through the space between the galaxies.

'I wouldn't get too close to that if I were you, Barney.'

The voice startled him, almost had the opposite effect and pitched him forward in fright. He scrambled away from the jet pool and climbed to his feet.

Lew Kramer stood before him, dressed in the suit he'd been wearing the last time Barney had seen him in the real world. He was a big, lantern-jawed man who carried his weight on small feet with surprising nimbleness.

Lew gestured at the slick. 'It's a rip in the reality of the virtual site, an area where the basal matrix has failed to mesh or knit properly.'

'That makes perfect sense,' Barney said, sarcastic. 'What causes them?'

Lew shrugged. 'Sometimes a lack of configuration, where a glitch in the system has ripped a rent in the matrix – in other words, where our calculations don't add up. Others are caused by viruses. There are a number of terrorist groups out there opposed to VR. They take great delight in trying to sabotage our systems.'

'And why the warning, Lew? Why shouldn't I get too near them? They dangerous?'

'Not as such, but they can cause certain short-term neurological anomalies and minor sensory dysfunctions should you find yourself caught up in one.'

Barney nodded. 'Thanks for the warning. I'll keep it in mind next time I feel like taking a dip.' He stared at the natty exec. 'Lew, what the hell's going on here? I want some explanations.'

Lew held up both hands. 'And I'll give you them, Barney. Why do you think I'm here?'

'Not for a holiday, I'll bet. This place'd drive anyone nuts.' He shook his head. 'What the hell's happening to me? Why can't I get outta here?'

Lew nodded. He had the slick PR man's repertoire of placatory gestures to reassure the concerned client. 'Right. That's why I'm here, Barney. I came to tell you that everything's under control. You don't need to worry about a thing.'

Barney shot him a glance. 'Listen, bud, when men in suits tell me that I got diddley-squat to worry about, I start worrying good. What gives?'

'There was a . . . let's say a minor glitch in the transfer routines when we attempted to pull you from the site.'

Barney spread his hands in a gesture of heartfelt relief. 'Well, thank Christ for that, Lew. You know, for a minute there I thought I was really stuffed.' He stared at the man. 'What the fuck,' he said, 'do you mean by a minor glitch?'

Lew cleared his throat. 'Sometimes subjects . . . clients . . . become too fully integrated into the matrix. It's a one in a million occurrence.'

'That's good to know—'

'And we're working around the clock to amend the situation.'

'Around the clock?' Barney stabbed a stubby forefinger into Lew's barrel chest. 'You tell me you're working round the clock? I've been here days, Lew! What's the upper-limit immersion time? Four hours?' He shook his head. 'What kind of state will I be in when you finally get round to pulling me outta here?'

Lew was holding up both hands and shaking his head. 'Barney, let me reassure you on that score.'

Barney stared. 'This should be good.'

'I know you might find this hard to believe, Barney, but although you've subjectively experienced seven days in this site, only one day has elapsed out there in the real world. As soon as the glitch appeared, we reconfigured this site into what we call a time-extension matrix. That's why it appears I've taken my time in getting here. In actual fact we had a few hours' work to do to stabilise the matrix before I could immerse myself.'

Barney shook his head. 'So I've been in here one day, real time? That's still way over the safe immersion limit, buddy.'

'Barney, let me tell you that the upper limit set by the VR companies is merely a safety measure. We've been conducting experiments with subjects who've been tanked for in excess of two days without any ill effects.'

Barney stared at the ground, trying to take all this in. 'So let's get this straight. The bottom line is, I'm stuck in here, living a long holiday while time dawdles by in the outside world, right?'

'That's about the size, Barney.'

'So when are you guys gonna get me out?'

'Believe me, we're working on it. We're confident that any day now we'll make a breakthrough.'

Barney matched his gaze. 'I hope so, Lew, for your goddamned sake I certainly hope so.'

'In the meantime, if there's anything I can do to make your stay here any easier—'

'Can you transfer me to another site? You wouldn't believe how dull paradise can be.'

Lew shook his head. 'Sorry, Barney. No can do. If we

could achieve that, we could get you out. But I might be able to transfer things into this site for you.'

Barney laughed. 'Sounds great. Like what, a troupe of dancing girls?'

Lew pursed his lips. 'Something like that might not be out of the question.'

Barney waved. 'Forget it, Lew. Know something? Along with the ability to feel, I've lost all those other human urges, too. To tell the truth, I can't even bring myself to feel that pissed with you – now ain't that something?'

'I'll be in touch, Barney. Rest assured, we're working to get you out pronto, okay?'

Barney nodded wearily. 'Sure, Lew. Anything you say. See you around.'

As he watched, Lew Kramer sketched a wave in the air and dematerialised like a holo-image breaking up.

Barney turned and stared down at the obsidian slick. What had Lew called it? A rent in the basal matrix?

It seemed to draw him closer, invite him to dive head-first into its inky depths. He wished he'd asked Lew about that, now. Why did it seem so alluring?

He thought of Lew's warning, and the explanation the exec had proffered for his imprisonment here. Barney had developed an astute ear over the years for what some people called the adept management of the truth, and others, lies. He preferred the much simpler term, bullshit.

Lew Kramer was hiding something, he was sure of that.

He stared into the basal rent, and it came to him suddenly – from nowhere – that the rip in the matrix might afford him a means of escape from this site.

Ten

Halliday was woken by the persistent summons of an alarm.

He rolled over onto his back, still half asleep. He'd incorporated the alarm into his waking dream: he was in a burning building, searching in vain for Casey, with the alarm bell shrilling in his ears.

He blinked up at the ceiling, banishing the dream images. The noise persisted, a constant, high-pitched shriek. He recalled quitting the Virginia site last night, pulling himself from the tank and vomiting before passing out. He must have come to his senses at some time and made it to bed.

He tried to ignore the alarm. It seemed to be coming from the office. He had no idea what might be making the noise, but it wasn't going to go away. He rolled out of bed and dressed, his vision blurring with the sudden exertion.

He stumbled into the office, light-headed. The noise seemed to be coming from the case that Wellman had given him the other day, on the desk where he'd left it last night.

He slumped into his swivel chair and opened the case. The alarm cut off instantly. The computer screen flared and flashed a two-word message: *Status Alert!*

Halliday tapped the touchpad. The screen cleared, the flashing warning replaced by the nano-med program showing Anastasia Dah's physiological status.

He tried to make sense of the horizontal slide-bars.

Where before each bar had extended itself into the middle of the screen, dipping when she had entered VR, now each bar had retracted to within one per cent of the range.

Halliday shook his head in an attempt to clear his mind and think straight. He found an option on a menu that read: *Report*, and selected it. A text window opened and he read: *Subject status: comatose. Traumatic physiological destabilisation. Emergency condition.*

Into his head came the vision of Anastasia Dah, glamorous in her scarlet wrap. What the hell was happening to her?

He opened the program that he hoped was still tracking the woman. He expected to see a map of Manhattan on the screen, with Dah's position indicated by a flashing red star. Instead, a map of New York State appeared. The star was flashing, but not in the city. It appeared that Dah had travelled upstate during the night, and was now somewhere in the vicinity of Nyack.

He zoomed in. Dah was situated three kilometres north of Nyack, in the country overlooking the Hudson River. He expanded the map even further. The red light pulsed in an area that had once been woodland, at the end of a dead-end road.

He returned to the nano-med program. There was no improvement in Anastasia Dah's condition.

He moved to the bedroom, strapped on his body-holster and took his automatic from the drawer beside the bed. He returned to the office, closed the case and carried it with him down into the street.

It was dawn, around six, and to the east the sky above the city was discoloured with a huge and sulphurous sunrise. Already it was hot, and the humidity made each drawn breath a physical effort.

On either side of the street the food-vendors were preparing for another long day. They set out their stalls with the bored, economical movements of people who had gone through the same routine a thousand times before.

Halliday bought a coffee and, recalling his resolution to look after himself a little better from now on, handed over an amazing ten dollars for one apple.

He drove north out of El Barrio and took the slip lane onto Interstate 87, set the cruise control at fifty and settled into the slow lane. He took one bite from the apple, then spat the pulpy mouthful through the window and pitched the rest of the fruit after it. He washed the taste from his mouth with an invigorating draught of bitter coffee.

His was one of the few cars on the road this morning. The highway curved ahead of him like the deserted set for a post-apocalyptic holo-movie. Not having to concentrate on other traffic, his thoughts wandered.

He recalled the feeling he'd experienced last night in the Virginia site with the Casey construct. He had felt shame, a disbelief that he had allowed himself to program a companion. He looked back to the time immediately after the Vanessa Artois case, when he'd been at his lowest. Perhaps it had been his only way of coping back then, his only hope of staying sane.

Later, tonight some time, he'd go over to Casey's apartment and apologise for his behaviour the other night. He'd try to explain to her why he had acted as he did, and tell her that he was sorry. He'd suggest they see more of each other, maybe go out for a meal from time to time. Try to get back to how things had been in the old days, when they'd been good friends and could chat for hours on end.

Hell, she had come searching him out yesterday. She had split with her boyfriend, lost her job, and had been worried about Kim – and he had lost it with the boxer in a fit of jealousy and hate.

When she had needed someone to talk to, someone who understood and who could sympathise with her, he'd acted like a thug.

He entered Westchester County, passing through what once had been great tracts of forest. He recalled that, just twenty years ago, plantations had patchworked the land around here. Now the trees were blackened and stunted, and even the once-green grass had a sear and unhealthy appearance.

Living in Manhattan as he did, and rarely venturing beyond the city limits, he had become accustomed to the lack of greenery in his day-to-day life. There had been few trees in the city anyway, so when they began dying fifteen years ago their absence was hardly noted. Only when he left the city, heading north, or over to Long Island where his father had lived, did the enormity of the devastation hit home. Plagues and blights had decimated the natural world of the North American continent, and the meltdowns five years ago in Raleigh and Atlanta had placed a greater strain on the already labouring ecosystem. He lived in a world that was slowly dying, despite the work of scientists and environmentalists to develop new strains of disease-resistant flora. He'd read optimistic reports that a corner was being turned, that all was not yet lost, and that in five to ten years the recovery of the country's devastated environment would be under way.

And he'd read other reports that claimed there was no hope, that the poisoning of the system had gone unchecked for so long that there was no chance of recovery.

Was it little wonder that he and millions like him sought solace in the dream realm of virtual reality?

He thought of Casey, who had turned her back on VR after experiencing it a couple of times. He admired her strength of will to resist something that was so easy and, at the same time, so gratifyingly rewarding. She had gone through a lot after losing her family in the Atlanta meltdown, had lived rough on the streets before he had taken her in. Perhaps the reality she lived now was safe and secure compared to the life she had led; perhaps she did not need the artificial succour of VR.

He crossed the Tappan Zee bridge high above the mud-coloured waters of the Hudson. The coastline ahead stretched left and right, dim behind the grey morning mist. For the most part the foreshore was denuded of trees, but here and there, where affluent landowners had the means and the desire, areas of holographic forest covered the slopes in displays at once beautiful and banal, an electronic homage to a lost cause.

He motored off the bridge and turned right along the coast, passing through the town of Nyack and heading north towards what had once been the Hook Mountain State Park.

He considered Anastasia Dah and what might have happened to her. He had last seen her, fit and healthy, entering a Chinese restaurant with the silver-haired Charles last night. Halliday had seen nothing to suggest that the guy had had any ill-intent towards Dah; in fact, quite the reverse: he had formed the impression that they were complicit, working together in something he had yet to fathom. The Methuselah Project . . .

And now Dah was somewhere not too far away, in a comatose state on the borderland of death. He found it hard to square the facts as reported by the nano-med program with the vision of her last night, so full of life and beauty.

He recalled something he had overheard in her apartment, as she and Charles made to leave. He had asked her if she needed anything other than her handbag, and she had replied, 'How much do you think I need, where I'm going?'

What the hell had she meant by that? Was it a reference to the restaurant they were dining at? But her answer had suggested that she was going somewhere alone.

At least he had made inroads on the case. He had leads. Dah and Charles were implicated in something which he was sure involved the disappearances of both Kim and the Charlesworth kid. It was more than just a start.

He pulled into the side of the road and opened the case on the passenger seat. He accessed the map. The flashing red star was situated a kilometre ahead, on a rising headland that Halliday could make out from where he sat. The promontory bristled with the remnants of a once extensive forest, a thousand dead trunks creating an eerie, nightmare landscape.

He eased the Ford back onto the road and motored north, aware of the sudden sweat that soaked his skin and had nothing to do with the heat of the day.

He slowed the car when he came to the headland. A narrow track led from the road at right angles and climbed through the dead trees. In the distance, on a rise of land overlooking the river, he made out a big, three-storey weatherboard house, sliced into sections by the intervening tree-trunks. Three cars and a white van were parked beside the building.

He checked the map on the computer screen. The red star indicated that Anastasia Dah was somewhere within the house.

He sat for a while and considered his options. He would take a look around the place, unobserved if he could manage it.

First he had to find somewhere to conceal the Ford.

The dead woodland continued over the road to his left, though it offered little in the way of cover. A hundred metres ahead, however, set among the dead trees a little way off the road, was a derelict filling station.

He started the engine and drove until he reached the station and pulled off the road. He parked the car in the lot behind the tumbledown building and hurried across the road.

He stepped into the bare forest, the leaf mould of centuries giving like a soft carpet beneath his feet. There was a rank smell in the air, the bitter reek of diseased woodland. Very little grew on the forest floor, other than the occasional bramble or courageous flourish of bindweed. There was no birdsong, no sound of any kind other than the scuffing of his footsteps. The air was filled with a silence which, when he stopped to listen, seemed far more profound than the mere absence of sound.

His hand strayed involuntarily to the automatic in his body-holster. He found himself creeping through stunted undergrowth, loath to make any more sound than was absolutely necessary. Ten metres ahead he made out a high mesh fence encircling the grounds. It seemed as old as the house, he was relieved to see, and in places it had worked free from the concrete pillars. If he chose, he could enter the grounds without difficulty. Beyond the fence, the house stood in quiet isolation, surrounded by extensive lawns, green and well-tended.

Halliday concealed himself behind the trunk of a blackened pine, staring through the mesh at the side wall of the house. The upper windows were shuttered, but the windows on the ground floor revealed two white-walled rooms.

He decided to take a closer look. He scanned the grounds to ensure there was no one in the vicinity, then moved quickly along the fence until he came to a rent in the netting. He grasped the wire mesh, pulled it back further, and stepped through. Doubled-up, he sprinted towards the house, heading for the wall between the two ground floor windows.

He made it and flattened himself against the timber, breathing hard and grimacing at the pain that shot the length of his left thigh. He took deep breaths, heart pounding. There had been a time, two or three years ago, when he'd prided himself on his fitness. Now he felt nauseous. He knelt, hanging his head and closing his eyes in a bid to banish the dizziness.

Perhaps five minutes later he suspected that he might survive the exertion, after all.

He stood and, his back pressed against the weatherboard,

edged towards the nearest window. He peered cautiously inside. The room was empty except for minimal furnishings: half a dozen uncomfortable-looking vinyl armchairs. The place had the appearance of an institution, a residential home for the elderly or handicapped.

He moved along the wall towards the back of the house, came to the corner and peered round. He made out more windows, a brick extension that might have been a kitchen.

He reminded himself of the vehicles parked around the front of the house. Someone was obviously inside, other than Anastasia Dah.

He moved along the rear of the house until he came to the first window, and peered in.

He backed off immediately, pressing himself against the wall and breathing hard. He'd caught a glimpse of a female nurse in baggy blue overalls, tending to someone in a narrow bed.

When he chanced a second look minutes later, the nurse was no longer in the room. He stared through the window at the figure on the bed.

Anastasia Dah.

He drew back, wondering what the hell to do now. Was this some kind of clinic, to which she had admitted herself voluntarily? Would that explain her comments to the silver-haired guy last night, that she would need nothing other than a handbag where she was going?

But she had been in perfect health last night, and now, according to the nano-med, she was at death's door.

Halliday took another look. Dah was hooked up to a battery of impressive-looking apparatus. He recognised a heart monitor and a respirator, but little else. Her head of luxuriant black curls had been shorn, and electrodes connected her skull to an array of monitors.

Before Halliday could react, the door opened and someone walked into the room. The man moved around the bed, his back to the window, and leaned over the woman.

It was the silver-haired guy, Charles.

As Halliday watched, he took Dah's hand and raised the long black fingers to his lips. Then he reached out and stroked the woman's cheek.

Two nurses, one pushing a wheelchair, entered the room. While Charles stood back and watched, they peeled the electrodes from Dah's head and arms, disconnected other leads, and between them lifted the woman carefully into the wheelchair.

Only then, as Dah sat upright and faced Halliday for a second, did he see that her eyes were open and staring without sight or seeming awareness.

He withdrew from the window, more shocked by the sight of her staring eyes than by the fact of her bed-ridden condition.

Shapes passed before the window, and when Halliday next looked he saw Charles pushing Anastasia Dah from the room.

There was little he could do now without knowing exactly what was going on here. He decided to follow Charles and attempt to learn just who he was. He'd return to the road and wait until Charles made his move and left the house.

He hurried along the back of the house, ensured the way across the lawn to the mesh fence was clear, and set off at a jog. He had almost reached the fence when he heard voices behind him. He turned, his heart hammering.

The front door of the house was open, and Charles was pushing Anastasia Dah across the drive towards the white van. Halliday ducked into the cover of an ailing bush and peered out.

Charles was accompanied by two men, a dark-haired man in his thirties wearing a smart blue suit, and a younger black man in casual slacks and a leather jacket.

Charles and the black guy lifted Dah into the back of the van, her unsupported head lolling horribly. Charles

110

climbed in after her. The other two men climbed into the front of the van and slammed the doors. A second later the engine started and the van crunched slowly down the gravel drive.

Halliday pushed through the mesh fence and entered the devastated forest, following the track he had scuffed through the loam. He slowed down as his lungs began to protest. There was no need to hurry, after all; he could allow the van to get well ahead of him and follow Dah with the tracking program.

He moved through the forest, listening to the engine of the van as it drove on a parallel course. He caught glimpses of the vehicle through the trees. As he approached the road, he crouched behind the cover of scant undergrowth and watched as the van turned and headed north.

He emerged from the trees and hurried up the road to the filling station where he'd left the Ford. He opened the case on the passenger seat, accessed the tracking program and watched the red star as it made its way up the coast road.

He drove slowly in pursuit, keeping a kilometre between himself and the van. As he drove, he reached out and opened the nano-med program. Dah's life-signals were still perilously low.

He switched back to the tracking program.

He recalled Charles' behaviour in the room. He had kissed the woman's hand, showed every sign of genuine affection towards Anastasia Dah. Where the hell was he taking her now?

He drove for a further kilometre, glancing at the screen from time to time. Five minutes later the red star slowed in its movement north and veered from the road.

He slowed, allowing the van to move further away. It was passing down another rough track in the denuded forest, heading towards the river.

Two minutes later Halliday drew to a halt at the turning. As he watched the screen, the red star stopped. He judged

111

that the van had come to a halt about half a kilometre from the road. He watched the star for a further three minutes, detecting no movement. Evidently they had reached their destination.

He looked along the length of the road, then drove north a hundred metres and concealed the car behind a stand of dying bougainvillea.

He switched off the computer and sat staring through the insect-encrusted windscreen for a minute. He touched his pistol in its body-holster, then left the car and walked along the road. He came to the gap where the track turned into the forest.

Using the scant cover of the dead trees, he walked into the forest on a course parallel with the track.

The trees were densely packed here. As a result there was more cover, but less light; a pallid twilight hung between the dead and stunted tree trunks.

He kept the track in sight, looking for the distinctive white bodywork of the vehicle as he hurried through the half-light, pausing to listen from time to time. The absolute silence would work both for and against him: it would be to his advantage in that he would be able to hear any noise made by Charles and the others; but by the same token they would be able to detect his approach. As he ran over the carpet of rotted leaves, he realised with surprise that he had drawn his automatic.

Something caught his eye up ahead. He slowed and stopped. Before him, miraculously, was a wild rose bush. A single red flower shone with an almost preternatural lustre. He looked about him and smiled. Once he'd seen the first rose, he saw all the others, a pointillism of blooms like a hundred beads of blood in the twilight.

He hurried on, eyes on the track three metres to his right. He slowed when he judged that he must have covered half a kilometre. If his calculations were correct, he was not that far from the western bank of the river. He paced through

112

the forest, automatic ready, scanning ahead for the slightest sign of movement.

He caught sight of the van, apparent as splinters of white between the trees. He stopped, concealed himself behind a trunk and gathered his breath. He listened, heard nothing in the silence but the sound of his own laboured breathing. He looked around the tree, then moved from the cover it afforded and crept cautiously forward.

The van was parked on a bluff above the river. There was no sign of Charles or the others.

He passed the van, keeping in the cover of the trees. He was at the very margin of the forest; here the trees petered out as the land descended towards the river. He looked down, over the gently shelving river bank, and saw Charles and the other two men.

They were standing in a slight dip or dell, surrounded by dead and dying sycamore trees. Anastasia Dah sat slumped in the wheelchair, and Charles knelt beside her, his hand in hers. He appeared to be speaking to her.

Halliday crouched, moved forward, and concealed himself behind the lightning-shattered bole of a pine, perhaps twenty yards from the van.

As he watched, his pulse loud in his ears, Charles stood and nodded to the black guy and the man in the blue suit.

Between them they lifted Dah from the wheelchair, and only then did Halliday see the shallow trench excavated in the leaf mould.

He wanted to stand up and shout something, somehow prevent what he knew was about to happen, but he could only watch as the black guy and the man in the blue suit carefully, almost reverently, laid Anastasia Dah in the shallow grave.

Charles moved forward and knelt beside the prostrate woman. He took something from the pocket of his jacket, pointed it at the woman's forehead, and fired. Dah spasmed, once, and a bloom of blood appeared on her

113

brow, as bright red as the roses in the forest. Then Charles knelt, reached out and touched the dead woman's cheek.

The black man took a spade and quickly covered the body with soil and leaf mould, and in seconds the woman was lost to sight. He scattered dead leaves over the discoloured soil, as if in a bid to conceal his handiwork. Then the trio made their way back to the van, passing within five metres of where Halliday crouched. He found himself unable to move, and prayed for the sound of the van's engine.

It seemed an age before the van started and backed up the track. The sound died slowly, leaving silence in its wake.

Halliday was aware that he was shaking. He fought to control his breathing. He had the gun gripped tight before him – he could have easily shot the three men before Dah herself died. What had stopped him firing? Self-preservation? Incredulity that what he was watching was actually taking place? He could have acted, but the fact was that he had been frozen to the spot with abject fear. He wondered what the old Hal Halliday might have done in the same situation. Surely he would have acted immediately, attacked and disarmed the men before Charles had murdered Dah. He felt a sudden and sickening spasm of self-disgust.

Later he wondered how long it was, as he stared down into the dell where the killing had occurred, before he saw the second grave, and then the third – leaf-covered mounds side by side.

Minutes, perhaps . . . and then perhaps another minute, or maybe even longer, while he stared and tried not to think about what the three graves might denote.

Slowly he stood and emerged from the trees. He walked down the banking, catching his feet in the undergrowth and stumbling more than once. He was aware of walking into the dell, but at a remove from reality, as if he were manoeuvring his body by remote control from a great distance. He felt cold, despite the heat of the day, and his heart thundered deafeningly in his ears.

There were, unmistakably, three graves ranged side by side in the loam of the forest floor. There was Anastasia Dah's freshly covered grave, and beside it another, much shorter disturbed patch of earth. Next to this was a third grave, and Halliday dropped to his knees beside it.

Then he began digging where he judged the head might be. He was aware of his tears, misting his vision, the painful tightness in his throat as he fought back his sobs. It came to him that to admit defeat now, and cry, would be to capitulate before he knew for certain, before his fears were confirmed. To cry now, he thought irrationally, might bring about the terrible actuality that he so feared.

His fingers came up against something, something at once harder than the soil through which he'd dug, but soft.

He cried aloud.

He brushed away the soil with the care and attention of an archaeologist excavating a precious treasure. Slowly, little by little, the outline of an oval face appeared in the earth. He wept and continued working at the soil with frantic, manic care; it seemed to him that he might in some way be able to communicate his love and grief with gestures as careful and delicate as those he had made when making love to her what seemed like such a long time ago.

He freed her face from the soil, and then her shoulders, and then reached beneath her and lifted her body into his arms.

A bullet hole marked the exact centre of her forehead.

As he held Kim's body to him, he looked up, perhaps subliminally aware of the noise, and saw the tall figure of the silver-haired Charles, staring down at him. In his right hand he held a single red rose.

Seconds later the casually dressed black guy and the blue-suited man appeared beside Charles, and looked down at Halliday with expressions of mixed distaste and disbelief.

Then the guy in the blue suit pulled an automatic from inside his jacket and fired at Halliday.

Three shots thumped into Kim's back, impelling her with a sick, ersatz life and saving Halliday from certain death. He cried and rolled away at speed, drawing his automatic and returning fire. He was up and running before he knew whether he had scored a hit. He dived from the dell, rolling down the bank of the river, then gained his feet and sprinted. He headed north, then turned and scrambled up the bank, making for the sparse cover of the forest. He heard cries behind him, and then shots, and ahead saw chunks of soil erupt from the ground. He made the trees and turned, knelt and aimed. When he fired he did so with rage and intent, and the shot connected. The black guy twisted and fell to the ground as if caught by an uppercut, crying out as he did so. Charles knelt and grasped the guy's shoulders, but the blue-suited man ran on.

Crouching, Halliday fired again, missing his target and hitting an intervening tree. The shot had the effect of sending his pursuer diving for cover.

He took the opportunity and ran, dodging through the closely packed trees on a zigzag course, his body protesting at the strain imposed, his lungs burning as if swamped with acid. He heard a flurry of gunshots, heard the thwack of bullets strike the trees around him. He turned and fired again and again, more in a bid to slow his pursuer than with any real hope of shooting him dead.

He came to the road and crossed it at a sprint. He dived through the trees on the other side, turning and heading in the approximate direction of where he'd left the car.

There were no further sounds of pursuit. He slowed, hardly daring to hope that he'd outpaced the gunman. He fell into a crouch behind the bole of a tree, taking in great lungfuls of air, and readied his automatic in a trembling hand.

He listened. The silence surprised him, more startling

116

than gunfire. He imagined the man, lying low out there, awaiting Halliday's next, fatal move.

Ahead, he could see the Ford through the trees. He chanced a glance in the direction he had come. There was no sign of his pursuer, and he allowed himself the insanely optimistic thought that perhaps he'd managed to escape.

He waited for what seemed like an age, probably no more than five minutes. He knew that sooner or later he must make his move, and in that split second he would know whether he was still being stalked, or not.

Crouching, he moved from the protective custody of the tree, and then ran doubled-up towards his car. He expected to hear the whine of a bullet, feel it smack into his body with deadly force.

He reached the Ford, hardly daring to believe his luck. He hauled open the door and dived inside, gunned the engine and accelerated at speed from the forest. He hit the road and spun the wheel, careering in a sprawling turn and sashaying across both lanes.

Ahead, he saw movement to his left. The blue-suited guy emerged from the trees and stepped into the road, levelling his automatic in outstretched hands. Halliday ducked and accelerated, heading directly for the bastard. He heard bullets impact the coachwork, saw a flash of colour as the gunman dived to avoid being hit. Then the car trundled into the ditch and Halliday fought for control as the vehicle veered towards the trees. He hauled the wheel clockwise and the car obeyed, fishtailing crazily onto the road again.

He turned in the seat. The guy was picking himself up, already a hundred metres away, a tiny figure diminishing rapidly in the distance.

He accelerated, leaving blue-suit in his wake. He headed south towards Nyack, hunched over the wheel like a madman as he stared through his tears at the blurred road ahead.

None of it made any sense. He could not banish from his

mind the image of Charles with the rose in his hand, nor the obvious affection he had shown earlier towards Anastasia Dah. And then he had simply shot her through the head.

What had happened to Dah, before her death, that might account for her comatose state? And Kim? Had Charles shown the same warped affection towards Kim before shooting her, too?

Into his head came a thousand memories of their time together. He was inundated with images of Kim, her face exhibiting a dozen emotions. He recalled the occasion they had entered VR for the very first time. Kim had taken him to a deserted beach where they had made love in the shallows of a perfect lagoon, and then lain in each other's arms on the golden sand.

He felt a cold emptiness in his chest, as if his heart and lungs had been excavated. Alternating with grief was the rage of revenge: he wished now that he had stayed and fought, had killed the man in the blue suit, and then the black guy – if he was not dead already – and then, last of all, the silver-haired Charles.

What eventually persuaded him that he had done the right thing in running was not so much the knowledge that he might later regret the killings, but that he had been in no condition to stay and fight. By fleeing, he had saved himself to fight another day.

Manhattan Island appeared in the summer smog before him, a compact wedge of grey high-rises and skyscrapers. He had never before thought that the sight of the ugly metropolitan build-up could be so welcoming.

He found himself driving along East 116th Street, coming to the turning to his own street and continuing east. He turned right and pulled into the kerb before a dilapidated brownstone.

Why had he come here? He had intended, on getting away from Nyack, to go straight to the NYPD headquarters on 42nd Street. But that could wait. How could he bring himself to dispassionately report the murder of someone he had loved to some bored, desk-bound sergeant he hardly knew?

He climbed from the car, then braced himself against the open door as a wave of nausea threatened to engulf him. He took a deep breath, his head clearing, and looked across the sidewalk to the steps leading up to the entrance of the brownstone. The physical act of making the short walk seemed beyond him. He felt sick, and it seemed that every muscle in his body was protesting at the mere fact of standing, never mind having to exert himself to climb the steps.

He pushed himself from the car and moved to the tenement. He took the steps one at a time, pausing halfway up. He must have presented a strange sight to the kids playing basketball in the street, as he stood trembling before the door, summoning the strength to turn the handle.

He opened the door and stepped inside, and faced the long climb to the first floor. He made himself do it, lifting one foot after the other until he reached the top. He stood before the steel-plated door, trying to rehearse the words he needed to convey what he had experienced.

He rang the bell, and again.

A voice issued from a speaker beside the door. 'Who is it?'

'Halliday,' he said.

The door clicked open automatically. He pushed it open all the way and stood on the threshold, unable now the time had come to summon a single word.

Casey sat on a chair in the corner, staring at a computer screen, her legs wrapped around the legs of the chair. She was wearing, he noticed inconsequentially, blue jeans and a white T-shirt.

She was smiling at him. 'Hal! Good to see you. I meant to get in touch. I wanted to apologise about . . .'

He shook his head and said, 'Kim . . .'

119

'. . . the other night.' She stopped and stared at him. 'What?'

He just shook his head, unable to find the words.

Something in Casey's expression, an awful dawning realisation of dread, seemed to compound Halliday's pain.

He had told himself that when the time came he would be able to tell her what had happened, but when he opened his mouth, now, all that emerged was a strangled sob.

She stood up, tipping the chair, and came to him.

'Kim's dead,' he managed at last, and collapsed into her arms.

Eleven

Halliday walked around the dell, unable to bring himself to look upon what it contained. He stood on the bank and stared down at the river, unseeing.

He felt a small, cold hand slip into his and squeeze. He put his arm around Casey and she looked up at him, smiled bravely. Her face was white with shock, her eyes raw with shed tears.

He was aware of activity behind him as the Scene of Crime cops, forensic and homicide detectives, moved around the dell.

'What you said earlier, Casey . . .' he began.

She shrugged, the tiny movement of her scrawny shoulders beneath his arm at once pathetic and touching. 'When?'

'Back at the apartment. You said you wanted to apologise.'

'For last night, Hal. I was being silly—'

He moved so that she was facing her and held onto her shoulders. 'You wanted to apologise? Chrissake, Casey. I was a mindless bastard. You were right. I needn't have hit King with the incapacitator. I don't know. Perhaps I hated him for being with . . .' He could not bring himself to say her name.

She reached up and touched his hand. 'We were both wrong, Hal. You for doing what you did to King, and me for going off like that.'

He pulled her to him and kissed her forehead. 'You were right to do what you did, Casey. I was stupid, heartless.'

She smiled at him through eyes filmed with tears.

'Christ,' he said, 'you've grown up a lot in one year. You look so much older, and so damned . . .' He had been about to say *pretty*, but stopped himself. 'I feel like the past year's been a waste, Casey. A hell of a waste.'

'Hey, you can put it behind you. Take more cases. Throw yourself into your work, okay?'

He smiled at her. 'Okay, counsellor. When I get to the bottom of this damned case, I won't look back.'

He made to turn, look into the dell, but Casey restrained him. He held her hand and stared across the river at the parched grassland sweltering in the early afternoon heat.

On leaving Casey's place that morning he'd contacted Jeff Simmons, an old friend from his NYPD days, and given a full statement.

Once he'd started speaking, going over what had happened minute by minute, he was amazed at how much he recalled, and with every objective statement of fact came the painful freight of recapitulated emotion.

Halliday heard a throat being cleared behind him. Jeff Simmons joined them, nodded at Casey and looked Halliday in the eye. 'Hal, if you'd care to come with me . . .'

Casey looked from Halliday to the Lieutenant. 'If you want, Hal, I'll go and do the identification . . .' She shrugged. 'If that's okay with you.'

Jeff was rubbing his jaw. 'There's only one problem, Casey,' he said, and glanced at Halliday with an odd, almost suspicious, expression. 'There's nothing to identify.'

Halliday felt his vision swim. He pushed past Jeff and stared down into the dell. The grave where he had found Kim, and next to it the grave where he had seen Anastasia Dah shot dead, were exposed to the light of the day and empty; a third grave – Suzie Charlesworth's, he had presumed – was also unoccupied.

Casey took his arm and, accompanied by Jeff, they walked into the dell. Halliday was aware of the Scene of Crime squad and the forensic team, ranged around the natural amphitheatre like a redundant Greek chorus, staring down at him.

He paused before the shallow grave where, just hours before, he had held the body of Kim Long.

'Nothing,' Jeff Simmons said. 'Not even blood traces. But we'll conduct tests to confirm that.' He stared at Halliday. 'Hal, I don't know how to say this . . . But are you sure about what you saw?'

His voice caught in his throat. 'They were here . . .' He pointed to the empty graves. 'I saw the guy shoot Dah. Then I found—'

'Okay, Hal,' Casey said, squeezing his arm.

'So how do you explain . . .' Jeff gestured at the empty grave.

'What do you think? They moved the bodies, obviously. I got away, didn't I? You don't think they'd leave the bodies, once I knew they were buried here?'

Jeff pulled a 'maybe/maybe not' face.

'The nano-receiver,' Halliday said, feeling relief. 'It's in my car, back in Manhattan. It'll lead us straight to wherever her body is.'

Jeff nodded. I'll get someone onto it.' He hesitated, then said, 'You spend a lot of time in VR these days . . .'

'What's that got to do with anything?'

'Hal,' Jeff said, and his expression was pained, 'you ever heard of engramatic hallucinations?'

'Yeah, sure I have. But I know what I saw, and it was no hallucination.' He thought of Eloise, his dead sister, and the hallucination of her that had haunted him immediately after his first VR experience.

But he had held Kim in his arms, felt the weight of her body . . .

A car drew up and a uniformed sergeant climbed out and gestured down to Jeff Simmons. The big cop climbed from the dell, panting, and spoke with the sergeant.

Halliday turned to Casey. 'I know what I saw, Casey.' Even to his own ears, he sounded desperate.

She reached up and touched his cheek. 'I know you did. They came back and moved the bodies, like you said. I believe you.'

Jeff was nodding at what the sergeant was telling him. He stared down at Halliday.

'Christ, what now?' Halliday said.

Jeff returned, negotiating the incline in a series of side-steps. 'They just got back from the house where you said you saw Anastasia Dah,' he said. 'Nothing. Not a thing, no beds, no medical equipment . . .'

'So they've moved everything in the house. They had plenty of time.'

'Or maybe you hallucinated the house, too?' He reached out and took Halliday's arm. 'You were a cop, Hal. You know how this must look from where I stand, right?'

Halliday shook his head. 'I know what I saw.'

'Let's go over the facts again. You were working on a missing person's case. You were looking for this kid—'

Before Halliday could argue that he'd been over the facts half a dozen times already, a cop appeared on the ridge overlooking the dell and waved down at them. 'Sir! We've found something.'

Halliday looked at Casey and hurried up the incline.

The cop was waiting for them on the edge of the lifeless forest. He gestured through the trees. 'About a thousand metres west,' he said. 'A body.'

Jeff Simmons led the way through the trees, Halliday following with Casey by his side. Her hand found his, squeezed as if with reassurance.

Two minutes later they came to a knot of forensic scientists and Scene of Crime cops gathered in a small clearing. A couple of sniffer dogs sat on their haunches, pink tongues lolling. The group parted to let Simmons through.

Halliday stared down at the mound of earth. Emerging from the loam, half-buried, was a single red rose.

Two cops were digging with hand-trowels, uncovering a body. Halliday watched the operation, Casey leaning against him and observing the exhumation with a sour expression.

Halliday braced himself as a head emerged from the crumbling subsoil, a bullet hole marking its right temple.

Jeff looked at Halliday. 'Recognise?'

It was the black guy he'd shot. But he was sure, thinking back and re-running the incident in his mind, that he hadn't shot the guy through the head.

He nodded. 'He was with Charles and the guy in the blue suit.'

Jeff regarded the body as the forensic team began an examination. 'You said that when these guys came after you, you fired, right?'

'Sure I fired. What do you think I did, threw stones?'

'You think you might've hit this guy?'

'Listen, Jeff. I admit, I shot him. I even heard his cries as he went down. If I'd caught him in the temple, he wouldn't have been able to utter one damned word. And I didn't fire again until blue-suit came after me.'

A scientist looked up. 'The shot that killed him was fired at close range, sir. He was also shot in the upper arm.'

Jeff nodded. He looked at Halliday. 'You still have your automatic?'

Halliday stared at his friend. 'You don't think I . . . ?'

'Hal, I gotta cover every possibility. You know that.'

He gestured to a forensic scientist who took Halliday's automatic and placed it in a sterilised container.

He heard a shout from through the woods. 'Over here!'

They moved further into the forest, to where a knot of forensic scientists gathered about a barking dog. Someone pulled it away to let the digging team through.

Halliday hung back, Casey next to him, gripping his

125

hand. He had a terrible presentiment that this time the body they would unearth would be Kim's. The odd thing was that, though he knew he had held her in his arms that morning, he did not want the fact of her death to be confirmed.

Jeff Simmons glanced back at him from where he knelt beside the grave. 'Dah,' he reported.

He stood and joined Halliday and Casey.

'So now you believe me, Jeff?'

'I never disbelieved you, Hal. I just had to be sure.'

Halliday felt a sudden, overwhelming urge to be away from the dead woods before Kim's remains were found. 'I'm outta here, Jeff. Is there a car—?'

'I'll drive you back to the city, Hal. I'll contact you for further questioning as and when that's necessary, okay?'

They rode back to Manhattan in an unmarked cop car, Halliday relieved that the questioning was over for a while. He went though what he'd experienced that morning, relived every second of the two hours from arriving at the house to escaping from the guy in the blue suit. Okay, so he'd suffered hallucinations in the past – but Eloise had never been as real as what had happened to him that morning. He'd never held his dead sister's phantom in his arms, for Chrissake. This morning he'd felt the weight of Kim's body in his embrace, experienced again the keening agony of knowing that she was dead.

He closed his eyes and pulled Casey to him.

He must have dozed. He awoke with a start at the sound of a voice. 'Where you want dropping, Hal?' Jeff Simmons asked. They were motoring through Harlem on Fifth Avenue.

He looked at Casey. 'Where's Kim's apartment?'

'Hal . . . You shouldn't—'

'I need to look around, see if I can find anything.'

'Okay, but I'm coming with you.' She leaned forward and gave an address off East 86th Street.

Five minutes later the car pulled up outside a five-storey apartment block in Yorkville. Jeff turned in the driver's seat. Halliday made to get out. 'Hal, I'll be in touch, okay?'

'Sure, Jeff. I'll contact you if I come up with anything.'

'Likewise. Take it easy, okay?'

Halliday nodded, not particularly enjoying the look of concern on the cop's face.

He climbed from the car and followed Casey across the sidewalk. He showed his ID to the doorman and rode the elevator to the third floor.

He leaned against the mock-timber panelling and massaged his eyes.

Casey was watching him. 'You okay, Hal? You sure you want to go through with this? Why not some other day, huh?'

'I need to find out who did that to her, Casey. I can't waste time because I happen to feel like shit, okay?'

Casey shrugged. 'Just thinking of you,' she whispered.

He mimed a right hook to her chin. 'I know you are, and I appreciate it, okay?'

They alighted on the third floor and Casey led the way to Kim's apartment. Halliday swiped the lock with six of his pass-cards before the door clicked open.

He hesitated, for no more than a second, then pushed open the door and stepped inside.

It might have been the apartment of a stranger, for all that it reminded him of his ex-girlfriend. She had left most of her possessions – the few pieces of furniture she'd scavenged from the Salvation Army store – in the loft above the office when she'd walked out, taking only toiletries and clothing.

She'd done well for herself since then – no more sale purchases from the Salvation Army store. The five-piece suite looked brand new, along with the plush throw rugs and expensive lamp stands.

He stood in the middle of the big lounge and looked

around. The furnishings might not have reminded him of Kim, but the strategic placement of everything in the room certainly did. He saw wind chimes hanging in the north-west, the picture of a sunrise on the south wall . . . and he could not prevent a sore tightness burning his throat like a draught of acid. Kim had been obsessed with feng shui; she had never entered a room or building without whispering to Halliday how she could improve the energy flow, the chi, to bring about prosperity, health and happiness to the owner. He wondered how she would have squared her obsessional quest for good fortune with what had happened to her in the forest north of Nyack.

He swore to himself. Strange, but why was he angry at her for going and getting herself killed?

He moved to a shelf above a heater. A line of pix showed Kim with friends and a couple of guys. There were no photographs or holo-cubes of Kim and him.

What the hell had he expected, he asked himself.

'So,' Casey said. She was standing by the door, watching him. 'What're we looking for?'

He stirred himself. 'I don't know. Letters. Pictures. A diary.'

Casey smiled. 'Kim never kept a diary.'

'She didn't? Well, whatever. Anything that might point to contacts you might not've suspected she had. Anything to do with a silver-haired guy. Or something called the Methuselah Project.'

'The what project?'

'Methuselah,' he said. 'A guy in the Bible who lived a long time. It was something she was into with Dah and Charles. God knows what. Okay, where do we start?'

Casey went through the little paperwork Kim had accu-mulated, and then her possessions, knick-knacks and clothes. Halliday overrode the password to her personal com and accessed her letter file. He found scads of business letters but nothing of relevance, and not the slightest hint of anything about any Methuselah Project.

'Hey, Hal,' Casey called from another room. 'You know she had a jellytank?'

He looked up from the com. 'News to me.' He stopped reading through Kim's letters, a lump in his throat at her quaint use of the English language, and considered.

A jellytank?

He stood and moved to the bedroom.

A red dress lay across the bed. Halliday picked it up, crushed the material in his hand. She'd had the same dress, or one very much like it, when she had lived with him.

The sudden vision of her, standing with the dress pinned against her naked body as she asked for his opinion, flashed into his head.

He dropped the dress on the bed. Casey was leafing though an old photograph album. 'Some pictures here of when Kim was a little kid, Hal.'

He nodded. 'I know. I've seen them.' They had traded histories, and gone through their respective albums, shortly after she had moved in with him. He couldn't bring himself to look at the pix of Kim as a cute kid just yet.

The jellytank was a fashionable Mantoni model, all streamlined curves and silver flashing – as if the damned thing had been modelled to fly through the air.

He activated the tank and accessed the history file.

He stopped, his hand poised above the touchpad, and stared at the blank screen.

Casey looked up from the album. 'What is it?'

'The history file's blank.'

She shrugged. 'So?'

'So . . . It's been wiped, cleared. And I mean purged, cleaned right out of the system.'

'So she wiped the history file,' Casey said. 'So what?'

'So, Casey, there's no need to clean your history file like

129

this – unless you've got a good reason. Like you want to hide where you've been.'

'Like sex zones?' she said.

'Only if you're a prude. And Kim certainly wasn't that.'

'So why'd she wipe the history?'

'Good question.'

Maybe she – or whoever else wiped the file – didn't want people to know she'd entered the site he'd been denied access to the other day? The same code he'd found in the history of Dah's tank. What was it again? Vrus~mp/ss/797 . . .

Or maybe he was leaping to wild conclusions?

They finished the search of the apartment and came up with nothing, no mention of the Methuselah Project, or of a silver-haired guy called Charles.

'What now, Hal?'

'Couple of things I have to do. I need to pick up the car over at the office. What you doing?'

She shrugged. 'Nothing. How about I come with you?'

He planned to check the history file of Anastasia Dah's jellytank, to see if that had been mysteriously wiped, too. Then he'd go up to White Plains and question Suzie Charlesworth's mother. Today should be the day she spent out of the tank – if, of course, she didn't cheat and spend it tanked in some VR Bar.

He shook his head. 'You'd just be hanging around, getting bored. It's just routine, Casey.'

A year ago she might have complained, pestered him to take her with him. Now she just nodded, trying not to show that she was put out.

'Hal, I was thinking. You can't go back to your place tonight. You can't spend the night alone, not after what happened.'

'I'll be fine,' he said.

'Listen to the big man!' She scowled at him. 'Look, I've a

130

spare sofa-bed. Why don't you spend a night or two at my place?'

He hesitated, torn between hurting her and giving in and accepting her offer, when all he really wanted to do was to get the interview with Anita Charlesworth out of the way, have a few beers, and sleep for a long time.

'I'll see how things turn out, okay? I might be back late.'

She was determined not to let him see her disappointment. She nodded. 'Hokay,' she said. 'If I'm asleep, just use your key-cards to get in, okay?'

He smiled. 'If I'm not held up, it's a deal.'

They left the apartment and shared a cab back to El Barrio. She got out at her place, waved fingers at him and ran up the steps of her brownstone. Halliday continued to the office, picked up the Ford and drove downtown on Fifth to Houston Street.

The concierge recognised him. 'Ms Dah's out of town for a few days,' he said.

Halliday flashed his police ID. 'I'll let myself in.'

He ignored the guy's protests and rode the elevator to the fifth floor. He opened Dah's apartment with one of his spare card-keys and made his way to the VR room.

He accessed the history file and seconds later stared down at the screen.

Surprise, surprise, he told himself. The file had been deleted, purged from the system.

Either Anastasia Dah had done it herself immediately before leaving the apartment with Charles, or someone had returned since last night and wiped the file.

He took the elevator to the foyer and leaned through the hatch of the concierge's cubby hole. 'You let anyone into Dah's apartment last night or today?'

The guy peered at him. 'You a cop, right?'

He produced his ID. 'What does this say, pal?'

The concierge nodded. 'Matter of fact, I did. VR tech, said

131

he was. Come to fix Ms Dah's tank. She said he might be around some time.'

'Remember the guy?'

He shrugged. 'Just a regular-looking guy. Couldn't describe him to save my life.'

Halliday returned to the Ford and sat behind the wheel for five minutes, going over the facts of the case and trying to work out what the hell was going on.

He gave in, started the car and drove north on Park Avenue. He left Manhattan on Interstate 87, slipping the car into cruise control and sitting back. He glanced at the digital on the dash. It was six, and the nightly rains were threatening. Just twelve hours ago he'd taken the same road north to Nyack. Just twelve hours ago, so far as he'd been aware, Kim was still alive, the case a simple Missing Persons investigation. Now Kim and Dah were dead and he was trying to find out why, why the silver-haired killer had taken Dah's life after such a show of affection, why he'd killed Kim Long.

There was an explanation, no matter how complex and convoluted; there was a reason for Charles to have acted as he had, a series of motives which were obscure now but which, given time and patient investigation, would become apparent. It was always a question of time and hard work.

He arrived in White Plains as the sun was going down through the summer smog, casting a bloody glow over Maple Street and the avenue of artificial trees.

He parked the Ford outside the Charlesworth residence just as the heavens opened. The monsoon deluge drummed on the roof of the car, deafening. He jumped out, hunched, and ran through the rain to the protection of the porch.

There was a light on in the front room, and when he rang the bell the hall light came on, too.

The door opened a grudging five centimetres. 'Yes?'

He showed his PI card. 'Halliday. I'm investigating your

daughter's disappearance. If you could spare ten minutes . . .'

A thin, gaunt face peered out at him, suspicious. 'You a cop?' Anita Charlesworth asked.

'Private investigator,' he said.

'Ten minutes,' Charlesworth said, opening the door and leaving him to close it as she retreated down the hall. He followed her into the front room. She was already seated by the window on the high-backed chair which the holographic Suzie had occupied on his first visit.

Her appearance confirmed what he'd been able to see of her in the tank the other day. She was a bad advertisement for VR addiction. She stared at Halliday from a withered face that once might have been attractive, and the tragedy was that her bright blue eyes, or rather the intelligence behind them, seemed aware of the terrible fact of what she had done to herself.

'I hope I haven't called at a bad time . . .' he began.

She clutched a dressing-gown around her withered body. 'I want her back, Halliday.'

'I'm doing my best to find out what happened to her, Ms Charlesworth.' He recalled the short grave in the dell, and wondered what effect the news of her daughter's death might have on her already fragile grasp of reality.

'I know what happened to her, Halliday!'

'You do?'

'Someone was around yesterday, some cop. Neighbour saw him nosing about. When I got out of the tank, Suzie was gone.'

'She disappeared four days ago,' Halliday began, and stopped. 'Who was gone?'

'Suzie. Who else? No doubt the cop took her, wanted to question her about where her sister might've gotten to.'

Halliday stared at the woman, slowly shaking his head. 'You mean the holographic Suzie?' he said. 'You want the holographic Suzie back?'

She clutched at the collar of her dressing-gown with an emaciated hand. 'Of course I want Suzie Two back, who the hell do you think I want back? Her sister?' She laughed. 'Suzie One's no company for me, Halliday. At least Suzie Two talked.'

He nodded. 'I'll get Suzie Two back for you, Ms Charlesworth. Don't worry yourself on that score.' He hesitated, wondering how to phrase what he had to say. 'I actually came here to talk to you about Suzie One.'

She shook her head. 'I don't know anything about her, Halliday. She never spoke to me, never told me what the hell she was thinking. She wasn't a daughter to me.'

'Even so, I need to know a few details.'

She seemed not to have heard him. 'Know what she did, before she left for good? She tried to turn Suzie Two against me. They spent a lot of time together – Suzie One filled her head with all sorts of fanciful notions, big words. Suzie One spoke to her, but not to her own mother, and by the time Suzie One had finished with her, Two hardly had the time of day for me, either.'

'I'm sorry. I'm sure everything'll be okay when I get Suzie Two back to you.'

'You promise me you'll do that?'

'If you answer just a few of my questions about Suzie One, then I promise.'

'I'll do my best. But like I said, I don't know the girl.'

'I just want to know if she ever went out, and if so where? Also, did she have any friends, or rather contacts? People she saw from time to time?' He paused, realising that he was speaking of the girl in the past tense.

'Friends? The girl doesn't know the meaning of the word.'

'She never went out, other than to work and college? She had no contacts?'

'Every fortnight, on Tuesdays. She went into the city to see her psychiatrist.'

'Suzie had a psychiatrist?'

'He called himself something else, but that's what he was. A shrink. He worked with people like Suzie, people with autism.'

'You don't happen to have his address?'

She looked over at the mantelshelf, nodded towards a small white business card propped against a carriage clock. 'Take that, if it'll do you any good.'

Halliday stood and took the card. He read: Edward L. Tallak, Behavioural Psychologist. Beneath this was an address in Lenox Hill.

'And she never went out other than to visit him, to work and to college.'

She shook her head. 'Never.'

'Did she by any chance use VR?' he asked.

'On occasion. I know she used the tanks over at Cyber-Tech, but she used my tank from time to time.'

'Could I examine it?'

She looked at him, as if wondering why the hell he was interested in her jellytank. 'If it'll help. It's upstairs. I'll show you.'

He followed her as she made her way slowly up the staircase, and he had to remind himself that the shambling, skeletal figure before him was just thirty-eight years old.

She opened the door to the VR room and switched on the light. She shuffled over to the tank and stood beside it, something almost defiantly proud and proprietorial about the way she lay a hand on the crystal cover.

'Do you mind if I access the history file?'

'Go ahead, I've got nothing to hide.'

He moved to the head of the tank and tapped the touchpad. A list of sites visited, stretching back almost a year, appeared on the screen.

He read through the sites, his disappointment mounting as he failed to find the site he was looking for.

No vrus~mp/ss/797 . . .

So the site was a dead end, a promising lead that had taken him nowhere, despite his high hopes.

He looked up as something occurred to him. 'Do you know if Suzie One had a separate history file that listed her own sites?'

She laughed. 'Of course. You don't think I'd let her have access to some of the sites I use, do you?'

He checked the tank's memory for any sign of a second history file. 'I don't see anything here.'

'There must be, Halliday. She used the tank just a week ago.'

He searched a dozen files, but found nothing.

'Have you had a VR tech come in to service the tank since last week?' he asked.

'Two, three days ago. I told him the tank was perfectly okay, but he said Suzie One had called him out.'

Vrus~mp/ss/797 . . . Perhaps that was the link, after all. Or perhaps he was clutching at straws.

It was the only real lead he had, and so far it had led him to nothing.

'Thanks for your time, Ms Charlesworth.'

They made their way back down the stairs and into the hall. She opened the door for Halliday, and laid a hand on his arm as he was about to step out.

'You'll get her back, won't you, Halliday?'

'Just as soon as I possibly can,' he said.

She restrained him a second time, her hand claw-like on his sleeve. 'You know, don't you?'

'Excuse me?'

'You're a detective. You know, don't you? I can see you use the tank yourself.'

'I know . . . ?' he began, then stopped and stared at her. 'You use the VR Bars as well?' he said.

She smiled, and there was something tragic in the smile that, very briefly, showed a woman in her late thirties.

136

'Wouldn't you, if you had two daughters like mine, Halliday?'

He nodded, lifted a hand in farewell, and then stepped from the house.

As he drove through the rain towards Manhattan Island, the glow from its neons and holo-façades lighting the horizon, he considered the inaccessible code.

A year ago he'd accepted a commission from a strange woman called Kat Kosinski, who turned out to be the brother of Joe Kosinski, a cyber-genius Halliday had worked with just six months before that. Kat was opposed to VR in some way that he had never quite figured out – though he suspected that her opposition was more active than she admitted. He'd been to her apartment a few times, and he'd never seen so much VR equipment, tanks, computers, and even stranger cyber-paraphernalia, outside of a VR store.

She'd once admitted, out of her head on spin and alcohol, that she was a VR hacker. What had she called herself? A vracker . . .

They'd lost contact not long after that, and he'd never got to know the full story.

But if anyone could crack the inaccessible code, Kat was the woman.

He drove into El Barrio, considering Casey's offer of a sofa-bed for the night. He parked in the street outside the office, then locked the Ford and ran through the driving rain to Olga's.

It was quiet in the bar, just a couple of familiar faces occupying favourite seats like sentinels. He ordered an ice-cold Ukrainian wheat beer and a couple of ham on ryes, with a side-salad as his concession to a healthier diet.

He carried the beer to his booth at the back of the bar, sat down and took a long, wonderful swallow.

The beer cut through his thirst like a scalpel.

He fished out his com and got through to Casey.

Her face peered out from the tiny screen. 'Hey, Hal. Where are you?'

'I won't be able to make it back tonight, kid. Sorry. Still up in White Plains.'

'You come across anything?'

'Maybe, maybe not. I'll fill you in later, okay? I'll be in touch.'

'Sure, Hal. Take care.'

He cut the connection, then sat staring at her fading image on the screen.

He told himself that he had to be alone, that the last thing he needed right now was company.

He considered Anita Charlesworth, and her request that Suzie be returned to her. How lonely and desperate must she be to consider a pre-programmed hologram as a substitute for her only daughter?

He got through to Wellman's heavy, Roberts, and asked him to have a copy of the Suzie holographic device sent up to White Plains as soon as possible.

Then he sat back and ordered another beer.

Twelve

Kat inserted the aerosol into her left nostril, prepared herself for the hit, and sprayed. The icy rush of spin seemed to blast the top off her head. She laughed crazily, reeling around the single room of her apartment. Her head was spinning, and for a few minutes the world seemed like an okay place.

She sat on the mattress and hugged her shins, staring into the darkness. It was daylight outside, but when she'd taken the apartment she'd spray-painted the window matte black to shut out the sunlight. All the monitors of her com-system were switched off, and without their glow the room was midnight dark. Without the sound of their motors, the room was utterly silent, too. She could make believe she was in space, floating through the vacuum. What about stars? She was glad there were no stars in her universe. Stars meant planets. Planets meant people. And people meant only heartache and trouble and loneliness . . . Loneliness? She thought through that convoluted logic again. How could people mean loneliness? If there were people, then you were not alone. But . . . she smiled to herself . . . she had it: you could be lonely in a crowd, so people did mean loneliness. Especially those people who walked out on you and left you lonely.

She ran the suicide fantasy number again. She was in a jellytank in Times Square, a freeze-dried mummy in the suspension gel, a warning to all who took for granted the easy pleasures of virtual reality.

She held her head in her hands and wept.

Colby, the bastard, had failed to show.

He should have arrived from Canada yesterday, but he'd neither shown nor called to explain himself. But that was Colby all over, a great guy, but as unreliable as hell.

He said he was a free soul, tied to nothing, a drifter through the cosmos – as if this excused him any responsibility towards others.

To make matters worse, she'd worked for the past few days with the needle that Temple had given her. The needle routed her to a few sites, and she was supposed to record the specifics of these sites, log the streams of data like some fucking mind-zapped wage slave. She could have done it in two days, two days of solid hard graft, but the job was so mind-numbingly tedious that she'd spread the work-load out over four days, and then downloaded it to some Virex source God knew where. And good-fucking-riddance.

The work had been made bearable, though, by the knowledge that soon Colby would arrive. He wanted to see her. Something big had gone down. He would be here by the weekend.

Only, the weekend had come and gone and there was still no sign of the bastard.

She cried herself to sleep.

She had no idea how long she'd been out. Something woke her, something loud and insistent. She rolled onto her back, feeling like shit. The room was totally dark. Christ, what'd happened to the com-system? Then she remembered. She'd killed everything to prepare herself for the spin hit.

She heard it again. Some crazy fuck was banging on the door.

She staggered to her feet and hauled the door open. She'd expected sunlight, but it was night out there. She must've slept for hours.

There was no one standing outside, no crazy with a gun

ready to shoot her in the head. She banged the door shut and reeled towards the mattress.

She thought she heard a shout. 'Kat!'

The banging started again.

With an effort of will she thought beyond her, she stood woozily and again made for the door. The banging continued. This time she'd catch the bastard. She pulled open the door and a thin, wiry, hairy, gap-toothed ugly son-of-a-bitch stood on the threshold, staring at her with concern.

'Kat, what the hell? When you didn't answer I thought I had the wrong place, so I tried down the street.'

She blinked. 'Colby?'

He stepped inside, found the light switch and filled the room with dazzle.

He looked into her eyes, then around the floor of the room littered with discarded aerosols. His eyes took in the evidence of her slide, but did not censure her.

That was one of the things she loved about Colby. He never took the moral high ground. He knew that humans were frail things, that everyone needed some crutch or other.

He settled her on the mattress, then sat cross-legged before her. He pulled a small stove and a kettle from his backpack and brewed some disgusting-smelling – and tasting – herbal concoction, which Kat drank only because it was Colby's special cure-all.

'Thought you were never gonna get here, Col,' she said.

'I was delayed, Kat. Long way down from Saskatchewan.'

'You been to Sas— to Sask—'

'Never mind, I'm back now.'

Her heart nearly stopped. 'For good?'

He hesitated, both hands clasped around his mug of herbal effluent. 'I found a place I want to settle down, Kat. It ain't New York.'

She could only shake her head, disappointment beyond her. 'Then why you back?'

'Because I want you to come with me.'

She stared at him. 'To Canada?' She shook her head. 'But I can't leave—' she began.

He said, 'That's what I came to talk to you about, Kat. Things have been happening. Big things.'

She smiled at his seriousness. 'Big things?' she mocked.

He shook his head, nibbled at the overhang of his moustache. He looked around the room. 'Not here. Might be bugged. Let's go some place else, okay? We'll talk then.'

She nodded. Her head was still tender from the spin. She needed coffee. She needed Colby to talk to her, his gentle Arizona drawl lulling her senses.

She found her shoes and locked the door and walked through the dark, wet streets with Colby. How often had they done this before, gone to some all-night place, drank coffee and herbal tea and traded backgrounds?

What had he said? That he wanted her to come with him . . . ? To Canada?

'Time's it, Col?'

'Four.'

She laughed to herself. They found an underground coffee shop on Bowery, and they were the only customers. Colby bought an espresso for Kat, and a mug of boiling water for himself. He sat across from her, adding a sprig of this, a leaf of that, for all the world like some ancient, bedraggled sorcerer.

She took a hit of coffee and felt instantly less dead.

He rolled a raspberry leaf cigarette with nimble, expert fingers. The process always fascinated her, just as the smoke always smarted her eyes.

'So, Col, what were you doing in Canada?'

'Checking something out, like I said. I'd heard about this place, up in Saskatchewan . . .' He talked real slow, careful, looking up from time to time as he built his roll-up. 'Town Called Barton, out beyond nowhere. Full of real people,

142

people like me, Kat. Back-to-Earthers and travellers and nature-freaks and what have you. And you know what?'

'No . . .' Mesmerised by the dexterity of his fingers, the sound of his drawl. 'Tell me.'

'The people of this good town have declared it a VR-free zone.'

She stared at him. 'A VR-free zone?' she echoed. 'Always thought there wasn't a place on Earth free of VR.'

'Well there is now, Kat, and it's called Barton, Saskatchewan.' He raised the almost-ready cigarette to his lips, licked quickly along the outside of the column, removed strands of excess leaf from one end, lit up and inhaled and stared at Kat though the resultant fug.

Her heart began a slow pounding. 'You quit Virex, Col?'

He nodded. 'Sure did, Kat. I got out. I found out something, and I reckoned I couldn't stay a second longer.'

'Found something? Something big, right?'

'Something mighty big,' he said. 'You know how a while back the bombing was vetoed, and then they quit with the viral attacks, just when we thought we were getting somewhere?'

She nodded, sipping her coffee.

'And then they start giving us VR sites to analyse, like we were company spies or something, and we send all the information down the line to some mysterious big organiser, some big wheel, head of Virex.'

'Where's this leading, Col?'

'Leading to this, Kat. Couple of months ago who drops by but Koviak. Remember me talking about Koviak, my cellpartner before you?'

She nodded. 'Sure I remember. You and him were big buddies.'

'Well, out of the blue he shows and he wants to talk, but not anywhere we can be overheard. He's all jumpy and nervous and not at all like himself, so I take him to Central Park Zoo, and he tells me.'

143

He stopped. His roll-up was burning unevenly. He remedied this by dabbing spittle onto the charred column with a smoke-stained forefinger.

'What'd he tell you?'

He looked at her through the smoke. 'He told me that Virex was being infiltrated. One by one the controllers were being replaced by other controllers, people belonging to a big, powerful, and rich organisation. You see, they knew we had mucho expertise. I mean, Virex had – still have – some of the best cyber-brains working for them. They reckoned that if they could take over, infiltrate, get us working for them . . .'

'What, Col? What they want?'

'They want the information we've been sending down the line to who knows where. The information on every big VR company in existence.'

'So . . . that sounds pretty much like Virex to me, Col. And when they have all that data, we use it—'

She stopped. Colby was shaking his head. 'They aren't Virex,' he said, 'or rather they aren't Virex any more. The organisation that's been using us is into VR itself.'

She regarded him, thought through what he'd said. 'Paranoia,' she pronounced at last, aware of the flutter in her throat. 'Conspiracy theory. I mean, what proof do you have, Col? What proof did Koviak come up with to make you believe all this?'

'He showed me pix,' he said. 'These pix, they showed Temple, your controller, in the company of a guy called Connaught. Now this Connaught is a big fish in financial circles. He has his fingers in lots of pies. One of these pies is the VR pie—'

'Hearsay.' Her hands were shaking, bad now.

'The pix show Connaught handing over needles to Temple, Kat. The needles he passed on to you and me, the needles that we used to get into the secure Mantoni, Cyber-Tech and Tidemann's sites.'

She felt sick to her stomach, and her protests sounded feeble even to herself. 'You can't be sure. A few pix aren't hard evidence.'

'They're evidence enough for me, Kat. Along with how things've been going for the past six months.'

They talked for the next couple of hours, going through half a dozen herbal teas and as many espressos until Kat was wired with the granddaddy of all caffeine ODs.

They went through what Koviak had said, and argued the evidence back and forth, and the end result was that Colby had quit Virex, gone north and found paradise, and wanted Kat to join him.

He was catching the eight-fifteen express to Montreal, and at seven they quit the cellar bar and walked through the quickening streets to Grand Central Station.

She stood with him on platform four, just like in some ancient weepy movie. 'So, Kat . . . You joining me up there some time?'

'I need to think about it, Col. I need to think about it hard, okay?'

The train was about to leave, and she hugged him to her, considered everything she would lose if she quit the city, and everything she would gain.

She waved him off as the train drew from the station, and then walked back to Chinatown, all the way, working off the caffeine high and trying to convince herself that what Colby had told her was nothing more than baseless supposition.

How could it be true? How could she have been working for what was in effect another VR company, the enemy? The thought was too terrible to contemplate.

Colby had given her his address in Barton. If she found that Virex had been infiltrated, that they had indeed been used like pawns, then she knew where to find him.

But how the hell could she find out? And, she asked herself, did she really want to know the truth?

How could she live with the knowledge that everything she had worked for, over the past year and a half, was for nothing?

She reached her apartment. A can of spin lay on the mattress, inviting her.

Kat inserted the aerosol into her right nostril, prepared herself for the rush, and sprayed.

Thirteen

At two that morning, before he got too drunk and maudlin, Halliday found Kat Kosinski's code in his com and tried to get through to her.

A message flashed on the screen informing him that the code was no longer in use.

He considered his options. He could stay here in Olga's bar, drinking until daylight, or go back to his room and try to sleep. If he kept on drinking he would only make himself angry, and if he went back to the office, haunted by the ghost of Kim Long, he would only succeed in making himself sick with grief.

Or he could try to find Kat Kosinski.

He quit the bar and drove south to Chinatown.

Back when he'd done a little work for her, Kat had spent a lot of time in a cellar bar off Lafayette Street. Most nights she could be found there, on a stool in the shadows at the end of the bar, nursing a beer and taking the occasional hit of spin.

She had once told him that she never spoke to anyone in the bar, that she had nothing in common with anyone she had ever met. He'd been intrigued by her self-imposed isolation, curious as to the reason for it. He'd often wondered what had caused her cynicism, her world-view in which trust played no part.

A year back she'd hired him to track down someone she merely referred to as Levine, a business partner – though when he'd tried to find out more about Levine and exactly what business they were engaged in, Kat had been reluctant to tell him much more. He'd found Levine, or rather his bullet-riddled body had turned up at the city morgue. Kat had taken the news stoically, without the slightest show of emotion – as if to exhibit feelings would be to admit to weakness. Six months before that her brother, Joe, had died – Halliday had known and liked the kid – and after the death of Levine Kat had retreated even further into herself, and Halliday had found her long silences and bitterness oppressive. He'd called round at her apartment from time to time, reluctant but sorry for her, and at the same time intrigued by the air of mystery that surrounded her like the ever-present reek of spin. Then, one day, he dropped by to find the apartment deserted, all the VR equipment packed up and removed, with no message or forwarding address apparent. Halliday had been secretly relieved.

He parked the car on Lafayette Street, crossed the rain-slick sidewalk and descended the steps. He pushed into the cellar bar and peered into the gloom; there was no sign of Kat Kosinski. He ordered a beer and asked the barman if he'd seen her about.

'Kat? She's been ill. Hasn't been in for a week.'

'You know where she's living now?'

The guy gave him the once over. 'You into VR?' he asked.

Strange question. Did he assume that Kat was likewise into VR, from her frail and wasted appearance? He nodded.

'Can't tell you where she lives. Kat wouldn't want that. But I'll give you her com code, okay?'

He scribbled the code on a beer mat and flipped it across the bar. Halliday finished his beer and returned to the Ford.

He entered the code and watched the screen.

Kat answered a minute later. The screen remained blank. 'Who is it?' Her voice sounded rough, marinated in bourbon and spin.

'Kat? It's Hal, Hal Halliday.'

'Jesus Christ. Ghost from the past. How long's it been, Halliday?'

'A year. How's things? Heard you been ill?'

'Just flu. I'm okay now. What you want?'

'I need to see you.'

Silence from the other end of the line. 'You don't have my address?' she said at last.

'You never contacted me when you moved out of your last place.'

She gave a humourless laugh. 'I didn't? Never was any good with the social graces. You know me.'

'Any chance of seeing you? I can wait till morning, whatever.'

'Shit, Halliday. What's wrong with now? You know I never sleep.' She gave her address and cut the connection.

He drove a couple of blocks and eased the Ford down a narrow alley. Kat's place was a basement apartment beneath a Chinese supermarket. He climbed down steps slick with rotten vegetable peelings and assorted litter and rapped on the door. The barred windows were blacked out, something he recalled from her last apartment.

She opened the door. Blue light spilled out, turning Kat into a dark waif-like figure. 'Hal Halliday, the man himself. Get yourself in here.'

He slipped into the small room – small, he told himself, only because of the amount of equipment that lined the walls, reducing the floorspace. A jellytank, banks of computers, monitors, touchpads and headphones.

A single mattress lay in one corner, Kat's only concession to furniture. Empty bottles of Jack Daniel's and canisters of spin littered the floor, along with congealed take-out trays.

Kat stood in the middle of the room, hugging herself. She seemed even thinner and more wasted than he recalled. As ever, she was dressed all in black, a baggy T-shirt and tights that made her legs seem spider-like.

She indicated the mattress. 'Take a seat. Drink?'

He sat down. 'I'm okay.'

She upped the lighting and peered at him as she sat on a

swivel chair before a desk of touchpads and poured herself a bourbon.

'Shit, Halliday. You look terrible.'

'Thanks, Kat. You know how to make a man feel great.'

'No, I mean it. You oughta stop, you know. It's no good just cutting down. It's like a drug. You can't quit an addiction by cutting down. It's gotta be sayonara to whatever's your kick.'

He stared at her. 'Listen to you.' He pointed to the spin canisters littering the floor like bowling pins. 'That stuff isn't exactly soda pop, you know.'

'Fuck yourself, Halliday. You know what I'm talking about.'

'Actually, you've lost me.'

She leaned forward. 'Quit VR, big boy. Get out while you can. Turn your back on it and wave goodbye.'

'Listen, I can handle it. I'm on a new fitness and health kick. Eating well, cutting out the booze. I'm joining a gym next week.'

She was shaking her head, as if in despair. 'Halliday, it isn't your body I'm thinking about. It's up here.' She tapped her head.

He mirrored the gesture, mocking. 'Hey, I'm fine up here.'

'Fine? Hell, look at society . . .'

He recalled this from a year ago, her magpie flitting from one disconnected subject to another. She might come back to her original premise, but it often took time. He wondered if it was an effect of the spin.

'What the hell has society got to do with me using VR?' he asked.

'Can't you see it, Halliday? You blind? Look at how society's been affected by the fucking plague. Look at how people interact . . . They don't.'

'They never have,' he muttered.

150

She pointed at him. 'Let's take you,' she said. 'You got a lover at the moment?'

'No. But I don't see—'

'You got friends?'

He opened his mouth to speak. Casey? Who else? Certainly no male friends, not since Barney died.

'Well?'

'So I'm a miserable lonely bastard, but what does that prove? Look at you. You don't use VR that much, so where're all your friends and lovers?'

'Difference is, Halliday,' she said, staring at him seriously, 'I chose my lifestyle, but the poor bastards who're addicted to tanking, they're affected without even realising it. Their social skills are eroded – their very need for human contact's diminished by what they experience in the sites. So you think you interact in VR, but what really happens is that you do what you want. It's a fact, Halliday, that ninety per cent of VR users now don't choose user-interactive sites – they use sites where they interact with constructs, artificial personas often programmed by themselves for their own gratification. People in VR don't have reciprocal relationships with other people, with a two-way flow of giving and receiving – they take what they want and give nothing in return. The ability of people to give themselves is being lost, Halliday. We're becoming a nation of loners.'

'So you foresee the ultimate breakdown of society?' he said, sarcastic.

'Look around you, Mr Private Eye. Don't you see the breakdown happening now?'

He shrugged. 'I see what I've always seen.'

'That's 'cos you're too out of it with VR to notice the fucking difference, Halliday.'

He looked around the room, part of him wondering if she had a point. When it came down to it, what the hell did he know, ultimately, about anything?

151

She hoisted the bottle of Jack Daniel's. 'Sure you won't have a drink, Halliday?'

He shrugged. 'Go on. Why not?'

She found a chipped mug on the floor and poured, then sat beside him on the mattress.

The alcohol burned his throat. Across the room, lined against the wall, he saw half a dozen cans of spray paint.

'Tell me. I've always wondered. Who pays for all this equipment, the coms and the tank? You pay for all that yourself?'

She stared straight ahead. 'Let's just say that it's paid for, okay?'

He smiled to himself, took a sip of bourbon. 'How long you been working for Virex?'

She looked at him quickly. 'Halliday the Private Eye. You been snooping around, doing a bit of detective work on the quiet?'

He shook his head, lips pursed around a mouthful of corrosive bourbon. 'Just put two and two together. I've seen the graffiti. "Virex Against Virtual Imperialism" and whatever. So what does it stand for? Virex?'

'Know something, Halliday? I don't know. Honest. It's just a name the cells have always worked under. I've often wondered. VIRtual EXperience? VIRtual EXtinction?'

'You in a cell?'

'Something like that.'

'So a year ago, the guy you wanted me to locate, Levine? He was a cell-mate, right?'

'Wrong, Halliday. He was a controller.'

'So who'd you think wanted him dead?'

'Who else? The big three. The bastards who run the virtual empire.'

Try as he might, he just could not imagine Wellman sanctioning the assassination of people opposed to VR.

She was looking at him.

'What?' he asked.

'You're working for Cyber-Tech now, right?' she said.

'Hey, I should employ you. Could use a partner with your ability.' He tipped his mug and swallowed, grimacing. 'How'd you know that?'

'We have monitors, people who swim in the cyberverse ocean, disguised, of course. We call 'em sharks. They make it their business to scavenge information, keep an eye on all the big operatives.'

'You're not the rag-bag collection of misfit anarchists and anti-capitalists I took you for.'

'I'll consider that a compliment.'

'So what else you know?'

'About you? Oh . . . That you use a semi-private site, with a construct of a kid you once knew.'

He felt his face burning.

'That you have almost a third of a million in the bank. That you haven't worked for six months.'

'What do you know about the case I'm working on now?'

She shrugged. 'Not much. Just that a Cyber-Tech employee went walkabout, and big shot Wellman himself got you in to track her down. Which,' she went on, 'is probably why you dropped by today? Or am I wrong and it's really just a social call to see how I'm doing?'

'You're right. I have a lead, a code I need to crack. I've tried accessing it myself, but all I get is an access denied warning.'

She hung her head between her legs and laughed.

'What's wrong?' he asked.

She looked up, still shaking her head. 'Think about it, Halliday. You want me to help you help the people who I'm fundamentally opposed to in political principle . . .'

'That's a long way of telling me to go take a flying fuck, Kat.'

She stared at him. 'What's the code?'

He told her.

She nodded. 'I'll do it.'

'What's the catch?' He cocked an eye at her. 'What about those principles?'

'No catch,' she said. 'Just fifty thousand dollars to make me forget my principles, okay?'

He whistled. 'That's a lot of dollars to pay for something that might not lead anywhere.'

'That's the deal, Halliday. Fifty thou if I can break the code. Take it or leave it.'

Fifty thousand dollars . . . He could always charge it to Wellman. So why not? It might not lead anywhere, but then again it might provide him with the break he'd been looking for.

'Okay, Kat. Fifty thousand it is.'

She jumped up and crossed to a swivel chair beside a bank of consoles. She sat cross-legged, a pair of headphones clamped to her ears. Halliday drew up a chair next to her and watched as she began work.

She pulled a touchpad onto her lap and tapped in the code. The screen on the desk exploded with colour, illuminating the room. Against a bright blue background, white script scrolled at a rate too fast to read.

From time to time Kat reached out and touched the screen, and the script changed, scrambling and snowing down into a rearranged configuration.

Kat regarded the screen and twisted her lips. 'Mmm . . . Access denied to casual users. It's a code I've never come across before, Halliday. It has nothing to do with any of the VR operatives I've had anything to do with. But there's a thousand smaller fish out there. I'm trying to break the code down into its individual properties, trying to find out where it came from.'

She pushed herself across to another burning screen and ran her fingers over the touchpad. She scanned the text that appeared.

'Technically, it's not on-line. Every potential user who

employs the code goes through an elaborate filter, and then gets shunted into a private matrixing system.'

She turned to the monitor, reaching out to touch the screen.

It detonated with a sudden flare of colour, an explosion of orange, followed by green; a hundred subliminal images flashed in a dizzying rush.

She looked across at Halliday. 'I've connected with the site, but I'd advise against going in there.'

'Where is it?' he asked.

She laughed, gestured. 'It's just . . . *out there*, Halliday. It's impossible to learn anything about the site, other than its matrix configurations, which wouldn't mean anything to you. Thing is, it's protected with so many guard systems and alarms that they obviously want to keep whatever's in there a secret.'

'There's no way of getting a visual representation of the site on screen?'

She shook her head. 'No way, José.'

'What about getting me in there? Can you do that, Kat?'

She stretched, cracked her fingers above her head, considering. 'I can get you in there, but like I said I wouldn't advise it. It'd be ve-ry risky. You'd be detected sooner or later, even if I employed all the shields and decoys I can. I'd give you a couple of minutes, three tops, and then the alarm bells'd start ringing and you'd be chased by the electronic equivalent of the hounds of hell.'

'I've got to try it.'

'Listen, when I mean it's risky, I mean it's like *dangerous*, you know? It's loss-of-life scenario I'm suggesting here. I had a friend, he was burned bad once, only good luck got him out in time.'

'If I get in and out inside a few minutes . . . ?'

'Easier s than d, Halliday. See, these guards and alarms don't announce that they're coming after you, don't tap you politely on the shoulder and say, "Excuse me, there's the door . . ." They sneak up and start burning, right back to your brain in the tank.'

He thought of Kim, shot dead in a shallow grave north of Nyack . . . He had no choice, really.

'I need to go in.'

She nodded. 'Thought you might say that. Okay. I'll be with you all the way, talking you through it. You'll be able to hear me, but won't be able to reply. I'll be monitoring things from this end, trying to detect strikes before they're launched. But look, don't sue me if you end up brain dead, okay?'

'Hey, I trust you. You'll get me out alive.'

'You sound pretty confident, pal.'

He smiled at her. 'If you don't get me out in one piece, Kat, how will I pay you?'

She pointed across the room to the jellytank. 'Just take your clothes off and get into the tank, Halliday.'

He stripped, his back turned to Kat. He attached the leads to his arms and legs, then pulled on the faceplate.

Kat glanced up. 'I don't know what you'll see in the site. There might be anything in there. Could be you won't be able to make sense of it visually. The readings I have here are all over the place.'

He gave a thumbs up signal.

'And another thing before you go,' she said. 'You won't be yourself in there, for obvious reasons. I'm inserting you in some kind of disguise. Thing is, I don't know what, yet. I'm cloaking you in a mimic program. So you might be anything, any size. Good luck, Halliday.'

He stepped over the side of the tank and placed his foot on the surface of the gel. It resisted his pressure initially, then gave suddenly and oozed up his leg. He brought his other foot down, then sat and lay back. He sank through the gel, lying on his back and staring through the visor as the warm amber goo sealed over him.

'I'm putting you through, Halliday.' He heard Kat's voice, tinny, in his ear. 'Three, two . . .'

One by one his senses departed. He was blind and deaf, and then his sense of touch deserted him. He was an intelligence, nothing more, afloat in an infinite dark void.

On his ear-piece he hard, '. . . one. Inserting!'

He felt a sudden heat in his head as he made the transition.

He was surrounded by silence, a silence that seemed to stretch away from him for ever. The sensation was more than the mere absence of sound. He felt the absolute quietude as his eyes might apprehend a vast ocean, stretching away in every direction. The more he thought about it, the more he came to realise that it was more than just that he was failing to detect any sound: the silence existed within his head, an utter and perfect peace.

A voice shattered his meditation. 'No sign of anything nasty yet, Halliday.'

The words echoed, reverberated away into the distance like thunder.

He was surrounded by darkness, but a darkness pierced here and there by minuscule points of bright light, like a starscape.

He moved towards the nearest light, and only then realised that he was in possession of a physical form.

He was enclosed within the chitinous armour of some kind of insect, in control of a body he knew was tiny but which, from his own perspective, seemed entirely normal. Without conscious thought he steered himself towards the rapidly expanding light in a blur of furiously fanning wings.

As he flew, he was aware of other insects moving towards the light, and then, in the distance, a million others heading in the same direction. Except, when he looked again, they were not insects but insect-shaped objects, reflective with oleaginous jet surfaces. On the thousand facets of every bodily surface appeared scrolling columns of numerals. He twisted his eye-stalks and saw with wonder that he too was no more than an aggregate of alpha-numerics, a constantly changing series of chitinous screens comprised of a million sequencing calculations.

'So far so good,' Kat's transistorised voice told him, from another world entirely.

Ahead, the insects were flying into the closest ball of light, hugely expanded now and radiating a fiery effulgence like the sun. Without slowing, one by one the insects disappeared into the light, as if this were their sole mission in life.

He approached the ball of light, so huge now that it filled his entire field of vision. All he could see, other than the glow, were the specks of jet that were the other insects, winking out of existence as one by one they hit the light.

He felt no fear; it seemed right that he was moving in concert with the million other numerical insects. He soared towards the surface of the sun, and was consumed in a great actinic blast that seared his vision and filled him with elation.

He was no longer an insect, he knew. He had adopted a human form now, an amorphous figure without identity. He beheld before him a rolling idyllic landscape of hill and vale, the clichéd default geography of some third-rate fantasy site.

A woman stood before him, naked. She walked forwards, across a sward of emerald grass, reaching out to him as if in greeting.

Then the woman, until that second merely the essence of womanhood, a female paradigm upon which individuality had yet to be bestowed, changed in an instant.

Kim stood before him, wearing the scarlet dress he knew so well. Her long jet hair hung past her high cheeks, and her large, brown Oriental eyes looked out at him with concern.

The sight of her was like a physical blow to his solar plexus.

'Hal,' she said, stern, almost accusing. 'You shouldn't be here.'

He reached out, took her hand. Her fingers were so warm, so real. 'How . . . ?' he began, wondering at the coincidence of finding her here.

'I read your signature as soon as you entered,' she said. She looked alarmed. 'Hal, you're in danger. Get out of here now.'

He shook his head. 'Who did this? Who constructed you?'

Her frown was so familiar. 'I can't begin to explain. You wouldn't understand.'

'I want to know what's going on . . .' He couldn't bring himself to call her by her name, for all she seemed a miraculous likeness of the woman he had loved. He was in VR, and the real Kim was dead, and this was some clever construct fabricated for some unknown reason by persons just as unknown.

She stared at him. 'How did you get in here, Hal? How did you find the code?'

'Where am I? At least tell me that!'

She bit her lip, prettily, and the gesture brought tears to his virtual eyes. 'You shouldn't even be here.'

'Tell me, is this the Methuselah Project?'

Her eyes grew wide in alarm, and he felt the grip of a hand on his arm. He turned, saw a face he recognised. The silver-haired Charles.

His grip was like iron.

When he turned again towards the Kim construct, he saw that she was no longer there.

'What's—' he began.

He tried to struggle, but the sensation was as if he were in a dream. He knew what he wanted to do, but he was robbed of volition, powerless to act or react.

He raised his hands, searched in vain for an exit decal.

Charles pushed him forward, and he was no longer on the greensward. In a dizzying, dream-like transition he saw that he was being marched down a corridor between empty, barred cells. A part of him wanted to cry out that this was VR, that what he was experiencing was not real but some vivid hypnagogic dream, but at the same time the pressure of the grip on his arm, and the absence of reassuring words from Kat back in the real world, filled him with fear.

Charles bundled him into a cell. He stumbled forward and fell to the floor. When he regained his feet and turned, the silver-haired man was gone.

He sat down against the wall. He was in a square, windowless cell. The only light came from a fluorescent strip in the corridor.

He knew he was in VR, lying suspended in gel in Kat's tank. This was nothing more than a dream, albeit a very real dream. What frightened him was that, unlike every other experience he had had in VR, he was not in control of this dream.

'Kat!' he shouted. 'Kat . . .'

He closed his eyes, and when he opened them again he was no longer in the cell.

He was in a familiar attic bedroom. It was his room, the room in the three-storey weatherboard house his parents had owned on Long Island.

How the hell, he asked himself, are they doing this? How were the controllers of this site reaching into his mind and making his memories so real?

He stood and walked to the window, and out there in the middle of the back garden was the majestic oak tree he had loved to climb as a kid.

He turned from the window, and his heart almost stopped.

Eloise and Susanna sat on the floor, Eloise reading a book,

160

Susanna poring over a chessboard. As he stared, she looked up.

'Come on, Hal. Finish the game!'

He opened his mouth to speak, but no words came.

Then he was aware of the odour of smoke, drifting up the stairs.

'No!' he screamed. 'You can't do this!'

As if in sadistic delight, whoever was in control of this nightmare chose to accelerate the vision of the attic and the two innocent children. As he watched, frozen, smoke filled the room and flames leaped up the steps, twisting around the wooden balustrades, dancing over the stair carpet. Eloise stood and screamed and Susanna made to dive for the window.

And then the vision halted. The flames stilled mid-leap, Susanna came to a halt, one foot on the ground, her mouth open in a silent scream. Eloise was a statue, paused in the act of standing, knees bent, alarm eloquent in her eyes. Halliday looked around the room. It was as if time had stopped. Flames hung in unnatural suspension, great lianas of brilliant orange twisting through the air, drifts of smoke stilled like floating phantoms . . .

He saw, then, the young boy he had been. He was sitting on the floor, staring at Eloise.

'Don't make me live through this again . . .' he pleaded.

He could not relive again the choice he'd had to make, at the height of the house fire in his fourteenth year. Eloise or Susanna? He could only take one at once down the crumbling, fire-swept stairs, and then come back for the other.

He had made that choice. He had chosen Susanna, and by the time he had returned for Eloise she was dead.

But how did *they* know that?

He saw movement. Through a torque of flames like twisted golden silk he saw the figure of the silver-haired man, Charles, stride towards him.

'Do you really want to go through this again, Halliday?'

'How . . . ?' he managed. 'How are you doing this?'

'Oh, we have the power to have you experience the flames all over again, Halliday, and this time die a terrible death in the conflagration. This time, even, we can have both your sisters burn with you.'

'What . . . what—'

'What do I want?' Charles smiled. 'I want you to get out of here, Halliday. Leave the site. Don't come back. Don't even think about coming back. And then when you're safely in the real world, drop the case. Forget about Charlesworth and the Methuselah Project. Forget about Dah and Long. Go back to your safe little existence with your trips to the Virginia site . . .' He paused there, and smiled at Halliday. 'Because if we find out that you've defied us and continued with your investigations, then you're a dead man, Halliday.'

He vanished then, with such speed that Halliday almost doubted he had ever beheld the threatening spectre.

And the flames suddenly leapt to life, and the roar of the conflagration deafened him. The heat of the fire singed his skin, scorching the air from his lungs, and his sisters' screams became unbearable.

He screamed – and then he was no longer in the burning attic.

The vision ceased, replaced by darkness, and the heat of the flames died suddenly. He was in the jellytank, struggling through the cloying gel, Kat's voice loud in his ears, '. . . I lost you, Halliday. What happened in there?'

He emerged with a cry from the gel, standing and ripping off the leads, struggling with the mask until it came free. He stumbled from the tank. The images of the burning room played on in his head, even though he was back in the real world now, back in the safety of Kat's basement apartment. She assisted him over to the mattress, where he sank down thankfully and accepted the mug of bourbon she forced to his lips.

'They have a construct of Kim in there!' he said. 'They got into my mind . . .'

'Who?' Kat asked. 'Who did, Halliday?'

He shook his head, remembering the threat.

'I don't know,' he said, but he knew that it would take more than threats and visions of hellfire to stop him from finding out.

Fourteen

Barney Kluger sat on the edge of the bed and stared through the window at the sunlit coastline. Another perfect day in paradise. He had been here around eight days now, each day exactly like the one before. Until, that is, Lew Kramer showed up with that half-assed explanation as to why he was imprisoned here.

He turned and stared at the sleeping Estelle. He tried to recall the feelings he had experienced during his first hour in this site, when he had made love to the construct of his wife. He was sure he had felt something, then – but now when he looked upon her sleeping form he felt nothing. He had been deprived of his other emotions, too. He knew that he should have felt rage towards Lew the other day, anger and frustration at the predicament he was in. The fact was that he felt nothing, nothing at all.

He knelt on the bed, reached out, and slipped his fingers around his wife's neck. He felt her warm flesh in his grip, her fluttery pulse beneath his thumb. He saw what he was doing, but was unable to summon any consequent self-censure. He knew that Estelle was only a computer-generated simulation, with no life of its own, but he wondered what he might feel if he were to perform the same act on a conscious, living human being. It would be an interesting experiment. Would he feel nothing then, too?

He increased his grip on the construct's warm neck, throttling her. This, in its own way, was an experiment. How might the construct react to his attack? Would she refer to it later?

He felt the muscles of her throat collapse realistically beneath his fingers. Will the woman wake up and scream at him to stop? Any reaction, he thought, other than her bland repertoire of platitudes and niceties, would make a welcome change.

He dug his fingers into her neck.

She opened her eyes and smiled up at him. 'Hi, Barney. Let's go and have breakfast, shall we?'

He let go of her, rolled away and moved from the bed. He felt nothing, not even despair.

'I'm going for a walk. See you later.'

'Okay, hon. Back around lunchtime?'

He made some non-committal reply and hurried from the bedroom. He left the villa and walked through the dunes towards the sea.

He tried to work out why the fact that he was imprisoned in this site should have robbed him of his ability to feel anything, love or hate, joy or anger. He had been perfectly capable of having human emotions during that first hour, so what had happened to him since then?

He watched the sea push scalloped lace petticoats up the hard-packed, shelving sand towards his feet. He inhaled, tasted the brine in the air; the wind was warm on his skin. He wondered what was missing from this site to make it truly paradisiacal.

Real people, he thought. Human beings he could talk to and react with. What was paradise, without friends with whom to appreciate it? He thought of Hal, out there in the real world. Was he right at this minute investigating the disappearance of his missing colleague? Barney smiled at the irony of the situation.

Perhaps not. According to Lew Kramer, he was in a time-extended zone. In the real world he had been missing for only a matter of a day or so.

He turned and stared up the coast, towards the stand of pine where, the other day, he had come upon the largest basal rent in the matrix yet. Even now, at this distance, he felt compelled to make his way towards the rip in the fabric of the site, drawn towards the jet-black slick.

He set off, hurrying up the beach and across the foreshore.

He came to the plantation of pines and slowed, peering through the trees. The rent was still there, surrounding a pine tree like a geometrical, inky shadow. He walked towards it, his steps careful as if with a combination of trepidation and respect. He braced his arms against his knees and peered into the fathomless midnight depths.

His vision lost all sense of perspective; he seemed to be pulled into the darkness. He got down on his hands and knees and pressed his nose to the skin of the pool. What had Lew told him about the rent? That close contact might result in short-term cerebral anomalies and sensory dysfunctions? Something like that.

He wondered why he thought that the exec had been trying to hide something . . .

He focused on the tiny golden flecks swirling like spiral galaxies within the blackness, and had the irresistible urge to tip himself head-first through the rent. He felt himself leaning forward, and knew that if he wished to stop himself from falling, then now was the time to call a halt.

But a part of him *wanted* to fall, to embrace whatever mysteries lurked within the depths. He realised, with a giddy vertiginous rush, that he could no longer help himself. He was toppling through the hole in the fabric of this site. He felt himself drop with a sensation at once helpless and euphoric.

Unlike his first occasion of falling through the darkness, when the techs had tried to pull him from the site after his first hour, now he seemed to be in control of his fall. He had no idea quite how, or by what means he was able to manoeuvre, but it appeared that if he merely thought what he wanted to do, then it would happen. He saw a coruscating swirl of light nearby, and *willed* himself in that direction.

A second later he was rushing towards the light, and it expanded enormously before him like a supernova. Then he passed through the light and seemed to be flying through the air. He was above a vast concourse crowded with a thousand citizens. They were consulting screens that floated in the air at head height, reaching out and touching the screens and instantly vanishing.

He looked down, to where his body should have been. He had no body. He was merely a discorporeal packet of consciousness, free to wander.

He willed himself to move, and he moved.

He descended towards one of the floating screens. It displayed a dizzying succession of images, a hundred different worlds, it seemed. People were reaching towards certain scenes, and at the second their fingertips made contact with the image, they vanished from sight as if edited from reality.

He was in some vast virtual reality clearing zone, he decided, a concourse that was the gateway to a thousand worlds.

He never realised that VR was this advanced. Or was this merely a Mantoni research and design site, the citizens around him no more than constructs?

He approached a screen. It showed what looked like the devastated surface of an alien planet, crawling with what appeared to be war machines, vehicles like trilobites discharging photon pulses towards other fighting machines. Soldiers in exo-skeletal armour plating danced across the war-zone, firing in a frenzy of destruction. As he watched, individuals selected this site and disappeared.

The scene changed. He looked upon a mountain scene, Earthlike but for the sudden appearance of two tumbling moons in the sky. This screen seemed to show nothing but extraterrestrial sites.

167

He moved on, taking in a dozen floating screens and their varied contents. He realised that he had somehow attained the ultimate freedom of the virtual world, the ability to roam at will, pick and choose the sites he wished to visit.

He came upon a screen showing what appeared to be a hundred naked people disporting themselves on the beach and foreshore of a site designed expressly for sex. He watched in mixed fascination and horror, the orgy scene offending his old-fashioned sensibilities. The scene changed, thankfully, to be replaced with the image of people skiing through blindingly white snow in a mountain landscape.

He had always wanted to go skiing with Estelle, but for some reason they had never made it.

Now he willed himself to move towards the screen, and he moved. He passed into the image, found himself hovering a metre above the piste as a dozen multicoloured skiers swished by.

What was the advantage of being able to visit all these sites at will, he asked himself, if he did not possess the corporeal form with which to enjoy them? It was all very well being a disembodied viewpoint, but it lacked excitement.

It came to him that he could summon form in the very same way that he willed himself to move – merely by *thinking* it.

No sooner had the thought occurred to him than he was moving down the mountainside, in possession of a body clad in garish salopets and jinking with the skill of a life-long skier. He felt the rush of the wind on his cheeks, the exhilarating speed as he raced downhill. Pines flashed by in a vertical blur. He heard a scream in his ears, and realised that it was coming from his own throat.

After perhaps twenty minutes of skiing downhill on a

never-ending slope, he moved on. He simply willed himself to leave this site, and instantly he was above the concourse again, bodiless.

It was a measure of his conventional thinking that he began to worry, then, about what Lew Kramer had told him. What if what he was doing did have side-effects? Some unforeseen neurological dysfunction? Would it affect his eventual release from virtual reality, or worse?

He moved himself away from the concourse, and a second later he was rising through the inky blackness of the basal rent. He was moving towards a source of golden light, something within him intuiting that he was heading in the right direction.

The light expanded, momentarily dazzling him. He was still blinded, and blinking, a second later as he stood beside the jet-black slick of the rent in the matrix, staring down into its depths and wondering if he had really experienced the vast concourse, the snow-covered mountainside.

He stood for a time, lost in thought, and then made his way back along the beach. If he was locked in VR, as Lew Kramer had said, unable to escape, then how was it that he had the freedom of the virtual world? Lew had told him that he could not be transferred to other sites – so why had he lied?

What the hell was happening to him?

As he came through the dunes and approached the villa, another thought occurred to him. When he'd entered the tank back at the Mantoni headquarters, virtual reality had been in its infancy. The first VR Bars had just opened that week, each offering a choice of a few dozen different sites. So was what he had experienced merely some research facility still under development by Mantoni, or . . .

He recalled the periods of blackness he had suffered three times since finding himself here, the sensation of plummeting though the universe similar to, but different from, the sensation of movement in the matrix he had just experienced. After these occasions, he had the subtle but nagging sensation that great periods of time had elapsed.

Had Lew Kramer lied to him about how long he'd been incarcerated in the site? Had he been in here for months?

For the first time in a while, he realised that he was looking forward to a strong coffee.

Fifteen

Halliday stared at the screen of his desk-com.

He had built up the face slowly, little by little. The eyes had been the hardest part. In the index of eye-types from the Identi-fix program, which he'd pirated from the NYPD a couple of years ago, there were over five thousand different eyes to choose from. Many he'd tried this morning had appeared as near as dammit identical, but each pair altered the appearance when placed in the context of the face he was building up.

Now he thought he pretty much had the likeness of the silver-haired guy called Charles.

Grey eyes in a well-fed, fleshy face, a big, hooked, Roman nose, a wide mouth.

He'd seen the guy twice in the real world, once in Anastasia Dah's apartment, and again up at Nyack. He'd got a closer look at him in VR earlier that day, and it was on this image of the guy, threatening him with death in the virtual reality construct of his childhood attic bedroom, that he based the Identi-fix.

Of course, it was a very real possibility that the face that Charles presented to the world might be nothing more than the disguise of a capillary holographic unit.

He saved the image and printed a dozen pix for future use, then fixed himself a coffee in lieu of breakfast and stared at the pix.

The silver-haired guy was his only real remaining lead. Find Charles, and he would be a good way to finding out what the hell was happening.

Not for the first time he considered the threats Charles had issued in VR, and he wondered how they had managed to enter his mind and create the image of the fire with such accuracy.

His com chimed. 'Halliday here.'

Casey smiled out, waving fingers before her face. 'Hi, Hal. Good to see you back.' She peered. 'You okay?'

'Sure, Casey. Fine.'

'You had breakfast yet?'

'Ah . . . No, as a matter of fact.'

'Well, is it okay if I bring something round?'

He hesitated. Hell, why not? It was still only nine, and he hadn't planned to hit the streets till midday anyway. He nodded. 'Sounds good.'

'Great! I'll be round in five minutes.'

She was around in two, making him think that she'd snuck up the stairs to see if his office light was on, and then called him from outside the deli.

She burst in bearing a box of food in both hands. She hooked her leg around the door and kicked it shut, smiling at him above her purchases.

Halliday fixed her a coffee and sat beside her on the chesterfield, the breakfast box between them.

'Wholewheat cheese and salad, egg mayonnaise on rye, yoghurt . . .'

'You trying to feed me up, Casey?'

'Someone has to.'

She was dressed in jeans, and a T-shirt a size too small for her so that it pulled tight across her small breasts and revealed a strip of skinny belly.

He concentrated on breakfast.

It felt like old times, not long after Barney's death, when Kim had left him and he'd found Casey out on the fire escape, trying to sleep in the pouring rain. He'd let her in for the night, a scrawny Georgian refugee, and one night had turned into months as they shared the bedroom on a shift system. Who would have thought that the cynical, street-wise urchin he'd befriended that night would turn into this pretty, personable teenager inside a year?

'How's the job hunting going?'

She gulped down a mouthful of sandwich, bobbed her head and waved a hand. 'Ah . . . terrible, Hal. Nobody wants to employ an ex-refugee with only three months experience of restaurant management. They all want older people with years and years of experience.'

'So what you doing for money?'

'Oh, I have a little saved. I'll manage.'

'The rent on your place must be pretty high.'

She shrugged, munching. 'Was okay when I was living with Ben, but since we split . . .'

'Didn't work out, huh?'

'And I thought it would last for ever. Am I a dummy or what, Hal? What did I do wrong? Everything was okay, and then after a few months when the physical side of things . . .' She shrugged, blushing. 'We just drifted apart.'

'It happens, Casey.' He finished his sandwich, considering. He wondered why he had never given her a cut of the Artois money a year ago, as he'd intended. Was it because she'd moved out, shacked up with Ben? Had he felt jealous, resentful, and one way of getting back at her was to withhold the money he would have given her had she stayed?

It sounded like him, he thought.

He pulled open a drawer in the desk and found his cheque book. He wrote a cheque for twenty-five thousand dollars, which should set her up, see her okay for a few months at least.

She watched him. 'Hey, there's no need. Breakfast's on me, okay?'

He tore the cheque and passed it to her. 'I got a big pay-out on a case a while back. Been meaning to give you this for some time.'

She took the cheque and stared at it, her mouth shaping the sum of twenty-five thousand dollars in disbelief. She looked at Halliday. 'For me? Twenty-five grand?'

'Unless you want to donate it to charity.'

'Twenty-five thousand dollars?' she whispered.

She pulled the box separating them onto the floor, leaned over and took him in her arms.

He held her, comparing this experience with that of holding her construct in the Virginia site, and realised that there was really no comparison at all.

'Don't know what to say,' she said, the words muffled against his shoulder.

He ran a hand up and down her slim back, feeling the notched cord of her spine. 'Don't say anything. How many times you bought me breakfast? How many times you sat up with me after Barney died and Kim walked out?'

She gave a teary laugh, pulling away to look at him. 'Not twenty-five grands' worth, Hal!'

'Who's to say? Values are relative, Casey. I'd've paid more than that to have you around, back then.' He pulled her to him again, stroking her hair.

'Christ, Hal . . .'

'What is it?' he asked.

She pulled away, kneeling on the cushions now, and rubbed at her eyes. She sat on her legs and stared at him. 'It's frightening. I mean, how things might've turned out. Like, if eighteen months ago I hadn't decided to sleep on *this* fire escape. If I'd try to get in the homeless hostel on 87th, only I'd heard it was full . . . so I walked down the back alley, looking for somewhere to spend the night. It was destined, Hal.'

He laughed.

'What? Don't you believe in destiny?'

He shook his head. 'Everything's accidental, far as I can make out. Random. Things happen and we call it good luck

174

or bad, but they happen nevertheless. Events don't consider human feelings, they just happen.'

'That's frightening, Hal. I mean, I like to think if I'm good and I work hard, then good things'll come to me, know what I mean?'

He smiled, gave her worried face a playful hook on the jaw. 'Sure I know. Don't listen to me. You were good, you worked hard, and look what happened.'

She held up the cheque. 'I'll bank it,' she said. 'Maybe buy a few clothes, save the rest.'

He wondered if, all along, on some subconscious level, he'd meant to ask her if she wanted to move into the loft above the office? It made sense, the rent was dirt cheap, and food stalls and the laundry were nearby . . . and she would be close to him.

Was his gift of the cheque no more than a bribe to get her back? Or was it nothing more than a subconscious desire to enable her to leave him for good?

She reached out, silent now and her eyes downcast, and ran the back of her hand up and down his thigh, and something in him was appalled that she wanted to pay him back in the only way she knew.

Or perhaps she was genuinely lonely and needed his love and affection?

He took her hand. 'Hey, how about more coffee?' he said, breaking the spell, and Casey smiled and nodded. 'Yeah, great . . .'

He refilled the mugs. She sipped, peering over the rim at the face on the desk-com. 'Who's that, Hal?'

He looked into the face of the silver-haired guy. 'Pretty sure it's the guy who killed Kim.'

Her eyes expanded. 'It is?' She looked at him. 'What happened last night? You get anywhere?'

Where to begin? 'I'm looking for someone called Suzie Charlesworth,' he said, and he outlined the case in detail, as much for his own clarity of mind. When Barney was about,

175

they had talked through assignments constantly, going over every detail no matter how insignificant and seemingly inconsequential. He'd missed that over the past eighteen months.

He told her about the inaccessible VR code he'd found in Anastasia Dah's jellytank, and how he thought it might be a lead.

'I have a contact who hacks into VR sites,' he said. 'She got me in.'

Casey shook her head. 'What happened, Hal? Something bad, right?'

'There was a construct of Kim in there,' he said. 'I was discovered, locked in a cell. I couldn't get out. Imagine that, imprisoned in VR . . . Then the scene changed and I was in the attic bedroom I had as a kid.'

He paused as he realised that he had never spoken with anyone, other than his sister and his father, about the fire that had killed Eloise. For so many years he'd blocked it from his memory, and when he did finally access the truth of what had happened all those years ago, Barney was dead and Kim had left him.

Now he told Casey. He described the fire as he recalled it, and how he had a choice. Susanna or Eloise? He had made his choice, and Eloise had died.

Casey stared at him, shaking her head.

'But how did they know, Casey? How the hell did the bastards get into my head?'

'How did you get out of there, Hal?'

'He—' Halliday indicated the face on the screen. 'He appeared and gave me an ultimatum. He said that if I continued with the case, then they'd kill me. Then I was no longer in the attic.'

Casey opened her mouth, but no words came. 'So . . .' she managed at last. 'What now?'

He regarded her. 'What would you do in my position, if

the guy who'd murdered your ex-girlfriend told you to drop the case, let him walk free?'

She whispered, 'I don't know.'

'Would you just shrug your shoulders and let him get on with whatever he's doing, or would you try to nail the bastard?'

The silence stretched. At last Casey said, 'What are you going to do?'

'What do you think? I'm going to nail the bastard.'

He drained his coffee, stood and switched off the desk-com.

He took his jacket from the coatstand by the door. 'I've a couple of things I need to follow up. What you doing now?'

She shrugged. 'I have an interview, just waitressing. Still, I could waitress part-time now I have this.' She folded the cheque and slipped it into the back pocket of her jeans.

He took an automatic from the top drawer of his desk and stowed it in his body-holster. 'You ever thought of going to college?'

She made a 'who-me?' face. 'As if. What do I know about anything!'

'That's the whole point. You go into college not knowing anything, and you come out knowing something. At least, that's the theory. You could try management. You want to run a restaurant, don't you?'

She shrugged. 'But I don't want to study, Hal. I mean, Kim never studied, did she? She just worked at it. And look at how successful she was.'

He smiled at her. 'She was lucky. She got the breaks.' She was lucky, he thought, until she no longer got the breaks . . .

'I dunno. I'll see what happens, okay? Maybe I'll fall on my feet and land myself a good job. Say, what you doing tonight?'

'Nothing planned.'

'Not working?'

'Don't think so. Then again, in this job . . .'

'Well, if nothing comes along, how about we go out? There's a great new holodrome opened around the block, showing all the old dramas. We could see what's playing.' She tapped her butt pocket. 'I'll buy you a meal.'

'Why not? I'll be back sometime after six.'

'I'll drop by around seven, okay?'

He collected his cheque book. He'd go visit Kat later, pay her what he owed and see if she could tell him anything more about the site he'd been imprisoned in last night.

He opened the office door, let Casey through, and locked it behind him. 'Need a lift?'

She looked over her shoulder as she descended the staircase. 'Nah, the diner's just around the corner. I need the exercise.'

They reached the sidewalk and Casey waved and walked off, fingers inserted into the hip pockets of her jeans.

Halliday watched her until she turned the corner, then climbed into the Ford and eased his way through the pedestrians in the street and headed downtown.

As he drove he tried to calculate how many times, over the years, his life had been threatened. Once or twice when he was a cop, by thugs too drunk or drugged to realise what they were saying. Maybe two or three times when he'd worked with Barney, warned off cases by parties with vested interests. He'd always discussed the situation with Barney, assessing the risk, the likelihood of whether or not the concerned parties were serious in their threats. Only once had Barney advised to leave a case well alone, the threatening parties being the type of people who would think nothing of mincing two private investigators and feeding them to the fish.

Halliday was in no doubt that Charles meant what he said, and would have no compunction about carrying out his threat. He'd seen him kill Anastasia Dah, and knew that at least two other victims had suffered at his hands. What

178

was different about this case, as far as Halliday was concerned, was that he had a personal stake in seeing the killer apprehended.

He'd just have to be more vigilant, was all; he'd keep a wary eye out for anything untoward, the attitude of strangers, the possibility that he was being tailed. In his line of work, it helped to be careful at all times: now, considering the situation he found himself in, he would have to be extra careful. Trust no one, question everything. Stay alive.

He drove down Park Avenue and parked outside the ComStore.

He booked a private booth at the rear of the store and patched himself into the NYPD network. Using a restricted code, he slipped into the known-felons file. He scanned the Identi-fix pix of the silver-haired killer into the com and requested the closest hundred matches from the library of stored identities.

Seconds later he was scrolling through a rogues' gallery of middle-aged, silver-haired offenders. It was a long shot, of course. Even if Charles were not hiding behind the assumed visage of a chu, the chance that his man might turn up on this file was remote, to say the least. But it was another one of those avenues of investigation that had to be ruled out in order to proceed along the right track.

There were three or four very near likenesses, but even these Halliday discounted. He'd caught a close look of the guy in Dah's apartment, and then in VR, and he thought he'd recognise him again in a mugshot.

Fifteen minutes later he closed the file and cut the link. He could discount the possibility that the mysterious Charles had a police record, which was not much help at all. The next job would be to try to match the pix against an existing likeness in business journals, newspapers, or any other online publication. It would be a long and painstaking business, with no guarantee of success at the end of it.

He was about to initiate the search when his com chimed.

Jeff Simmons stared out at him, his heavy face filling the screen.

'Hal. Where are you?'

'Park Avenue, the ComStore. What is it?'

'Get yourself down to the station, Hal.'

Something turned in his stomach. 'You've found the other bodies, right? Kim and the kid's?'

'We're still searching. Something else has come up. I don't want to talk about it over the link. See you in ten minutes, okay?'

Halliday pocketed his com and left the store. He drove down to the police HQ on the corner of Fifth and 42nd, wondering at the summons.

Jeff Simmons had a big office in the basement of the old library building, an interior room without the luxury of a window. He sat behind a big desk, his ruddy face washed in the blue glow of his com-screen. A fan turned on the ceiling, stirring his grey hair.

'Hal, Christmas's come early this year.'

'Yeah? What's Santa brought me?'

Jeff leaned over the obstacle of his belly, reached out and flipped his desk-com so that it faced Halliday. The screen showed the likeness of the black guy he'd potted in the woods north of Nyack.

'The guy we found in the grave . . .' Jeff began.

'My bullet didn't kill him, right?'

Jeff nodded. 'The bullet from your automatic winged him – caught him in the upper arm. The bullet that killed him was fired at point blank range, like the forensic people said at the scene.'

Halliday nodded. So why the hell had someone shot the guy dead?

'Turns out he was one André Connaught,' Jeff was saying, 'a big fish wanted on a list of charges as long as your arm.

He was into big money scams, laundering, stock exchange frauds . . . you name it. We suspected he was behind a lot of financial crimes in the city, but we've never had the evidence to prosecute. You know how it is with these guys, they employ some high-profile attorney who knows all the tricks, ties the case up for a decade. So anyway, when the Fraud Squad found out he was dead . . . hey, it was Christmas for them, too.'

Jeff hesitated, looking uneasy. 'Ah . . . Forensic examined the graves you found, Hal. They came up with minute blood samples. They matched those on record for Suzie Charlesworth, Anastasia Dah, and Kim.' He looked away, shrugged. 'I'm sorry.'

Hal heard the words and felt a strange hollowness within him. He told himself to snap out of it. He'd held Kim in his arms, hadn't he? He'd known all along that she was dead.

He wondered if some part of him had been holding out the hope that the events of two days ago had been a hyper-real hypnagogic hallucination, after all.

'Suzie Charlesworth as well . . .' Halliday said.

'We're investigating multiple murder,' Jeff went on. 'Anything you find out, we'd be interested in sharing. Strictly off the record, Hal, the same goes the other way round, okay?'

'Sounds like a fair deal to me,' Halliday said. He passed a pix of Charles across the desk. 'This is the guy I saw in the woods north of Nyack.'

Jeff took the pix and stared at it, nodding. 'Any other leads?'

Halliday hesitated. 'A VR site,' he said. 'I found it in Dah's tank. Only when I checked again, it'd been wiped. I checked Kim's tank and Charlesworth's. Guess what? They'd been cleaned, too. So I hacked my way into the site.'

'And?'

Halliday described what he found in there, leaving out

181

the fire in the attic scenario but reporting the silver-haired guy's threat.

Jeff nodded as he tapped a touchpad and relayed Halliday's report to his desk-com. He read something on the screen, then looked up. 'You know anything about something called the Mercury Project, Halliday?'

'Mercury? I keep coming across something called the Methuselah Project, but that's all I know about it. Kim Long and Dah mentioned it in conversation a couple of times, and were overheard by a third party.'

Jeff shrugged. 'Dunno, might be linked.'

'You got anything on the Mercury Project?'

'A little. Connaught was behind the legitimate funding of a consortium of like-minded business contacts – they called themselves the Mercury Project.'

'Like-minded in what way?'

'They were funding research into von Neumann technology.'

'Interesting . . . or it might be if I knew what the hell von Neumann technology was.'

'Hey,' Jeff said, 'where you been hiding yourself, Hal? You don't keep up with the times? The technology's been around in theory for some time now. Apparently von Neumann machines are devices that self-replicate, spaceships that go among the stars, using what they find to make more of themselves.'

'And Connaught was behind this?'

'Behind the *funding*. Hal.'

'You think it's linked to the deaths of Dah and the others?' He thought it highly unlikely.

Jeff nodded. 'We think maybe, yes. See, Dah was also funding the same project. Her father was the billionaire tycoon George Dah, the holo-drama mogul. When he passed on, guess who got his billions? We checked her assets and found she was siphoning off millions into the same account as Connaught used to fund the Mercury Project.'

'Curiouser and curiouser.'

Jeff grunted. 'And that's as far as it goes, Hal. The principal players apart from our Mr Charles are dead, and we've linked no one else with what's going on, as of yet.'

'What do you think Kim and Suzie Charlesworth were doing mixed up with these people?' For the life of him he could not see Kim knowingly involved in any underworld activity. She must have been an unwitting accomplice in whatever was going on, the Suzie kid likewise.

The cop shrugged. 'Search me, Halliday. I was hoping you might have some ideas.'

'If I come up with anything, you'll be the first to know.'

'Sure thing. Keep in touch.'

Halliday smiled. 'Just like the old days,' he said.

'Get outta here, Hal,' Jeff grumbled.

He quit the office and made his way back through the maze-like warren of corridors, at once nostalgic for the times he'd spent here, the memories of the cases he'd worked on with Barney and Jeff, and at the same time relieved that he was no longer part of the vast and inefficient mechanism that was the NYPD.

He started the Ford and headed uptown, towards Lenox Hill. Five minutes later he drew up in the shadow of the Lincoln Tower, erected ten years ago and for a short while – perhaps six months, until the Japs finished the Mitsubishi Stratoscraper in Tokyo – the tallest building in the world.

He stood on the sidewalk and gave himself a sore neck trying to look all the way up to the top. It was like peering along an infinite length of polished steel, and left him dizzy when he looked away. Then he saw the elevator shaft, a diaphanous column on the outside of the building, and he hoped that Edward L. Tallak's office wasn't on the top floor.

He passed into the building. A receptionist in the busy

183

lobby told him that Tallak had his office on the 297th floor, a mere three quarters of the way up the tower.

He rode the elevator with half a dozen secretaries and business suits who didn't seem in the least concerned by the fact that New York City was falling away from their feet with alarming speed. He felt his stomach roll, threatening to dispatch his breakfast, and resisted the urge to plaster himself against the inner wall. He glanced down, at his feet, and knew he'd made a mistake; the floor was gratuitously transparent, and the flank of the tower seemed to fall in a long, graceful parabola all the way down to the miniaturised avenue far below.

He stared ahead, at the spectacular panorama of Manhattan stretching away into the summer smog. Somewhere out there, among the high-rises and sunken streets, the silver-haired killer of Kim and the others was quietly going about his business.

Revenge would be so terribly sweet.

He stepped from the lift onto the safe, non-transparent solidity of a carpeted corridor with the sensation of stepping onto *terra firma*. A brass plaque listing the various business concerns on this floor hung on the wall opposite the elevator exit.

Edward L. Tallak, Child Psychiatrist, occupied suite twenty-five. Halliday made his way along a series of wide corridors before he found the office area, positioned on the corner of the floor with dizzying views over Manhattan to the south and New Jersey to the west.

A receptionist with all the poise and hauteur of a fashion model sat at a desk like the console of a spaceship. Halliday passed his card. 'I need to talk to Mr Tallak.'

She glanced at the card with disdain. 'I'm afraid Dr Tallak is with a client at the moment.'

'Fine. I'll see him when he's through.'

'Do you have an appointment?'

184

'When he's finished, tell him I'm investigating the disappearance of one of his patients, Suzie Charlesworth.'

He moved off before she could reply. He sat in a recliner well away from the view and tried to interest himself in a plastic-paged magazine. It seemed to consist of nothing but images of women like the receptionist sporting fashions that cost more than he might earn in a good week.

When he looked up, the woman was murmuring into a microphone and sliding a quick look in his direction.

Five minutes later a door beyond her desk opened to reveal a plush office with a floor-to-ceiling window full of nothing but sky. A slim, suited man in his fifties appeared, signalled to the receptionist and slipped back into the office.

She looked up. 'If you'd care to step into the consulting room, Dr Tallak will see you.'

Dr Edward Tallak was seated behind a vast desk, silhouetted against the sky. He was perhaps fifty, his hair greying at the temples, his face tanned and unlined. The word impeccable seemed coined to describe him. Halliday often wondered, on the few occasions he came across examples of human perfection such as the one enthroned before him, if the contents of their psyches were as well-ordered as their physical aspects.

He passed his card across the desk, then sat down and watched as Tallak picked it up and examined it between thumb and forefinger. The doctor's hand was tanned and beautifully manicured, exhibiting an attention to detail that Halliday found vain and vaguely distasteful.

Tallak looked up from the card. 'I understand you're here in relation to Suzie Charlesworth?'

Halliday decided not to tell Tallak that Suzie was dead. 'She disappeared last Friday. I've been hired to find her. She had a regular appointment with you, I take it?' He concentrated on looking directly at Tallak, ignoring the view of Manhattan beyond the doctor. If he glanced through the window immediately to his left, he had a vertiginous view down the plummeting flank of the tower.

Tallak nodded. 'One hour, every Thursday morning.'

'She was here last Thursday, right?'

'She never missed an appointment, Mr Halliday.'

'The last time you saw her, did you notice anything unusual in her manner? Was she at all agitated or distracted? She didn't say anything to you about future plans?'

Tallak smiled. 'Mr Halliday, Suzie was autistic. One of the features of the severe form of autism as exhibited by Suzie Charlesworth is a chronic inability to communicate states of mind, feelings, emotions. Whatever she did say to me would have been factual, and often only in response to questions I asked. Last Thursday was like every other session I've had with Suzie Charlesworth for the past two months.'

'How exactly were you treating her, Dr Tallak? I understand there's no cure.'

'Autism is congenital, a condition hardwired into the system during the development of the embryo in the womb. There is no cure, only various means of helping someone with autism make sense of a world in which everyone else seems to communicate in a language they are unable to understand, a language of gestures and tacit codes, subliminal messages indicating empathy with and understanding of other human beings. People with autism are unable to comprehend the emotional existence of others, because they themselves do not function within the same range of emotions as do you or me.'

'So how did you help Suzie Charlesworth?'

Tallak smiled. 'I'm not at all sure that I did, Mr Halliday. I tried to facilitate her abilities and stimulate her interests in fields allied to those she was already studying.'

'Cybernetics?'

'Computational theory, mathematics, quantum theory . . .'

186

Halliday shook his head. 'It seems amazing that she had no difficulty with these fields, but the act of communicating her emotions was beyond her.'

Tallak gestured. 'We're all products of our hardwiring and environmental conditioning, Mr Halliday. It's just that the preponderance of citizens happen to be non-autistic. It's only a theory, but some researchers hold that the hardwiring of an autistic's brain is not wrong, aberrant, but merely different.'

'Did Suzie ever mention her work to you – or rather did you question her about her work?'

'Occasionally, but merely as a ploy to facilitate some form of conversation. What she talked about, when she was in full flow, was way over my head. I'm no computer scientist.'

'Do you know if she was happy with Cyber-Tech?'

Tallak smiled. '"Happy" is not a word I would associate with Suzie. Her interests were sufficiently stimulated by the work she did there, and to that extent you could say that she was content.'

'Did she ever mention whether she'd been approached by other companies, wanting her services?'

'She said nothing about that to me, no.'

Halliday nodded. 'Did you know that she was interested in discovering . . .' He paused, trying to recall how the holographic Suzie had described it the other day . . . 'in discovering whether the human soul existed as a material fact?'

'I didn't, but it doesn't surprise me. Suzie, despite appearances, has a brilliant mind. That kind of question would fascinate her.'

'The night before she disappeared,' Halliday went on, 'she was seen at a restaurant in White Plains, accompanied by two people. One was a woman, and the other a man in his sixties. We know him only as "Charles".' He drew the

Identi-fix pix of the silver-haired man from his pocket and slipped it across the desk to Tallak.

'Did Suzie ever mention anyone who might fit this description?'

Tallak regarded the pix, his lips pursed. He shook his head. 'She'd very occasionally mention her mother, and the hologram of herself, and now and again her co-workers at Cyber-Tech. But I never heard her mention anything about anyone called Charles.'

'Did she ever refer to something called the Methuselah Project?'

Tallak repeated the name, shook his head. 'Not to my knowledge, no.'

Halliday shook his head. How much of his time was spent in conversations like these, interrogational cul-de-sacs that were a necessary part of investigations but which ninety-nine per cent of the time led nowhere?

For the first time, Tallak asked a question of his own. 'Do you have any idea what might have happened to Suzie Charlesworth, Mr Halliday?'

He had a flash vision of the grave in the dead forest north of Nyack. 'It's too early in my investigations to tell, yet, Dr Tallak. I'm following various leads, and with luck something will turn up.'

He stood, making to leave the office.

Tallak reached into the breast pocket of his blue suit and produced a card of his own, a wafer of silver metal inscribed with his name and business address. He passed it across to Halliday, tweezered between his perfect fingers.

'If you need to know anything more that you think of relevance to the case,' he said, 'don't hesitate to get in touch.'

Halliday nodded. 'I appreciate that, Doctor.'

He smiled at the receptionist as he made his way out, but she deigned not to return the compliment. As he stepped into the elevator along with a dozen other beautiful people, he considered the many and separate worlds inhabited by the citizens of the same city, from which one was excluded by the arbitrary rules of things like wealth, appearance, age . . . He recalled something that Kat Kosinski had told him when they'd first met, a year ago. According to her, far from VR breaking down prejudices in people's minds about things like colour and class and sheer *difference*, the facility to assume any persona in virtual reality, to adopt perfect physical alter egos at will, was having an unforeseen effect in the real world: people were becoming ever more conscious of the perceived privileges of colour and class, wealth and beauty. Instead of leading to an egalitarian society in which everyone was seen as equal in one realm at least, VR was reinforcing old prejudices, leading to even more rigorously defined divisions in real life, as citizens strove to gain physical perfection and wealth.

Halliday hardly noticed it, spending most of his time in the ghetto of El Barrio. Only when he ventured into the more affluent enclaves of Manhattan, and observed the lives led by others, did he begin to think that Kat might have a point.

He plummeted down the side of the Lincoln Tower, doing his best to ignore the startling rate of descent, and considered Suzie Charlesworth and her world. She was – or rather had been – in the position of being excluded from society by an accident of birth. He wondered at the hell of being unable to interact with others because of some essential deficiency within yourself, and knowing that something was wrong without being able to understand quite what, or to effect a change. He considered the mess of his own life, the emotional troughs he suffered as a matter of course – but surely it was better to be able to experience the emotional highs and lows of life than to live solely an existence of pure intellect?

He left the Lincoln Tower and drove south, towards Chinatown and Kat Kosinski's place.

After he'd dropped off the cheque and talked to Kat about last night, he had a date lined up with Casey. A holo-drama and a meal somewhere . . .

Nail Charles and he'd be a happy man.

He turned onto Houston Street and seconds later noticed the black Merc in his rear-view mirror. It'd been tailing him all the way down Fifth . . . Okay, he was being paranoid. He'd travelled only a couple of kay, and on a main thoroughfare at that, so what was wrong with a Merc on his tail? But he'd been idling along, day-dreaming, and the car had had plenty of time to overtake him . . . and had declined to do so.

He decided to take a few turns, find out for sure if the Merc was on his tail.

He eased the Ford over to take the next right, and in the rear-view mirror saw the Merc signalling right, too. He turned and accelerated. The car followed, allowing him to open a distance of some five hundred metres.

He was not far from Kat's place. He could always ditch the Ford and head for her apartment, hole up there until the heat was off. He thought about it, decided against that option.

He turned left down a quiet sidestreet, considering the alternative. He had no doubt that he was being followed, now. The question was, who was it? His stomach turned at the thought that Charles might be making good his promise . . . They'd been watching him, following him, as he met and questioned Tallak. The shrink's office would have been the obvious place for them to stake out. He cursed himself. He should have thought of that, been more careful.

He took a sharp left down another quiet street and raced the Ford to the end. He could turn right or left now. The Merc had yet to show itself at the end of the street. He could easily lose his pursuer and be home free. Instead he idled, and only when the black car showed in his rear-view did he turn right.

Why run away when this was the perfect opportunity to find out who was following him?

He needed a good lead, something substantial to advance his understanding of the case, and if he played his cards right he would soon be in possession of the best lead of all.

A principal player in the game of cat and mouse . . .

On either side of the street were the recessed loading bays of various stores and warehouses. He turned the Ford into an empty bay, then climbed out and ran back down the deserted street in the direction he had come. He slipped into the cover of the next bay and ducked behind a plastic trash container.

He waited, heart pounding. Any second now the Merc would drive past in pursuit of the vanished Ford. He would get the car's plate, maybe even a glimpse of the driver.

He counted off the seconds, and then the minutes. Either the driver had taken a wrong turning and lost him, or he was clever and playing a game of double bluff.

The car did not appear. Halliday cursed, tried to work out how he might have done better. He could have stopped and remained in the car, inviting his pursuer to approach, but that would have been just too much of a risk. If it was Charles, or one of his minions, out to kill him . . . Then perhaps he should consider himself lucky that he'd evaded the Merc.

Five minutes later he chanced a glance up and down the quiet street. It was deserted, still but for the scurrying shape of a rat in the distance, and a scrap of litter twisting through the hot air like a kite.

He stood and hurried back to the Ford. He would have to be extra vigilant from now on, now that he knew he was under surveillance. Maybe he should think about relocating his base, and making use of the chu Wellman had given him.

He heard the sound, then – a footfall behind him, and he stopped in sudden alarm and with a terrible sensation of vulnerability and fear. He saw, in the distance, the same wind-borne sail of litter float through the air in slow motion, and it struck him, absurdly, as a thing of supreme beauty.

He made to turn, but the shot punched a hole through his back and chest and sent him pirouetting through the air. He landed on his back, and pain like molten lead being poured through his torso pulled a scream from his throat.

He lifted his head in a bid to see who had shot him.

His pursuer was perhaps three metres away, staring at him with an expression of disbelief, as if unable to comprehend the enormity of having shot another human being.

Halliday felt tears sting his eyes.

What had he counselled himself, earlier? That he should be extra careful from now on. Trust no one, and question everything. Stay alive.

Stay alive!

His hand moved to his chest, as if to check the damage done by the bullet. He was oddly surprised to encounter a feeble, pulsing flow of warm liquid.

Already he was finding it hard to breathe and his vision was misting.

His hand came up against the butt of his automatic, and his assailant saw the sudden movement and raised his gun to fire again.

Halliday gripped his automatic and, firing through his jacket, loosed off half a dozen shots, each one finding its target. The man fell to his knees, staring down with incredulity at the shattered remains of his chest.

Halliday closed his eyes. What a futile way to die, he thought.

He remembered the silver card Tallak had given him, and he knew then how the bastard had traced him.

He opened his eyes. Tallak sprawled before him, one arm outstretched. He heard a sound. The doctor was crying, and Halliday felt a sudden and quite involuntary stab of pity.

He stared in wonder at the man's outstretched right hand.

He reached into his jacket, found his com and pressed the emergency code.

Tallak's hands, he thought as oblivion claimed him. He should have known.

Tallak's hands were so young . . .

Sixteen

Barney climbed the steps to the verandah of his beach-front villa, and in that second Lew Kramer materialised before him.

He felt a sudden start of guilt at the thought that the exec was here to reprimand him for his jaunts through the cyberverse, but something in Kramer's attitude suggested that he had other things on his mind.

'Barney, good to see you again. Let's sit down. We need to talk.'

'I'm fixing a coffee. How about you?'

'Ah . . . no. No, I'm fine.'

Despite his curiosity, Barney moved into the kitchen anyway and brewed himself a coffee. It was a small and futile act of defiance, but one he found very satisfying. Christ knew, he had precious few other means of demonstrating his will.

Unless, of course, he made more of the basal rents.

He carried a mug of steaming black coffee out onto the verandah and joined Lew Kramer at the table.

'So what's the score, Lew? Your whiz-kids worked out a way of getting me outta here yet?'

He sipped his coffee, watching Lew, enjoying the guy's discomfort.

'That's why I'm here, Barney. There've been developments.'

'Good news?'

Lew hesitated, and Barney thought, uh-oh . . .

'Okay, bud. Let's have it. What gives?'

'Let me start by saying that I was against this from the start. Someone above me in the R&D hierarchy okayed the procedure, and my team had little choice but to go ahead with it.'

'You're talking in riddles, Lew,' Barney said, not liking the sound of what Lew was saying one bit.

'From time to time, as a matter of procedure and for the benefit of research, we copy the volunteers who help us out at Mantoni—'

'Hold on there. Slow down. Did I hear you right? You copy volunteers?' Barney lowered his mug to the table. 'What the fuck do you mean, *copy*?'

Lew cleared his throat, shifting in his seat uncomfortably. 'I mean, we make an e-download of the volunteer's mind – thoughts, memories, personality, the whole package that makes up an individual's unique identity.'

Barney nodded. He was curiously calm. He understood intellectually what Lew was saying, and could work out the consequences, but he was unable to bring himself to *feel* anything.

He said, 'Is that legal, Lew?'

'Well, actually, there's no precedent in law as things stand at the moment. It's one of those grey areas where the technology has stolen a march on the judicial process.'

'So what you're saying is that it isn't illegal?'

Lew nodded. 'As a matter of fact, in the contract that all volunteers sign there's a clause which states that the Mantoni organisation is within its rights to make e-copies—'

'I never read any such thing, Lew.'

'Maybe it isn't stated as baldly as that,' Lew said, 'and it is hidden away in a sub-clause somewhere.'

'Like all big businesses everywhere,' Barney grated, 'you're just a set of scheming, cheating, immoral bastards.'

Lew coloured. 'Like I said, I personally was against—'

'Spare me the protests of innocence, bud.' He stared across the table at the exec, marshalling his thoughts.

'Okay, so where does that leave me? Let me guess. You made a copy of me, right?'

Lew nodded. 'That's right, Barney.'

'And then you couldn't get me outta here?'

Lew glanced down at the tabletop. 'That's not exactly true.'

Barney sipped his coffee. 'So,' he said, 'what you came here and told me the other day. All that crap about . . . what was it? "clients becoming too fully integrated into the matrix . . . "? And the baloney about the time-extension site – that was bullshit, too, right?' He waited. 'Why all the lies, Lew?'

The exec exhaled noisily. 'Look, I felt that I had to tell you something. I mean, Christ . . . I knew you out there in the real world. I felt I owed you something, an explanation at least.'

'Even if that explanation was a lie?'

Lew nodded. 'I guess so. At least a reassuring lie was better than ignorance, or so I reckoned.'

'So if that was the lie, Lew, then what's the truth?' He forced a laugh. 'It's got to be something pretty fucking awful, if being stuck in this place was a *reassuring* lie . . .'

'The truth is, Barney, that we pulled you from the tank after your allotted hour with Estelle.'

Barney nodded. He had seen it coming. He had guessed. That moment of dislocation at the end of the hour with Estelle . . . 'What you trying to say, Lew?'

The exec could not bring himself to meet Barney's gaze. 'You're the copy,' he said.

Not surprisingly, he felt nothing now that his supposition was proved correct. He *felt* nothing, no rage, anger, fear . . . But he was curious, very curious indeed.

He lifted a hand, stared at it. He clenched his fist, felt the blood flow through his veins. The taste of the coffee was strong on his palate.

'Remarkable,' he said. He considered all his thoughts, his

196

memories. They were all so many pieces of electronically coded information, now.

He smiled to himself. What had they been before, though, technically speaking, but just so much electronically coded information, only housed in a flesh and blood receptacle?

The remarkable thing about the whole process was that humankind possessed the ability to make such copies.

'So I guess the fact is,' Barney said evenly, watching Lew across the table, 'that I'm no longer human?'

'Technically speaking,' Lew said, 'I suppose that's correct. I mean, in the strictest definition of the law, that is. Of course, things might change in the future. And, if you look at it another way . . . what exactly defines the parameters of what is or is not a human being? You have your thoughts, feelings, memories, you have your own sacrosanct sense of self, your identity.'

Barney almost stopped him when he mentioned *feelings*, but resisted the urge. Let him think he had feelings, if it would make him feel any better. Barney smiled at the irony of the situation.

The exec was running off at the mouth in relief that Barney, or rather the electronic copy that was now Barney, was taking the revelation in his stride.

But how could I possibly do anything else, he thought, when I've been robbed of my ability to feel?

'Let's cut the bull and get to the bottom line,' Barney said. 'So I'm no longer, technically speaking, human. I'm a copy. I exist in the Mantoni cyberverse, or whatever the fuck you call it. I guess that makes me your property, doesn't it?'

Lew shrugged. 'Well, I wouldn't exactly phrase it quite like that.'

Barney laughed. 'I'm sure as hell certain that your legal boys would, though. In fact, they've probably already got it down in black and white somewhere – no doubt tucked away in a sub-clause.'

He took another long draught of coffee. He tried to analyse his thoughts. The old Barney would have said, what do I feel about this situation? But feelings were useless to him now. All that mattered now was what he *thought* about the situation.

He was a copy of a human being, with a set of memories he considered his own, an identity. He seemed to have a physical existence, even if that was only an illusion maintained by a very sophisticated cyber system.

Had he been restricted to this site and this site alone, then he might have complained, but since having discovered the rents in the basal matrix ... he foresaw an interesting existence ahead of him.

'So why the change of heart, Lew? First you tell me I'm imprisoned in here, can't get out, but you're working on it. Now you spring the big surprise – I'm no longer human, I'm a copy. What happened? You said there's been developments?'

Lew nodded. 'You see, a while back in the real world, the original Barney Kluger died.'

Barney nodded, calm. Hell, how was he supposed to react to the news of his own death?

'Don't tell me, the old ticker went, right? Doc Symes was always warning me to lay off the wheat beer.'

Lew shook his head. 'We don't know the details, but we heard he died in a shoot-out.'

'Died with his boots on, doing his job.' Barney shook his head. 'That's how I always wanted to go, you know?' He stopped, stared at the exec. 'So where does that leave me?'

Lew nodded. 'You ever heard of an NCI?' he asked.

'Nano-cerebral interfaces? Sure.' He'd done his research. An NCI was a cyber skull-augmentation, wired into the brain of VR technicians to facilitate interaction with the cyberverse.

'Right. You see, it's possible to download information into NCIs – any kind of information.'

'What are you trying to say, Lew?'

'We have a body, out there in the real world. Victim of a cerebral haemorrhage. Brain dead, but the body's in perfect working order. We've fitted it with the latest model NCI.'

Barney stared at him. Just as he was anticipating the possibilities of surfing the cyberverse . . .

'Another one of your big fucking experiments, Lew?'

'With your permission, of course, we plan to download you into the new body tomorrow.'

Barney raised his mug, smiling across at the nervous executive. 'So let's drink to my resurrection,' he said.

Seventeen

The first thing he was aware of was the absence of pain.

Only then did it come to him that he was still alive. He lay on his back with his eyes closed, and where before a searing agony had lanced through his chest, now there was no pain. More than that, his body was no longer racked with the aches, the nausea and dizziness that had plagued him for months.

It came to him that he was still lying on the deserted street, that he was so close to death that his body had shut down, sluicing natural analgesics around his system as life slipped away.

But that was impossible. The surface beneath his body was not hard. He moved his right hand and felt the soft texture of linen beneath his fingertips.

Somehow, he had survived.

He opened his eyes.

The sight that greeted him was almost as surprising as awaking to find himself alive and in no pain.

He lay on a raised bed in a circular room. No, he thought, not a room as such, but a dome. The arching inner hemisphere of the dome was opaque, a milky hue shot through with iridescent threads of green and red, like opal. There seemed to be no entrance to the dome, and no other furnishings apart from a chair placed next to the bed.

He lifted a hand, stared at it and then at the material covering his arm. He was dressed in a pair of beige chinos, a blue T-shirt and sneakers. He sat up, expecting pain but experiencing none. He drew back the covers of the bed and swung himself into a sitting position.

He unbuttoned his shirt and stared down at his chest. There was no wound, no sign at all that a bullet had ripped through his back and exited through his ribcage.

He took a deep breath, and had to admit that he felt wonderful.

The bed was positioned in the middle of the room. He stood and walked across to the curving inner wall, to where a touchpad console was set into a waist-high pedestal. Experimentally, he reached out and touched a red square.

Instantly the wall of the dome deopaqued. He looked out on a familiar scene: ice-bound Tethys, with the gas giant of Saturn on the horizon.

He turned. 'Wellman?'

'Halliday.' A head and shoulders vision of Wellman appeared in the air before him. 'Just give me a minute while we adjust the programs. The sites are running at different time-scales. I'll be with you shortly.'

Before he could reply, the vision of Wellman vanished.

He wondered how long he had been in VR, if his well-being was nothing more than a trick of technology to ease him through his dying moments. It came to him in a burst of panic that that was exactly what was happening. He was dying, and Wellman had inserted him into a time-extended site so that his last few hours might be prolonged.

What kind of compensation was that? To know that he was rapidly dying in the real world, but had been resurrected to live out a period of grace in VR?

It would be a torture he'd find hard to endure. Far from being in heaven, he was in hell . . .

Then he recalled what Wellman had said about the sites running at different time-scales. Wellman existed in a slowed-down site. Given that, then this site could not be time-extended, like Wellman's. This must be a regular VR site, which meant that out there in the real world he might not be dying, after all.

An oval opening appeared in the wall of the dome diametrically opposite him, and the dapper figure of Wellman, dressed in a crisp white suit, stepped through.

'Halliday, it's good to see you up and about.'

'What's happening? Why all this ... ?' He gestured around him at the dome.

Wellman sat on the chair and indicated the bed. 'Sit down, Halliday.'

He remained standing. 'What's happening in the real world?'

'Don't worry. I'm taking care of everything. You're recovering remarkably, considering what you've been through.'

'I'll live?'

Wellman smiled. 'You were lucky. An emergency team was a kilometre away when your call came in. They were there in three minutes. Any longer and ...' Wellman gestured. 'Well, we wouldn't be talking now.'

A sensation of relief swept through him. He crossed to the bed and sat down.

'The bullet missed your heart by a centimetre. You lost a lot of blood. As soon as I found out what had happened I had you transferred to a private clinic. You're doing fine.'

'How long have I been in here?'

'In VR? A day. But you were in hospital five days before we thought it safe to transfer you here. You were unconscious all that time, after the operation.'

He thought back to the shoot-out in the deserted street. It could so easily have been the end. For some reason he thought of Casey, and how she might have taken the news of his death.

'We got you the best treatment that money could buy, Halliday. It was the least we could do.'

'You said I've been in here a day?'

'Just over.'

'When do I get out?'

Wellman raised a hand. 'One further day should be enough. We've found that around two days in VR greatly facilitates the healing process of trauma victims.'

Halliday shook his head. 'I thought the safe limit was twenty-four hours?'

'The legal limit for the protection of citizens who might wish to over-indulge is twenty-four hours, but the body can exist in suspension for three or four days before the first signs of adverse reactions. We've been working on extended immersions for the past year.'

'Why, Wellman? You want people to live in VR permanently?'

Wellman laughed. 'That wouldn't be at all practical. Think about it. The economics wouldn't work, for a start. Society would fall apart. Oh, I know there are doom-merchants who foresee a society of haves in VR and have-nots in the real world, working to keep the privileged in their safe dream worlds, but that's not what we at Cyber-Tech are working towards.'

'So why the research into extended immersion?'

Wellman smiled, and Halliday thought he saw a light of sadness in his eyes. 'Many reasons. To ease the plight of those with terminal illnesses, to aid post-surgical recovery, and of course – why deny it? – as a leisure facility. We're working on ways to keep the body active in suspension, so that the disadvantages of immersion, muscle atrophy, post-VR fatigue and nausea, will be a thing of the past. We hope to be able to introduce safe week-long immersions to the world in six months or so.'

Halliday wondered what Kat Kosinski might have to say about that scenario, and its effect on society at large.

He considered his earlier reaction, when he thought that he might be dying in the real world, and that he was living a time-extended period in VR before the inevitable end.

He looked up at Wellman. 'How can you live in here,' he asked, 'knowing what's happening to you out there?'

Wellman said, 'What's the alternative? That I return to the real world, to my emaciated and pain-racked body, and die in a matter of days?'

'I don't know . . . If I were dying, perhaps I'd rather go quickly than live out this . . .'

'This lie, Halliday?' Wellman shrugged. 'It's a hell of a lie, my friend. I have everything I have in the real world, and more besides. Friends visit. I have the run of the most amazing sites . . . I can't complain.'

Halliday considered something Wellman had said earlier, about the sites operating at different time-scales. He asked him about this now. 'Have you left your time-extended site to visit me?'

Wellman shook his head. 'Your site, this dome, was running on a real world time-scale. We reconfigured the matrix just after you awoke so that I could step through without losing any precious time. When I return, the techs will adjust this site back to how it was.'

Wellman looked through the dome at Tethys, then touched the decal on the back of his hand. Instantly, the icy moonscape vanished, to be replaced by a sun-drenched stretch of grassland, with a lake to the right and a range of snow-capped mountains in the distance.

Halliday made out animals drinking in the shallows of the lake, rhinos and what looked like wildebeest, a herd of giraffes galloping with somnolent negligence perhaps a hundred metres from the dome.

Wellman moved towards the oval opening in the curved wall. He paused, turned and gestured for Halliday to follow him, and stepped outside.

Halliday stood and approached the exit.

He was immediately hit by the heat of the African day. A distinctive odour, sun-baked dust and the musky scent of wild animal, filled the air.

Wellman had seated himself beneath the awning of a khaki tent. Halliday left the dome and joined him at a table laid with a teapot and two bone-china cups.

'Where are we?'

Wellman poured him a cup of Earl Grey. 'Serengeti. What do you think?'

Halliday nodded, impressed. 'Quite something. It looks so damned real.' He accepted the cup and sipped the tea.

In the distance a herd of elephants, led by a magnificent bull, trundled past, harrumphing and bellowing with a good imitation of disgruntlement.

'We've set you up with a new office,' Wellman said, 'a couple of kilometres south of where you were. So you won't be needing to go back to your old place. We thought it wise, after what happened to you.'

Wellman paused, then said, 'Now, I'd like to know what's going on out there.'

Where to begin? Halliday tried to order his thoughts. He was in possession of so many facts, so much information. Trouble was, no matter how he arranged the details of what he'd discovered, he could make out no pattern to the series of events.

'I wish I knew,' he said. 'All I can do is tell you what I've found out, and we'll take it from there. I haven't seen you since Nyack, have I?'

'What happened at Nyack?'

So he gave Wellman the rundown, how he'd traced Anastasia Dah to the house in Nyack; he told him about Charles and the killing of Dah, his discovery of the graves.

'So you think they killed Suzie?' Wellman asked, his gaze fixed on the distant horizon of the Serengeti.

Halliday nodded. 'Forensic found traces of blood matching hers.'

Wellman looked across at him. 'And you've had no luck trying to track down these people, Charles and the others?'

'The guy I winged at Nyack was known to the police:

André Connaught. He was into big money scams. He was also behind something called the Mercury Project.'

Wellman looked at him. 'He was? That's interesting . . .'

'You heard of it?'

'My techs have been studying the holo-device you brought back from White Plains. Unbeknownst to anyone at Cyber-Tech, Suzie Charlesworth was doing some independent work for someone – we have no idea who – who was involved with the research and development of von Neumann machines. They're—'

'Self-replicating devices theorised by some physicist in the twentieth century,' Halliday said. 'I found that much out when I discovered who Connaught was.'

Wellman poured more tea. 'According to Suzie's holo,' he said, 'the Mercury Project aims to send an unmanned probe to Mercury within the next year. We can only theorise that they'll be taking von Neumann machines along too.'

'I thought they were still only theoretical?'

Wellman shook his head. 'We've been hearing reports from various usually reliable sources that a couple of labs in Japan have succeeded in developing prototypes. If that's so, then the technology is extant, and if Suzie Charlesworth was working on it, then I can only assume that someone somewhere in the US is onto something big.'

'But how does that tie up with the deaths of Dah, Kim and Suzie? I can see why opponents to the Mercury Project might want Suzie out of the way . . . but Connaught was behind the damned project. Why the hell would his accomplice, Charles, kill her?'

'You've come up with nothing on this Charles character?'

'Nothing – except, I did come across him in the VR site.'

Wellman lowered his cup in surprise. 'You managed to access the site?'

'With a little help from a friend, yes.'

'I had a team of techs working round the clock trying to get in there. They finally managed it, for about three seconds flat. Then they were ejected. You say a vracker got you in? Would he like to come and work for Cyber-Tech?'

Halliday smiled at the thought of Kat's reaction to the job offer. 'It's a she, and she's strictly independent.'

'So . . . what happened when you got in there?'

'There was a construct of Kim. She tried to tell me to leave the site, that I was in danger.'

'And you took her advice?'

'I couldn't quit,' he said. 'I couldn't get out of there.' He told Wellman about the appearance of Charles, the burning attic, Charles' threats.

'Thing that gets me is, how the hell did they know this? How did they reproduce the attic, right down to the pattern on the damned carpet?'

Wellman looked at him for a second or two before speaking. 'Good God, Halliday, we're certainly not dealing with amateurs.'

'You know how they did it?'

'When you entered the site, they mapped the contents of your mind, charted your memories.'

Halliday stared at him. 'They can do that?'

'Believe me, they can do that. They dug into your memories and found the attic fire and used it to try to frighten you off the case.'

Halliday sipped his tea. The clean heat of this ersatz Africa was refreshing after the polluted humidity of New York.

'So anyway, when I got out I checked up on a guy called Tallak, Edward L. Tallak. He was Suzie's psychiatrist or whatever. I asked about Suzie, showed him some pix I'd made up of Charles.' He shook his head. 'Should have known something was wrong, Wellman. I should've been more alert. It was his hands. See, this guy looked about fifty, maybe older, but his hands were the hands of a guy twenty years his junior.' He smiled to himself. 'I should have worked out he was wearing a chu, that he had something to hide. I should have been suspicious when he gave me his card, a flash metal job. He traced me with the damned thing.'

'You got the guy, Halliday. You did enough to save yourself.'

Halliday shook his head. 'It wasn't professional. Barney would never have fallen for that.'

He stopped, looked up at Wellman as a thought occurred to him. 'Hey, if Tallak was wearing a chu, and working for the people who ran the site ... maybe he was our mysterious silver-haired Charles?'

Wellman shrugged. 'I had someone run a check on him. He operated under a number of aliases. In reality he was one Benedict Stevens, a psychiatrist. I suppose it's possible that one of his guises was Charles.'

'I hope not,' Halliday said.

Wellman looked across at him, an eyebrow cocked in query.

Halliday smiled. 'I want the satisfaction of finding Charles and having him know that there's no way out.'

There was a silence from the executive. 'You wouldn't kill him?'

Halliday considered. 'In the heat of the moment, perhaps I would, and I'd feel no guilt about it either. But I don't want the satisfaction of killing Charles, just nailing him.'

'I wish I could be there with you, Halliday.'

A silence developed between the two men. Wellman refilled Halliday's cup, then his own.

At last Wellman said, 'What are your plans when you leave here?'

Halliday considered. 'I'm not too sure. The leads've dried up again. You know, there I was thinking I was getting somewhere ... If I'd managed to get Tallak alive, or tail him back to some place, maybe I would've had something big. Now he's dead, it's back to square one. I'll just keep on

208

digging, trying to turn something up. I'll come across something, sooner or later.'

'Don't forget, if you need anything, anything at all, just contact me.'

Wellman stood and made to enter the tent, then hesitated. 'Oh, if you lie down and rest awhile, when you wake up you'll have a visitor.'

'A visitor? Who—?'

Wellman smiled. 'I'll keep you guessing. Good luck with the case. I'll see you later.' He gave a wave and hit the decal on the back of his hand.

Halliday watched as the executive vanished, then he returned to the relative cool of his room. He opaqued the dome and lay on the bed, considering who his visitor might be.

Within seconds he was asleep.

Eighteen

The day after Barney was informed that he was to be downloaded into a nano-cerebral interface wired into the head of a brain-dead corpse – a cyber-zombie, as he thought of it – Lew Kramer materialised on the beach.

Barney had spent an interesting last day in paradise – or rather surfing the cyberverse via the basal rent in the virtual matrix beneath the pine tree.

He'd visited dozens of varied sites, fighting wars on Beta Hydri IV, sightseeing in ancient Greece, climbing Everest with Hillary and Tenzing . . .

Then, that morning, he'd come across something even more interesting. Moving back through the obsidian depths towards the basal rent in this site, he had noticed a golden light brighter than all the others. It was situated at the centre of all the tiny flecks of lights, like the sun-packed core of a galactic cluster. Out of curiosity he had diverted and made his way towards the light, almost blinded by its intensity as he made the transition to its interior.

It was not a virtual reality site, as such, but the vast core of the Mantoni Entertainments network. Lew had described the core to him when he had shown Barney around the Mantoni headquarters, shortly after he'd volunteered to help Lew recreate Estelle in VR. He'd indicated a chamber like a bank vault packed with more computer processing power than had ever before been assembled anywhere on Earth. The room was surrounded by armed guards and an array of sophisticated surveillance equipment.

210

Now Barney was in the unique and privileged position of finding himself inside the very mind, as it were, of the core.

The virtual engine room of the Mantoni cyberverse appeared to him as a network of interrelated skeins and vectors linking all the thousands of scattered sites. Visually it resembled a more tightly packed version of the galactic-analogue outside. He moved from light to light, expecting to find individual sites. What he discovered instead were mysterious realms which presented themselves to him in images of visual symbols: one light bombarded him with a thousand calculations, like a confetti of digits and mathematical code. Another site came to him in a welter of colours, each one of which corresponded to an emotion: the red of rage, the blue of intense grief, the orange of joy. The effect on him, after so long without feeling such things for himself, made him thankful that he was no longer prey to such irrational influences.

These sites made no real sense to him: he guessed that whatever they were in the cyberverse was beyond the conceptualisation of the human mind; his consciousness processed what he saw and interpreted it in symbols of what it understood, much as an animal might view the human world.

And then he found a site that did make sense to him, and more: it was a site he knew he would come back to, given the opportunity.

It was simply a long, low, white-walled room, containing a table and perhaps twenty men and women seated around it.

Lew Kramer was present, listening to a grey-haired man talk about productivity and development targets.

He had happened upon the Mantoni VR conferencing centre.

He listened in for an hour. They seemed to be worried about a group calling itself the Methuselah Project, though who these people were and what threat they represented to the Mantoni organisation, Barney was unsure. The people around the table were discussing the means by which they might find out more about the Project.

He was about to leave when the grey-haired man turned to Lew Kramer. 'And how's the e-identity download progressing, Lew?'

'The NCI and the donor somaform are ready and waiting, sir. We'll be initiating the download procedure this afternoon.'

'No snags? Everything going down smooth?'

'Everything's AOK, sir.'

'Very good. Keep me informed . . .'

Barney would have smiled to himself, had he had the means to do so. He wondered if, once back out in the real world, Lew would allow him the use of a jellytank. The opportunity to eavesdrop on such conferences was too good to miss.

Now he stood on the wet sand and stared out to sea, waiting for the download procedure to begin. He wondered if the transition would be instantaneous: one second he would be standing here in paradise, and the next inhabiting the NCI in the head of an animated corpse. He wondered how long the rehabilitation might take, if he would have to suffer weeks or months of physical pain as he learned to control the donor body.

He wished the bastards would just leave him alone to roam the cyberverse. But what choice did he have in the matter? He was, after all, their property now.

'Barney, good to see you again!'

Lew Kramer had materialised five metres up the beach, waving.

'Lew, when's the great switcheroo scheduled to take place?'

'That's why I'm here, Barney. We're initiating the procedure in about fifteen minutes. I thought I'd better come and give you advance warning. Thought you might want to say goodbye . . .' He gestured towards the villa.

'Thanks,' he said. But no thanks, he thought.

He looked up the beach, avoiding eye contact with Kramer. 'You know, in a way I'll be sorry to leave this place. I'll be able to come back, won't I?'

Lew nodded. 'You'll have your own tank, Barney. I'll see to that.'

Barney looked at the exec. 'How much freedom will I have, Lew? I mean, will I be allowed out without a chaperone?'

Lew shrugged uneasily. 'I don't know quite how we stand on that one, Barney. But I can assure you that you'll be well looked after. You'll want for nothing.'

'But I'll still be a prisoner, right? After all, I'm the property of the Mantoni organisation now, aren't I?'

Lew eyed him. 'Look at it this way, Barney. If we hadn't copied you back then, you wouldn't be here. You'd be dead—'

'Correction, Lew,' Barney interrupted. 'I wouldn't be dead. The real Barney Kluger is the poor schmuck who's dead. I'm just his copy, remember?'

'The fact remains – thanks to the Mantoni organisation, you exist to experience all this.'

Barney shook his head. He tried to look into himself and determine how he felt about that. Would he rather not exist, or did he gain something from the experience of being – what could he call it? – of being e-live?

He felt nothing. He could enjoy nothing. They had robbed him of his emotions . . . or rather they had made an emotionless copy of his original, which *had* felt emotion.

He neither wanted to die nor to live. He would exist, recording what he experienced, until he ceased to exist. He felt no fear of the end, merely occasional intellectual curiosity as to what might come before it. Perhaps that was what gave him the impetus to look ahead, a curiosity about what was happening to him.

'So how will it be, Lew? The transition? What can I expect?'

'Quick and painless, as all the best surgeons say.' Lew smiled. 'We'll actually be putting you into a quiescent state until the period of transfer is completed.'

Barney smiled. He liked that. Quiescent state.

'So I'll suddenly wake up in my new flesh suit? I can't wait.'

Lew smiled, unsure. 'Right . . . Okay, so I'll leave you to it, Barney. It'll be about ten minutes from now.'

'See you then, Lew,' Barney said, as the exec touched the quit decal on the back of his hand and dematerialised in an instant.

For what felt like a long time Barney sat on the beach and stared at the crushed sapphire effect of the breaking waves, waiting for the commencement of his new life.

Then, the bright scene of the sunlit beach was ripped away from him. He experienced a sudden sensation of falling through darkness, of existing through a timeless duration, which he recalled from the time when the technicians had originally copied him.

He opened his eyes. He was lying in bed. He felt his body, much as he had been aware of his virtual body what seemed like seconds earlier. There was no pain, no discomfort even. He blinked, staring up at a white-painted ceiling.

In fact, he had no way of distinguishing this, his real somatic existence in the real world, from his e-existence in virtual reality.

He looked around him. He was in what looked like a small hospital room, though surrounded by banks of computers and casually dressed techs. Lew Kramer stood at the end of the bed, smiling at him – identical to the Lew who had paid him courtesy calls in paradise.

He attempted to sit up, and to his surprise managed to do so with no ill-effect.

He nodded to Lew. 'You boys certainly know how to do a good job.'

He swung his legs from the bed, and then for the first time noticed his new body.

He looked down on well-muscled legs, tanned forearms. He seemed to be younger than the original, real Barney Kluger – younger even than he had been in virtual reality. This body seemed to be about thirty-five, leaner and fitter than his original.

He turned his right hand, clenched it into a fist. He felt muscles and sinews working, stretching.

He looked at Lew. 'I thought I'd be hospitalised for weeks before I could control this thing.'

Lew smiled. 'We've had the body slaved to a functioning program in the NCI for months, Barney. Today it was only a matter of downloading you into the NCI.' He looked around at the techs in the room. 'And that seems to have been achieved successfully. Well done.'

Barney reached up, touched something trailing from the back of his head. A hank of leads and wires fell down his back like dreadlocks. He traced them to a cold arrangement of metal spars implanted in his skull. The NCI, evidently.

The leads trailed across the bed and connected him to the com-system. A dozen techs monitored the screens and read-outs.

'How long have I been out, Lew?' he asked. 'How long since the original Barney tanked for one hour that time?'

'The original tanked in . . . what? January '40.'

'And it's now?'

'July, '41.'

Barney frowned. 'So you copied me back in '40 . . . and turned me on, when . . . ?'

'We activated the copied program for three or four short periods over the past year to ensure that it was in full

215

working order.'

'And yet to me, in VR, it all seemed like one consecutive stretch . . .' Except, of course, for those infinitesimal black-outs that had lasted only nano-seconds, and yet paradoxically seemed in retrospect to have lasted for aeons.

Those, obviously, had been the periods during which the copy had been switched off.

He parted the hospital gown that covered his chest. He was broad, well-developed, his stomach hard and flat.

'You picked a good one, Lew. Who was the poor bastard?'

The exec shook his head. 'That's doesn't matter, Barney. The person who had this body before you is dead. It belongs to you, now.'

'Nearly new body,' Barney grunted. 'One previous owner. Well-maintained. Suitable for any homeless e-copy.'

He stopped. His voice, to the best of his knowledge, sounded just like his old one.

'Hey, how'd you do that? I sound like the original Barney.'

'Coincidence. It's a couple of semi-tones higher, though. The donor was a life-long New Yorker. Happy with it?'

Barney shrugged. 'It'll do, bud. I mean, what good would it do if I complained?'

Lew laughed and consulted a couple of techs.

'We'll be through here in another ten, fifteen minutes,' he told Barney. 'Then I'll show you to your rooms, okay?'

The techs disconnected the leads from the NCI, the sound conducting hollowly through the bone of his skull. He dressed in new clothes: casual slacks, a white shirt, black mock-leather shoes. As he worked the unfamiliar fingers, pulled clothing over strange contours of muscle and bone, he wondered why the physical sensations of the real world felt no more real that those of VR. He thought that his experiences here would have had somehow more verisimilitude, more reality. It spoke volumes for the science of VR that he was unable to tell the difference.

The techs left the room, and Lew Kramer gestured to the door. 'This way, Barney.'

He stood and took his first steps. No dizziness, not even the slightest loss of coordination. He was taller than he had been. Now he looked down on Lew Kramer.

They left the room and ascended in an elevator. The display indicated that they were rising through floors numbered in the nineties.

Lew showed him into his new home, or rather his new jail.

For a prison cell, he had to admit that it was pretty luxurious. It was a suite of rooms overlooking Broadway – Barney worked out that he was in the Mantoni Entertainments HQ, a stone's throw from the Empire State building. A lounge with all the latest accessories, a bedroom, an adjacent gym and even, he was relieved to see, a small VR room equipped with a state-of-the-art jellytank.

He moved to the vast window and looked out. Far below, the occasional automobile crawled along the quiet street. The sidewalks were packed with pedestrians. He thought that Hal would be somewhere out there, working away. Christ, was Hal in for a hell of a shock when he was contacted by his old partner in disguise.

He turned to Lew. 'How much freedom do I have, bud? I mean, is this it? This suite?'

Lew gestured. 'For the time being, yes,' the exec said. 'You represent a valuable asset to the Mantoni organisation, Barney.'

'You don't want me to do a runner?'

'I was thinking more in terms of other interested parties who might take it into their heads to kidnap you. Until we've assessed the situation, I'm afraid we'll have to restrict your freedom of movement to this suite and the labs.'

'And if I decide I need a little recreation, slip out one morning?'

'We'd find you pretty damned quick and bring you back.

Your NCI's implanted with a tracer. Just to be on the safe side.'

Barney nodded. 'What about if I want to make a call, check up on an old friend?'

'I'm afraid that's out of the question. You're a top-secret project. Can you imagine the reaction of the media if word got out that we'd brought you back to life?'

'E-life,' Barney reminded him.

Lew shrugged. 'It'd be all the same to the sensationalist news stations.'

Barney moved around the lounge. 'So I'm pretty much a prisoner here. That's what it boils down to, I suppose?'

'A prisoner surrounded by luxury, with room service laid on – even a VR tank.'

Barney nodded. 'That I appreciate.' He looked across at Lew, feigning gratitude. 'It'll be nice to visit Estelle from time to time.'

Lew proceeded to outline Barney's day-to-day regime. 'From nine till one, six days a week, you'll be down at the labs while the techs run a few tests. After that, the time's your own. You can use VR up to the legally permitted twenty-four hours, just so long as it doesn't interfere with the lab hours. I'd advise you start working out, if you intend to make use of VR. You can order meals at any time, just as if you were in a top hotel. There's even a bar a couple of floors down. You're welcome to use it at any time.'

Barney nodded. 'For a high-security penitentiary, Lew, it's pretty damned civilised.'

'We try to be humane, here at Mantoni,' Lew said, sounding as though he were spouting the party line.

Barney stared at him. 'Yes, but am I, technically speaking, human?'

'As far as I'm concerned, Barney, you're as human as me.'

In that case, Barney thought, I pity you.

He moved to a full-length mirror on the wall and for the first time looked into the eyes of his new host.

Lew cleared his throat. 'What do you think?'

He stared at the face that regarded him with the look of a stranger. It was a hard face, tanned, dark-eyed; it appeared suspicious.

Barney turned to Lew. 'It looks mean. I'm not sure I like it. I don't suppose you have one of those . . . what the hell are they called? Chus? Programmed with my old appearance?'

Lew nodded. 'I'll see what I can do.'

Barney smiled, nodding. 'I'd appreciate it, Lew,' he said, and turned back to his reflection.

His life soon slipped into a regular routine. In the mornings he endured the attention of the tech team in the labs on the 90th floor. They jacked leads into his NCI and consulted read-outs and com-screens. They had him performing various isometric exercises to calibrate NCI-body compatibility. He underwent memory tests and psychological profiling. He wondered how long they would take to work out that, although on one level their experiment had been a remarkable success, it had failed to reproduce the whole human being. He wondered when they would come to the conclusion that they had created a human-like robot, and what they might do with him then.

In the afternoons, he retreated to his suite and immersed himself via his tank in virtual reality. He always made for the Californian idyll they had created for his original, ignored the villa and the construct of Estelle that presumably still existed there, and made his way up the beach to the rent in the matrix beneath the pine tree.

He headed for the Mantoni core site and sat in on their VR conferencing sessions. He learned that the conferences were daily and scheduled from two till four in the afternoons, and after that he made sure he was present every day for the next two weeks.

For the most part the business conducted was of little interest to Barney. What he could understand he found

219

mind-numbingly tedious, and likewise all of the technical jargon he was unable to comprehend.

They did, however, occasionally discuss the Methuselah Project – and anything that worried the Mantoni high-ups was of interest to him.

The grey-haired vice chairman, Sellings, demanded regular updates from his security team, and it was these reports that Barney found most fascinating.

They had established a link between the anti-VR terrorist organisation Virex and the Methuselah Project.

'A link?' Sellings repeated. 'What kind of goddamned link?'

'We're pretty sure,' the head of security reported, 'that they're now one and the same. The Project have infiltrated the ranks of Virex and are using the organisation for their own ends.'

'So where does that leave us?' Sellings asked.

'We're trying to crack the Methuselah site,' the head of security said.

Barney learned nothing more about the Methuselah Project for a while. He underwent tests in the mornings, and hurried to his tank every afternoon. For the next week, this set the pattern of his existence. Then one afternoon Sellings addressed the assembled management team.

'If the Methuselah Project have Suzie Charlesworth in their pay,' he said, 'then I'm worried. I want to know where she is and what they want with her, is that understood?'

The head of security said, 'Wellman's hired a private eye to trace the girl, sir.'

'Wellman? I thought that bastard was on his way out?'

'That's right, sir. Leukaemia. But he's living in time-extension VR.'

'So what has this private operative come up with?'

'We don't know. He makes all his reports direct to Wellman in VR.'

'Have you tried vracking the site?'

'That's the first thing we tried. It's secure.'

Sellings nodded. 'I want to know what this operative knows, understood? What's his name?'

'Halliday, sir. Halford Halliday.'

The meeting broke up. Barney left the site and emerged from his tank. He spent the rest of the afternoon seated by the window, staring out across the block-graph skyline of Manhattan as he considered his next move.

Nineteen

Halliday dreamed, and when he awoke later he recalled images of trees, stretching over the land for as far as the eye could see. In the dream he was walking with two people – and as was the nature of dreams he could not recall who these people were, only that they were friends. The wonder of the dream, which he understood while sleeping, was that the forested tract was not in VR. He was in Washington State, not far from Seattle. Last year his sister told him that scientists were sowing great swathes of land with genetically enhanced trees, and in a letter Anna had described the fledgling plantations that covered mountainsides in great patchwork quilts of sapling pines. In the dream he was filled with awe that he was walking among real trees in the real world.

When he awoke, reality flooded in on him. He was in New York, and there wasn't a live tree within a hundred miles of the city. Except, of course, for his bonsai oak.

There was movement across the dome. As he watched, a figure materialised and approached the bed. Halliday sat up, smiling at Casey as she sat on the chair and lifted her shoulders in a quick shrug.

'This is strange, Hal. I can hardly believe I'm here.'

He laughed. 'No kiss for the patient, Casey?'

She smiled shyly. 'Come here,' she said, standing.

He stood and held her for a long time. She was the real Casey he knew from the real world, the skinny kid he'd held on the chesterfield days ago.

She looked around her in wonder.

Halliday smiled. 'When was the last time you tanked?'

She shrugged, sat down again. 'Dunno. A year back, I suppose. It seems, I don't know . . . better now. More real.'

'Things have come on a long way in a year,' he said. 'Look.' He moved from the bed and approached a control pedestal. He touched a red decal and the dome deopaqued, revealing the magnificent sweeping panorama of the Serengeti.

She joined him by the curving dome and stared out. 'God, it's amazing. I never realised . . .'

'You want to go out?'

'We can? I mean, what about the animals? There're lions out there.'

Halliday laughed. 'You can't come to any harm in VR, Casey. The lions don't really exist. They're just constructions, clever computer animations.'

He made for the oval opening and Casey followed. They passed into the clean African heat and walked across the grassland towards a fallen tree trunk.

They sat down and Casey stared out towards the lake and the distant mountains. She looked at him. 'The frightening thing is, Hal, that it's impossible to tell this from real reality. I mean, if I didn't know I'd entered a tank, I'd think I was in some foreign country. Where are we?'

He smiled. 'You never seen lions before?'

'India?'

He told her, and she shook her head in silent awe.

'How did you find out about the shooting?' he asked.

'You said you'd be back at your place by six, right? So I called around seven and you weren't there. I waited an hour or so then decided to call you. A nurse answered your com.' She stopped suddenly, looked away and wouldn't meet his eyes. 'I was standing out on the street. When the nurse told me you'd been shot . . . my legs, they just collapsed. I sat on the kerb and tried to make sense of what she was telling me. You were shot bad and she couldn't tell me for sure that you were gonna live. I got the name of the clinic and caught a cab. You looked pretty bad when I got there, Hal. All hooked up to machines, your chest a mass of synthi-flesh. I stayed all night and in the morning they said you were gonna pull through. I visited every day, then they put you in a jellytank to help your recovery.' She shrugged. 'This morning they said I could have one hour in the tank, visit you in VR, so I thought why not? They took me to a room where you were tanked.'

'How'd I look?'

'Not as bad as I thought you were gonna be. I mean, your chest's all healed, but you're awful thin and pale. You're gonna have to start eating right when you get out, okay?'

'Whatever you say.'

'Hey,' she looked up from her fingers, 'guess what? They moved your office. Apparently this big boss called Wellman got you a new place just a few blocks south of my apartment.' She hesitated, then said, 'The guy who shot you, he was the same person who killed Kim, right?'

Halliday stared off into the distance. Here, New York seemed a very long way away. 'He was one of the guys involved with the deaths, yeah.'

'So they're moving you so that when you get out, these guys won't find you, right?'

'Something like that.'

She said in a small voice, 'I've been thinking, Hal . . . You know, when you get out, why don't you quit detective work, find some other job? You know lots of things. You could find something else.'

He smiled. 'Sometimes I think that'd be a great idea, Casey. Get away from it all. You know, I think I'd like to go to Seattle. Heard they're planting trees again out there.'

She nodded. 'That'd be something to see, wouldn't it?

Real honest to goodness trees.' She paused, looked up at him. 'So why don't you quit the job?'

He reached out and took her hand. He sat looking at it as it lay in his, palm up, inert. 'Maybe after I've found Kim's killer, Casey. Maybe then I'll think about settling down. Before that, I gotta get the bastard who killed her.'

She shook her head, not comprehending. 'But you could let the police do that, Hal. That's what they're there for—'

'The police are overworked and corrupt and not very good at doing what we think they're there to do. I couldn't leave them to find Kim's killer. Chances are after a couple of weeks the case'd get logged away with all the others, maybe one guy assigned to it for a month or so. Then he'd be transferred to something else, and the case'd be dropped. And Kim's killers would still be out there, unpunished for what they did to her. Casey, look at me.' He squeezed her hand, tugged it, until reluctantly she looked up at him. 'Try to understand, Casey, I just couldn't live with myself if I knew Kim's killers were out there somewhere, jack free and enjoying life. You understand that, don't you?'

It was a painfully long time before she replied. 'I understand about wanting to get the people who did it,' she whispered, 'but I don't think you should risk your life trying to do that, Hal. I don't know what I'd do if they killed you next time.'

He pulled her to him, pushed her head into his chest and kissed the top of her head. 'I promise I won't go getting myself killed,' he murmured. 'Trust me, okay?'

She stood quickly and strode off, then stopped and stared out across the lake, fingers tucked into the back pockets of her jeans.

She pulled out her right hand and rubbed her cheeks with her fingertips.

He watched her, wanting to tell her that it was okay, that when he got out they'd be together. He wondered what it was that wouldn't allow him to open up like that. He knew that once he got back to the real world, they'd be as they were before: friends who'd see each other occasionally . . . and then she'd meet someone her own age, and she'd drift out of his life as she had done before.

She returned to the log. Instead of sitting down, she lodged a sneakered foot on the tree trunk and inspected the rubber-capped toe.

'You know something, Hal? I don't understand you.'

Something lurched inside him. He had the feeling, then, that their relationship was about to change, that she was going to tell him something, admit something about her feelings for him, that would require from him a response, some affirmation of commitment that he was not prepared to give, and his pulse quickened at the thought.

He said nothing.

The silence lengthened.

At last she went on, 'What I don't understand is . . . you seem to be two people, Hal. One person's this kind and thoughtful guy. He took me in off the street when I needed some place to stay. He looked after me, bought me things, clothes and things, talked all night. I feel like I know this guy better than I know anyone in all the world, and I . . . like, I trust him more than anybody else, you know what I mean? Trust is the most important thing in the whole world, Hal. When you trust someone, it's like this great feeling somewhere in here . . .'

She stopped, gave the log a kick. 'And then, there's this other guy, same guy really but different. He has a strange way of looking at things. It's as if he hates the world and himself, he doesn't know what a good guy he is and always does the wrong thing. Like he gets hooked on VR because he hates reality, and then he has this death-wish about trying to find some killers . . . And it's all because really he wants to punish himself for something. I don't know what, and I don't pretend to understand it all. But . . .'. She shrugged and her voice almost cracked, then, 'but I wish he could see this other side of himself that others can see, and then he'd see what a good guy he is, and he might be a little happier. Or is that too much to hope for, Hal?'

She would not look at him, just stared down at her sneaker as it rocked back and forth on the camber of the log.

He could have come up with a dozen cheap lines then, but the last thing he wanted was to alienate her.

What hurt him the most, what hurt even more than being unable to tell her what she wanted to hear, was the knowledge that she was right.

But how could he tell her that, even so, there was nothing he could do change himself?

Instead, he did the cowardly thing, the only thing he could do in the circumstances. He said nothing, and stood and moved behind her and held her to him.

The moment seemed to last for ever.

At last, as if remembering herself, she looked at the back of her hand, then raised it to Halliday. 'Look, my hour's almost up. I'd better get going.'

'I'll see you out there in the real world, okay?'

She nodded, still facing away from him. She turned then and smiled.

She stood on her toes and kissed his cheek. 'See you later, Hal,' she murmured, then hit the decal on the back of her hand and vanished in an instant.

Halliday returned to the dome, sat on the bed for a while, and finally lay down. He stared at the curve high above him, at the cloudless blue sky beyond.

Somewhere, deep within him, he had always hated himself; he did not know why, but only that it manifested itself in a kind of quiet despair that allowed him no satisfaction with his life, his achievements. Even when he had Kim, and told himself that he was at his happiest, he had always wondered what she saw in him. Her leaving had

227

been inevitable, and something within him at the time had experienced a strange and masochistic sense of fulfilment.

He closed his eyes and slept.

Twenty

Over the course of the next three days, since learning of the security team's interest in Hal, Barney made preparations to escape from the Mantoni headquarters.

The only way he could see of getting away, other than via the drastic measure of climbing through the window and scaling the side of the hundred-storey building, was to walk out through the front entrance. To get past the security guard in the foyer he would need an identity card. The only way he could think of obtaining a card was to take one from a member of the Mantoni staff.

Also, it would help if he had the disguise of a chu – and Lew Kramer still had not made good his promise to get him one.

The next time he saw Lew, during one of the lab sessions on the 90th floor, he took the opportunity of a coffee break to draw Lew to one side.

'You know, every time I look in the mirror and stare into this ugly mug, I feel like I'm in the wrong body.'

Lew put an invisible pistol to his temple and pulled the trigger. 'The chu! Look, it clear slipped my mind, but I'll fix you up with one asap, okay?'

'I'd really appreciate that, Lew.'

'Otherwise, everything AOK? You settling in up there?'

'Everything's fine. The suite's comfortable, the food's great.'

'You taking the opportunity to tank, Barney?'

The question was asked, it seemed, without ulterior

motive – but Barney was wary. He didn't trust anyone who worked for Mantoni.

'I get along to the California site most days,' he said. 'You know, drop by, see how Estelle's doing.'

Lew grinned. 'Sure, Barney.'

'Say, when I'm in there with Estelle, you don't go snooping about, watching me?'

Lew clapped him on the shoulder. 'Word of honour, Barney. What you do in VR is your own affair, okay? Trust me on that one.'

He nodded. 'Fine, Lew. Just thought I'd ask.'

'Anything else I can get you?'

'As a matter of fact . . .' He'd need money, out there in the big bad world. He had no need for it in here; the meals came courtesy of the Mantoni organisation, and the drinks at the bar were free.

But there was a candy machine in the corner of the bar that took five-dollar coins.

Lew laughed when Barney said he'd developed a sudden sugar craving. 'Don't worry, I'll bring some coins up after lunch, okay?'

If Lew made good with the promise of the chu, and the cash, then he was halfway there. All that would remain would be to get hold of an ID card – which would be easier said than done. Most of the Mantoni staff he came into contact with wore their passes clipped to their clothing, reducing his chances of stealing one to virtually nil.

One morning in the lab, while he lay face-down on a padded couch as the techs rammed jacks into his occipital console, he noticed that a couple of the scientists had dispensed with their lab coats. As far as Barney could see, they weren't wearing their ID cards, either. As he made his way from the lab, after the session, he saw a couple of white coats hanging from pegs on the wall. On one of them he made out a card . . .

He almost took it then, but stopped himself.

If a card was reported missing today, then the chances were that the security-com in the foyer would be reprogrammed to alert staff in the event of its being used. He would have to take the card on the day he planned to escape, and use it before the tech noticed its absence.

The following morning he made his way down to the lab, wearing a jacket which he took off and hung on one of the pegs in the entrance. To his relief, he found that the same two techs who had deposited their coats yesterday had done so again today. Creatures of habit.

In a day or two, it would be a simple matter of taking his time with his jacket while he snapped the ID card from the lab coat . . .

That afternoon, Lew Kramer came up with the goods, as promised.

Barney had just emerged from an abortive session in VR – Hal wasn't mentioned in the conference: the management team had discussed sales – and was drinking orange juice in the window seat when the doorbell chimed.

Lew pushed in, his broad-shouldered bulk filling the doorway. He held up a shrink-wrapped package.

'I had this cooked up by the tech team,' he said. 'Take a look.'

Barney took the wrapping from the chu and held it up, a lightweight balaclava of fine capillaries connected to a small control handset.

'That's great, Lew. I should have fun with this . . .'

'Here, there's something I want to show you.'

He activated the handset and adjusted the slide. The chu, lying collapsed on the coffee table between them, displayed a ghastly series of shrunken faces.

'Here we go,' Lew said, and picked up the chu. He arranged it over his hand like a glove-puppet and said, 'Recognise?'

Barney looked into his old face. 'Never realised I was so handsome.'

'We downloaded it from images of your original we had in stock. It's enhanced, made to look around ten years younger than his true age. Suit you?'

'Great. It'll make looking in the mirror bearable again.'

'There are about a dozen other faces on the chu as well, in case you get tired of your old mug.'

Lew made to go. 'Oh, and before I forget.' He reached into his pocket and pulled out a small bag. He dropped it on the table beside the chu. 'Five-dollar coins. About a hundred dollars' worth. Should keep you in candy for a while. Tell me when you run out, okay?'

When Lew departed, Barney sat in his chair by the window and stared at the chu and the coins. When he managed to take the ID card, he'd be away. In the morning, he decided, he'd go for it . . .

Of course, the problem of the tracer implanted in his NCI remained, but Barney had a couple of contacts who might know how to fix the tracer. As soon as he left the building after the morning lab session, he'd head uptown and call on these guys. With luck, his absence would not be immediately noticed.

And if they couldn't fix the tracer? Christ, he'd worry about that later. The main thing was to get away, find Hal and warn him that the Mantoni security team was onto him, tell him to take extra care with who he talked to about the Charlesworth case.

Just before nine the following morning, Barney left his suite and took the elevator down to the 90th floor. If the techs had hung their lab coats, then at one o'clock he'd be on his way. As he pushed through the swing door to the labs, he felt a tight knot of expectation in his gut. Christ, he thought, am I actually *feeling* – or was it merely a psychosomatic reaction to the intellectual game he was playing?

He shrugged off his coat, turned the corner and

approached the row of pegs. There were no lab coats in sight. He left his jacket and told himself that there would be other opportunities in future.

The lab session passed without incident – the techs who usually ditched their coats were obviously feeling the chill of the air-conditioning this morning. At one he returned to his suite, disappointed. He ate a light lunch, then decided to check on what the Mantoni management team was up to.

He entered the cyberverse via the basal rent in the California site, and made his way to the glowing Mantoni core.

One hour later he hit the jackpot, and what he heard made him grateful that his planned departure had been delayed.

Halfway through the meeting, Sellings said, 'I hear there's been progress on the Halliday front?'

'We've devised a means of finding out what we need to know, sir,' the head of security said.

He outlined the scheme. Barney listened, knowing that he was unable to stop them implementing the plan. His only hope lay in getting to Hal in time – and his only hope of being able to do that lay in escaping from the building.

'Ingenious,' Sellings said. 'When do you start?'

'We'll send a team around to his office tomorrow afternoon at one, sir. There's just one thing . . .'

'And that is?'

'The status of the subject, Halliday. Is he expendable?'

Sellings nodded. 'We don't want him finding out that we had any involvement in the affair,' he said. 'He's expendable.'

When the meeting finished, Barney returned to his suite in the real world and thought through what he should do.

That evening, as he sat in his recliner and stared out at the light-show that was night-time Manhattan, he wondered why he was planning to help Hal like this. It had nothing to do with emotion, he thought. Nothing to do with old friendship, loyalty, duty . . . Then what, he asked himself? Could it simply be that he had weighed the morality of both sets of opponents, Halliday and the Mantoni organisation, and found one to be wanting? The organisation was corrupt and, like every grouping of human beings gathered to ensure the perpetuation of vested interest, evil and capable of any deed to get what it desired.

Halliday was a lone figure, pitched against a corrupt enemy, and he needed all the help he could get.

Or perhaps, Barney conceded late into the night, perhaps the NCI containing the copy of Barney Kluger did still possess, hidden deep somewhere in its convoluted sub-routines and programming, some vestige of loyalty towards his old partner?

The following morning he woke early and, as he showered and dressed preparatory to making his way down to the labs, it came to him that Hal's life depended on the success of his actions over the next few hours.

Twenty-One

When Halliday awoke he was no longer in the dome.

He lay in bed in a small room, its stark minimalism suggesting a hospital, though there was no evidence of surgical apparatus in sight, no monitors or diagnostic coms.

He sat up and swung his legs from the bed, and his head swam with the sudden movement. He ached in every bone of his body, and he experienced a familiar nausea that resulted from an extended period in VR.

He was bare-chested. He sat on the edge of the bed and looked down at his body, touching the neat line that vertically bisected his chest – the only evidence that remained of the shooting. He took a series of deep breaths, filling his lungs; he felt weak, and when he held his right arm out before him he saw that his hand was trembling uncontrollably.

A digital calendar on the wall told him that it was the twelfth of July, a week to the day since Tallak had shot him. Weak sunlight filled the room. A window looked out across a street to a row of town houses, and he heard the occasional engine of a passing automobile. So he was in the city, somewhere.

He felt suddenly tired and lay down. A nurse entered the room, smiled at him and applied something cold to the skin of his forearm. He wanted to protest that he was feeling fine, and didn't want to sleep, but seconds later he felt himself slipping . . .

Later he was aware of a doctor standing over him, examining him with devices that glinted silver in the overhead fluorescents. He drifted, heard the medic talking to him. He even replied, but recalled nothing of the conversation, other than the doctor's parting words, 'I see no reason why you can't leave tomorrow, Mr Halliday.'

When he came awake again, the calendar read the fourteenth of July. He felt better; the nausea was gone, and his body no longer ached quite so badly. A clock on the cabinet beside the bed read 10.45.

He sat up and swung his legs out of bed, and only then saw that he had company.

Casey sat on a chair by the window, her sneakered feet hanging centimetres above the floor.

'Hi, Hal. How you feeling?'

He smiled, shook his head. 'Better than I thought I would, considering.'

'They called me last night, said you could go home today. I've brought some things.' She indicated a neatly folded pile of clothes on top of the bedside cabinet.

'Great.' He looked across at her. She was swinging her legs, smiling at him.

If she harboured any resentment after their conversation in the Serengeti site, she gave no sign. It was so fresh in his memory that he could hardly bring himself to look her in the eye – but for her, he reminded himself, their meeting in VR had occurred five days ago.

He dressed slowly, the simple act of pulling on his jeans requiring an effort and degree of concentration that surprised him. When it came to buttoning his shirt, he found that his fingers had lost dexterity and coordination.

Casey sighed. 'Here, let me do that, okay?'

He didn't protest. She stood before him, lips compressed as she quickly fastened the buttons from the bottom up. He wondered whether he should hug her, tell her how good it was to see her again.

'There. You ready? Let's go, okay? I'll give you a guided

tour of your new office. Just wait till you see it, talk about swish! Makes your old place look kinda cheap.'

He had to think about walking, concentrate on keeping his balance as he stepped from the room and down a carpeted corridor. Uniformed nurses moved back and forth with a quick efficiency that left him vicariously exhausted. Casey slowed her pace to match his, taking his arm and glancing at him with concern.

When they emerged into the daylight, he saw a low morning sun emerging from behind a skyline of mansions to the east. He guessed they were on the Upper West Side somewhere. The sidewalk was quiet, with only the occasional pedestrian walking a dog or taking a leisurely stroll.

'What day is it, Casey?'

'Sunday,' she said, 'all day.'

He laughed. Now that he knew, the day did have that strange, indefinable atmosphere of lassitude possessed only by the traditional day of rest.

Casey had a cab waiting. As they motored east through quiet streets, she took his arm and squeezed. 'Hey, guess what?'

He looked at her. She seemed so young, so enthusiastic and full of life. 'Go on.'

'That interview I had, the last time I saw you in the real world—'

'Don't tell me, Casey. You got the job, right?'

'Right on. It's only waitressing, but it's in a big diner on Fifth and there's a chance of promotion. I work part-time, five afternoons a week. So I'll have my mornings free to come round and bug you, okay?'

He smiled. 'I couldn't stop you if I wanted to, could I?'

She punched him. 'I start today at two. I'll have time to get you settled in your new place, then I'm off.'

His office was in a plush three-storey walk-up off Lexington Avenue where El Barrio phased into Carnegie Hill, about ten blocks south of his old office. Ten blocks, but it might have been a world away from the poverty of his old haunt. There were no beggars or refugees in sight, no food stalls in the street; the buildings had the appearance of having been maintained over the years, and not allowed to fall into the decrepitude that had overtaken so much of the city north of 96th Street.

Casey paid off the taxi and led him across the sidewalk. 'Hey, he said, stopping. 'How'd that get here?' He indicated his battered Ford slumped in the gutter.

Casey smiled at him, unable to conceal an expression of pleasure. 'I had it brought back from Chinatown, Hal. Couldn't leave Barney's old banger down there to get broken into, could I? C'mon.'

They passed through a swing door into a spacious, mock-marble tiled corridor. They took an elevator to the third floor and he followed Casey down a short corridor to a door at the far end.

'Okay, Hal. Close your eyes.'

He did as she ordered. He heard her swipe a key-card through the lock and the door click open. She took his hand and pulled him inside.

'You can open them now. What do you think?'

He peered around a large, red-carpeted room that looked more like a doctor's surgery than the office of a one-man detective agency.

Potted plants, a landscape painting on the wall, a silver kidney-shaped desk . . . Barney would have died laughing.

'Well?'

'I'm impressed. Some place. I dunno, though . . . I feel like I don't belong here.'

'You'll fit in, Hal, given time. You feed yourself up, get fit again. Buy yourself some new clothes.'

She danced around the desk, fell into a big swivel recliner chair and lodged her feet beside the desk-com – his system from the old place, he was pleased to see.

She rocked back and forth. 'You'll attract a different kind of customer, Hal. Rich folk with dollars to burn.'

'Yeah, and commissions to find their missing poodles.'

Casey shrugged. 'It'd be safer than missing persons,' she said.

He ignored her, and sensed that Casey immediately regretted digging up that old bone of contention.

'I'll show you the apartment. Follow me.'

A connecting door gave onto a lounge furnished with what looked like a genuine black leather three-piece suite. A sound system was stacked in one corner, and a big screen covered the whole of the wall opposite the floor-to-ceiling window overlooking the quiet street.

Halliday whistled. 'Impressive.'

'It's leased for a year, with an option to renew next July.' She saw his look and explained, 'I talked to the realtor when I moved some of your clothes and stuff from the old place.'

She opened another door. 'And this is the bedroom, Hal. Bit more comfy than the old dump.'

Polished imitation timber floorboards, white walls, a bed the size of a tennis court. 'I don't think I can take so much luxury, Casey.'

'There's a bathroom through there,' she said, pointing to a door, 'and a kitchen off the lounge. You can give dinner parties that'll be the talk of the town.'

'You haven't tasted my cooking.'

He moved back into the lounge and stared around him. He felt a vague sense of discomfort at being the recipient of such largesse, when Casey was holed up in a one-room dive back in El Barrio.

He wondered if she had manufactured this guided tour in a bid to elicit the comparison and make him feel guilty. Then he told himself that it wouldn't have crossed her mind to set him up like that. She was merely delighted to be showing him around his windfall.

'Hey, where's the jellytank, Casey?'

She shrugged, affecting a sudden interest in the sound system.

'They didn't bring it along with the desk-com?' he asked.

'Dunno. If it isn't here . . .'

He wouldn't have put it past her, he thought, to have told the hauliers that the jellytank was staying behind.

He stepped through to the office and checked the desk. 'The oak,' he called back. 'Casey, did you bring the bonsai tree?'

She appeared in the doorway, a guilty grimace on her face. 'The movers must've shifted it from the desk when they took the com, Hal. I never saw it when I packed your clothes. I didn't think . . .'

'Don't worry, I'll pick it up later.' He felt a sudden and irrational fear that some harm had come to the tree, that the hauliers had decided to help themselves to it, or the office had been broken into in his absence, the tree stolen or vandalised.

Casey looked at the watch on her thin wrist. 'It's time I wasn't here, Hal. You okay? Don't need anything?'

'I'm fine. I'll just stick around and get used to the place.'

She moved to the door and stopped. 'Hey, you know the other day? The date we made, and then you went and got yourself shot?'

'Yeah, the things I do to get out of seeing you.'

'How about we take in a holo-drama tonight, Hal, then go dine some place?'

He felt a subtle weight of commitment settle upon his shoulders. I can't give you what you want, Casey, he almost said. Instead he just smiled and said, 'Sure, why not? Around seven?'

She beamed. 'Great. See you then.' She slipped from the room with a wave, and Halliday stood in the middle of the office and stared at the door.

He moved around the desk and lowered himself into the swivel chair, testing it. It was just too comfortable. He saw the coffee percolator, his old one – thank Christ they hadn't thrown it out and bought him some French state-of-the-art replacement.

He brewed himself a mug of Colombian roast and was thinking about going up to El Barrio and collecting the oak when his com chimed.

The small screen flared and a white-faced woman with jet-black hair peered out at him.

'Jesus, Halliday. Where the hell are you?'

'Kat, good to see you, too. How can I help?'

'I just called the hospital. They said you got out today. I need to see you.'

He gave her his new address. 'What's happening, Kat?'

'It's about the guy who called himself Tallak. But I can't talk now. I'll be around in five minutes.'

Halliday cut the connection and sipped his coffee.

He'd planned to take it easy today, go rescue his oak, not even think about the case. Allow himself a day of rest before he began work again from square one.

He opened the drawers of his new desk until he found his cheque book, then wrote out a cheque for fifty thousand dollars. He'd give it to Kat before she complained that he hadn't paid his dues.

Five minutes later someone rapped on the door, then opened it and stepped through before he had time to reply.

Kat hurried across the room as if someone was tailing her, all twitchy-nervous, eyes darting. Halliday guessed she was high on spin.

She paced back and forth before the desk, staring around the room. 'Jesus Christ, Halliday, you've gone up in the world.'

He gestured. 'Only the best for the best.'

'Don't bullshit me, pal. You're like a fish outta water. What happened? You sold out and pitched in with Cyber-Tech?'

He winced inwardly at her accuracy. 'You've no faith in

241

my ability as a private detective, Kat. I don't need to sell out. Coffee?'

'I didn't come here for afternoon tea, Halliday.'

'So . . . What about Tallak?'

She was still pacing, arms folded tight across her chest, hunched and peering at him.

'Kat, will you slow down. I just got discharged from hospital and you're making me exhausted.'

She ignored him, pulled a folded page of a plastic mag from the back pocket of her black jeans, and dropped it on the desk before him. He smoothed it flat. The page showed the pix of a young man, his face vaguely familiar.

'So?'

'Read the words, Halliday, or are you illiterate?'

He pulled the page towards him and read the caption beneath the pix. 'Benedict Stevens. Shot dead in a shoot-out with Private Detective Halford Halliday.'

He looked up at Kat, who had ceased her pacing and was watching him. 'So that's who he was,' he said, 'underneath his chu—' He looked at the pix again, and then he had it. He knew where he'd seen the face before.

The young guy in the blue suit in the dead forest above Nyack.

Two down and one to go. The black guy in the forest was dead, along with blue-suit in the alley . . . and now only Charles remained.

'What is it, Kat?'

She unfolded her arms long enough to point at the pix. 'Why did he want you dead, Halliday?' She folded her arms again, shivering with the effects of a spin overdose.

'Because I was onto him and his colleagues. They killed Kim, a woman called Anastasia Dah, and the Charlesworth kid I was looking for. They nearly burned me in the site you got me into the other day.'

She was pacing again. 'Jesus fucking Christ,' she said.

'Kat? What he hell's going on?'

242

She turned to him. 'This guy,' she stabbed a finger down on the plastic page, crumpling his face, 'I knew him as Temple.'

'You knew him?' Halliday said, incredulous. 'You knew Stevens?'

'Sort of knew him,' she said. 'See, he was my controller in the Virex Organisation.'

'Your controller?' he echoed. He held his head in his hands, elbows propped on the desk, and tried to work out how this latest piece of information fitted into the broader picture.

So far as he could see, it didn't.

'Let's get this straight. This Temple guy, or Stevens or Tallak or whatever the hell he called himself ... He was involved in the Methuselah Project, and the Mercury Project, working with people who're up in state-of-the-art VR technology ... and you're telling me he was your controller at Virex, the people who're trying to bring about the downfall of VR?'

'That's what I'm telling you, Halliday.'

He shook his head. 'Sorry. It doesn't make sense.'

Kat paced to the end of the room and leaned against the wall. She wasn't still for very long. She held the pose for about three seconds, then set off again.

'Except,' she said as she neared the desk, 'it does. It makes a kinda sense.'

'Well, do me a favour and fill me in.'

'This guy I know, someone I was close to once ... I worked with him in Virex a year or so ago. He told me we were being infiltrated. He didn't know why or who by. A few things had gotten kinda screwy, like decisions made on high had been reversed, plans scrapped, that kinda thing. We'd a plan of terrorism set up a while back. We were gonna bomb a few VR HQs, but the plug was pulled on that right at the last moment ... Temple was obviously one of the infiltrators.'

243

'But why would Temple, someone involved in his own VR site, get involved with Virex?'

'Hold fire, Halliday. I'm getting to that.'

She paced, thinking. She returned to the desk and stanchioned her arms, hanging her head, staring at him. Her pupils, he saw, were as large as dimes.

'For the past six months, say, I'd noticed that things were going in a different direction. About a year ago, we were trying to hit the big three and a few other smaller VR operatives with bugs, viruses, trying to get the bastards where it hurt, at their cores. We reckoned if we could down their cores, we would've scored a major propaganda coup. We were nearly there; we'd failed a few times, but the techs working for us were confident that we'd hit pay dirt sooner or later.'

She paused, shaking her head. 'Only, the policy changed. No more virus strikes on the cores. We were ordered to target certain sites within the big three and gather information, work out what they were doing and how. It turned into a game of espionage – and you know something, Halliday? Even back then I couldn't work out for the life of me who all this information was helping, 'cos it sure as fuck wasn't doing a thing for Virex.'

Halliday raised his cup to his lips and took a mouthful of coffee, knowing better than to interrupt her flow.

'A while ago I got curious about where I was uploading all this information to, so I put a trace on it. I tried to find where the Virex core was located, but it seems the core was well protected with anti-tracers. All I got was a few faint traces, paths through cyberspace where the info was routed before it reached its destination.'

'So . . . a dead end.'

Kat nodded. 'Then you come along and I get you into a nasty site that won't let you out and nearly burned you bad, and a few days later you shot Temple in self-defence. From what you told me about the threats made to you in the site,

I put two and two together. I go back and worked through the coordinates I used to get you into the restricted site, and guess what, Halliday?'

'Go on.'

'All the information about the technology of the big three I've been uploading for months . . .' Kat stared at him, eyes wide. 'It's been heading right into the core of the restricted site, Halliday. Me and however many other Virex operatives, we've been playing right into the hands of a big VR concern without even realising it! Talk about being duped good!'

She pushed away from the desk and paced to the end of the room.

'So what now, Kat? Where does that leave you?'

She slid down the far wall and sat on her haunches, staring across at him.

'Out on my own, is where, Halliday. You think I'm ever going to trust another fucker after this? Virex is rotten to the core, pal. Every fucking thing I've worked for over the past eighteen months . . .' She hung her head, then looked up suddenly, and the expression of despair on her face was alarming.

'So I'm on my own, now. I moved out of my old place last night, took all the equipment with me. I've gone to ground and the fuckers won't find me.' She stopped there, gathering her breath. 'I've learned a lot in eighteen months, Halliday. I have a lot of very valuable equipment, and I no longer have to abide by the rules made by people higher up. I'm my own free agent, and the first thing I'm gonna do is find out what the fuck the Methuselah Project is, and where it's based, and who's behind it – and when I do find out I'm gonna go in there and burn the bastards.'

She jumped up and moved to the desk, leaned over and stared at him. 'What I want to know, Halliday, is are you with me in this?'

He reached across the table and took her hand. 'Bet your life, Kat.'

'My man!' she said.

'Don't know how I'll be able to help, but I'll sure as hell do all I can.'

She moved to the door. 'That's what I want to hear, Halliday. I'll be in touch.'

'Hey, before you go . . .' He stood and moved around the desk. 'You forgot this.'

She stepped back into the office and stared at the cheque he held out to her. 'Christ, Halliday,' she said, taking it. 'Forgot all about the fifty grand . . .'

'Spend it wisely, Kat.'

She waved it in the air. 'It goes straight into the fighting fund, Halliday. Catch you later.'

He returned to the recliner, deciding that he might get accustomed to its comfort, after all. He brewed himself another coffee. He'd gone – what? – over a week without a caffeine hit, and his body was craving.

He thought about Kat and what she'd told him. It made sense; why wouldn't the Methuselah Project try to glean as much technological information from its competitors as was possible? Thing was, the big question still remained: what the hell was the Methuselah Project?

He found his car keys in the top drawer of the desk and locked the office behind him. As he drove north ten blocks, he considered Kat Kosinski. There was no doubting that she was as crazy as hell, and addled with spin much of the time, but she knew her stuff when it came to VR, and she was committed.

He was glad she was on his side.

He pulled up outside the Chinese laundry and sat behind the wheel for a while, just staring out at the old, familiar street. It was midday and sultry with that soaking, tropical heat that visited the city every summer. Perhaps a hundred food stalls lined the gutters, filling the air with the aroma of cooking meat. Families sat out on the steps of the tenement buildings, and crowds passed back and forth, a mixture of blacks, Hispanics, Chinese and the occasional Caucasian. Just another busy day in El Barrio.

A car was parked across the street, an electric blue Chrysler coupé. Halliday made out two people inside, a man and a woman eating spare ribs. For a brief, paranoid second he wondered if they constituted a threat. He dismissed the thought. He was getting jumpy, thanks to the shooting incident. He decided to treat himself to a take-out.

He lined up at his favourite stall and when his turn arrived he ordered chicken rolls and beef satay, along with coffee. The ancient Chinese woman jabbered at him in Mandarin, either welcoming him back or commenting on the heat. Halliday just smiled, handed over a fifty-dollar bill, and left without taking his change.

He climbed the stairs past the laundry and unlocked the office door. His possessions had been moved out, and the room looked bare, neglected. A couple of prints, which Kim had put up over a year ago, had been taken down, leaving pale patches in the paintwork. The dead flowers that had stood by the door were no longer there. He crossed to the desk, bare now of his com-system. There was no sign of his miniature oak.

He checked in the desk drawers, one by one, without coming across the tree. He experienced a sense of loss bordering on physical sickness. He'd treasured the damned thing, read texts on how to look after it, delighted like a proud parent when customers commented on its tiny, exquisite perfection.

He moved to the bedroom on the off chance that it'd been placed in there. His jellytank stood in one corner, his bed in the other, but there was no sign of the tree.

He stepped from the bedroom, and then saw it.

It stood in its terracotta trough on the window-sill behind the chesterfield. It seemed, in its minuscule, spreadboughed isolation, aloof and disdainful. He laughed with relief, retrieved it from the sill and sat in his swivel chair, just staring at the tree. It had become a powerful symbol in his life over the past year; its appearance of frailty was at odds with the fact of its hardy self-sufficiency. It could go weeks without water, and still flourished; it gained sustenance from stony soil. He wondered if part of his delight in the tree was admiration and respect.

He placed the oak on his desk, lodged his feet beside it, and started on his take-out.

Just as soon as this case was over, he promised himself, he'd move back here. The office off Lexington was all very well, but it wasn't him. He'd feel a fraud, operating out of such a swank establishment.

He was a creature of habit and the familiar room was a reassuring safe haven. He belonged here, and anyway the down-at-heel office held so many memories. Every stain on the carpet, every cigar burn on the chesterfield, reminded him of past incidents, of people now gone. For eight years he'd worked here with Barney, and to just up and leave would be an insult to his partner's memory. Barney was so much a part of the place that Halliday sometimes felt as though he was still here, watching him, often ruefully, as he went about his business. He felt a quick stab of guilt, then. Hell, he'd hardly done a week's work over the past six months. He'd slacked, felt sorry for himself, allowed the money from the Artois case to stand in lieu of regular, paid commissions. He'd escaped into the easy dreams of virtual reality and told himself that it was because life had been hard on him of late.

He knew what Barney would have said to that. 'Bull –' he could almost see his buddy forming the epithet '– *shit*. Halliday, you're a slacker.'

Barney had worked hard for nearly fifty years without complaint; his idea of a vacation was a week at Coney Island, and he'd still managed to feel guilty about that.

When he'd worked on a case he'd been dogged in pursuit of the goal. He'd never been the greatest detective brain in the city, but he was thorough and methodical and relentless.

And . . . what was it that Casey had said to him in the virtual Serengeti? That what mattered most of all was trust? Well, to know Barney Kluger for more than a day was to trust him implicitly.

Not that the guy didn't have his faults. He'd sink into black moods, especially after the death of his wife six years ago, and be surly and uncommunicative for a day or two, and Halliday would know better than to try to jolly him out of it. He'd just bide his time until Barney came round, returned to his dour old mock-cynical self.

And then the old bastard had gone and got himself shot dead one winter's night in a deserted back alley off Christopher Street . . .

Halliday took a deep swig of coffee and tried to banish the image of Barney, propped up against the trash cans, his chest a bloody mess of bullet wounds.

He felt a tightness in his throat and cursed himself for a weak fool. More coffee, that's what he needed, or maybe a wheat beer for old time's sake at Olga's bar on the corner.

He poured himself another coffee and was finishing his take-out – he'd have a beer when he went out with Casey tonight – when someone tapped on the door. He looked up, pulse quickening. The outline of a woman rippled through the pebbled glass.

'Yeah, what is it?'

The woman knocked again.

'Come on in,' he called.

The woman just stood there. Halliday cursed, hauled his legs from the desk and crossed the office. He pulled open the door. The dark-haired, pretty girl from the car across the street. She was smiling, saying, 'Sorry to bother you. I was just wondering . . .'

A figure emerged from the shadows beside her, and

before Halliday had time to react, before he had time even to register alarm, the guy had raised something and was spraying it into his face.

Halliday cried out, felt himself falling backwards into the office. A part of him was aware that he was about to strike his head painfully on the floor, but he was unconscious before the impact came.

Twenty-Two

Barney rode the elevator down to the labs on the 90th floor. He pushed open the swing door and saw with relief that two lab coats were hanging on the pegs, side by side. He removed his jacket and hung it next to them, then stepped into the working area of the laboratory.

The next four hours seemed to take an age to pass. He cracked a joke with some of the less up-tight techs, and hoped Lew would show so that they could trade some good-natured banter. They put him through all the usual tests and work-outs, comparing his performance, both mental and physical, with earlier results. Lew didn't turn up, and he took his coffee break alone, staring out through the window at the sparse traffic on Broadway. He wondered if it was the sight of the outside world that made him feel imprisoned, or the knowledge that soon, if all went well, he too would be out there.

At one point, around midday, one of the techs whose coat hung on the peg by the door left the lab carrying a com-board. All it needed now was for the second tech to go walkabout, and his plans would be scuppered. He tried to make a contingency plan in case that happened. He could always try to bluff his way through security, if the worst came to the worst, claim he'd left his card in his office.

He tried not to dwell on the chances of succeeding with that scenario.

One o'clock approached. The remaining lab coat was still hanging on the peg. If only the techs would finish what they were doing and let him go. He felt a mounting impatience as he lay face-down on the couch. One o'clock came and went. At five past he said, 'You boys anywhere near quitting yet?'

'Just another couple of minutes,' said the tech, inserting probes into his NCI.

He closed his eyes and willed the minutes to pass.

He felt a slap on his shoulder. 'That's it, pal, you're free.'

'Certainly hope so,' Barney muttered as he rolled from the couch and made for the exit.

He was aware of his heart, pounding like a jack-hammer, as he approached the pegs. He looked over his shoulder. The techs were standing around the lab, drinking coffee, chatting. No one gave him a glance as he reached for his jacket.

With his free hand he turned the lab coat. His heart leapt. There was no ID card attached to the breast pocket. He ran his hand down its length, feeling for the small plastic rectangle. He glanced back into the lab. The techs were still talking away. He wondered how long he could remain here before he attracted their attention.

In desperation he turned his back to the lab, lifted the coat from the hook and checked it back and front. Fact remained, no card. So how the hell had the tech made it through security that morning? Barney had checked that the guy wasn't wearing his ID card in the lab . . . So where the hell was it?

The bastard probably had it on him, he thought, tucked away in his pocket . . . That gave him an idea.

He checked the breast pocket, knowing that this was his last chance.

No card.

He replaced the coat on the peg and tried to order his thoughts. Plan B. Attempt to bluff his way through.

He was about to quit the lab when the swing door opened and a white-coated technician stepped through.

252

'Barney, still here?' the guy laughed. 'Can't get enough of the place?'

'After four hours, you kidding?'

He watched, with incredulity and amazement, as the tech removed his coat and placed it on the peg next to his own jacket. He nodded to Barney and continued into the lab.

Barney reached out, unclipped the ID card from the lapel and grabbed his jacket. He pushed through the swing door and made for the elevator, heart banging at a rate he was sure was far from healthy.

Doused in sweat, he hurried to his suite and changed his jacket and trousers, clipping the ID to his lapel. He pulled the chu over his head and looked into the mirror. He selected a face that approximately corresponded to the tiny pix on the ID, then slipped the bag of five-dollar coins into his jacket pocket.

He was ready to go.

He quit the lounge and strode down the corridor towards the elevator. There were security cameras on each floor, but he guessed that they weren't monitored all the time. And anyway, no one would recognise him in the guise of this blond stranger.

As he rode the elevator all the way down to the ground floor, he tried to work out what might possibly go wrong now. If he managed to get through security with his borrowed card, then that would, hopefully, afford him a few hours' grace before his disappearance was noted and the alarm raised. Around five every day either Lew Kramer or some other exec dropped by on some pretence or other. He had, he thought, about four hours.

Of course, if security was continually monitoring the tracer implanted in his NCI – or if it was linked to a com-system rigged to set off an alarm if he strayed – then he was well and truly stuffed.

He told himself to be optimistic. He would face adversity

if and when it arrived. So far, it had been plain sailing . . . well, almost. He told himself that he was as good as free.

The descent seemed to take an age, the elevator stopping at every floor to pick up other workers. They hardly gave him a glance. Barney stood at the back, his gaze fixed above their heads, conscious that if anyone looked too closely at the pix attached to the breast of his jacket, and then glanced up into his mismatched face . . . He told himself not to worry. The chances of some bored office worker being so vigilant was almost nil.

Then, on the fifth floor, the doors sighed open and Lew Kramer stepped aboard.

Barney thought he was about to suffer a coronary.

Lew looked straight into his eyes, seemed to hold his glance for a fraction of a second, then turned and faced the closing door. He wondered if something subconscious in Lew had half-recognised his soma-form, the shape of his body, something unmistakably *himself* in his bearing. If so, the contrary evidence of the blond stranger presented by the chu had put him off.

He closed his eyes and tried to control his breathing.

Lew Kramer alighted on the second floor and Barney felt as if an immense weight had been lifted from his shoulders. A minute later the elevator hit the first floor, bounced minimally, and opened its doors. He allowed his fellow passengers to step out before him, then squared his shoulders and emerged into the lobby. At least ten other workers were heading for the exit, and as Barney followed them he concentrated on the guards – two guards – standing beside the sliding glass door. They were eyeing the ID cards of everyone as they passed from the building.

The workers before Barney had come to a halt as they were processed through the exit. Barney slowed as he joined them, knowing that he had no chance. One of the guards would surely notice his dissimilarity to the pix on his card and raise the alarm.

The woman before Barney showed her card and was waved through. The guard had a habit of nodding at every passing worker, though his gaze seemed far away. Barney looked straight ahead, at the busy, beckoning sidewalk outside the building.

He approached the guard, heart pounding. The guy smiled, nodded . . .

Barney walked towards the door.

It slid open soundlessly and he stepped out.

He expected a hand on his shoulder, a polite, 'Excuse me, sir,' at every step. None came, and he was ten paces from the exit of the Mantoni tower before he realised that he was free.

He hurried across the sidewalk, stepped into the road and beckoned a passing taxi.

He slipped into the cab, gave his destination as 116th Street, El Barrio, and sat back, suddenly limp with nervous exhaustion.

As the cab drew away from the kerb, he looked back at the Mantoni tower.

As he did so, two men in black suits ran from the exit and crossed the sidewalk to a parked car. Something about their build and haste suggested that they were security guards charged with ensuring that the golden goose didn't fly away.

Barney leaned forward, thinking fast. 'Make that Monroe Street, Two Bridges. Let's move it!'

They car turned right, right again, and headed south. Barney looked through the rear window. There was no sign of the car in pursuit.

He'd get out in the area of warehouses around Two Bridges. If they were following his tracer, then it was inevitable they'd get him sooner or later. But . . . if he holed up, jumped them when they came for him, he could get away and hope that no other heavies had been sent after him.

It would mean silencing the two guys following him, but what the hell.

What had Sellings said about Hal?

'*Expendable.*'

If you chose the rules, you could hardly complain when the same rules were used against you.

He'd give the bastards *expendable* . . .

He peered through the rear window. At the end of the street, about two hundred metres back, the silver Lincoln appeared.

'Turn left. Drop me here!'

The driver turned. They were in a narrow street between a fruit and vegetable warehouse and some other, indefinable red-brick building. Barney handed the driver four five-dollar coins and jumped from the cab. He ran along the street, thanking Lew Kramer for bequeathing him such a fit body. He sure as hell couldn't have sprinted like this with his old, fat-bellied model . . . *His*? he thought. You're nothing but a copy, he reminded himself, a copy of someone whose memories had once meant something . . .

He came to a turning, a narrow walkway between two factories. There was nowhere to run to, he knew; nowhere to hide. He was looking for a place where he could play dead, then turn on the bastards when they approached.

To his advantage was the fact that they wanted to bring him back alive. When he attacked them with all the emotionless aggression he had inside him, they wouldn't know if what had hit them was human or animal, or some kind of hybrid killing-machine.

He stopped.

A trash can blocked the walkway. He smiled and kicked it over, then lay on the ground beyond it in a reasonable imitation of unconsciousness.

Seconds later he heard the sound of a car engine approaching, growing louder.

Then it cut out. Silence.

He braced himself to act, knowing that he was doing this for Hal. His partner's life depended on it. Hal was expendable, after all, in the eyes of the Mantoni organisation.

Was that anger he felt coursing through his NCI? Was such a thing possible? Or if not anger, then perhaps an intellectual appreciation of the iniquity of the situation?

He heard footsteps.

They rounded the corner, paused, then approached cautiously down the walkway. He heard a voice. 'Delgardo here. We got him. No problemo. We're bringing him in.'

The footsteps stopped before they reached him. He heard one of the guys approach, wary. They were playing it by the book, real pros. One guy going in, the other covering. Okay, so he'd play along with that, use it to his advantage.

A booted foot punted him in the midriff. He shut out the pain and lay absolutely motionless.

'He's out cold,' he heard. 'Okay, let's get the bastard back.'

He heard footsteps as the second guy approached, felt hands on his arms. They heaved, lifting him between them. For a second he hung, a realistic dead weight. He opened his eyes, made a decision. The guy on his left first.

Then he came to life.

He grabbed the guy to his left by the neck, squeezing his carotid and killing him in the prescribed three seconds. The bastard hardly made a sound. The second guy yelled and backed off, drawing a pistol.

Barney turned, holding the dead guy before him as a shield. As the second guy backed off, Barney felt for the dead man's weapon, found it.

He pulled the pistol and aimed at the retreating guy. 'Stop! Don't move a fucking step further. Drop the gun! I said drop the fucking—'

The guy dropped the gun, and Barney fired three times, fast and accurate, hitting the sucker in the chest. The guy

257

dropped something from his left hand as he fell to the ground, reached out as it skittered away from him.

Barney shot him again, in the head this time.

Expendable.

He dropped the guy he'd been using as a shield, then went though his pockets. He found the car keys along with a wallet stuffed with hundred-dollar notes. He decided they were better in his possession. He made to leave the alley, then stopped when he saw what the shot guy had been reaching for.

A com.

Barney picked it up, thumbed the command for a return call.

'Delgardo?' a voice said.

Barney held the com to his mouth. 'No problemo. We've got him. Bringing him in.'

'Well done, boys.'

He cut the connection.

He hurried from the alley without a backward glance. The silver Lincoln stood ten metres away. He climbed into the driver's seat, started the engine, and U-turned.

He headed uptown, towards El Barrio.

He wondered how much time he'd bought himself with the call. How long before security became suspicious that Delgardo and partner had failed to return?

If they were still monitoring the tracer, then they'd know pretty soon. But if, complacent after the reassuring call, they'd quit monitoring ... Maybe he'd given himself enough time to help Hal, after all.

Twenty-Three

Halliday rose like a swimmer through the depths of oblivion. Consciousness came slowly. He found himself blinking up at the nicotine-browned ceiling of the office, reliving again the split second before the attack.

He rubbed his face where the spray had hit him, then struggled into a sitting position. Whatever they had used, it had had an anaesthetising effect on his body. His mind felt distanced from the ache in his limbs, the nausea that had become a constant companion.

He climbed to his feet and looked around. He checked his pockets. He still had his wallet containing his cards and almost a thousand dollars, and . . . He hurried over to the desk. Either they had overlooked the oak, or had no botanical appreciation. The tree was still standing in its terracotta tray, unmoved by the drama enacted before it.

He looked around the office. Nothing had been touched, it seemed. He moved to the bedroom. The jellytank was still there. He glanced at his watch. He'd been out perhaps one hour, plenty of time for them to have arranged for the removal of his tank . . .

So why the hell had they attacked him, rendered him unconscious?

Opportunists? They thought they'd knock him out and ransack his office for valuables, but of course had found none. But why then had they left without taking his wallet? Perhaps they'd been disturbed before they got round to robbing him?

He took his oak from the desk and left the office. He locked the door behind him and hurried down the stairs.

There was no sign of the couple's car in the street. He slipped into the Ford, placed the bonsai on the back seat, and was about to start the engine when his com chimed.

He thumbed it to receive and stared at the tiny screen.

'Halliday,' a voice asked, 'is that you?'

He tried to make out the face. It was thin, its skin yellowed.

'Jesus,' he breathed. 'Wellman? What the hell . . . . ?'

The semblance of the smile was appalling on so ravaged a face. 'One last look at the real world, Halliday,' Wellman said. 'I went round to your new office, but of course you weren't there.'

He felt suddenly, irrationally, guilty for wasting the dying man's precious time. 'I'm at the old office.'

'I'm in the area,' Wellman said. 'I need to see you.'

Halliday thought it wise not to remain immediately outside the office. 'I'll be parked along the street outside Olga's, okay?'

'I'll meet you in five minutes, Halliday.'

He cut the connection and stared at the executive's stilled image on the screen. He had known that Wellman was dying, of course – but his image in virtual reality had belied the fact of his terminal illness.

He was not relishing the prospect of meeting Wellman in the real world.

He started the engine and U-turned, idled along the street and braked outside Olga's.

He wondered what Wellman wanted. Had he emerged from VR to say goodbye, incarnate, to friends and acquaintances? There was something formal and decorous about such a farewell gesture that would be entirely in keeping with the man.

Five minutes later a white Mercedes pulled up across the street.

A thin figure in a cream-coloured suit climbed with agonising slowness from the back of the car and crossed the street, leaning heavily on a walking stick. Halliday jumped from the Ford and assisted Wellman to the sidewalk.

'Should we go into the bar?' he asked.

Wellman took ten seconds to regain his breath. 'I won't keep you, Halliday. The car will do fine.'

He helped Wellman into the passenger seat and resumed his own seat behind the wheel, trying not to stare at the deterioration that time and an incurable disease had wrought on the executive.

He'd last seen Wellman in the flesh almost eighteen months ago, when the executive was in hospital after being injured in the firefight that resolved the Sissi Nigeria case. He'd looked the picture of health then, despite serious leg injuries. Wellman was in his mid-forties, but now he looked like a man in his eighties.

'Are you sure it's a wise thing to do?' Halliday asked, hesitantly.

'Hell, why not?' Even his voice was affected, little more than a croak. 'I'll get back into VR as soon as I've seen a couple more people. I reckon I'll have another week of virtual life before the old body gives up the ghost.'

'You said you need to see me?' Halliday said, conscious that, every minute he kept the executive in the real world, he was denying him precious time in VR.

'Sure do, Hal,' Wellman said.

'About the case?' Halliday looked at Wellman, wondering how much his mind had been affected by whatever drugs he was on. The man didn't seem himself; his speech was clipped and informal, unlike his usual precise, sometimes ornate elocution. And never before had he called Halliday by his first name.

Wellman sat hunched forward, clutching the handle of his walking stick with emaciated hands. Halliday noticed

261

the thin, pale skin stretched between the metacarpal bones like the etiolated membranes of a bat's wing.

He nodded. 'About the case, Hal. Indulge an old and dying man. I want to know what you've found out so far?'

'Everything?' Halliday asked.

'Everything you think relevant, Hal.'

He was about to point out that he'd gone through the details of the case point by point in the Serengeti site, but stopped himself. Obviously Wellman's memory was going the way of his frail body.

He marshalled his thoughts, sorted the many incidents into some kind of order.

He went through the case from the initial interview with the Suzie hologram, though his interrogation of Jimmy King, Anastasia Dah, and every other player in the drama. He recounted what he'd discovered in Nyack, his brush with the mysterious Charles in the restricted site, and his shoot-out with Tallak.

Wellman asked frequent questions, and it became obvious that the executive had forgotten much of Halliday's initial report. When he asked Wellman if his technicians had managed to glean anything more from the Suzie hologram, he was met with a blank stare.

'The device I gave Roberts,' Halliday reminded him. 'You said that you'd found out that Suzie Charlesworth was involved in the Mercury Project, working on the R&D of von Neumann machines . . .'

Wellman turned a watery gaze on him, and his hand trembled as he touched his brow in confusion. 'I did? Forgive me, Hal. You know, the failure of the body I can almost tolerate – I was never one of these people who pride themselves on their physical perfection. But what I find so terrible about my condition is the state of my mind. I've always thought of myself as a reasonably intelligent man.' He shook his head. 'I'm sorry, you were saying . . . ?'

'Things've come to a standstill since the shooting. I got

out of hospital this morning, so I haven't had much time to follow anything up. Oh, there is one thing.'

Wellman looked at him. 'Significant?'

He shrugged. 'Hard to say. I have a contact in Virex – or rather she was involved with them. It seems that for the past six months they've been infiltrated and run by members of the Methuselah Project. The Virex techs on the street have been raiding Mantoni sites, among others, and passing on what they find to the Methuselah people, unwittingly, of course.'

'That's very interesting. Who is this woman?'

Halliday hesitated. He doubted whether Kat would thank him for passing on her name to the head of Cyber-Tech. 'She uses a tag,' he said. 'But I can give you her com code . . .'

Wellman nodded. 'I'll have my people contact her, find out what she knows about the Methuselah Project.'

Halliday repeated the code.

Wellman reached out and tapped Halliday's knee with a trembling hand. 'I have faith in you. Keep up the good work.'

He pushed up the sleeve of his suit jacket and peered at his watch. 'It's time I was getting back.'

'I'll see you across the street. The sooner you're back in VR, the better.'

He took Wellman's arm and walked him slowly towards the Merc, feeling the slack play of sinew and atrophied muscle against bone.

He opened the rear door of the car and Wellman laboriously folded himself inside. He turned and looked up at Halliday. 'Farewell, Hal . . . if we don't meet again.'

Halliday raised a hand and stood in the street as the Mercedes started up and eased away from the kerb.

He returned to the Ford and sat behind the wheel, considering the executive and what he'd told him about his lack of success so far.

He had to admit that he was no nearer solving the case now than he had been ten days ago, at the very start of his investigations. He'd amassed a lot of diverse information, witnessed sufficient incident to keep a holo-scriptwriter busy for months, but he had nothing concrete on which to base further enquiries. He hated to admit it, but he was relying on Kat Kosinski to come up with the next positive lead.

Perhaps he was being hard on himself. Christ, he was only a few hours out of hospital after being shot in the chest. What did he expect?

Tomorrow he'd begin the round of routine investigation again, try to find out more about Tallak, or Temple, or whatever his real name was. He'd look further into the business dealings of André Connaught, see if that might lead somewhere.

He looked at his watch. It was four. He was due to meet Casey around seven ... He had some time to kill. He glanced up at the sign outside Olga's, neon tubes bent into the shape of a beer bottle ... How often had the lighted sign beckoned him through the darkness? Even deactivated, grime-encrusted and somehow sad in the hot afternoon air, the redundant beacon possessed an alluring power. Or perhaps he was just weak-willed? One for the road, he told himself. For old time's sake.

He descended the cellar steps and pushed through the swing door. The familiar smell of hops and stale tobacco smoke, the familiar low lighting and serried, cushioned booths. It felt like he'd been away for months.

A new girl was serving behind the bar, and Olga was nowhere in sight. Halliday ordered a wheat beer and carried it to his regular booth by the steps.

Although he'd just left hospital that morning after major surgery and six days in VR, he was feeling fine. Okay, so his body was wasted, and he was easily tired out, but what did he expect? It was improvement all the way from here, he told himself. This was the first day of his recovery. No more VR ... or only when it was absolutely necessary in his investigations. He'd work out a bit more, eat sensibly.

He sat back, took a long drink, and thought about Casey and what she'd told him in VR. He tried to work out his feelings for the girl. Did his reluctance to get involved stem from the fact that he was almost twenty years older than her, or was he reluctant to commit himself again for fear of being hurt a second time?

Stuff it, he thought. She'd find some young stud nearer her own age sooner or later. She was just going through the regulation teenage crush for an older guy, the father figure missing in her life for so long; it was merely a phase she'd pass through, given time.

He finished the beer, bought another at the bar and returned to his seat.

Five minutes later he heard a familiar voice. 'Long time no see, Hal.'

Vanessa Artois, the VR-queen, stood beside the booth.

'Vanessa . . .'

'Well, are you going to sit there gawping or are you going to buy me a drink?'

She slipped into the seat opposite with one svelte, practised movement, swept a tress of midnight hair from her eyes and smiled at him.

'I . . . sure. White wine, sweet, right?'

'You remember? That's nice.'

He escaped to the bar, his heart thumping. He ordered a wine and stared back at the beautiful woman in the booth. She wore a silver lamé dress that followed the curves of her body like waves of liquid mercury. She was even more stunning than he remembered her. Staring at her across the rapidly filling bar, he felt the renewal of the familiar and sickening emotion that had gripped him during the time he had worked with Artois a year ago.

He returned to the booth with her drink.

'Thanks, Hal,' she said, sipping and eyeing him over the glass.

He could not stop the laboured pounding of his heart as he stared across the table at the fine, angled planes of her face.

'What the hell,' he found himself asking, 'are you doing here?'

She laughed. 'I was in the city doing a little publicity.' She wrinkled her nose at him. 'And I thought, why not drop by and see how Halliday's doing these days? So I went to the office, and it's all locked up. Then a stall-holder told me you were here. It's great to see you again, Hal. How's work?'

He shrugged. 'Work's work,' he said, finding it hard to believe that she really was here. 'You know how it is. Cases come in, and some I solve and others . . .' He shrugged again.

She once meant a lot to me, he thought, and I blew it . . .

'I'm staying with friends up in Nyack,' she said. 'You know it?'

'Matter of fact,' he said, 'I was up there on a case the other day.'

'You don't say, Hal? How about that for a coincidence. Tell me about it.'

He shrugged. 'Just another missing persons case. A Cyber-Tech employee went walkabout, or was kidnapped, or whatever. I went up there on a tip-off, looking for this organisation.'

'You found where they were based.'

He looked at her. 'Yeah, yes I did.' He paused, wondering at her interest.

She nodded. 'You know who these kidnappers are?'

He shook his head. 'Enough of my work,' he said. 'Tell me about what you're doing these days.'

'Oh, nothing interesting. I'd rather hear about—'

For a fraction of a second, the image of her beauty froze. The drinkers around them in the bar stopped suddenly, drinks stilled before open mouths. The hubbub of the bar ceased, replaced by an eerie and absolute silence. Halliday felt himself lose his grip on this reality, felt his sense of touch depart him.

The image of the bar before him was locked. It was as if he was staring at a stilled holo-screen, the actors frozen in mid-gesture. He wondered, for a second, if he was going mad.

Then the bar disappeared, and the vision of Vanessa Artois with it, and he was aware of himself floating in the familiar medium of the suspension gel, rising from the tank as someone hauled him out by the arm.

He struggled to free his face from the visor. He felt hands on his arms and legs, pulling free the leads and sensors. Physical awareness returned to his body, filling him with nausea and sickness. As he stepped from the tank, the muscles of his legs protested.

Oh, Christ . . .

He felt his legs weaken and buckle and he collapsed against the side of the tank.

Then he heard a familiar voice. 'C'mon, Hal! This ain't no time for amateur dramatics. Get dressed!'

He clutched the tank, staring at the figure before him.

Christ, but it was Barney. Or rather it looked like Barney. The same face, only younger . . .

'Barney?' he said, incredulous.

The figure threw a bundle of clothes at him. Halliday caught them, for a second too stunned to act.

'Move it, Hal! We gotta get outta here!'

He dressed in a daze, working solely by touch as he stared at the figure of Barney Kluger before him.

This Barney was a little taller, not as paunchy. He had the same heavy-jawed face, the same receding hair . . .

'You look like you seen a ghost, Hal,' Barney said.

'I think I have.'

Barney embraced him, slapped his back. 'Solid flesh and blood, this ghost.'

Halliday felt the solidity of Barney against him, experienced a surge of emotion he could not name – the desire to believe that Barney had miraculously risen from the dead, together with an intellectual knowledge of the impossibility of that hope.

He shook his head, on the verge of tears. 'You're dead,' he said. 'You died back in . . .'

'So I came back to life, Hal,' Barney said. 'Look, I'll explain later, okay? It's a long story. For now, just trust me.'

Halliday screwed his eyes shut, but when he opened them again Barney was still standing before him.

'What the hell's going on?' he managed.

Barney – or whoever it was – stared at him. 'Remember the broad who called by your office earlier? The guy who jumped you? You've been in VR since then.'

Christ . . . He *had* come round feeling great, attributing it to some anaesthetic effect of the knock-out spray. All along he'd been tanked.

He pulled on his shoes. 'Okay, fine. I'm knocked out by two intruders and placed in my own tank. I wake up and continue my life as if nothing had happened . . . But why the hell did they do that?'

'Because they want to know everything you know about the Methuselah Project, the case you're working on at the moment. Why do you think they sent Wellman to question you?'

Halliday held his head. 'But Wellman knows all about the case. I mean, I told him everything the other—' He stopped.

'That wasn't Wellman you met earlier, Hal. It was a construct, to fool you into telling it what you knew about the case.'

He shook his head, dazed. 'But who wants to know about the Methuselah Project?'

'Mantoni. They're paranoid about the people running

the Methuselah Project. They want to know what they're up to, why they've been raiding Mantoni sites, rustling information.'

'How do you know this?'

'Couple of days back, I overheard 'em planning to dupe you.' He stopped. 'Hey, we're standing around here gabbing like old maids. Let's get the hell out.'

They left the bedroom and paused in the office. 'You still keep the hardware and ammo in the bottom drawers?' Barney asked, moving to the desk.

Halliday took the keys from the top left drawer and passed them to Barney. Seconds later Barney found a body-holster and his old automatic. He hurried to the door. 'You got the car?'

'Outside.'

'I need to take it for a while, okay? Come with me. I'll drop you off. You go to earth and stay hidden for a while, got that? We'll arrange to meet somewhere in a couple of days.'

'Why split up? Why not—?'

''Cos the bastards got a trace on me. They're on my tail right now. I plan to lead them a dance, pick 'em off one by one till they have no more operatives able or willing to risk themselves trying to track me down. Then . . . then I'll try to work out how to get rid of the fucking beacon. Let's go.'

He hurried down the stairs. Halliday looked back at the office, some vague thought niggling at him. The oak tree? He'd left it in the back of the car . . . But that had been in VR. Here, in this reality, it stood on the desk.

He ran to the desk, grabbed the oak, and locked the door after him.

Twilight was falling in the street outside. Barney stood by the Ford. He tossed the keys to him and slipped into the passenger seat, stowing the bonsai safely on the back seat as Barney revved the engine and hauled the car from the kerb.

He accelerated, missing a street-stall by centimetres, and headed south.

'Where you want dropping, Hal?'

He thought about it. 'Anywhere on Lexington.'

Barney nodded. 'You find somewhere safe and hole up for a while, okay? The bastards at Mantoni won't stop until they've got you. See, you know too much, Hal.'

He nodded. 'I'll do that.'

'You still got the same com code?'

'Yeah.' He stared across at Barney. Every intuition he had, every gut feeling, told him that despite all reason, all logic, his partner was sitting beside him, driving the Ford with reckless abandon, just like old times.

He felt a sudden reluctance to let Barney out of his sight. 'We should stick together—'

Barney grunted. 'You know the routine, bud. We being trailed, and what's the safest ploy? Right. We split up.'

'But they haven't got a trace on me,' Halliday pointed out. 'So once I get outta here, I'm free.'

Barney glanced across at him. 'What the hell you trying to say?'

'I'm saying your logic's flawed. Splitting up won't divert their attention or their forces, because they're after you right now, not me.'

'Okay, so maybe I don't want you to get yourself shot dead. I don't want to be responsible for the death of my partner just when we've teamed up again.'

'You've either got no faith in me, or the people who're tailing us are damned good—'

'It's just that we'll find it hard to shake the bastards, buddy.'

'We'll stand a better chance of getting away if we stick together. Think this through.'

Barney glanced up, into the rear-view. 'Christ! We're in it together now, Hal. The bastards've found me . . .'

Halliday screwed around in his seat and peered through

the rear window. In the twilight he made out a car about a hundred metres behind.

He recognised the car – the blue Chrysler coupé belonging to the couple who'd attacked him in the office.

'I lost 'em a while back, Hal. But they stick like limpets. There'll be others around, too. That's the hell of it. We just don't know where the enemy is.'

He revved, took a left, then a sharp right on First Avenue, heading south.

Halliday slipped his automatic from its holster and turned in his seat, staring through the rear window for any sign of the coupé.

'Looks like we've given it the slip.'

'Yeah, but for how long? See, thing is that they know where we are. They don't have to follow us, just find us by another route.'

'How're they tailing you?' Halliday asked, eyes on the road behind.

Barney tapped his head and smiled. 'Nano-cerebral interface, you remember those?'

How could he forget? The Sissi Nigeria case, eighteen months ago, which had led directly to Barney's death.

'You're implanted with a unit, Barney?' He glanced at his partner's receding hairline, but the light in the car was too low for him to make out any sign of spars or circuitry.

Barney nodded. 'How'd you think I came back to life, Hal?'

It made a kind of ludicrous sense. The NCI somehow contained Barney's identity, his personality . . . and the body? The body was a little taller than Barney's original, not as big around the gut.

'The people at Mantoni's, they installed a tracer in the unit. I'm a valuable possession to 'em, Hal. They didn't want me straying.'

'You any idea what kind of tracer's in there?'

'Search me, bud.'

'If we can get it out, Barney – or stop the signal . . .'

'Then I'm home free and laughing. Trouble is, Hal, that's a big *if*.'

Halliday thought of Kat Kosinski. If there was one person who might have the technical expertise to check out the NCI, and the desire to help the cause, it was Kat.

Halliday pulled out his com and entered her code.

Barney glanced at him. 'Who you calling?'

'A contact.' He glanced across at Barney. 'How'd you feel about someone digging about in your NCI?'

Barney opened his palms on the apex of the steering wheel. 'If it gets rid of the Mantoni mob, I'll love 'em for ever.'

The screen flared. A thin white face glared out at him with a good imitation of hostility. Her cheek twitched and her eyes were wide with the effects of spin.

'Oh, it's you, Halliday. I just talked to your friend.'

He stared. 'Friend?'

Kat sighed. 'Don't play the fool, Halliday. You got a friend in the world, no?'

'Kat, just hold on. I don't know what you're talking about.'

'This guy called. Said he was a buddy of yours, a private eye working on the Charlesworth case. Said he wanted to talk to me about what I know of the Methuselah Project, their restricted site. So I arranged to meet him in an hour.'

Understanding hit him. He'd told the Wellman construct about Kat and the Methuselah site. He'd even given the Wellman construct her com code.

'Kat, did you tell him where you are?'

'Do I look like a dummy, Halliday? Only trusted folk get to know where I'm based.'

'Okay, great. Look, don't meet that guy, okay? Don't go anywhere near him, and don't answer any more of his calls.'

Kat screwed her face up and stared at him. 'Halliday, what's going on?'

'Long story. Look, what do you know about NCIs?'

'Nano-cerebral interfaces? A bit. Girl in my line of work needs to keep up with the technology.'

'Okay. Listen, I've got someone with me who's on our side. Thing is, his NCI's implanted with a tracer, and we need to get it out, fast. You think you can help?'

Kat stared out at him, suddenly serious. 'A tracer in an NCI? Could be two or three things. If it's a deep implant, like sub-cortical, then no way, José. But if it's a needle plant or a simple tracking program . . . Then maybe I can help.'

'I hope so. Where are you? We'll pick you up.'

'I'll meet you on the corner of Canal Street and Bowery. Where're you?'

'About five minutes away. See you then.'

'Over and out, Halliday.' She cut the connection.

Barney glanced at him. 'Who was that?'

He told Barney about Kat.

'Sounds some kid. You think she can debug me?'

'If anyone can, she's the girl. Corner of Canal and Bowery.'

Barney glanced up at the rear-view. 'Might be a little longer than five minutes, Hal. We got company.'

Halliday turned in his seat. The electric blue coupé, as relentless as a scavenging shark, kept pace about two hundred metres behind.

'What now?'

'Let's try a few diversionary tactics, and if that doesn't shake 'em long enough so we can pick up the kid, we'll think again.'

Halliday peered out and raised his automatic as Barney hit the accelerator.

They turned left, heading towards the Lower East Side. Seconds later the lights of the coupé swept around the corner, tracking them. Barney turned a sharp right and

273

accelerated. Halliday swayed in his seat as the Ford careered around the bend. The coupé would not be put off; each time Halliday thought that they might have given the following car the slip, its dazzling headlights appeared in the distance.

'Find a quiet street, warehouses or whatever. Lose the coupé and drop me off.'

Barney glanced at him. 'What's the plan?'

'I get out and conceal myself in a doorway. When the coupé passes, I take out its tyres. Then I get outta there and head for the corner. You drive around the block and pick me up. It'll slow 'em down for a time.'

'And if they start firing?'

'Then I'll return fire – and I won't be going for their tyres.'

Barney nodded. He headed into the Lower East Side, making for Two Bridges. He turned left down a quiet street between looming factory buildings, the coupé turning with them and keeping pace. Barney accelerated, then made a quick right turn and slowed. 'Tell me when, Hal.'

Halliday made to open the door. The coupé was nowhere in sight. 'Okay, here!'

Barney stepped on the brakes. 'See you in two minutes.'

Halliday dived out, rolled across the tarmac and sprinted into the shadowed recess of a factory's loading bay. Barney sped off down the quiet street and Halliday waited, struggling to regain his breath.

He heard an engine, and seconds later the searchlight beam of its headlights swept around the corner. He dropped into a crouch and held his automatic at arm's length. The coupé was speeding now, attempting to gain on Barney's Ford. A second later it flashed past and Halliday aimed low and opened fire, a dozen bullets smacking into the tyres and hubcaps. The car swerved, wallowing on dead rubber for fifty metres before smacking into the side of a building.

274

The second he quit firing, he was up and running towards the end of the street. He slowed, exhaustion like two fists gripping his lungs and squeezing. He looked over his shoulder. The guy was staggering from the smashed coupé, hauling open the passenger door and dragging the woman out.

Ahead, headlights showed. Halliday slowed his pace. In seconds they'd be on their way, safe for a while at least. The ambush had bought them time enough to pick Kat up, see if she could work her magic on Barney's NCI.

The car up ahead was turning the corner, and Halliday wondered what the hell Barney was thinking about. He came to a halt, dazzled by the headlights as the car sped towards him. Barney should have stopped on the main drag and waited for him there. The way up ahead was blocked by the coupé and the vengeful Mantoni duo.

He wondered if Barney was being pursued by another car, and no sooner had this struck him than he realised, in a second of surging panic, that the car bearing down on him was not the Ford. A white Mercedes came to a halt ten metres from him with a squeal of brakes and the doors flew open, upwards like the wing-cases of a beetle. Two dark figures jumped out and began firing, and Halliday fell flat, rolled and returned fire. He caught one of the men in the chest, sending him sliding across the hood of the Merc in a syrupy slick of blood.

He dived into the partial cover of a doorway and heard shots rain around him like metallic hail. The second guy was kneeling in the cover of the Merc, loosing the odd round to keep Halliday pinned down. He wondered how long it would be before the man and woman from the coupé decided to join in the turkey shoot.

He heard a cry, and the firing stopped.

A sudden silence fell over the scene. Then he heard a quiet hiss: 'Hal, where the hell are you?'

'Barney?'

'Over here. Let's get the hell out!'

Someone appeared from behind the Merc, recognisably the taller, slimmer figure of the resurrected Barney Kluger.

Halliday stood and moved past the Merc, glancing at the guy he'd hit and the one Barney had accounted for. The second guy lay face down on the tarmac, arms parenthesising the place where his head had been in an accidental gesture of protection.

Halliday stared at the guy on the hood of the Merc, a sick feeling in his gut. Barney grabbed his arm. 'It was him or us, Hal.'

Halliday nodded, silent. Barney put two bullets through the rear tyres of the Merc and led Halliday to where he'd left the Ford on the main drag.

Halliday drove in silence. He made for Canal Street. At last he said, 'You think that's it, or they'll be sending more cars after us?'

'I'll be surprised if they give up that easily.' Barney was quiet for a while, then said, 'Tell me how I died, Hal.'

Halliday glanced across at his partner. He was staring through the windshield, something unreadable in his expression, blank in his eyes.

'It was January, '40, Barney. Eighteen months ago. We were working on the Sissi Nigeria case, you recall?'

Barney narrowed his eyes, as if trying to see that far back. 'I remember taking the case on, doing a bit of leg-work.'

'You've no memory of finding the dead woman? You recall the rogue AI, LINx?'

Barney shook his head. 'That's impossible, Hal. I must have been downloaded before any of that.'

Halliday suppressed a shiver. 'Downloaded?'

Barney ignored him. 'So, January . . . What happened?'

'We were working on the Nigeria case with Wellman. A rogue AI had uploaded itself into the NCI of a Mantoni technician. It came after you. It shot you in an alley off Christopher Street, left you for dead.'

'I didn't die immediately?'

Halliday shook his head. 'You managed to call me. I found you, pretty near dead, and got you over to St Vincent's. You died about thirty minutes later.' He stopped, hearing the words he'd just spoken, recalling the time in the emergency unit.

They turned onto Canal Street and approached the corner with Bowery. Halliday saw a fidgety figure striding up and down the sidewalk. She wore her customary black leggings and the same colour T-shirt, a small backpack lodged between her thin shoulder blades.

Barney said, 'That the kid?'

'That's Kat.'

Barney reached into his hair, and as Halliday watched he seemed to grasp his scalp and lift it from his skull. His receding hair came away, along with his fleshy face. The expression on the chu became one of elasticated surprise as it elongated, then snapped off to reveal a stranger's face beneath.

Halliday stared at the man in the passenger seat. He was in his mid-thirties, swarthy and handsome in a hard kind of way. His head was shaven, and his domed skull was traversed by the spars and input sockets of a nano-cerebral interface.

The stranger looked at Halliday. 'Don't be alarmed, Hal. It's me, Barney, okay? Only a little changed, is all.'

Halliday nodded, wordless. He pulled into the kerb and sounded his horn.

Kat turned, saw the car and hurried over.

She hauled open the back door. 'Christ! What the hell kept you guys? I've been propositioned three times. Could've made a fortune.'

'We had a bit of a hold-up, Kat.' He started the Ford and pulled into the street. 'Kat, this is Barney.'

'Pleased to meet you, Barney. You the guy with the bug in your brain?'

277

She shrugged the pack from her back and pulled it open. Halliday glanced over his shoulder. She was taking glittery things from the backpack and laying them on the seat beside her.

'You can do this on the move, or should we stop?'

'Hey, I'm not responsible if I poke his brains out while you're speeding, okay? We'd better stop.'

Barney said, 'Head over the bridge. We'll make for beyond the airport. There's some quiet stretches out on the coast. If anyone's following us we'll see 'em coming.'

Halliday glanced at the stranger and nodded, turned the bend and headed for Manhattan Bridge. It was disconcerting to hear Barney's speech patterns issue from the unfamiliar face of the stranger beside him.

'Hey, Barney,' Kat said, 'lean your head back on the rest so's I can get a good look at the hardware.'

Barney obeyed. As Halliday accelerated on the fast lane of Interstate 278, Kat hummed a tune to herself and examined Barney's NCI.

She stopped humming and said, 'Hey, this is a real neat piece of hardware, Barney. Must've cost you an arm and a leg.'

He smiled. 'More like an entire body, in a manner of speaking.'

Kat kept up a running commentary from then on. Halliday caught only the occasional fragment, and it meant little to him. 'Latest VR interface, Hal. Multi-parallel programming. Some great formatting . . . Enough ports to run a fucking spaceship.'

'You think you can debug the thing, Kat?' Halliday asked.

'Don't rush me, Halliday. I'm getting to that. These things take time.'

He turned off the highway and took a quiet road north of the airport. High above, the lights of arriving planes spiralled through the night-time darkness like Christmas baubles in a whirlwind.

Halliday heard clunking and whirring sounds from the direction of Barney's head, and when he glanced at Kat she was inserting what looked like knitting needles into the NCI.

'I thought you wanted me to stop?'

'It's okay. I'm just playing about in here for now.' She whistled. 'Christ, Halliday. The things I could do with this kind of augmentation. This is state-of-the-art stuff.'

They passed the airport and approached the coast around Valley Stream. Halliday turned off the road, taking a track through dunes and marram grass. The area reminded him of the long walks he'd taken further along the coast as a kid.

Ahead he made out a concrete jetty extending arrow-straight into the ocean.

'How about the end of the jetty, Barney? If anyone approaches we'll be able to see them coming for miles.'

'Let's do it.'

Halliday eased the car onto the narrow jetty and headed for the end, tyres rippling noisily over the ribbed concrete.

He braked the Ford, facing the dark immensity of the ocean. Kat switched on the overhead light and in its feeble glare set to work. Barney closed his eyes, his head back against the rest, as if asleep.

'Okay,' Kat said. 'Let's see what we've got ourselves here.'

She slipped three short needles into the NCI's ports, wires trailing to a device like a com which she held in her left hand, and glanced at it occasionally.

Halliday looked through the rear window, uneasy. He was about to leave the car and patrol the area when Kat said, 'Hey, jackpot, Halliday! It ain't no sub-cortical implant, you'll be delighted to know. It's a plain old-fashioned needle device. Trouble is, it's fitted with a retrieval code, so I'll have to hack through that to get it out.'

'You think you can do it?'

She nodded, tight-lipped. 'I'll do it. Just give me time, okay?'

He left her to it and climbed from the car. He walked back along the length of the jetty, aware of the weight of his automatic in its body-holster.

He sat on a concrete capstan and stared inland. The coast on this stretch of the island was dark, the approaching tracks unlighted. If a car tried to reach Barney at the end of the jetty, it would have to get past him first.

He thought about the stranger in the car who sounded like Barney, seemingly had all the memories of Barney, and with the chu even looked like his old partner. But the body of the man in the car was not Barney's – so was his partner nothing more than a set of memories and behaviour patterns downloaded into the NCI? And, if so, then what of the body? Who had the body belonged to before Barney's occupancy? Did it still have its own memories and thoughts, its own identity, locked somewhere within its skull?

The twin cone projection of a car's headlights appeared in the distance, swinging wildly through the night as the car bounced along the rough track. Halliday tensed, then ducked behind the capstan and watched as the car approached.

If it tried to drive onto the jetty, he decided, he'd shoot out its tyres and hope its occupants were from Mantoni, not a couple of lovers looking for privacy.

He drew his automatic.

The car approached the jetty and swept on by, heading for a line of beach chalets about five hundred metres away. Halliday stood and watched, just to make sure. The car halted before the first chalet and four figures climbed out, laughing.

He breathed a sigh of relief and wondered how Kat was doing.

To the west, Manhattan showed as a lighted blur on the

horizon, a pastel halation of combined neons and holo-façades. It looked like some kind of fabulous ocean liner bedecked with party lights, about to embark on some epic voyage. It was a wonderful lie, he thought; beneath the lights it was more a rotten hulk, becalmed.

He looked up. Overhead, rainclouds gathered in preparation for another evening deluge.

He heard a noise from the end of the jetty as the car door opened and slammed shut. A small, slim figure strode towards him.

'Halliday!' Kat called. 'Got a present for you!'

She stopped before him and swept a strand of jet hair from her eyes, holding it in place against the warm breeze.

She held out a small needle.

Halliday took it, examined the innocent-looking object. 'That all it is?'

She nodded. 'That's all. Simple tracking device.' She continued staring at him, hand to her forehead to pin back her hair. 'Halliday, I want to ask you something.'

He drew his arm back and flung the needle into the ocean. 'Yeah?'

'That guy back there,' she said, hesitant. 'Barney or whatever he calls himself . . .'

'What about him?'

'Well, I don't really know how to ask this . . . But what the fuck is he?'

He stared at her. 'What do you mean?'

'I mean, the people who're implanted with NCIs, techs and scientists and whoever, well . . . they're usually alive.'

He was suddenly aware of the salt tang of the sea air, the sound of the waves soughing on the beach beneath the pillars of the jetty. The first warm drops of rain, harbingers of the torrent to come, pattered down around them.

'You mean Barney isn't?'

She shook her head. 'He's brain dead. He's a zombie. It

281

isn't his cerebellum running his autonomic nervous system, or his cortex controlling all his higher functions, it's the fucking NCI. I've never seen anything like it in my life, Halliday, and it's sure as hell spooky.'

He shrugged. 'He's on our side, Kat. That's all that matters.'

'Yeah, but I'd like to know exactly *what* it is that's on our side.'

'He's on the run from the Mantoni organisation,' Halliday said. 'He was my business partner, before he died.'

She looked at him. 'So he's some kind of Mantoni experiment?' she said. 'Christ, Mantoni are bringing the dead back to life?'

Halliday pointed to the car. 'Let's get going, Kat. I don't want the bastards to find us now.'

They returned to the car through the strengthening rain. Barney was staring out at the darkness of the ocean. Or rather the stranger was staring out, expressionless.

Halliday started the Ford and backed the length of the jetty, then spun the wheel and careered along the track, heading for the highway and Manhattan.

Thirty minutes later they crossed Brooklyn Bridge and passed through a riotously illuminated Chinatown. The rain had let up and a festival was in progress, a giant dragon undulating down Centre Street. Neons and holo-façades lit a thousand beaming faces packed onto the sidewalks.

'Drop me here, Halliday,' Kat called out.

He looked over his shoulder. 'You gonna join in the carnival?'

'Sure . . . Do I look like the partying type? I'm still trying to trace the Methuselah people, Halliday. I'll be in touch.'

She jumped from the car, and Halliday watched her as she vanished into the crowd.

Barney was quiet as they headed north. The stranger

closed his eyes, feigning sleep. Halliday wished he'd put his Barney chu back on.

He almost drove past Carnegie Hill and on to El Barrio, before remembering his new office-apartment on Lexington.

He parked the Ford in the street and indicated the building. 'What do you think, Barney?'

'Certainly gone up in the world. Business must be good.'

'As if. This is courtesy of Wellman. I had to get out of the old place. It's a long story.'

They rode the elevator to the third floor and Halliday showed Barney through the office and into the lounge. When he checked the cooler, he found a dozen bottles of Ukrainian wheat beer.

'Well, what do you know?' he called back. 'Wellman certainly did the job right.'

He carried two beers to the lounge and passed one to Barney. He sat on a lounger before the floor-to-ceiling window.

Barney stood in the middle of the room, bottle in hand.

Halliday stared at the stranger. He raised his bottle and said, 'So, you gonna tell me what happened?'

As if drawn from a reverie, Barney half-smiled. 'You'd feel better if I put the chu back on, right?'

Halliday shrugged. 'Whatever makes you feel comfortable.'

Barney sat on the sofa and stared down at his beer. He placed the deactivated chu on the cushion beside him. 'Know something, Hal? I thought that being in control of this body, reborn, human again . . .'

'Yes?'

The stranger shrugged, took a slug of beer. 'Something's missing. I have all my thoughts, my memories. As far as I know I am Barney Kluger, but something's missing.'

Halliday tipped his beer and felt the ice-cold liquid kill

his thirst. 'Look, why don't you start at the beginning? You said you were downloaded . . . but where the hell from?'

Barney stood and moved to the window. He stared out at the holo-façades that lined Lexington Avenue, stared through the reflection of the stranger in the plate glass window.

'Remember those sessions I had with the Mantoni people?'

'You said you were studying VR,' Halliday said. 'But I found the pin, after your funeral. You were in VR with a construct of Estelle.'

Barney smiled. 'That's the last thing I recall. I was in the villa with Estelle, and I never got out, back to the real world.'

Halliday shook his head. 'What happened?'

Barney's eyes focused on his reflection; Halliday saw the sudden start of surprise in his eyes, before he turned from the window and sat down on the sofa.

He took a long swallow of beer and said, 'The bastards at Mantoni recorded the contents of my head while I was in the tank. A while back, they switched me on . . . only from my point of view I'd never been switched off. I was still in VR with Estelle, but I'd lost the ability to experience emotions. I knew something was damned wrong.' He paused, regarding his beer.

He told Hal that a few days later Lew Kramer had turned up and said that Barney'd been copied, that out there in the real world the original Barney Kluger was dead.

'Of course, I didn't feel dead. I had all my memories, personality, preferences . . . Then Kramer told me they had a body waiting for me – I'd be able to function again in a real, live body.' He paused, took another swallow of beer.

'So a few days ago they downloaded me into this – but I was imprisoned in the Mantoni building. I had my own tank in the apartment and I surfed the sites . . . Back when I'd been in VR, I found the Mantoni core site, where the

284

management team met. So while I was imprisoned, I accessed the site, heard what they were planning. I had to get out, warn you.'

'Christ, Barney, no wonder they want you back so bad.'

Barney shrugged. 'I'm a security threat. They don't want competitors getting in on the act. That's why they're so paranoid about what the Methuselah Project is up to – they're scared shitless that the Methuselah people have already, or soon will, come across their secrets.'

Halliday finished his beer, saw that Barney was well down his. He fetched two more from the cooler and sat back on the sofa. 'You said you were missing something, Barney. I don't understand. You look like you've got it all. A new body, better than the old one. Christ, come back into partnership with me and we'll clean up!'

Barney smiled. Halliday was getting accustomed to the stranger's face. How long could it remain unfamiliar when his every gesture, expression and mannerism was informed by the consciousness of the man he had known so well for so many years?

'Hal,' Barney said, looking across the room at him, 'the real Barney Kluger died eighteen months ago in some back alley. The essence of him, the real Barney, ceased to exist when he died. All I am is a copy. How can I be real, when the original Barney died after I came into existence?'

Halliday lifted his beer bottle. 'That's one for the philosophers. So you might not be the original Barney Kluger, but you're the only one in existence now. Isn't that enough? I mean, you have all your memories, thoughts and feelings, and the things that make you unique to yourself.'

Barney shook his head. 'That's just it, Hal. I don't . . . I mean, I don't feel any more. It's as if when they copied the original, they could copy everything but the ability to express emotion.'

Halliday stared at the man who had been Barney Kluger. 'You want another beer, Barney?'

They talked until midnight, when Barney yawned and complained that the big drawback of being physical again was the demands of the body. Halliday showed him to the bedroom, then returned to the lounge and dimmed the lighting.

He was stretching out on the sofa, staring out at the lights of the avenue, when he remembered Casey with a sudden pang of guilt.

He'd meant to meet her tonight, go to a holo-drama, then have a meal. He considered calling her, apologising and arranging another date.

It was too late, now. And anyway, he'd sound feeble if he tried to apologise. She'd just bawl him out, and right now he could do without that.

He'd ring in the morning, make it up to her then.

He lay back and tried to sleep.

Twenty-Four

Kat Kosinski hurried along Canal Street. She passed a VR Bar, all lit up like a porn parlour. A few people were drifting in, to immerse themselves in the delights of other worlds, other times. Something in her wanted to rush across the street, start preaching about the folly of virtual reality. But another part of her was tired; she knew when she was defeated.

She called into the Jade Garden. 'Hi, Mr Xing. Chicken rolls and French fries. Take-out.'

'Hey, Kat. You quiet today.'

'I am?' She shrugged, smiled. 'Thinking about the future, Mr Xing.'

She had wondered, briefly, after Colby had spouted all that stuff about Virex having been taken over, if it'd been nothing more than a ploy on his part to get her to leave New York. She'd wondered if she should hate Colby for that, or feel gratified that he liked her enough to make up such an elaborate story. Thing was, he had never said that he loved her, never. What they had was unspoken between them . . .

And then Halliday had turned up, and was almost burned bad by the Methuselah site. She had traced the site, discovered for positive that it was the site she'd been routing the stolen information to for months.

So Colby had been telling the truth, and Kat had experienced a yawning pit of emptiness and despair inside her. She had been working for the enemy. Not only that, but Colby hadn't made up the elaborate story to lure her away from New York. Maybe he didn't love her, maybe there was nothing there but friendship. He wanted her to come to Saskatchewan not because he loved her, but because he didn't like to see her living like she was. Because he pitied her.

So what was she going to do?

Mr Xing pushed the take-out across the counter. 'And this, Kat. Take this.'

'What is it.'

'Fortune cookie, for future.'

She took the cookie, slipped it into the pocket of her leggings. 'Thanks, Mr Xing. See you later.'

She hurried through the streets. She seemed to be seeing things with a greater clarity these days, noticing the city around her, the beauty of the old architecture not plastered with holo-façades. Maybe she was seeing the place for the first time, she thought to herself, because something in her subconscious knew she was also seeing it for the last time . . . Well, maybe.

She unlocked the door of the new place she'd moved to a few days ago. It was a dive: one room with an adjacent shower unit, no kitchen. Her mattress was in one corner, the jellytank in the other, and all around the walls were her monitors and com-systems.

She stared around the room. This was all she'd had for so long, no real possessions, no comfort. For that long it'd been all she'd needed, all she'd really cared about. There was something about the intricacy of the system, and her total knowledge of it, that had empowered her, given her an identity, self-esteem. Now, all the hardware was nothing but a symbol of the futile game she'd been playing for so long.

She knew people who would give her good money for the stuff. She could sell it and clear out and head north, fast, before the bastards at Virex realised she'd shafted them. That'd be sweet.

But when she got to Saskatchewan, what then? Did Colby really want her? If not, then what the fuck would she do with herself out in the middle of nowhere?

She poured herself a bourbon, then sat cross-legged on the bed and ate her chicken rolls and fries.

All she knew was the city, New York. She'd lived here all her life, first in Brooklyn and later Manhattan, moving around various places, never still for very long. How would she adapt to a one-horse town on the prairie?

Choices, she thought. Never was any good at making choices. She had always found herself drifting into making decisions, found herself so far down a road towards a certain possibility that it seemed like too much hard work to turn back.

She finished the take-out and sat holding the bourbon in both hands, staring into the disc of golden liquid. She remembered the fortune cookie Mr Xing had given her and dug it out.

She unwrapped it, bit into the biscuit and pulled out the rolled message.

Go west for happiness, she read.

She smiled. Strange thing to find in a Chinese fortune cookie. Go west ... Saskatchewan was west of New York, wasn't it?

She was filled with a sudden heady impulse. She leapt to her feet and found her backpack. She raced around the room, digging out her old clothes and full canisters of spin. Five minutes later she had all her worldly possession stowed in the backpack.

She'd leave the pack here and go look up a few contacts who'd buy the hardware; she wouldn't get the full price, but they'd pay her fast. She could be out of here on the eight-fifteen to Montreal ...

She stood in the middle of the room and looked around. A bunch of needles glinted in the light of the fluorescent.

The two dozen viral programs she'd used over the past year and a half.

She had a idea.

Why not? she asked herself. Christ, why not?

She sat on the swivel chair and powered up her com-system for the very last time. It'd be sweet, she thought. She might not succeed, but it'd be so sweet trying. And who knew, but one of the viruses might find its way through, undetected.

The irony of it, she thought. Virex, or whoever the hell they were, burned by their very own bugs . . .

She pulled on her headphones and touched the screen. She traced the route through the cyberverse to the now redundant zone where the Methuselah Project had had their site, where Halliday had nearly got himself burned. The site was no longer there, but that didn't stop Kat. For the next two hours she worked through a thousand sub-codes, translating the program traces the Project techs had left scattered across the cyberverse like spoor. She came across a big zone, loaded with a site that was restricted, as she'd fully expected.

She worked at vracking through the defences. She had the advantage of not needing to enter the site through VR; it would be enough merely to establish contact with the site via her system.

An hour later, around four in the morning, Kat found her way through. The screen before her flooded with code which she speed-read in an attempt to make sense of where she was.

She smiled to herself. The site bore all the signatures of the Project, the bastards who'd robbed her of the past eighteen months.

There was a lot of activity on the site.

She decoded the text, wondering what the hell they were doing in there.

The site was emptying, fast. A billion bits of information

– more, Kat was unable to tell quite how much – was leaching away from the zone every few minutes. They were sending a barrage of coded signals out of America, right across the Pacific, to Japan.

She picked up the needles and inserted them with loving care into an array of ports on her touchpad. They slipped home with satisfying ease. She fingered the pad, instructing the attack to commence.

She launched the viruses together, intending to hit the site in a rapid, quick-fire blitz. One by one the viral programs would easily have been repelled; but they stood a chance of causing damage if they arrived *en masse*.

And even if nothing happened, the act of trying would be cathartic.

She watched the screen as the viruses hit home and, one after the other, were rendered harmless, fizzling into oblivion like spent fireworks.

She smiled to herself. At least the bastards knew, now, that she had seen through their duplicity.

She was about to cut the connection when the screen filled with text. She speed-read the code, translated the information. Something was coming down the line, fast. She thought it was a burn, at first. She was about to kill the system and quit when a woman's face appeared on the screen and stared out at her.

'Who the fuck,' she said, 'are you?'

The woman was pretty, Oriental, maybe Chinese. She smiled. 'I'm Kim Long, Kat. We need to talk.'

Kat pushed her swivel chair away from the screen, as if the Chinese woman posed a physical threat. 'How'd you know who I am?'

Kim Long wrinkled her nose. 'Come on, Kat. How do you think? We've been following you as you traced us through the 'verse. Very well done. You're a star, Kat.'

'You're Virex?' she said in a small voice.

291

'We prefer to call ourselves the Methuselah Project,' Kim Long said.

Kat shook her head, not quite believing that she was having this conversation. Wasn't Kim Long the name of Halliday's ex-girlfriend? Hadn't she died a week or so ago?

'Hey, I thought you were dead. Murdered, right?'

'That was part of the project—'

'Hal took it real bad, you know that?'

'How is Hal?'

Kat shrugged. 'He's . . . like, he's okay. Uses VR too much, but he's surviving.' She stopped and stared at the image of the Chinese woman. 'So . . . what do you want?'

'We want to show you where we are,' Kim Long said, smiling out at her. 'I'll give you the geographical coordinates, okay? Then, will you contact Hal Halliday and tell him that I want to see him, one last time, and say goodbye? Okay, here's where we are . . .'

Kat recorded the woman's words, shaking her head. 'You're leading us to the base of the Project?' she said.

'We're leaving now,' Kim said. 'But I know that Hal's been trying to find us, and I want to talk to him before I go.'

'What—' Kat began, leaning forward.

But Kim Long had cut the connection.

All thoughts of Saskatchewan forgotten for the moment, Kat reached for her com and got through to Halliday.

Twenty-Five

They picked Kat up on the corner of Bowery and Canal Street.

Halliday pulled into the kerb and Kat leapt into the back. 'Hiya, Barney. Halliday, how's it going?'

'Give,' Halliday said, turning in his seat and glaring at the woman. 'Information, now. Why the hell you hang up like that?'

'Back off, Halliday. You think I was gonna spill everything over the airwaves with who knows what fuckers listening in? Get real.'

Barney said, 'First things first, Kat. Where they based?'

'Nyack. Somewhere three kays north of the town.'

Halliday U-turned and headed north. 'I know it,' he said. 'I was there the other day. So how come the cops found nothing when they searched the place?'

'You know the cops,' Kat said. 'Couldn't find their ass in the john.'

'You sure about this? I mean, one hundred per cent absolutely positively certain?'

Kat rolled her eyes. 'Listen up, Halliday. There was enough e-activity going out that place to light up New York at Christmas.'

Halliday got through to the NYPD and asked for Jeff Simmons. Seconds later his big face filled the screen. 'That Hal? How's things?'

'Some information you might be interested in, Jeff. We've traced the Methuselah people.'

'No kidding? Good work. Where the hell are they?'

'You're not gonna believe this, Jeff. How about trying that big weatherboard place north of Nyack.'

Jeff peered out at him. 'This on the level, Hal?'

'According to reliable sources.'

'I'll get a team up their pronto. Don't go anywhere near the place until we've staked the house, okay?'

'See you up there, Jeff.' He cut the connection.

Halliday accelerated north on Madison. It was six in the morning and the city was coming to life. Dawn light duelled with the holo-façades, and won: the fancy front-ages wavered with shades of wan pastel in the weak sunlight, showing ghostly images of the original buildings underneath. Few vehicles were on the streets; they'd have a clear run up Interstate 87.

Halliday held fire with the question he most wanted to ask, in fear of hearing what he didn't want to hear. He'd held Kim's body in his arms in the dead woods above Nyack, and now she wanted to say farewell to him. Some kind of recorded image, he thought. Some kind of fucking lifeless construct.

Barney turned in his seat and looked at Kat. He hadn't worn the chu since yesterday evening, and Halliday was getting used to the face of the stranger.

'So how you locate the source of the site, Kat?' Barney asked.

She hung between the front seats, peering ahead. 'I'll be honest, guys. Technically, I didn't find it.'

'I thought you said—' Halliday began.

'Listen up. I was monitoring the old restricted site. You know, Halliday – the one that nearly burned you?'

'How can I forget?'

'They'd closed it down after you got in there, but there were still traces, faint links to another site they'd estab-lished since. I'd accessed it, and then I got a big incoming. Christ, I thought it was some kinda burn at first. Before I could disengage, there was this Chinese woman on the screen, staring out at me.'

Halliday gripped the wheel, staring at the road. They were leaving Manhattan, the sun rising through the smog to their right.

Why would Kim's construct contact Kat? Why, he wondered, would she want to say goodbye to him?

'What she say?' Barney asked.

She shrugged thin shoulders. 'She simply gave me the coordinates of the US base of the Methuselah Project.'

'Just like that?' Halliday said. 'I mean, it doesn't make sense. They've been trying to avoid us for weeks.'

'Yeah, but according to her things are different now. They've come to the end of whatever they're doing, and they're outta there.'

Halliday shook his head. 'She didn't tell you what it was they were doing?'

'Uh-uh. She wouldn't say.'

He nodded. Before long, maybe, when they arrived at the weatherboard place and Jeff's men made sure it was safe, they might find out what the hell was going on.

'Before she signed off, Halliday,' Kat said, 'Kim told me to tell you that she wanted to say goodbye. She said tell Hal that I want to see him.'

He felt his palms break into a hot sweat. He wondered who might have programmed the construct to say goodbye. It was a joke too sick to contemplate.

They passed the turn-off to the Cyber-Tech headquarters over at Archville. Eighteen months ago he had headed this way, for a showdown with the rogue AI, a shoot-out more bloody and traumatic than he'd feared.

The showdown this time, at least, would be far from bloody. No shoot-outs, he promised himself.

They passed over the Tappan Zee bridge, the wide Hudson a muscled, muddy brown beneath them. The far bank of the river was stippled with an array of dead tree trunks. He made out, pale in the morning light, the artificial holo-forests south of Nyack. It seemed a long time since he had last been this way, not just a week or so but a lifetime ago.

He turned the Ford right and followed the coast road north through Nyack, heading towards the Hook Mountain State Park. They passed through the desolation of the dead forest, as devoid of life as a war-zone.

Kat shivered. 'This place gives me the creeps, Halliday.'

'Perfect location for a hideaway. Who'd think of coming out here for a quiet Sunday afternoon picnic?'

A kilometre from the turn-off to the weatherboard house, they were stopped by a police road-block. A state trooper stood beside a low-level laser-cordon. Halliday rolled down the window and showed his ID.

The trooper waved them through and they headed up the deserted road. In the distance to the right, through the denuded masts of a hundred pines and firs, he caught sight of the white-painted house.

They passed a line of police cars and a couple of armoured vans. Kat seemed to shrink in her seat. 'Christ, all these cops give me the jeebies.'

Halliday slowed and turned down the narrow, rutted track.

Barney looked at Kat. 'Hey, you're working with the cops now. I'll be surprised if they don't give you a commendation.'

'Can't wait,' she muttered.

A cordon of lasers lanced through the forest, surrounding the house in a vast purple hexagon like a computer graphic. The cordon was patrolled by armed cops at regular intervals. A dozen cars, squad vehicles and unmarked, jammed the track. A personnel carrier, its rear doors open wide, stood beside the open gate of the perimeter fence.

Halliday saw Jeff Simmons and three other plainclothes

cops standing just inside the gate, wired up with head-phones and mics. They were staring up at the weatherboard house, talking among themselves.

He braked the Ford and accompanied by Barney and Kat crossed to Jeff and the others.

The lieutenant nodded at Halliday. 'We've a team going through the place, Hal.'

'Found anything?'

'They checked the ground floor and upper floors first. Nothing. Just like the other day.'

'And the basement?'

'Like a World War Three bunker down there, Hal. No wonder we never found anything the other week. Vault doors a metre thick. We went in with cavity detection equipment, found the chamber and blasted the doors open.'

'No resistance?'

'They've been in there ten minutes now and not a thing.'

'What've they found?'

'Lots of VR equipment, com-systems . . . you name it, it's down there.'

'But nobody at home?'

Jeff shook his head. 'Place is empty. They're going though it now for booby traps. Should be clear in ten, fifteen minutes.'

Halliday turned at the sound of a car engine approaching along the track. He experienced a sudden sensation of *déjà vu* as he watched a cream-coloured Mercedes halt beside the personnel carrier.

A burly bodyguard jumped from the passenger seat and opened a back door, and a thin figure dressed in an impeccable grey suit stepped out and approached, leaning on a walking stick.

Halliday looked at Barney. 'Tell me this is the real world,' he whispered.

Wellman raised his stick in greeting. 'Halliday, good to see you.'

'Christ, Wellman. You're the last person I was expecting to see up here.'

'My people have been in touch with Simmons for the past week. As soon as you contacted him, he informed my staff.' Wellman's face was thin, marked with lines that had not been there at their last physical meeting, eighteen months ago. But he looked fitter than the construct Halliday had encountered in VR yesterday.

'Seems like you've done it again, Halliday.'

He shook his head. 'Nothing to do with me. Meet my technical assistant, Kat.'

The thin, black-clad woman stared at Wellman. 'You knew my brother, Joe,' she said. 'He worked for you.' And died for you, too . . . Halliday saw the unspoken accusation in the woman's eyes.

'He was a brilliant mind, Kat. We were very close.'

Kat opened her mouth to say something, a look of hatred in her eyes.

To defuse a potential scene, Halliday took Wellman by the elbow and assisted him towards the gate. 'There's a team going through the place. They've found a bunker full of VR stuff and com-systems . . .' He told the executive what Kat had discovered that morning.

He hesitated. 'It's been a long time, Wellman. It's good to see you in the flesh at last.'

'Eighteen months? A lot has happened.' Wellman glanced at him. 'You look ill, Halliday. Cut down on the VR, okay?'

'I think you told me that once before.' Halliday hesitated, wanting to ask Wellman something but unable to find the right words. 'You're taking a risk,' he said at last. 'I mean, venturing out . . . Wouldn't you be better off in VR?'

'Better off? VR's all very well, Halliday, but it isn't the real world, where things happen, things that matter.' He laughed. 'But don't quote me on that.'

He paused, then went on, 'But things are changing, Halliday. Very soon, believe me, it will be the place where things will happen that matter.'

'You mean,' he glanced over at the stranger who was Barney, 'recorded identities, or whatever they're called? Copied personalities actually living in the Net?'

Wellman gave him a quick glance. 'So you know,' he said. 'I never had you down as the technical type, Halliday. Yes, that will certainly change things. The world will never be the same again.'

Halliday said, 'Have you thought about . . . ?'

'What?' Wellman sounded surprised. 'Recording myself, my identity?' He waved. 'Of course, the board think it would be a good idea, to ensure that I was still around to steer the ship, as it were.'

'But you're not so sure?'

'What would the recording be, Halliday? It wouldn't be *me*, would it? It would be a copy, a lifeless copy. The real me would be dead and gone . . .' He smiled. 'No, Halliday. I know when to give in and call it a day.'

Halliday looked into the face of the dying executive and saw not the slightest trace of sadness or self-pity. He wanted to say something, to communicate to Wellman that he was sorry . . . but how could he possibly do that when the man himself would admit to no such emotion on his own behalf?

Jeff Simmons moved past them, walking into the grounds of the house and then coming to a halt. He spoke into his microphone. 'Check. I'm sending someone in.'

He turned and gestured. 'Get Michaels in there now!' he called.

Seconds later a police paramedic raced past Halliday. He was met outside the house by an armed marksman who escorted him in through the front entrance.

Despite himself, Halliday felt his stomach turn.

Jeff approached Halliday and Wellman. 'They've found someone down there.'

Wellman said, 'Injured?'

'In need of medical assistance,' Jeff said.

'Male or female?' Halliday asked.

Jeff shook his head. 'That's as much as I know.'

Barney and Kat joined them. 'What's happening in there?' Barney asked.

Halliday reported the situation. He was aware of a tension building within him. He told himself that he was a fool to hope that there was anything else in the house besides a holographic simulation of a woman who wished to say goodbye.

Jeff moved away, touching his ear-phone and listening intently. He spoke into his mic, then turned to the others. 'That's it. The place is clear. We can go in.'

He led the way up the drive towards the open front door. Halliday followed, a knot of apprehension in his stomach. He was hardly aware of the others behind him. He watched Jeff's broad back and wondered what the hell they might find in the basement chamber.

Armed guards stood outside every doorway in the house, their faces expressionless yet watchful. Halliday followed Jeff along a corridor. His first impression, a week ago, that this had been some kind of clinic or nursing home, seemed pretty much borne out by the rooms he glimpsed through open doors: drab institutional paintwork, serviceable linoleum floors, armchairs and settees solid and functional rather than comfortable.

A short staircase led down to what seemed to be a cellar. When Halliday reached the bottom he found himself in a dank, whitewashed space perhaps the size of a small washroom. Before him, however, the entire facing wall was missing. In its place, a colossal vault-like door stood ajar. The adenoid-pinching reek of explosives filled the air.

He passed though the opening, into the bright chamber beyond, then stopped and stared about him.

Twenty jellytanks were spaced across the white-tiled floor, and banks of computers lined the walls. Positioned before monitors and screens, a dozen empty swivel chairs gave the impression of recent abandonment.

Kat edged past him, whistling to herself. She moved from the nearest tank to the bank of controls, her eyes wide like a kid in a toy store on Christmas Eve.

'Some place,' she said. 'Would you look at those tanks, Hal! A few million dollars' worth of com-systems, here.'

A knot of armed cops stood at the far end of the room, surrounding the medic. He was attending to the figure of a man lying prone on a black-padded couch.

Halliday made his way down the aisle between the jellytanks. The figure on the couch was unmoving, as if dead, but his eyes were open and staring blindly at the ceiling.

It was the silver-haired man they had known as Charles. A mass of electrodes snaked from his head, giving him the aspect of some cyber-age Medusa.

'He's technically brain dead,' the medic reported to Jeff. 'There's no cortical or sub-cortical activity. He's being kept alive by the functioning of his autonomic nervous system, no more. I'd have to examine him more thoroughly, but he seems to be in the initial stages of a persistent vegetative coma.'

'What happened to him?' Jeff asked.

The medic shook his head. 'That's impossible to say as yet, sir.'

Halliday asked, 'Is he wearing a chu?'

The medic shook his head. 'No, sir.'

Halliday nodded. Had Charles known that he would soon die like this, and so had dismissed the need of a disguise?

He stared at the comatose figure on the couch. He was reminded of Anastasia Dah. Charles looked as lifeless as had

301

Dah, immediately before he had put the gun to her forehead and pulled the trigger.

So what the hell, he asked himself, was going on?

He stared around the room, overcome with a subtle sense of disappointment. What had he hoped for, a miraculously resurrected Kim, even a copy of her, restored not to any old body as Barney had been, but to her own slim, child-like form?

He felt a soft touch on his upper arm. It was Barney. He was pointing across the room, towards a bank of com-screens.

One of the screens was lit, and with a heart-wrenching shock of recognition Halliday made out the head-and-shoulders image of Kim Long.

He stood immobile for long seconds, unable to bring himself to move. His mouth ran dry and he felt a painful constriction in his throat.

So this was it, then: the final farewell. A taped goodbye from the woman he thought he had once loved.

Slowly, he approached the screen. He paused, his fingers resting on the back of a swivel chair, and stared at the image of the beautiful woman before him.

He had assumed that the image was a still, so little movement was there on the screen as he approached, but now he saw that the picture was moving; that Kim was staring out at him, blinking, a slight smile playing on her lips.

He stared at the wide-apart eyes, the snub nose, the high fringe of jet-black hair . . . and the sight of her was almost too much. He slumped into the swivel chair and stared up at the iconic image of Kim Long.

'Hal,' she said, her voice a soft breath as he always recalled it. 'It's good to see you, Hal.'

He wanted to shout that she was lying on two counts. Neither could she see him, nor would she be pleased to do so . . . She had walked out on him eighteen months ago,

302

had never sought him out after that; it had always been he who had attempted reconciliation.

'What's going on, Kim?' he asked wearily, sick with himself for playing the game with this empty, meaningless computer-generated image.

'First of all I want to apologise, Hal. When Charles threatened you . . . I want to say that many of us were opposed to the threats. We doubted that your investigations would harm the Project. But Charles argued that the threat was merely that, just a threat that would persuade you to drop the case.'

'And I suppose that you'll apologise for what Tallak tried to do to me? He tried to carry out Charles' threat and kill me, Kim.'

'We were appalled. You can't imagine my horror. Tallak . . . Stevens – he deserved to die for what he tried to do.'

Halliday gestured, as if to wipe away what had happened on that day. He looked at Kim, and saw again the dead woman in the shallow grave.

'Just over a week ago,' he began, his voice almost breaking, 'I found you buried . . . buried in the forest. And now this . . .'

'I'm so sorry, Hal. I want to explain.'

'If you could, that'd be great. I'd really appreciate that. But I don't want an explanation from some recorded construct—'

'I'm not a construct, Hal.'

He stared at her, and thought he understood, then. Before her death, before Charles had assassinated her as he had so callously killed Dah before her, she had had her personality copied, recorded, in the mistaken belief that it would grant her an immortal e-existence. Was that what the Methuselah Project was all about?

Was Kim an e-identity now, living a virtual life in the cyberverse?

'I know what you are, Kim—' he said, and wished that he

303

could stop calling this thing before him by the name of the once living woman. 'I know what you are, and no explanation will be good enough.'

'Hal, please listen,' she said, leaning forward and looking down on him from the screen. 'I am not dead.'

He laughed, almost losing it. He wanted to stand and throw the chair at the screen, to shatter the mocking image of the woman he had once held in his arms.

'I found your body in the woods!' he said. 'Don't tell me you're not dead, for Chrissake!'

'Hal,' she went on, looking pained, 'I'm not dead, and I'm not a construct, and I'm not merely an e-copy, a recording of my identity and memories and personality. I'm more than that.'

He shook his head, not wanting to listen to this zombie's futile rationalisations, the words it used to try to convince itself of its own humanity.

'Of course you would say that,' he said. 'You seem alive and human to yourself. You *think* you're Kim Long. What else could you think? You have her memories and thoughts, her encoded personality. But all you are is a clever copy.'

She was silent, staring at him, and the sudden pause in the dialogue brought Halliday up short. He was reminded of the few occasions on which they had argued, how there always came a point when she would realise the futility of words. Then she would either throw something at him, attack him with her child's balled fists, or point out with sweet and simple logic that he was wrong.

'Hal, you saw Charles shoot Anastasia,' she began.

'I don't see—'

'Three days earlier he shot me, and then Suzie Charlesworth.'

'I don't want to hear this.'

'Hal, we were all part of the Methuselah Project, we three and Charles and perhaps a hundred other citizens. I was

Charles' lover. I'm sorry to hurt you like this, Hal, but I knew when I met him that I had found someone I'd always been looking for. A soul-mate—'

He turned away, sickened.

'Anastasia was his former lover. Charles was a scientist specialising in neuro-science. His dream was to map the human brain, to be able to record the mind, to eventually make a copy of an individual's very personality.'

'And he succeeded, and copied you, and then killed you ... What happened?' he said, flinging a gesture back towards the comatose figure of Charles. 'Did the process go wrong when he used it on himself?' He was aware that he was not alone; Barney stood behind him, and Kat, and next to her was Wellman. They were staring at the image of Kim Long on the screen, as if mesmerised.

She ignored his outburst. 'He realised, of course, that to copy the contents of the brain was one thing, but actually to succeed in capturing the subject's very self, the essence that made one human, was quite another. So he funded the Methuselah Project, and recruited Suzie Charlesworth and two or three other leading scientists. A month ago their work came to fruition. The team led by Suzie succeeded in copying not only the seat of human consciousness, the brain, but along with it the essence of our very humanity, the soul.'

He stared at her. He opened his mouth to object, but no words came.

Wellman stepped forward, a hand on Halliday's shoulder. 'You've succeeded in uploading the human soul?'

'What do you think has happened to Charles, Hal?' Kim said. 'And you saw Anastasia – and the same happened to myself and all the other members of the Project. We had our identities copied and uploaded, but when, for want of a better word, our "souls" were recorded and uploaded, the essence of our selves, what made us human, departed from our bodies and left what you can see across the room.

Charles, like the rest of us, is no longer alive in the accepted sense. He is here, with us.'

At last Halliday found his voice. 'Where is "here"?' he asked.

She smiled. 'Last night we moved to a secure site in Japan, preparatory to the launch of the Mercury Probe. At midday we leave for Mercury, Hal. There we will set up a beachhead, and von Neumann machines will manufacture other ships, and in time – how long we do not know, but we have all the time in the universe – in time we will head for the stars.'

Wellman stepped forward and said, 'You will leave . . . taking with you the secret of immortality?'

Kim laughed, a pretty laugh Halliday knew so well. 'How in all conscience could we do that?' she said. 'Why do you think I am talking to you now? As well as saying farewell to you, Hal, I also want to give you the results of Suzie Charlesworth's research. You can do with them as you will, give them away, sell them to the highest bidder. I will relay them to your com before the launch. It is my gift to you, Hal . . . and what greater gift can anyone give to a person they once loved?'

The screen blanked suddenly, and Halliday was staring up in disbelief at his own reflection.

He turned, and on the face of Wellman he saw the look of a man within reach of salvation.

Halliday reached out and took Barney's arm.

'Told you,' Barney said, quietly, his stranger's face staring down at him. 'I told you there was something missing.'

Halliday left the chamber. Slowly he climbed from the basement and stepped from the house. He stood and stared through the dead woods towards the smogged blur of Manhattan on the horizon.

He heard Kim's words again, and tried to consider the implications of what she had told him.

306

He knew only that the world had changed immeasurably, now, and he was gripped by a terrible fear, and at the same time a strange and undeniable exultation.

Twenty-Six

He heard the hiss of an aerosol spray, followed by a relieved inhalation.

Kat leaned between the front seats. 'Hey, Halliday, Barney – guess what?'

Halliday glanced at her. 'Go on.'

'There's this place in Saskatchewan, small town middle of bug-fuck-nowhere.'

Barney smiled. 'What about it, Kat?'

When she spoke, her voice held a note of awe. 'It's declared itself VR-free, is what. Can you imagine that? A whole town without a single fucking VR Bar or jellytank?'

'Bizarre,' Halliday said.

'And guess what?' Kat went on. 'I'm gonna pack up and head off there, just as soon as I can. I'm outta here, man. Won't see me for dust . . .'

Halliday hesitated, then said, 'You should've taken the money Wellman offered you, Kat.'

She snorted. 'What? Take money from the enemy? Fuck that, Halliday.'

He pulled into the kerb on the corner of Canal Street and Bowery.

'Call by before you head off, okay?' he told her.

'I'll do that, Halliday. See you around, Barney.'

She jumped from the car and strode along the busy sidewalk with the jerky, uncoordinated strides of a manic marionette.

Halliday drove around the block and headed uptown.

'Drop me off at Olga's, Hal,' Barney said.

'A Ukrainian and a ham on rye?' Halliday asked.

'Sounds good to me. You coming in?'

He thought about it, finally shook his head. 'I should've seen Casey last night. I'll call around now, apologise.'

'Hey . . .' Barney looked at him. 'You two . . . ?'

Halliday concentrated on the empty road. He shrugged. 'I dunno . . . I mean, she's a great kid. We get on fine. I get the impression she wants to, but . . .'

Barney shook his head. 'Then what the hell's stopping you, Hal? Go for it. Listen, you need someone. You know how you were before Kim came along – she saved you, Hal. Way you're looking now, you need saving again.'

Halliday gripped the apex of the wheel, shrugged again. He drove in silence, contemplating Barney's words.

Five minutes later they drew up outside Olga's bar. He turned to Barney. 'What you said back there, in the chamber . . .'

Barney looked at him. The stranger's eyes were becoming familiar . . . if not exactly the windows to his soul, then the windows to whatever made this new Barney what he was. 'I meant what I said, Hal. I've always felt there was something missing. What Kim said back there explains it all.'

'You know what the Barney I knew would've said about the soul?'

Barney smiled. 'Go on.'

'He'd've said that it doesn't matter what we call it. What matters are our memories, our identities. Listen . . . how the hell do Kim and Charlesworth and all the others know that they've succeeded in recording the soul? Perhaps they've just come up with a better way of recording the personality, so that it leaves the original completely wiped?'

'So what does that make me, Hal? An incomplete recording?'

Halliday paused. 'It makes you whatever you think you are, Barney. You've got your thoughts, memories, personality. You've got a better body than the one you had. Look

. . . come back and work with me again, okay? It'll be just like old times.'

Barney smiled. 'I'll think about that over a couple of beers, Hal. I really will.'

Halliday watched the stranger who was Barney Kluger climb from the car and disappear down the steps to Olga's. He pulled from the kerb and drove around the block to Casey's apartment, then braked and sat behind the wheel, lost in thought.

Perhaps emotions, feelings, he thought, can be learned. Christ, he knew they could . . .

Ten minutes later, having almost driven away twice, he climbed from the car and crossed the sidewalk. He took the steps to the first floor slowly, wondering at the reception he could expect from the kid.

He knocked on the door and waited. It was eleven o'clock, a few hours before she was due to begin the afternoon shift at the diner. He wondered if she'd left early.

Then a small voice said, 'Who is it?'

'Casey,' Halliday said. 'It's me, Hal. I need to—'

'Go away.'

As simple as that. He felt something tighten within him, a familiar pity for himself alongside a pity for Casey and the hurt he'd caused her.

'Casey, we need to talk. I'm sorry about yesterday. Something came up with the Charlesworth case. I couldn't make it—'

'You could've at least've called!' she cried.

He felt a stab of hope: at least she had replied. She was giving him the chance to explain himself, extend the dialogue.

'I know, and I'm sorry. You wouldn't believe how crazy it's been.'

Suddenly, without warning, she snatched the door open and stood there, staring at him. She seemed even tinier

310

than he recalled. She wore shorts and a misshapen T-shirt, and her eyes were swollen and sore from crying.

She turned and retreated to a couch, where she curled herself up and snatched a cushion, crushing it against her chest and staring at him.

He walked into the room and drew up a chair.

He sat in silence, staring down at his hands. Christ, but now that the time had come to say something, all thoughts had fled. He knew what he felt, but the words required to articulate these thoughts were impossible to find.

Finally, as if exasperated by his silence, Casey stood up and flung the cushion on the floor. She strode across the room, turned at the window and stared at him. 'God, Hal, are you so totally blind?'

He looked up. 'What?'

She was slowly shaking her head, tears tracking down her cheeks. 'Jesus, isn't it obvious? Look, there I was . . . I had nothing, and you took me in, gave me a room, shelter. And we got on great . . . And all the time I'm thinking, why's he doing this? Does he think I'll be an easy lay? Is that what he wants?'

She stopped, twisting her fingers, unable to bring herself to meet his eyes.

He began to protest, but she went on, 'But it wasn't. You did it 'cos you were a good person, because you cared. And anyway, then I met Ben . . . That was great, but you know something, Hal? You know, all the time I was with Ben, I was thinking, I wish I was with Hal, I wish things could be different and I was more his age.'

She leaned against the wall and pushed at the tears on her cheeks with her fingertips. 'And then Ben walked out, and I got back in touch with you again, and I thought, I don't know . . . maybe now it'll happen. But you acted like a friend, nothing more. And I wanted more, Hal. Are you so totally fucking blind that you can't see that, or don't you really like me? Is that it? Do you feel sorry for me, this ugly, ignorant little street kid—'

'You aren't ugly,' he said. 'Casey—'

She stared at him, defiant. 'What?'

It surprised him, then, what he said next. He hadn't planned it, and yet it seemed so right.

'I want to show you something.'

Her eyes narrowed. 'Show me what?'

'It's . . . It's hard to explain. Come with me and I'll show you, okay?'

'Where? Where we going? What d'you want to show me?'

'We're going to a VR Bar. I want to show you a site I spent a lot of time at.'

'In VR? I don't see . . .'

'It'll tell you a lot about me,' he told her. 'More than I can say with words, okay?'

She regarded him slantwise, almost suspicious. 'It's not a sex-site, is it?'

He laughed. 'Christ, no. It's a nature site. It's beautiful. But there's something there . . . I want you to come with me, please.'

He stared at her, and something in the intensity of his regard made her relent.

'Okay,' she said quietly, looking around the floor for her sneakers.

He watched her pull them on, his heart pounding. Then she turned away from him, pulled off her T-shirt and quickly drew a new one over her head.

They walked down to the busy summer street and he drove two blocks north to 116th Street. He was aware that he might be making a big mistake, but knew also that he had to go through with it.

He braked outside Thai Joe's VR Bar and climbed out. Casey stood beside him, timorous, staring up at the glitzy façade.

Thai Joe waddled up to them: with his loud Hawaiian shirt and sunglasses he looked like a Sumo wrestler on vacation.

'Hey, Hal! Long time no see! How you these days, friend? Where you been?'

'Out and about, Joe. How's trade?'

'Trade? Trade's bad, Hal. Everybody these days, they have own tank. Bad for business. You here on duty, Hal?'

'Pleasure, Joe'

Thai Joe glanced at Casey and winked. 'Sure, pleasure, Hal! Joe do you good deal. Discount, okay?'

'Sounds good to me.'

Thai Joe laughed and slapped him on the back.

Halliday took Casey's hand and passed through the neon-bordered portal into the VR lounge. He showed her into a booth and gave her the code to the Virginia site.

She touched his arm as he was about to step from the booth. 'There're two tanks in here, Hal,' she said, staring at him as if this were a test.

He nodded, closed the door and moved to the second tank. As he undressed and stepped into the suspension gel, he thought that this might be one of the very last times he used VR in life. After all, he told himself, maybe he would have an eternity in virtual-nirvana, once he was dead.

He watched Casey step naked into the tank, something expanding in his chest at the site of her skinny white body.

He lay back and awaited the transition.

Seconds later he was standing in the pristine pine forest of the Virginia site.

He was assailed by the resinous scent of the trees, the sight of the serried pines ascending the rise. The sun shone in a brilliant blue sky, and a clean warm breeze lapped at his face.

He looked around, and Casey was beside him. She gazed about her, eyes wide in wonder.

He contrasted the real Casey with the version he had

constructed. Physically, the construct was prettier, fuller of figure . . . but knowing that the Casey in VR was nothing but a construct had reduced his relationship with her, had made her nothing more than a plaything, a doll.

He had gained nothing from creating her simulation other than the transitory illusion of companionship, and the knowledge of his weakness.

'This is . . . it's so beautiful, Hal. I never realised that VR could be so beautiful.' She laughed at him. 'It's even better than the Africa site.'

He indicated the track that climbed to the ridge path through the trees. They walked. Something stopped him from reaching out and taking her hand.

'Are we all alone?' she asked. 'Where're all the other people?'

'I pay a premium to have this site more or less to myself. Sometimes other people come here, but it's a big place, plenty of room for everybody.'

'And you came here alone all the time?'

He hesitated. 'Most of the time. Sometimes I came with constructs, simulated people. But most of the time I wanted to be alone.' Which was true enough, in the early days . . .

She left the path, high-stepped through long grass, and touched the bark of a pine tree. She looked back at him. 'You know something, Hal? I've never ever felt a tree in the real world. In fact, I don't think I've ever seen a real tree.'

He watched her fingers trace the furrows of the trunk, a smile like he'd never seen before playing across her face.

She rejoined him and they climbed until they emerged on the ridge path. Casey gasped as they stood side by side and stared out across the burnished silver-blue expanse of the ocean.

'Years ago,' he said, 'all the world was like this. Natural, unspoilt. There were forests covering most of the land, full of animals, birds.'

'And no people?'

314

'There was a time when there were no people, yes.'

She whistled. 'I can't imagine a land with no people,' she said. 'I'm so used to seeing millions of people every day.'

Everyone, he thought, living identical lives.

But what the Methuselah Project had discovered would change all that, he knew. He looked around the natural beauty of the site and imagined a time in the future when he might live here, or some place like it, in a community of like-minded individuals, content with the knowledge that he was free, with no physical body to atrophy and deteriorate in the real world.

What a dream that was, he thought.

He indicated the path that wound down to the bay.

As they began the descent, she glanced at him. 'You said you wanted to show me something, Hal.'

'Down here.'

'What is it?'

'I can't explain. I want you to see it, make up your own mind.' He wondered then, fleetingly, if something in his subconscious had made him bring Casey here so that she would be repelled by what he had to show her.

He wondered if that self-hating part of himself wanted nothing more than to frighten her away for good.

He told himself that he had brought her here so that he might explain to her something about him that even he did not truly understand.

'Hey, Hal,' Casey said as they stepped out onto the pebble beach. 'Look, there's a camp. Someone's already here.'

'Shall we go and say hi?'

They walked towards the red blister of the tent beneath the fir trees. He felt a curious hollowness within his chest.

They halted thirty metres from the tent as someone emerged. The girl was dressed in blue jeans and a red and black checked shirt. She busied herself at a camping stove, then looked up and waved.

315

He wondered how he had ever been satisfied with this make-believe doll.

Casey stared. She walked forwards, her pace retarded with a kind of dawning disbelief. Halliday followed, heart racing.

'Hiya, there, you two,' the construct said. 'How about some breakfast?'

She knelt and turned on the stove.

The sight of the two Caseys, the construct and the real girl, was like viewing two versions of reality. The first was the reality of holo-dramas, where physical perfection was paramount, where feelings were subjugated to the primacy of image. The second reality was that of the real world, where imperfection was a part of everyday life, where the onus was on one's ability to deal with the sometimes impossible permutations of feeling and emotion – an ability which was, after all, the measure of one's ultimate humanity.

Casey turned to him, her expression shocked. 'I don't believe it,' she said.

'I had to show you.'

'How could you? How could you do this? You were using me!'

'Casey, I was lonely. I needed companionship.'

'Companionship? And everything else *she* could give you!' She flung an arm towards the construct. 'Look at her! She might have my face, but look at that body!'

'Casey, I didn't . . . It wasn't like that. There was nothing like that between us. I needed friendship. We talked, that's all.'

'You needed friendship? You talked? But you could've talked to me, Hal!'

He merely shook his head, words beyond him.

She was silent, staring at him.

'I'll leave you with her,' he said at last. 'Ask her about . . . about our time together.'

And before she could demur or protest, he turned and

walked along the beach, his heart hammering, palms sweating like a gauche adolescent.

He found a rock beside the waves and sat down, staring out to sea.

When he chanced a look back, Casey and the construct were sitting beside the tent, cross-legged, talking and gesturing like eerie mirror images.

He picked up a flat stone and skimmed it across the surface of the water. It bounced five, six times – a personal record – then sank.

What if she did not accept what the construct told her? What if she wanted nothing more to do with him, after this? He knew, if this happened, that a part of him would be secretly satisfied, would be content to return to the isolated, insulated and safe regime of old . . . but that part of him, he knew, would be the part least human and most constricted by the easy options of self-pity and self-hatred.

He heard the sound of pebbles grinding behind him. He stood suddenly and turned.

Casey was staring at him. 'She said that you were just friends,' she murmured. 'You walked and talked. She liked you, you know? She said you were a good person.'

He almost said then that the other Casey was nothing but a computer-generated construct, but stopped himself.

'Why did you bring me here, Hal?'

He hesitated, his mouth dry. At last he found the words. 'I . . . I had to show you what you meant to me, Casey.'

He stopped, gathered his thoughts, then went on. 'After Kim left and Barney died, I constructed her. You were the only person I was close to . . . but you had your own life with Ben. What could I do?'

'But for the past few weeks I've been alone. You could have—'

'I couldn't. I wish I had. I don't know what stopped me. The fear of losing you, of you walking out like Kim. Sometimes I told myself that I was happiest being alone,

317

with no emotions to sort out, no one's feelings to consider but my own.'

'And now?'

'Now . . .' he began. He stared at her. She was watching him closely, wonderingly.

Now, if he was to grow as a human being, if he was to turn his back on the facile dream promised by this site and others like it, he would have to learn to explore the extent of his flawed humanity, and the humanity of others, too.

He reached out and drew her to him. 'I want to do this in the real world,' he said.

And, to his relief, she did not protest as he held her.

He gazed out over the bay, and in the distance, high in the clear blue sky, the graceful shape of an eagle soared towards the horizon.

Epilogue

Halliday stood by the floor-to-ceiling window of his new apartment and stared out at the sparse traffic on Lexington Avenue. It was another hot day in New York City, and bright – only the low cloud cover kept out the sunlight.

'And now we see the first of the auto-probes venturing from the ship and traversing the hostile, sun-washed plains of Mercury . . .'

Halliday turned and stared at the wallscreen at the far end of the room. The screen showed a craggy, desolate landscape, silver-grey beneath the glare of the sun, contrasting with the utter blackness that began at the horizon.

The remote camera showed the bulky shape of the Mercury Project mother ship in the foreground, and the smaller, trilobite form of an auto-probe scuttling across the surface of the planet.

And to think that, somewhere within the memory banks of the mother ship, Kim and hundreds like her, reduced to mere bytes of information, and yet at the same time something much more, were stored in some virtual realm, before their *en masse* migration to the stars . . .

He had watched the launch ten days ago with Casey curled on the sofa beside him. She had been curious at first why the event had fascinated him, until he had explained the significance of the launch.

That day, two hours before the take-off of the Mercury probe, his desk-com had flared and the serene face of Kim Long had smiled out at him.

'You ready for the download, Hal? I've secured the link.

Copy this information to file, and guard it with your life, okay?'

'I'll do that.'

'You decided who you'll sell it to, Hal?'

He had smiled. 'Wellman has made me an offer I can't refuse.'

'Here goes, Hal. Goodbye.'

He had opened his mouth to say something, to ask her if some day they might meet again . . . But the image of her face had vanished then, to be replaced by a screenful of meaningless text. One hour later the download had finished, and Halliday got through to Wellman with the news.

Now he watched the auto-probe scuttling over the aluminium-burnished bedrock of the planet Mercury, and considered the future.

Barney had showed himself only once over the past week. He had turned up at the apartment drunk and incoherent. He'd slept the night on the sofa, Halliday remaining with him until the early hours, attempting to come to some understanding of what his friend was going through.

But in the morning, Barney had vanished.

Casey appeared in the doorway to the bedroom, all tousle-haired and sleepy-eyed, and dressed in a long T-shirt. She yawned and tottered across to him, robot-fashion, and hung her arms around his neck.

'Mornin', Hal.'

He hugged her to him, reliving the night they'd spent.

'You still watching the probe?' She yawned again. 'Don't you ever get tired of it? I mean, the pictures aren't even very clear.'

'It's what the pictures mean that's so fascinating, Casey.'

She shrugged, smiled. 'Guess so. I'm taking a shower. You had breakfast?'

'Not yet.'

'Good. We'll have something later, okay?'

He kissed her and watched her run back to the bedroom, knowing that, just one week ago, he would have found it hard to believe the degree of affection he would feel towards the scrawny street kid made good.

He was still daydreaming, five minutes later, when his com chimed.

The small screen remained blank. 'Yes?'

'It's me – Barney. I've been lying low for a while, Hal. You at the apartment? I need to talk.'

'Sure. Great. Come on up.'

Barney cut the connection. A minute later the door opened and he walked in.

It *was* Barney, Halliday told himself. He might not be wearing the Barney chu, or physically look much like his old partner, but the things that made him Barney Kluger were still there – the thoughts and memories, behaviour and mannerisms.

All that was absent was the soul – whatever the hell that was.

He looked rough, as if he'd spent the past week drinking hard and sleeping rough. His shaven head had grown a covering of dark stubble, matching his scrubby beard.

'Hal, good to see you, buddy.'

'Sit down. Can I get you something?'

'Could kill a coffee. You got Colombian roast?'

'What else?'

Halliday fixed two cups and sat on the armchair across from Barney. 'It's good to see you again. I've been worried.'

Barney laughed, holding the cup in both hands before his mouth and blowing. 'Worried? I can handle myself.'

Halliday shrugged. 'Even so . . . Look, you decided what you gonna do yet?'

It was a while before Barney replied. He eyed his coffee for a long time, then looked up. 'I've been thinking about what you said the other day, outside Olga's.'

'And?'

He shrugged. 'You know what I've always despised in people, Hal?' Before Halliday could reply, he went on, 'I always hated self-pitying bastards who bewailed their fate and did nothing to alter things.' He shook his head. 'The past five days, that's been me. So something's missing? So what? I might not be complete, might not have a soul, whatever that might be . . . But what I have got are my memories, even if they're really another Barney Kluger's memories. They're all I have. I remember working with you, all the cases we took on.'

He paused there, and Halliday wondered whether he should say something. Before he could find the right words, Barney continued.

'Back when I was imprisoned in the Mantoni HQ and I found out what they planned for you . . . You know, I asked myself why I was trying to get out to warn you. I mean, I must've felt something, right? I could tell between right and wrong, between what was fair and what was not . . .' He shrugged. 'I had to do something.'

'I appreciate that, Barney,' Halliday murmured.

Barney regarded his cup. 'What I'm trying to say is, maybe feelings can be learned. That was a start, back there in the Mantoni HQ. And over the past few days, I've been thinking. What matters to me is what I have in here – the memories of the past. What happened between us. For some reason they're important. They're what matter.'

Halliday nodded. He let the silence stretch, then said, 'So . . . what've you decided?'

Barney looked up. 'What you said the other day, about joining you again, starting over. You're right, we'd make a good team.'

Halliday nodded. 'So let's do that. Hey, how about another coffee?'

Five minutes later Casey breezed in from the bedroom, covered in nothing but a towel knotted beneath her right armpit. 'Oh, you gotta guest, Hal. Aren't you going to introduce us?'

'Sure.' He smiled. 'Ah, Casey, this is Barney. Barney, Casey.'

'Good to meet you, Barney. Hey, I knew a Barney once. Isn't that a coincidence?'

Barney laughed. 'Big coincidence, sweetheart.'

She perched herself on the arm of the chair next to Halliday. 'So how do you know Hal, Barney?'

He smiled. 'Hell, that's a long story, Casey.'

Halliday's com chimed. 'Halliday here.'

A familiar face, which he could not at first place, stared up at him. Then he had it. Roberts, one of Wellman's heavies.

'Halliday, Roberts here. Ah . . . Wellman died today at nine,' he said. He hesitated. 'He wants to talk to you. I'll put him on, okay?'

Halliday patched the call through the wallscreen, and a second later the inflated image of Wellman's face replaced the Mercury landscape. He appeared much younger, fitter, than the dying man Hal had met up at Nyack. Behind the executive, he made out the sear plains of the Serengeti.

'Halliday,' Wellman said. 'It's good to see you.'

Halliday smiled. 'I'm glad to see it worked, Wellman. How's things?'

Wellman laughed. 'Never better, my friend. You don't know how wonderful it is to be reborn. I want to thank you for everything you did.'

Halliday shrugged. 'It was a team effort, Wellman. Barney, Kat . . .'

'The money should be safely in your account by now. Have you decided what you're going to do?'

He looked across at Barney, and then up at Casey. 'Matter of fact we're about to discuss that right now . . .'

'Then I'll leave you to it. Thanks again. I'll be in touch.'

The executive's image vanished, replaced by the scene of

323

planetary exploration relayed from Mercury. Halliday killed the sound.

Casey was staring at him. 'Discuss what?' she said. 'What we gonna discuss, Hal?'

To Casey he said, 'Barney's my new partner, Casey. You'll be seeing a lot of him in future.'

'Neat,' she said. 'Say, that's another coincidence. You know, Barney, Hal's last sidekick was a guy called Barney, too.'

'Ain't that something, sweetheart,' Barney laughed.

Halliday said, 'Wellman's just transferred five million dollars into my account.' He looked from Casey to Barney. 'And that's just the start, the first down payment. Thing is . . .' He shrugged. 'What're we gonna do with it?'

Casey was staring at him. 'Five million dollars? You joking me, right?'

'No joke, Casey. Five million.'

Barney said, 'What you want to do, Hal?'

Halliday considered. He'd been dreaming of late of moving out west, over to Seattle. He'd been looking at real estate on the Net, checking up on the reforestation projects going on over there.

He looked across the room to where his bonsai oak stood, alone and aloof, on the table.

'We need to talk this over,' he said. 'I mean, we could stay here, in New York . . .' Casey was shaking her head. 'Or we could try Washington State. I've heard great things about Seattle.'

Casey was wide-eyed. 'Seattle?' she said. 'Sounds good to me.'

'And then of course there's always the problem of what we're gonna do when we get out there, if Seattle is where we decide to go.'

Barney shrugged. 'Why don't we talk about that when we get there, Hal?'

'Seattle okay with you?'

'Sure, why not? People go missing in Seattle.'

Halliday smiled. 'You keen on continuing in this line of business, Barney?'

The thought, as he considered it, appealed. Part-time, with breaks to enjoy life out there, get fit again . . .

'Hey,' Casey said, 'what do you mean, "continuing"? You worked in missing persons before, Barney?'

Barney laughed. 'You could say that.' He looked across at Halliday, as if to say, 'You tell her . . .'

'It's a long story, Casey,' Halliday said.

She shrugged. 'So we'll have breakfast and you can tell me all about it. I know a great little diner on Fifth. I'll hand in my notice while I'm there.'

Barney said, 'Sounds great, Casey. I'm starving.'

Halliday considered the future, life in Seattle . . . and then he tried to think about life beyond Seattle, and what that might hold.

Virtual immortality in the Net, a life among the stars.

The future, he thought, begins here.

He reached out and took Casey's hand.

Outside, for the first time in weeks, the sun broke through the low cloud cover.